MORTAL THREAT

A. J. TATA

Cover Illustration by Larry Rostant
Cover Layout by Stanley Tremblay
Book Design by Stanley Tremblay

Published by A.J. Tata

For Brooke, my talented and beautiful daughter

Praise for Mortal Threat

MORTAL THREAT is tomorrow's news today! While some people working in the dramatic arts try to snatch stories from today's headlines, Tony Tata has fashioned a riveting plot with compelling characters that is also *prescient. MORTAL THREAT* grabs you, shakes you, and doesn't turn you loose.

—George Galdorisi, *New York Times* bestselling author of
Tom Clancy Presents: ACT OF WAR

"AJ Tata's *MORTAL THREAT* reads at a blistering pace while weaving a cure for Ebola, a 30,000 year old religious document, a president who thinks he's of divine origin, and a burgeoning ISIS threat into a tightly knit plot. Amanda Garrett is a new breakout heroine as she races across the Serengeti to save the cure from the evil men who seek it. Great stuff."

—Jeremy Robinson, International Bestselling Author of
ISLAND 731 and *SECONDWORLD*

"…captivating, riveting. Once you start *MORTAL THREAT*, you won't want to put it down."

—Grant Blackwood, *New York Times* bestselling author of
The Briggs Tanner series

"When I'm not writing, I like to read, and I read books in my genre. I'm very choosy in my reading and there's a lot to choose from. That's why I like Tony Tata. There is a 'been there, done that' feel to his storytelling, his characters are vivid and engaging, and his plotting is tight and well-paced. So I highly recommend *MORTAL THREAT* and *FOREIGN AND DOMESTIC*."

—Dick Couch, *New York Times* bestselling author of
ACT OF REVENGE

Praise for A.J. Tata

"An explosive, seat-of-your-pants thriller!"

—W.E.B. Griffin and W.E. Butterworth IV,
#1 *New York Times* bestselling authors

"Topical, frightening, possible and riveting!"

—James Rollins, *New York Times* bestselling author

"Powerful and timely. Great stuff!"

—John Lescroart, *New York Times* bestselling author

"Anthony J. Tata is the new Tom Clancy. . . . Electrifying!"

—Brad Thor, #1 *New York Times* bestselling author of *BLACK LIST*

"Every military thriller writer wants to be compared to Tom Clancy, but to be called better? That's what Anthony J. Tata is hearing . . . very realistic."

—Paul Bedard, *U.S. News and World Report*

"Riveting entertainment at its best!"

—The Military Writers Society of America

"Vince Flynn and Brad Thor better watch out because there is a new player in the genre. A must read!"

—*Author Magazine*

Advance Praise for Foreign and Domestic:

"**FOREIGN AND DOMESTIC** delivers!

"Anthony Tata's new thriller *FOREIGN AND DOMESTIC* is absolutely fantastic! It captures the pulse-pounding intensity of *Lone Survivor* and wraps it in a brilliant, cutting-edge plot that will keep you on the edge of your seat until the very last page. This is the kind of thriller writing that will remind you why you fell in love with reading, and reasserts why Tata <u>truly</u> is the new Tom Clancy. Turn off your phone, lock your doors, and jump into the phenomenal new book that <u>everyone</u> is going to be talking about."
— Brad Thor, #1 *New York Times* bestselling author of *BLACK LIST*

"Tony Tata writes with a gripping and a gritty authority rooted in his matchless real-life experience, combining a taut narrative with an inside look at the frontiers of trans-national terrorism. The result is so compelling that the pages seem to turn themselves."
— Richard North Patterson, #1 *New York Times* bestselling author of *IN THE NAME OF HONOR*

"General Tata's story mixes high-threat combat with an intriguing and surprising mystery. Disgraced Delta soldier Jake Mahegan finds himself tied to a crime that proves to be much larger and more dangerous than anyone suspects, involving national security, and hitting far too close to home. Vivid and complex characters make this a fascinating read."
— Larry Bond, New York Times bestselling author of EXIT PLAN

"Grabs you and doesn't let go . . . written by a man who's 'been there,' this vibrant thriller will take you to places as frightening as the darkest secrets behind tomorrow's headlines. The enemies in these pages are, indeed, 'foreign and domestic,' and it's hard to say which are more frightening.

Bound to be a breakout book for a gifted storyteller who served his country as splendidly as he writes!"

Prologue

As Iraqi Army tanks prowled the barren streets like hungry jackals, American media mogul Jonathan Beckwith watched his hired document thief through the lens of one of his many satellites orbiting the earth.

Tonight, Beckwith's task for Mohammed Aktar was to secure documents that could hold the most sacred truth ever hidden from mankind. Beckwith believed his target, thirty-thousand-year-old sheets of animal skin called vellum, contained undeniable proof of God.

Thus, his "consulting payment" to Aktar, a part-time guard at the ancient library of Ashurbanipal in Northwest Iraq, had been one million dollars. Beckwith used a toggle switch to pan and zoom the video feed so that he could watch his money in action. He could see the worry etched onto the man's wizened face as Aktar stood in the dark alley by the loading dock behind the library.

Beckwith had chosen Aktar because he was on a closely held list of document thieves, and it helped that he was also an anthropologist, linguist, and world civilizations teacher at a prestigious high school in Mosul, Iraq. One of Beckwith's Internet miners had hacked Aktar's home email and gained access to the man's hundreds of communications into the dark nether regions of document thievery. Beckwith's interest had been piqued when he'd found an exchange from Aktar to a friend in Egypt, "The victors write history, while the vanquished are forever condemned to the scrap bin."

True, Beckwith thought, like so many strips of silicon littering a film producer's floor, the powerful decided which ancient texts and documents to preserve and which to discard.

Beckwith watched as Aktar stood nervously in the dark alley. The man was thin and lanky, and his jacket flapped like a loose sail fluttering against its mast in a gale-force wind. Aktar's target was in Sennacherib's Palace in the ancient, Old Testament walled city of Nineveh. Directly across the Tigris River from Mosul, this fortress was to Biblical Mesopotamia what Luxor and Karnak had been to ancient Egypt. In 1847, Sir Austen Henry Layard had unearthed this palace to discover over twenty-two thousand cuneiform tablets, most of them etched in Sumerian, the oldest documented language in the world. Layard had secreted them back to Great Britain like so many treasures stolen from this land to advance political careers or enrich already fattened purses.

Beckwith planned to best Layard with this mission.

A watchful moon cast a silvery glow onto the khaki-colored dirt street in front of Aktar. The man pressed himself against the ten-meter-high mud and brick wall, built thousands of years earlier. The stone pillars of the vaunted historical fortress stood erect, perfectly cylindrical in their countenance, like sentries on guard.

At nearly two o'clock in the morning, Beckwith watched from his massive yacht, the *Intrepid*, cruising peacefully in the Red Sea as Aktar retrieved bolt cutters from beneath his coat and cast one more skittish glance in each direction. Beckwith had instructed Aktar not to use his key so that the theft would appear to be a burglary. With a quick move, Aktar placed the pincers on the master lock securing the hasp to the loading dock at the rear of the museum. With the lock removed, he was soon inside the cluttered storage room adjacent to the loading dock.

Beckwith switched displays to the cameras inside the library, which his Internet miner had manipulated to upload live streaming video so that Beckwith could follow his thief. Aktar passed through multiple hallways, and Beckwith was glad to see the man leave the gold crowns and chalices untouched.

Beckwith had studied the *Book of J* and the *Book of E*, the Torah, the Bible, the Koran, the Hebrew Tanach, and many other religious texts. What he had learned was that all of the scriptures had been eventually recorded from memory after being passed along by the oral traditions of tribal chiefs or religious scholars. The hierarchy of those who determined the canonization of Biblical texts fascinated him. To him, it seemed that all of the religions essentially agreed on the basic pretexts of a God creating the universe and man. It was this particular issue, the creation of man, which had captured Beckwith's attention.

In November 2012, one of his Internet miners had pinged on a secure email from an Al Rhazziq Media server farm in Morocco that had mentioned the location of the Book of Catalyst, a fabled alternative to the Book of Genesis that had been dismissed as fairy tale. However, Beckwith wanted it, and had vetted document thieves until landing upon Aktar, who was now making his way down the marble staircase that led to the cavernous storage area.

The building Beckwith was watching shuddered. Beckwith scanned another screen, where he was monitoring the combat actions between Iraqi troops and insurgents in nearby Mosul, and the library appeared safe.

Looking back at the internal cameras, Beckwith watched Aktar shine a powerful flashlight on a steel cage. Retrieving the bolt cutters, Aktar snapped the thick-gauge steel around the key lock, reached through the newly fashioned gap, and turned the deadbolt to open the door.

Aktar moved quickly. His flashlight found the third row of wooden containers sitting atop a graying pallet, and he removed the top wooden box and used the bolt cutters a third time.

Zooming in now, Beckwith watched as Aktar carefully removed the brittle protective cover from what was essentially a humidor. But instead of housing cigars, this container stored the secrets of civilization, Beckwith believed. He was reassured when he watched Aktar rub his thumb and forefinger across the material and nod his head, confirming that the parchment was vellum and not papyrus. Vellum had been used throughout Africa prior to the birth of Christ, whereas papyrus, much more fragile, had been common in Egypt and Greece after Christ's birth. Beckwith watched his motivated thief gingerly sort the documents. About two-thirds of the way into the box, Aktar stopped. Beckwith gripped the camera, his palms sweating on the camera controls. Aktar must have found the targeted pages.

The thief stared at the documents. Beckwith felt his hands shaking. If these papers were indeed what he believed, then his understanding of them might be the first since the author had penned the originals, or perhaps since a fearful tyrant thousands of years ago had locked them away in the trash pile of history.

Beckwith watched Aktar use the flashlight to study the six pages of the text and drawings, and he zoomed the camera even closer so that he could see the script. It looked like a mix of hieroglyphics, Sumerian, and something that closely resembled Swahili. He saw a sun and a starburst followed by legible script in aging ink, perhaps henna, that the author had used to pen the words.

Beckwith pictured the Book of Catalyst in his hands. He had so many questions. Could this be one of the many religious books that had not been included in the King James Bible? Why was it hidden deep in the bowels of this museum? How was it that Layard had taken over twenty thousand tablets back to Britain and yet left these boxes? Was he unaware of its significance? Concerned about political ramifications of a holy text that gave credence to the import of sub-Saharan Africa in man's origin?

Beckwith clasped his hands as he watched the thief carefully place the vellum parchments in a wax envelope the size of a manila folder. He secured the envelope in a cardboard protected casing like a FedEx envelope, closed the box, took the lock, replaced the other container on top of it, and retraced his steps out of the museum.

Beckwith switched satellites to follow Aktar through the streets of Nineveh. The thief ran east, crossing the river and scampering through the narrow, dusty roads toward the Ark Church. He finished the two-mile trek back to his home, much of the distance due to his circuitous route to avoid ISIS ambushes.

Again, Beckwith switched to another set of monitors in his yacht command center. He watched Aktar quickly lock himself inside his study after ignoring his wife, who seemed to be pleading with him as she gestured for him to stop. Beckwith's excitement disappeared when Aktar placed the documents on his scan/fax/copier machine. Aktar then looked into the hidden camera, took a step away and aimed an AK-47 at the fiber optic lens. Suddenly Beckwith's eyes were gone inside Aktar's office.

But Beckwith had been ready for this. He knew not to trust a thief. Aktar would not be making a fool of him today.

He turned to Styve Rachman, the redheaded, earring wearing, twenty-something kid who he paid three hundred thousand dollars annually to mine for emails that could benefit him. One day it might be a patent application that he could steal; the next it might be a message about a rare document.

Aktar's digitized packet of information he thought he had securely faxed, now relayed off Beckwith's satellite to his mini-server farm aboard the *Intrepid*.

Rachman said, "Got it."

"What's it say?"

"He's sending it to the language guy in Egypt. Raul Akunsada. He punked you."

"I get that. What's the email say?"

"Well, he attached the scan and a cover page, so in a way, you've got the documents."

"I need the originals."

"Some strange stuff here. I'm just going to read the cover page with the hand written translations: Baba Yetu Mungu. *Our Father God.* Kitabu Wakati Moto. *Book of Fire Time. In the beginning there was a Catalyst, which produced life. This Catalyst was God who created the earth and the stars and water and fire and life.*

"*There is a beginning, a middle, and an end.... The black footprints are timeless. In 1436 he will walk the path toward peace.*

"There's a drawing of a heart and then *going to the sky.* Then...*the mortal threat will be no more.*"

"That's got to be the Book of Catalyst," Beckwith gasped.

"Could be. If it's real," Rachman said.

"Real? Shit, son, this is where Layard found the tablets. I need you to destroy Aktar's and Akunsada's computers with a virus, and I'm activating my go-team to retrieve the originals."

"Roger that, boss."

Beckwith watched Rachman's fingers skitter across the keyboard as he sent a text to his two-man private military contractor team that was waiting in a Humvee not far away. He leaned back and looked at the ceiling of the command center, where an image on the corner television caught his eye.

He had totally forgotten a new president was being inaugurated today. Jamal Barkum stood before the masses of the Washington, D.C. Mall. Beckwith punched up the volume using the remote.

"And I say to all of you that today we march on toward a better destiny. Our footprints are timeless. Thank you and God Bless America."

And suddenly Beckwith thought he understood.

1

Amanda Garrett used her heel to kick open the plywood emergency room door. Her two rubber-gloved hands were holding one end of a medical stretcher while her protégé, Kiram Omiga, held the other.

"She doesn't have much time," Amanda said. The small African girl on the litter was huddled in the fetal position, Ebola-infectious drool seeping from her mouth. The girl was wearing a pink T-shirt and green shorts. Amanda noticed the dilated pupils and white salt stains on her face from a sweat that had stopped hours ago.

"Age is eleven. Name is Likika," Kiram said in a calm voice. At nineteen years old, Kiram had grown up in the Mwanza orphanage. He had known Amanda since he was fourteen after her first summer volunteering to assist the war orphans like him.

Amanda commanded, "Ready, lift."

She and Kiram lifted Likika onto a makeshift operating table. They were both wearing rubberized gloves, olive green U.S. Army chemical protective suits with charcoal liners and gas masks. Amanda's initial research had been on finding a cure for the Human Immunodeficiency Virus, which they believed they had done. They had accumulated over ninety positive-to-negative seroconversions on orphans and truck drivers riddled with HIV. Those were substantial results for her clandestine CIA program called *Project Nightingale*. Because the two viruses shared a common multiplying protein mechanism known as TSG101, Amanda had experimented on one dying Ebola patient two months ago. He had lived. Soon, truck drivers began dropping off infected Ebola patients at the "miracle clinic," hoping Amanda could save them. By her count, they had saved nine Ebola victims.

She was eager to alert the CIA that the mysterious formula was ready for mass-market production.

"Syringe," Amanda said, holding out her hand. Kiram moved to her left as she stared at Likika, whose eyes were open wide as if she were astonished. The gas mask eyelets blocked some of Amanda's peripheral vision, which caused her to grow impatient. "Talk to me, Kiram."

"Here, Miss Amanda," Kiram said. He reappeared holding a clear syringe and three-inch needle. The tube was filled with a substance the color and texture of tar. Through the gas masks, their voices contained a tinny, muffled quality.

"Need you to hold her, Kiram. If she's still with us, this is going to hurt like hell," Amanda said.

"I understand," Kiram said. He bent over Likika and gently held her by the shoulders while Amanda inserted the needle into her left shoulder, as if she were giving her a vaccination. Applying steady pressure to the plunger, she heard Kiram chant a native Swahili melody to Likika, who, as far as Amanda could tell, was unconscious and close to death.

Having transitioned from only performing HIV vaccinations and cures to also conducting Ebola testing, Amanda was painfully aware that her Spartan facilities were inadequate. But how could she deny the victims the potential of a cure or prevention of disease? She couldn't. While she was a Columbia University medical school student who'd spent the last five summer and winter breaks in Tanzania at this orphanage, she believed in the inverse of the Hippocratic oath. Instead of *first, do no harm*, Amanda's maxim was *first, help who you can*.

The needle puncturing Likika's arm created a trickle of blood, which cut a path through the salt stains onto the operating table. Amanda focused on the black serum she was injecting through the hypodermic needle into the young girl's system. As the plunger reached the bottom of the barrel, she was concerned that Likika hadn't responded at all. She retracted the needle and immediately dumped the entire syringe in a hazardous waste container to her right.

"Pulse?" she asked, looking back at Likika and placing an alcohol swab on the injection site. She carefully wiped at the blood.

Kiram looked at Amanda and removed his glove.

"Hook her up, Kiram. Don't do that," she implored.

"It's okay. I'm careful." Kiram gingerly grabbed Likika's wrist with his bare fingers and paused. Like HIV, Ebola could only be transmitted via contact with bodily fluids. *But still*, Amanda thought.

Amanda counted the seconds, holding the gauze on the puncture site. Once she hit sixty, she asked, "Anything?"

Kiram said nothing. His eyes were focused on the girl's blank face.

After another sixty seconds, Amanda took a deep breath, which was like breathing through a wet towel on a hot afternoon. "Come on, Likika. Work with us, honey," she whispered.

Kiram looked at Amanda.

Likika jolted, as if prodded by a defibrillator. Her arm rose off the table, and then her body went still. Amanda's pressure on the needle mark slipped with Likika's sudden movement. A spray of blood shot out but didn't appear to reach either of them. Slowly, Likika began to move. Amanda saw her blink. Likika turned her head and mumbled some words, which caused Kiram to smile.

"What?" Amanda asked.

"She said, 'That hurts.'"

Amanda nodded. "Good. She felt it. That's a good sign. Let's move her to quarantine."

First, Amanda carefully placed a full bandage on the injection site of Likika's arm. She used alcohol swabs to again clean the trickle of blood from her arm and the operating table. Kiram lifted the stretcher, and together they nursed Likika's body onto the canvas. Amanda walked backward toward the makeshift quarantine area adjacent to the operating room. They had sealed off a separate section of the building with tarps and clear plastic sheeting used in construction. Amanda felt the cot with the back of her leg and pivoted to her left as Kiram moved to his right. They placed Likika on the cot and stood the stretcher on end in the quarantine room. They would give that a thorough cleaning later.

As they quietly slipped from the room, Amanda watched Kiram pull the plastic sheet across the doorway.

Which was when she saw the droplet of blood on his hand.

"Kiram," she said.

"Yes, I know, Miss Amanda. I go wash my hand now."

"Now," she ordered.

Amanda knew that if Kiram did not have a cut or tear on his hand where Likika's blood had splattered, then he would ninety-nine point nine percent most likely be okay.

Most likely.

She watched Kiram pour a purplish medical cleanser onto his hand. Amanda grabbed the bucket they had recently filled from the orphanage well. "Let me help you," she said. She poured water over his hand and watched the purple liquid stream against his black skin. The blood droplet had mostly dried, so Amanda took a sponge to his hand and dabbed at the affected area. After three more applications of cleanser and flushes and dabs, Kiram smiled.

"I'm good, Miss Amanda. No cuts on me."

"Put this on just in case," she said. Still wearing her gloves, Amanda lightly taped a dry gauze pad that would absorb any remaining microscopic remnants of blood on his hand.

"Thank you," Kiram said. He looked at the plastic sheeting behind them.

"Good wins," he said like he did every time they saved someone even though the verdict remained undetermined.

"Let's pray that it does," Amanda replied.

"I'll be out in a bit," Kiram said.

As she walked outside, Amanda removed her gloves and gas mask. She walked to her wooden hut in the center of the orphanage. Before entering, Amanda removed her protective clothing and changed the filters on her gas mask. She dumped everything in a sterilization bag on her porch. She cinched the bag shut and slipped it into a plastic trash bag. She would wash the ensemble at her first opportunity. She used the sink on her porch to wash her hands and face, then went around back and stood inside her jungle shower, stripping naked and then pulling the chain link to serve a trickle of water over her body. She used shampoo and soap to clean every pore of her body and then dried herself with a threadbare towel she had hanging on a cable. She reached in her window and grabbed a folded pair of shorts, underwear, and a T-shirt from a shelf, checked them for insects, and then dressed again. She dropped her soiled clothes in another plastic trash bag, cinched it, and walked around front, where she dropped it next to the other.

Stepping inside her "home," she spied her cot with a sleeping bag, a power strip wired to a generator she could hear purring in the dirt next to her shower, and two duffle bags—one for clothes and one filled with books and magazines. She traveled light. Looking to her left, she considered her computer and monitor that were connected to a satellite antenna on her roof.

Exhaustion got the best of her, and she lay on the cot, grabbed a book from her entertainment duffle, and began flipping through it. Anything to take her mind off the trauma of the last hour.

Great, she thought, de Tocqueville. She read a few pages, laid the book on her bare stomach just below her already sweaty T-shirt, and let her mind drift. *More than anything, mankind seeks freedom*, she considered. Looking down at *Democracy in America*, de Tocqueville's magnum opus, she found his writing pedestrian but still necessary. The search for escape from that which tyrannized, oppressed, or otherwise shackled the spirit defined the human existence. That was the "take away," she thought in her med school vernacular.

Whether it was the pilgrimage from the United Kingdom to the United States or the migration of so many millions of Africans to clinics where they prayed at empty altars for cures to the diseases that plagued their land, mankind sought to unleash itself from that which spiritually or physically constrained them. That was her take on it, anyway.

Similarly, she thought about her patients. Preparing and delivering the cure to a young child was always an emotional event. Each time, she thought, *what if it doesn't work?* But it always did. Freedom from disease was perhaps as important as political or religious freedom, she considered. Ever since Kiram and her other able helper, Mumbato, had brought the black paste from what they called, *Mahali*, or *The Place*, the same serum had been effective in patients positive for Ebola *and* AIDS. The two nineteen-year-olds refused to disclose the location of the active ingredient in her serum, claiming they feared for her safety. Yet Amanda's patience was wearing thin, as she needed to know so that they could go into mass production to stem the viral tide.

For their part, the boys assured her that their only limitation was how much they could carry in one trip, which took two days. As the Ebola outbreak worsened on the west side of the continent, she had experimented with the new recipe and achieved encouraging results. She prayed for the same with Likika. Where HIV was a stealthy, indirect attack on the immune system, Ebola was a bold frontal assault that killed rapidly. The common intersection was that both viruses used a protein called TSG101 to hold open the host cell door so that the virus could multiply and emerge, like invaders from a Trojan Horse. Her serum shut that trap door, forcing the virus to ultimately smother and die.

She plugged her iPhone earphones in and listened to some old Rolling Stones tunes as she dropped de Tocqueville and now thumbed through a *People* magazine from last year. She drifted off briefly into sleep and then awoke. She heard the children on the soccer field. Curious that she had not heard from her husband, Jake Devereaux, for two days, she used her phone to tap out a quick email to him:

Hi, love. I miss you and wish you were with me. We solved another puzzle today. Keep praying. I love you, all ways and always. A.

Amanda stood from her wooden frame bed and walked outside. Solved another puzzle. That was her code for *saved another human being. Project*

Nightingale was a top secret mission, and she had to be circumspect, even with her husband. The Tanzanian heat slapped her in the face as she walked the short distance to the patch of dirt that doubled as a soccer field. She saw the orphans kicking the new ball that she had brought them for Christmas this year. Kiram was jogging past her to the field and smiled as he held up his bandaged hand.

"No problem," he said.

"You scare me, you know?" Amanda said, half joking. Having experienced so many close calls with Kiram and Mumbato, Amanda and the boys had developed a gallows humor among themselves.

"Miss Amanda, why you always on white phone?" he asked, laughing and changing the subject.

"Gotta keep in touch with my peeps," she said, patting her safari vest pocket.

"Never see me using one of those. Black magic." He showed her a toothy grin of crooked teeth.

"Get out on the field, K-boy," she teased.

"No longer boy. Big man now," he called over his shoulders and then flexed his muscles, showing her a broad, bare back that was as cut as any weight lifter on the cover of *Muscle* magazine.

She watched him immediately get into the game, steal the ball, and then nurse it past a few of the other boys from the orphanage as they chased him. His mahogany-black chest was sinewy as he rolled the ball along the dirt patch that doubled as a soccer field. He cast a glance in her direction directly before flipping the ball up using his right heel and left toe. The ball arched behind him and then over his head. He nudged it gently with his head past the last defender, spun to his right, and then rifled the ball into the worn net. The ball shot through a hole in the webbing and flew deep into the Tanzanian jungle that abruptly began where the dirt field ended.

Situated between massive Lake Victoria on the west and the Serengeti Plain on the east, the orphanage was on the eastern edge of the Mwanza Province. Tectonic faults riddled the terrain, which gave way to the wind-swept Serengeti a few miles in the distance. Pockets of dense foliage and African acacia trees spotted the low areas where condensation collected. Mount Kilimanjaro could be seen in the distance on a clear, cloudless day.

"Not again!" Amanda laughed, clapping her hands.

Meanwhile, Kiram was running with his hands in the air, the triumphant smile on his face beaming as he screamed, "Goallll!"

"Go get the ball, Kiram!" Mumbato yelled, standing there with his hands on his hips, an aggressive pose, sweat pouring down his dark face and wide nose as the sauna that was Tanzania in January enveloped them. Mumbato was wearing a yellow and green mesh soccer shirt with black shorts and remained standing in the middle of the field. The two boys had their moments, yet mostly they got along just fine. For the past year, as the boys had begun to sprout into young men, she had witnessed what she called a "testosterone duel" between Kiram and Mumbato. They were her two most able helpers with the program, and if the time came that she ever needed assistance, she knew she could trust both of them.

"What is the American saying, Miss Amanda? Losers walk?" Kiram laughed as he came jogging toward Amanda.

"Nobody's a loser here, Kiram, remember?"

"Okay, no losers. But he still walks into the jungle to get the ball."

Amanda had learned the local dialect but had mentored the children over the last five years to learn English. And so now they spoke with an African lilt to their English words sounding not unlike a Caribbean accent.

Kiram and Mumbato stood barely taller than Amanda in her Humvee-brand khaki vest and cut-off paratroop pants. Her skin was deeply tanned from nearly five years of mission work. After her high school graduation, she had spent five consecutive summer and winter breaks here in Tanzania. In her first year of a combined medical and PhD program, Columbia had agreed to give her credit for her service in the orphanage. Her thesis being the intersection of virulent pathogens, her faculty had begrudgingly allowed Amanda to gain course credit for her time in Tanzania. Of course, her faculty advisor had no idea that Amanda's uncle, CIA operative Matt Garrett, had recruited her into *Project Nightingale*. Amanda was more than happy to accept the position and the funding provided by her uncle's organization.

Directly after her graduation from Columbia University pre-med, she had married Jake, her high school sweetheart, in the Citadel chapel. Jake and Amanda's wedding had been the first of his class after graduation. Now, Jake was at Fort Bragg serving as a paratrooper platoon leader, having endured Infantry Officer Basic Course, Airborne School, and Ranger Training. Until they could live together again in a few years, while they each built their own professional foundations, they had agreed to settle for irregular visits and daily communication by email and Skype.

"So who gets the ball?" Kiram asked impatiently.

"Why do you need me to make the decision?" Amanda smiled. She put her hands on her hips and put on her best poker face for her two teenagers. "For the past five years, we've been trying to teach all of you to make your own decisions. Good decisions," she emphasized.

Kiram laughed again. "But Miss Amanda, going into the jungle is not a good decision."

"Then don't kick the soccer ball in there anymore."

She recalled with fondness how just five years ago, Kiram had drawn a picture of her father, who, at the time, she'd believed was dead, killed in Afghanistan. Kiram had sketched a coal caricature better than any Virginia Beach boardwalk artist, conjuring her father's image exactly. But it hadn't been a psychic vision on Kiram's part. Suddenly, her father had been behind her. She had turned, closing her eyes, when she'd heard the words, her father's words: "We're good to go, baby girl."

Framed by the wandering river behind him, her father had stood tall, his arm in a sling. He had been leaning against a walking stick. Her uncle, Matt, and her psychologist, Riley Dwyer, had been with him.

She remembered running to him, hugging him so tightly, and crying. The years of confusion and estrangement had floated away with the sneaky-swift river. Her mother and grandmother now in prison for their crimes, all she had left, and all she had wanted, was her father. And now she had Jake, with whom she planned a long life and large family.

The images raced back to her as she watched Mumbato, with a scowl on his face, step carefully into the dense underbrush, behind the same curtain from which her father had reappeared those five years ago. She turned and looked at the river flowing behind her. The stump where Kiram had roughed out the sketch of her father was still there as well. Waiting for Mumbato to reemerge from the dense foliage gave her a moment to consider the past five years. How much progress had she and Dr. Arthur King made in this village? Was her mission accomplishing their goal of finding a cure and vaccine for the relentless diseases of this plagued land? Or was this a black hole that sucked away energy and resources in a hopeless spiral of despair as evidenced by Ebola rates doubling every twenty-four hours?

She hoped not. Her optimism burned brightly at the notion of Kiram and Mumbato one day becoming doctors for their people. Already, both teenagers had shown incredible aptitude in the field of medicine. She thought that if she could make a difference with just a few of these children, then there was a chance, because there were others out there equally pure-hearted and driven to help. And if she could verify that she and Dr. King really had found cures for Ebola and HIV, maybe she could be content with having done her part.

And she knew they were close.

She had learned to believe that good could triumph evil. It would not necessarily happen by itself, but in the end, with proper steerage, *good wins.* If she could escape the byzantine labyrinth in which her mother and grandmother had placed her, then anything was possible. She was neither optimist nor pessimist; perhaps she was a realist who believed the best would happen, or at least was possible.

Her blond hair was bleached from years of swimming competitions. Freckles across the bridge of her nose darkened under the searing heat of the African sun despite bush hats and sunscreen. Luminescent green eyes, like her father's, radiated her mood; they were brilliant emeralds when she was mad and changed to a green-tinted azure, like fiery diamonds, when she was intensely focused. She could dress to the nines in something trendy—say, a vintage Tracy Reese silk top matched with a pair of Gucci denim shorts. Or she could wear with authority the Humvee safari vest and Abercrombie and Fitch cut-off paratroops she had donned this morning.

While not a member of Mensa, she had graduated pre-med at Columbia University with a 3.95 grade point average and had scored an impressive forty-two on her Medical College Admissions Test. One of only seventy-five applicants accepted out of the twenty-seven hundred who'd applied, the next year she had entered as a student in Columbia University's College of Physicians and Surgeons. Her goal was to graduate and join *Médicins Sans Frontières,* Doctors Without Borders. She figured that a couple of years as an emergency room surgeon, coupled with her experience at the orphanage, would readily gain her admission into the elite organization. Her father was a Special Forces soldier, and this was her way of following in his footsteps. She would join the special forces of doctors, and she and Jake would find a way to make it work.

Amanda was snapped from her introspection when Mumbato raced from the jungle onto the field, his soccer ball clutched in his arms. He was screaming something in his native Swahili tongue that even Amanda did not immediately recognize. *Afriti! Afriti!* Then: *Damu! Damu!* His wide eyes and open jaw were nearly frozen in fear. Amanda looked at Kiram, whose cocky grin disappeared when he saw and heard Mumbato.

"What's he saying, Kiram?"

"He's saying he saw the devil and blood. He's scared. Wait here." Kiram ran toward Mumbato, who stopped mid-field when Kiram approached him. The two teenagers spoke in their native tongue, Amanda only picking up on pieces of the conversation.

Something about a dead man in the jungle.

2

"Take me to the body," Amanda said.

The three of them stood at the edge of the clearing. Amanda had immediately executed a well-rehearsed battle drill, as she had labeled it, and had Sharifa, an assistant, hide the children in the most secure building in the orphanage. She'd ensured she had accountability of everyone for whom she was responsible and then had contacted the village constabulary, called Askari. Now, two Askari wielding M16 rifles walked toward them as they prepared to confront the dead man in the jungle.

"Miss Amanda, it's a white man," Mumbato said. "I think it's the doctor."

"Take me there now," Amanda directed. Her mind raced. *Dr. King? It wasn't possible.*

Amanda tucked her headphones into the top of her khaki fishing vest, the necklace still hanging loosely around her neck. She pushed her hair behind her ears as her determined face looked west toward the jungle. She set her jaw and began striding stubbornly across the dusty soccer field, her squad of Mumbato, Kiram, and the two Askari in tow.

Mumbato, machete in hand, led through the forest, and in a few minutes, they arrived at a small clearing.

"Here," he said.

Amanda kneeled next to the rapidly decomposing body of Dr. Arthur King. She had always found his name a cute play on words: King Arthur, Arthur King. Accordingly she had always called him King Arthur as a sign of affection. Every time she had traveled to his laboratory to compare notes, she would ask, "So where's the round table and all those cute knights?"

To which, Dr. Arthur King would respond, "You've got the cutest knight of all waiting for you in America."

Of course, he had been right when speaking of her husband, Jake, and the thought of Dr. King's compassion and friendship caused a tear to well at the back of her eyes.

She had worked closely with King Arthur over the past five years as part of her medical training. Necessarily, they had labored in secrecy in two laboratories. She had been King's partner in the CIA's *Project Nightingale*. King had mostly lived in the village as Amanda did, but he had spent about a third of his time at the backup facility near Lake Victoria, where he had focused on the Ebola cure once Amanda had experimented on that first patient.

Mumbato and the other orphans were proof of the success of the natural remedy. Two years ago, their positive HIV blood draws had turned negative, and remained so today. Kiram had never tested positive but had appeared in the orphanage after the Rwanda bloodshed. Still, every day, they were obtaining positive-to-negative conversions. King Arthur had been a fundamental link in the discovery process. The elements of their contract were to work on these orphans, using them as experimental subjects. Amanda discussed with each child the risks involved. Yet to a person, they considered the chance that the formula might work was a far greater benefit than perhaps an accelerated death if it failed. And it was King Arthur who always received the funding and did the bulk of the research at his facility seventy miles away on the eastern side of Lake Victoria. For security, though, he wanted to do the testing at Amanda's facility in this village near the Serengeti, away from civilization.

"Someone is after the formula," Amanda whispered to herself.

Mumbato and Kiram, benefactors of the research and experimentation conducted by Amanda and her medical colleagues, knelt next to Amanda while the two Askari, perhaps ignorant to the significance of yet another dead body in the jungle, provided guard.

"King Arthur. Good man," Kiram said.

Amanda turned and looked at her two protégés. She had lost a friend; to them, they had lost a man who had brought back comrades from death and given them hope for a future without disease. Certainly she had contributed to the work; however, it was Dr. King who had labored for so many years in the privacy of his laboratory in hopes of saving the thousands, if not millions, of HIV-positive parentless children and, now, even the victims of the budding Ebola outbreaks. He had eschewed the luxuries of the medical profession in America, and instead of joining an immunology practice there and easily making a half-million dollars per year, he chose to live in a small shack in Tanzania.

To Amanda, King Arthur was a hero second only to her father, Zachary Garrett. And even then, they were heroes on the same scale, each fueled by their respective talents with a pure, driven desire to make a difference in the world.

The two Askari suddenly turned at a noise in the brush a few feet away. They relaxed when they heard the child's voice but kept their weapons ready. But Amanda tensed, leaning over the body to protect her from the sight of King Arthur's bloodied body.

"Miss Amanda!" she cried. "Come quick!"

It was Shenia, a twelve-year-old girl, who also had been riddled with HIV until recently, when her test results had come back negative. She had transformed from anemic to healthy in a matter of two years.

"Please, lower your weapons," Amanda said. The Askari dropped the muzzles of their M16 rifles.

Shenia appeared, her dark skin glistening with sweat. She wore a red scarf across her forehead, tied in the back into a carpenter's knot. A potato sack with holes cut in the sleeves was draped over her shoulders.

"*Mzimu!*" she said.

Amanda placed her hands on Shenia's shoulders, which were shaking with fear. Yet she had been brave enough to run into the jungle to seek help. Frustrated, Amanda turned to Kiram.

"She's saying she saw a ghost," he said. "*Mzimu.*"

"Where did you see this ghost, Shenia?" Amanda asked.

Shenia tried to open her mouth, but no words formed, as if she were experiencing a seizure. Amanda had worked with the children on their English, and most had progressed nicely, but when the adrenaline flowed, they naturally gravitated back toward Swahili.

"Calm down, honey," Amanda said, holding her hand. "What's happening?"

"A bad man," she finally said. "Burning village!"

Amanda dipped her head, thinking. She believed she had so much to make up for since her selfish childhood days that she worked overtime, ensuring she didn't waste a minute. She had once visualized herself as pulling a rope against a ratchet; with each tug, she locked in more gains for those she could help.

And now, with the orphanage under apparent attack, it was as if someone had released the flywheel and the rope was whipping wildly backward through her hands, burning them as she tried to get control. With that image, Amanda looked down at her hands. Then, she quit feeling sorry for herself and refocused.

"Mumbato, please stay here with one of the Askari and move Dr. King's body to the village. Kiram, you come with me."

She pulled on the arm of one of the constabularies while Mumbato grabbed the other. Soon, Amanda, Shenia, Kiram, and the armed guard were moving back toward the ghost who was destroying the village.

If the village was under attack, Amanda suspected the worst had happened: someone had learned of the formula for the cure and was trying to steal it. She knew the value of what she had developed and its lucrative potential. Carpetbaggers would kill for the formula. After all their work to cure disease in the people she had come to know and love, Amanda sensed that their entire operation could now fall prey to violent criminals.

Running, she thought of Jake and her father. She could desperately use an encouraging word from either or both of them right now. Briefly, she wondered if she would ever see them again.

Second Lieutenant Jake Devereaux's mind swooned with the seemingly endless yaw of the C-17 Globemaster aircraft. One moment he was dreaming about his beautiful, new bride, Amanda, and the next he was painfully aware of the weapons case wedged against his legs from his paratrooper stick buddy, Sergeant First Class Willie Mack.

He shook his head to clear the cobwebs as he nudged the gun away from him with his knee. One hundred of America's finest paratroopers from the 82nd Airborne Division were crammed into the hulking jet with six other C-17s following. Jake looked at his watch and realized they had been in the air for over four hours. The sway he was feeling was from the aerial refueling they were conducting en route to their drop zone in Al-Qaim, Iraq, along the Syrian border.

Jake was a platoon leader in the airborne and considered himself lucky to have been on Division Ready Force One when the president had made the call to send troops to secure the Special Forces base in Iraq. While he wasn't a foreign policy master, Jake thought that defending against thirty thousand Islamic State, or ISIS, zealots was going to require a lot more than seven hundred paratroopers, as good as they were.

Their drop time was near 2 a.m. Iraq time, and he knew that he and his men had a few hours to get some rest. As soon as they jumped, they would be all business. So he laid his head against the red netting and thought about Amanda.

3

Moroccan media mogul Zhor Rhazziq looked at his phone as it pinged with a text message from his informant near Fort Bragg, North Carolina.

Seven birds are flying.

To Rhazziq that meant a battalion of paratroopers were headed to Iraq or Syria. He logged the information in the back of his mind as he stood in one of his many studios in Marrakesh. However, the more pressing situation at the moment was what he was seeing on the giant plasma television screen, which was showing real time footage of the burning orphanage in Tanzania. As the primary competitor to Beckwith Media, Al Rhazziq Media dominated the Northern Tier of Africa, most of the Middle East, and parts of Southern Europe.

With the orphanage attack as his trigger, Rhazziq nodded to his friend, Dr. Hawan Quizmahel, who stood in front of a television camera with an indistinct blue tarp and AK-47 assault rifle as his background. The doctor began speaking.

"I say to all of our African brothers who can hear me over the radio and the television and by any other means that I have discovered a cure for your dreaded diseases, AIDS and Ebola. As you know better than the Zionists, one African dies every ten seconds of AIDS and one African contracts HIV every fifteen seconds. Thirty-five million Africans have died from the disease, and another ninety million are dying a slow death from HIV infection. That is nearly one half the population of the African continent.

"In the same way, Ebola threatens to kill the entire western region of the continent. Every minute, another African is infected with Ebola. These are weapons of mass destruction brought to you by the Zionists. Islamic State scientists and doctors, including those in ISIS, began experimenting many years ago to find a way to help the people that the infidels have left behind. They treated you as their slaves, and now they have abandoned you in your time of greatest need. Over fifty percent of our continent's population is suffering from these terrible viruses, yet where is the wealthiest nation on earth? Where are the others who can marshal the resources to help you? They are nowhere to be found. Worse, they use the Ebola affliction to send armed invaders to your countries. They use you for their own materialistic and imperial purposes to fund their crusade against Muslims. They only come to you to help now that they fear the far-reaching spread of the Islamic State's good work. As we promised, we have used the money from our leadership and your support to work diligently to find the cure to the Ebola and human immunodeficiency viruses that plague your people. We have good news for our African brothers and sisters today. We have *found* the cures. Africa will soon be out from under the grip of both plagues that have taken the good lives of your family and friends for decades. Soon, we will begin mass production of these formulas so that they are easily ingestible or otherwise introduced to the suffering subject's body. We will establish outreach clinics in your most remote regions, and we will provide the cures and vaccines free, of our own goodwill. Rest assured, the Islamic State and ISIS seek to bring medical relief and unity to the African continent, God willing, and to rid the world of these Zionist viruses spread by their immoral ways."

Rhazziq watched Quizmahel remove the small, black foam-covered microphone from his white tunic and walk toward him. He left the AK-47 leaning against the blue tarp. He wouldn't need it where he was going, Rhazziq thought.

"Your words will live beyond our lifetime, Doctor," Rhazziq said.

"*Inshalla.*" *God willing*, he said. "Is there any progress on finding the American formula?"

"Soon, very soon," said Rhazziq.

They had better find it soon, Rhazziq thought, as he had just directed the doctor to tell the world he had the cure, when, in fact, they possessed no such thing. Though he had taken the necessary steps to secure the recipe.

In addition to being a wealthy media tycoon, Rhazziq was also the diaspora leader of the Islamic State, which was a broader transnational entity than ISIS, making ISIS a subset of Rhazziq's organization. Rhazziq's goal was to dominate the Northern Tier of Africa and link it to the burgeoning ISIS movement in Syria and Iraq. Like a pincer movement, the Northern Tier fighters would connect with those on the Arabian Peninsula to crush the American coalition invaders. Then, a true caliphate would provide sanctuary for terrorists to slowly bleed the Western world of its treasure, both human and financial.

"Rhazziq, my brother," said Quizmahel. They hugged.

"I will miss you, my friend," Rhazziq replied.

"I am ready to be martyred," Quizmahel affirmed. "But you are too valuable to be near my broadcast. Please, you must leave, Rhazziq."

"Morocco is my home. But I will go upstairs as you walk outside and rise to the holy place where we will one day meet again. Your announcement will further strengthen the caliphate. All Muslims will follow those, such as you, who are leading the way."

"*Inshallah.*" *God Willing.*

"Go in peace, my friend."

He hugged Quizmahel one last time. He watched his friend step outside into the teeming streets of Morocco's Red City. Shimmering waves of heat rose from the mud street of this Marrakesh *Souk el Kebir,* leather market, like the hypnotic sway of a tamed cobra rising from a basket. Out of the corner of his eye, Rhazziq saw the rooftop sniper and flinched as he visualized the man squeezing the American-made .50-caliber weapon's trigger.

But no shot came immediately. This momentary lapse gave him time to cycle through his Koranic verses and to visualize the virgins who awaited his friend. Quizmahel had cancer and had been given less than a year to live. It had been Rhazziq's idea for his friend to martyr himself and stage the assassination. The time had come.

Rhazziq had once met the American president, Jamal Barkum, after his election in 2012. The president had visited several African nations to better understand the culture and seek understanding between the West and the Arabic populations in Africa and the Middle East. He believed the man to be an Arabic sympathizer and wondered how he would react to Quizmahel's murder, if at all. Regardless, the true targets for his operation were the people of Africa. He needed fresh manpower to fight.

Just like those who had hijacked the airplanes on 9-11 had altered the course of history, so would Rhazziq. He knew his plan was massive, something he called The Greatest Mind Game in History. He had one major goal: to establish the caliphate. The best way to accomplish that goal was to keep America at bay.

Rhazziq's mind reeled from the thought of a bullet entering his friend's head. But he knew that death would be immediate, as would be the release of his friend's soul.

From the partially opened curtain, Rhazziq watched the doctor walk across the dusty street. He found himself mentally picturing the shot. He eyed the sniper across the street on the rooftop, waiting and expecting.

Quizmahel continued forward, slowing a bit as if wondering why the shot had not occurred, when suddenly a young boy on a buzzing moped sped past him in the opposite direction. Rhazziq's last thought before his friend's head blew apart was that he had indeed created the most masterful psychological operation of all time.

The high-pitched whining of the moped's engine muted the shot, but as planned, the NATO caliber bullet had entered the doctor's skull and killed him instantly.

He watched his friend tumble to the ground as the moped raced by. Immediately, Rhazziq removed his satellite-enabled wireless device from his vest pocket and sent a note to his operative in Tanzania. Even Rhazziq feared the man he called The Leopard. Better to have him hunting for the HIV and Ebola cures in Tanzania than prowling the streets of Marrakesh or Rabat.

If The Leopard failed at the mission, which was unlikely, Rhazziq's backup plan was to spring Paul Inkota, a man he called The Cheetah, from the Rwandan war criminal prison in Arusha. Known for killing with two swords swinging like a pendulum in the Rwandan killing fields over twenty years ago, The Cheetah would be ready for a fresh kill.

But first, The Leopard. Rhazziq's message to him simply read: *We need the medicine.*

4

Amanda held the secure satellite iridium phone to her ear as she knelt behind a generator and watched the thatch huts of the orphanage burn. Kiram and Mumbato flanked her with two Askari securing her position, just as they had rehearsed. The afternoon sun seemed to propel the fire from hut to hut. The jungle was about a quarter mile away. Thankfully Sharifa had gathered the orphans in the safe house, then had begun moving them to rally point number two. Amanda had instructed one of the guards to don the protective gear and drive the lone Land Rover with a barely conscious Likika and Arthur King's body in the back. Amanda had rehearsed this evacuation plan with Sharifa just a few weeks earlier, minus the concept of a dead body.

Amanda watched the procession diminish to the east as she dialed her father's number.

When he answered, she said, "Dad, we're being attacked. We think it's just one person, but we're not sure. He killed Dr. King, and now he's burning the village, which we are evacuating. Sharifa is on her way to our rally point with the kids," she said in a calm voice that belied her fear.

Her father, Colonel Zachary Garrett, listened, she presumed, from his Special Forces command post in Djibouti in the Horn of Africa. "Have you executed your defensive plan?" he asked.

Amanda stared intently at the flames engulfing two huts. "I did all that before calling you. We've got Dr. King's body in the Land Rover moving to the rally point with the main group. I'm with Kiram and Mumbato, and we're executing Broken Needle. There's no doubt in my mind that whoever is doing this is after the recipe."

Broken Needle was their code word and a reference to *Broken Arrow*, a common military contingency plan enacted when an enemy was about to overrun a defensive perimeter. The commander would call in *Broken Arrow*, which would result in the Air Force dropping danger-close bombs to attempt to repel the attackers and, sometimes, to destroy equipment so the enemy could not use it in the future.

She had prayed she would never have to implement *Broken Needle* but always understood it was a possibility. But still, the impact would be felt far and wide. They were close to solving the riddle of HIV and Ebola. In addition to finding positive-to-negative conversions in the children, they had proven both the cure and the vaccine worked by testing a portion of the truck drivers who delivered their supplies on a weekly basis. Over the years, they had been able to identify about twenty HIV-negative men of the 111 drivers that would sojourn along the trade route past their village. They had inoculated the twenty men with the vaccine and, for the other ninety-one, had provided the cure. All but one of the twenty vaccine recipients had remained HIV-negative. There was some question as to whether the twentieth man had already been infected and had not yet turned seropositive when initially tested with the Western blot test. When he'd showed positive months after receiving the vaccination, Dr. King had ordered that Amanda provide him the natural remedy, which had worked. Later he was deemed seronegative and given the vaccine.

Of the ninety-one cure recipients, twelve had died and the remainder eventually converted to serum negative. Some required repeated testing. Of the nine Ebola victims they had treated, all had survived and recovered after administration of the same formula Amanda and King had developed to cure and vaccinate against HIV. They had reams of data stored on the computers in both laboratories. She was proudest of the fact that she was training Kiram to be a doctor. Kiram had helped with nearly every administration of the vaccine. He would look the children or the truck drivers in the eyes, holding them by the shoulders, reassuring them in their native tongue while Amanda inserted the special serum into their arms.

Amanda knew and had recorded all of the ingredients to the recipe except for one, and that was the black paste that Kiram and Mumbato would bring back from their "special place." She had tried to conduct a chemical decomposition of the substance and found that her results kept coming back as what biologists called angiosperm xylem. She preferred to call it the insides of a hardwood tree. She'd found properties such as potassium, calcium, magnesium, nitrogen, and a mystery element she so far had been unable to identify. She had been close to making the boys take her on the trek to the special place, but now this.

"Okay, which rally point?" her father said over their secure satellite link.

"We're moving toward rally point two. Rally point one is unsafe right now," Amanda said. Rally point one was the laboratory where Dr. King had been working. She presumed it would be risky to go there.

"Okay. And?"

"We're taking all necessary supplies," Amanda said, then paused. "I mean *all*," she emphasized.

"Okay, honey, I will have a team link up with you at rally point two, and you'll be good to go. Be safe. Love you," her father said.

"Good to go. Love you."

They each hung up the phone after speaking in partial rehearsed code. Her father had instructed Amanda to use the iridium phone only in extremis. Nothing could be more extreme than an attack on the village where someone was seeking the recipe. She knew that her uncle, Matt, and her father were two of only a few people who had access to and responsibilities regarding *Project Nightingale.* Typically they communicated in coded, innocuous texts and emails such as the one she had sent to Jake earlier, or "Solved two puzzles today, Dad. Love you…"

Amanda rallied her charges. Like a football coach talking to a quarterback in a big game, she snatched Kiram by the arm and shouted, "You and Mumbato check the orphanage one last time with the Askari, then we will link up at the cellar and move out to rally point two from there."

"Yes, ma'am. Everyone else is already gone, but we make final check now. Rest of Askari took villagers away, also."

"Good. We'll shut down the lab, grab our supplies, and then move out."

"Everything is on fire, Miss Amanda. Hurry."

As if to emphasize his point, a thatch hut burst into flames as the wind pushed the fire from one structure to the next like a fireball from hell rolling through the village. Amanda flinched at the warmth cast upon her face as they knelt in the center of what would soon be a ghost town. The Mwanza orphanage sat on the outskirts of a small village, which served as a truck stop on the north-south artery of eastern Africa. Less than one hundred villagers actually lived in the town that was nearly a mile away. Amanda was glad to know that the local police forces were protecting those people as well. The CIA paid for her two guards at the orphanage, yet the intelligence organization had eschewed deeper security so as to not overtly reveal *Project Nightingale* as an agency operation. Her uncle, Matt, had called it *hiding in plain sight*, which had worked well until now. Amanda knew that the image the CIA wanted to project was that *Nightingale* was just another of thousands of American humanitarian projects around the continent. Yet once she'd begun achieving results, the word must have begun to spread.

"Go now," she said quietly. She gave Kiram a gentle shove and watched Mumbato follow. In truth, she didn't want either of them to see what she was about to do. The laboratory was isolated and might not catch fire like the huts. She couldn't take any chances. As part of *Broken Needle*, her CIA instructions were to destroy the laboratory to conceal any evidence of *Project Nightingale*. Since the Tanzanian government had no knowledge of the program, they could not run the risk of anything from the research remaining behind. Amanda ran across the dirt road toward one of the burning huts and grabbed a three-foot-long chunk of flaming acacia that had been used as a support beam. The wood was hot to the touch but manageable. Holding the burning branch at a distance, she jogged to the laboratory and tossed it onto the wooden porch. She watched the flame licking at the parched planks of the steps and then the building behind it. Soon the façade of the laboratory was lit, and Amanda knew it would not be long before the entire building was destroyed. Burned with the building would be any linkages to the HIV and Ebola vaccine program, save her go-bag.

Now Amanda ran in the opposite direction and turned the corner toward the soccer field. The blackened embers of a former mud and thatch hut lay at the farthest end of the orphanage from the laboratory. She had deliberately constructed a cellar on the back side of her hut, where she kept a go-bag of the recipe's essential ingredients: small quantities of the mixed vaccine they called "ready-vac," larger quantities of the cure, vials of the black paste, and several small glass bottles of live HIV and Ebola for testing. These were the key elements of their program, which had been weeks, if not days, from going operational. Now, without Dr. King and with thieves in pursuit of their work, who knew how long it would be?

She stepped quickly into her hut, took thirty seconds to grab her external drive, and pressed two buttons that wiped her computer.

As she heard the Askari either exchanging gunfire or shooting blindly at someone she couldn't see, she ran from her home, clutching the external drive containing all of her test data. Taking the steps in one leap, she dashed for the secret facility beneath the storm doors less than fifty meters from her hut.

Two doors on hinges that lay at an angle protected the stairwell that led to an underground room that had been built with sturdy mahogany boards. She had padlocked the door, so she slid the key attached to the necklace of her locket to her front where she could unlock the hasp. She pulled back the shutters, which were constructed very similar to a Kansas tornado shelter.

Instinctively, she patted her breast pocket to ensure she still had her satellite iPhone secured in her vest, which she did. Amanda also subconsciously tapped her cargo pocket to reassure herself that she had the iridium satellite phone, which she did. She climbed down the steps into the shelter, the sounds of gunfire snapping through the village. Amidst the chaos, she stopped what she was doing, pulled her iPhone from her vest pocket, and typed out a quick email to her husband, Jake.

Jake, Love you. Under some stress now. Call my dad. Be safe. Always and all ways, Amanda.

She watched the data wheel spin her email to Jake and tucked the iPhone back into her vest pocket. Regaining focus, Amanda spotted the green Army rucksack and the small medical supply cooler plugged into the wall. The generator powered the cooler, which effectively served as a refrigerator. She calculated that the batteries would last about forty-eight hours before the viruses died and the serums decomposed if they did not get to a new refrigeration source or electrical power. She hoisted the ruck onto her back and then, at the last moment, unplugged the cooler.

In the rucksack, which she had inspected weekly since creating their emergency plan, were a smaller backpack, called an assault pack, and all the essentials for restarting the program and keeping their work alive. Laboring in secrecy had been a tough call. There were many who wanted to claim credit for what she and Dr. King were doing, which was not a big concern to Amanda. However, those who wanted to claim credit wanted to do so for financial or nefarious purposes. Amanda's work was purely humanitarian and funded by the CIA, which came with strings attached. One of those strings was to keep the operation secret until they could reliably mass-produce the formula. Their rapid success was unexpected, catching Amanda, Dr. King, and the agency unprepared for a full-scale attack.

Also, she knew that there were those who did not want the cure or the vaccine to come to fruition. Amanda did not understand the reasons people might have this distorted vision. The vaccine in particular represented a sort of Rosetta stone. It would forever change the course of history, especially on this continent.

Amanda scrambled up the steps of the cellar and was met by a hot wind blowing into her face.

"This way, Miss Amanda," Kiram screamed. She saw Kiram and Mumbato running toward her, but with clear intent to continue beyond her. The fire was belching from the windows of a nearby hut like greedy orange arms reaching skyward.

With the Askari providing covering fire, Kiram snatched the cooler from Amanda as the three of them gathered and began trotting to the southeast, toward rally point number two, an abandoned airfield forty miles away.

5

The Leopard watched the blond American woman through his riflescope as he received the message from Zhor Rhazziq, his current employer. He felt his left arm vibrate, causing him to look at his new satellite Al Rhazziq Media wearable sleeve, or ARM-Sleeve. The device was a high-tech carbon fiber sheath, much like a football quarterback's forearm playbook, that covered his massive left wrist and part of his arm. He saw the message.

We need the medicine.

No shit, he thought. He would deliver. He had already killed the white-haired doctor and left him in the woods for one of the orphans to discover.

He used the camera function on his ARM-Sleeve to quickly snap two pictures of the American girl tossing the log onto the medical clinic. Those would prove valuable for the propaganda war and would keep Rhazziq off his ass. Essentially a wearable iPhone, his ARM-Sleeve enabled him to immediately email the photos to Rhazziq. He knew that Rhazziq had developed the cutting-edge wearable technology to compete with Google and Apple. The Leopard could watch streaming video, download email, browse the Internet, and make phone calls on his ARM-Sleeve.

He pressed the fabric to shut down the device and save battery life, though the batteries were constantly recharging via solar energy. Looking up, he studied Amanda Garrett and waited for her to make her move for the cure. Like the sniper he was, The Leopard lay perfectly still four hundred meters away. As he waited, he thought about how he had killed Dr. King yesterday.

Yesterday, The Leopard had pre-positioned himself near Lake Victoria, Tanzania, where he'd found a different small village that was teeming in the day with young African children and a few constabularies smoking cigarettes. The target folder Rhazziq had provided him identified this village as containing the production facility, while a woman named Amanda Garrett ran the testing program some seventy miles away. The altitude, near eight thousand feet, and the fact that they were in the wet season had made for a brisk drive in his open-air vehicle. But the sun had brought temperatures into the mid-nineties during the day as he observed through binoculars from a distant hilltop the patterns of life in the town. As night had fallen, he had watched the constabularies retire to a mud hut, probably to chew on some qhat. The children had all vanished inside similar structures as if on cue.

The Leopard repositioned his vehicle on the backside of a small forest about a half mile from the village. He followed the edge of the dense foliage toward the ersatz community.

He stood at the end of the tree line, no less than one hundred meters from the village. He saw a dirt road framed by single-story mud structures with open doorways and windows. Set apart from the huts was a wooden building, much more recently built, though its architecture was similar to the other buildings.

This was his target.

Walking behind the huts, he passed trash and feces and the usual flotsam of an underfunded and forgotten orphanage. He ascended the steps of the medical clinic and opened the door.

There he found Dr. Arthur King sitting with his back to him staring at a computer monitor, apparently so deep in thought that The Leopard's presence did not register.

"Where is the cure?" The Leopard asked.

The man looked like his dossier photo, The Leopard thought. Arthur King, a wiry immunologist from Ohio, calmly turned around and looked at his hulking presence in the doorway.

"Excuse me?"

"You've got five minutes to give me the HIV and Ebola recipes or I will kill you. It's that simple."

The Leopard's English was nearly perfect, but he could weave the Maghreb octave into a heavy Middle Eastern accent when necessary, as he did now under the assumption an Arabic voice might project more fear into the American.

"Seems like two shitty options," the doctor replied. A wave of understanding crossed over his face. "Who sent you? A pharmaceutical company?"

The Leopard said nothing.

"It's not here." King shrugged. The Leopard almost believed him, but the defiance in the doctor's eyes told a different story.

The Leopard was large, about six and a half feet tall and close to 250 pounds. His ripped muscles flexed beneath the silken sheen of his black T-shirt that hugged his frame like body paint.

"Besides, you're going to kill me anyway," Dr. King smugly responded. "And with me, you will kill millions of people who will never get the treatments that I can deliver. AIDS is wiping out this country, and Ebola could wipe out the world."

"Such a tragedy," The Leopard said, sliding a Ka-Bar knife from its sheath. "Last chance. Are you going to tell me what I want to hear?"

Dr. King eyed the knife, swallowed hard, and shook his head. The Leopard slid behind the small man, grabbed his chin, and lifted it upward as he pressed the finely honed blade against King's carotid artery.

"This knife will cut your artery, and you will die in less than a minute," he said.

"I'm a doctor. I know. But neither the recipe nor the ingredients are here."

The Leopard pulled some rope from his tactical vest and tied the doctor to the chair. In five minutes, he trashed the entire lab, then came back to the computer, which he noticed had a blue screen. The blue screen of death, he thought. The doctor had, at some point, erased everything on the hard drive.

"Sorry about that," King mocked.

The Leopard used one hand to lift Dr. King's neck upward, as if he were about to bleed out a pig. Placing the knife against the left carotid artery midway down King's neck, he whispered, "I know you have another laboratory, Doctor."

He felt the man shiver under his arm, perhaps wondering how The Leopard knew, or realizing his work and colleague could all be lost, making his heroic silence useless. Or perhaps he was just scared.

With a quick push, he slid the knife into King's throat. He pulled it out and wiped the blade with a lab towel. Death was everywhere, he thought, especially on this continent. What was the difference between a black kid dying of Ebola or a white man dying from a cut neck? Not much, he reasoned.

Though he was aware of the task he had just performed and of its impact on millions of people, he had more work to do. With this lab destroyed and still no filled memory stick or vials of formula to show for it, he needed to move quickly.

He untied the doctor from his chair and wrapped a towel around the dead man's neck to absorb what blood had not already left his body. Lifting the featherweight man over his shoulders as if carrying a bag of seed, The Leopard pushed through the screen door of the wooden building filled with beakers and spectrometers. From the outside, the shack looked like a French mountain still. On the inside, however, it boasted the most recent advancements in medical technology.

Standing on the porch, he noticed the Tanzanian firmament above him. Brilliant arrays of white and yellow stars swirled around the sky like artwork. He saw Orion and the faint hint of the Southern Cross. Billions of pinpricks viewed him with a steady gaze, as if some powerful being were on the other side shining a spotlight against the black curtain.

Having already poured the gasoline, walking away from the building, he flicked the lighter lid upward and nudged the switch that would hold open the butane aperture. He tossed the burning lighter into the doorway. To his satisfaction, flames immediately licked upward and spread like demons running scared along the plywood floors.

He stepped into the jeep and cranked the engine, which idled roughly. He had about a two-hour drive to his final stop. This time he would employ tactics, not a direct assault. He would envelop the area in an indirect approach to allow him to observe the young doctor's movements, which he believed would lead him to his goal. She wasn't even a doctor; she was just an idealistic medical student whiling her summer and winter breaks away in Tanzania.

Clearly the frontal assault had not worked on Dr. King; The Leopard had not secured the formula. He'd suspected that approach might not be the most productive, given the import of the project King and the girl had been developing. Yet, of the two dossiers he had developed on his targets, he had selected King as the one who would be most responsive to direct threat, if either of the two would respond to such a tactic.

Nonetheless, King had not, and part of The Leopard respected him for that.

Last night he had laid the doctor's body in the woods to employ an indirect approach. He needed the girl to grab the cure, and then he would make his move.

Now, observing Amanda Garrett from a thicket outside the village of Mwanza, he watched a second village burn in less than twenty-four hours and laid the crosshairs of the scope affixed to his rifle onto the stairwell opening into which Amanda Garrett had descended. *Like smoking out mice from a sugarcane field*, The Leopard thought.

The two African boys ran from behind one of the burning huts toward the cellar. The constabulary quit securing the cellar and began trying to extinguish the fire that was devouring Amanda's hut. The Leopard could see a vehicle and the band of orphans heading away quickly in the distance to the south.

He noticed movement in the dark hole, just the slightest flicker of blond hair, as if she had started up the steps and then dropped back into the cellar. Perhaps she had forgotten something.

Moving the scope to one of the two African boys, he assessed their stature. They were strong and able and seemed loyal to the girl. So he moved the weapon to the constabularies, who had drifted farther into the village, which was nothing but a raging inferno. His plan was working perfectly. He fired two accurate, silenced shots, killing the Askari.

As he moved the scope back to the cellar, he saw that he had missed the girl's exit. She and the two boys were running south toward the lead group of orphans, who had a thirty-minute head start on Garrett and her companions.

Then he heard the sound of a gasoline engine in the sky. A white Sherpa airplane banked low over the village, like a gull seeking safe purchase but finding none.

His brilliant plan was suddenly askew as he noticed the airplane line up for a landing on the road that led south from the orphanage.

6

Amanda watched an airplane circle low once and then again. It looked like the small wings-above-the-fuselage Sherpa cargo plane that did the resupply runs. She wondered if the pilot and his crew were watching the fire or coming to rescue them. Either way, she knew it wasn't the resupply day, and even if it were, the airfield was forty miles away. The planes usually did not travel this far north.

By now they were jogging as best they could with the cooler and backpack. The cooler was about the size of a small Igloo Playmate that would carry a six-pack of beer. Amanda saw Mumbato look at Kiram hauling the cooler. Not to be outdone, he tried to grab the backpack from her, but she refused to transfer her precious cargo to the teenager.

"You can help when I get tired," she told Mumbato. "Rotate carrying the cooler with Kiram."

She looked at the airplane that was now lined up directly to their six o'clock as if it were on a strafing run. The plane lowered gradually and continued on azimuth in their direction. Now only one hundred meters or so behind them, she began to worry that the airplane could have someone aboard who was after *Project Nightingale.*

"Quick, get off the road!" she commanded as the airplane buzzed over them. They scrambled to the side and landed in a small ditch that was filled with briars. Amanda moved the hair out of her face and checked on her two boys. They were scared but focused.

As the small airplane buzzed low over their heads, dust and debris sandblasted them. Amanda turned her head in the opposite direction and closed her eyes. She could feel the prop wash from the airplane blow grit into every unconcealed portion of her body, mostly her ears.

"Airplane land," Kiram said softly. He pointed in the direction they were traveling as they dared to turn into the dust storm created by the landing aircraft. Amanda opened her eyes, carefully wiping grime away from her face.

She watched the airplane land and roll to a quick stop. The dust billowed around the white fuselage as a form emerged from the craft. Amanda wiped her eyes again, removing more of the dust she could feel caking against her skin.

Stepping from the cloud was a vaguely familiar form that she couldn't quite place. Her mind was immediately drawn to her college memories at Columbia University, and she realized who it was.

"Amanda!" called Webb Ewell.

"Webb?" she answered against the din of the spinning airplane propellers.

"Amanda, are you okay?" he asked as he jogged toward her.

She stood and climbed the short distance out of the ditch.

"Webb?" she asked again, though she could plainly see it was him. He approached from a few yards away.

"Seriously? What's going on?"

Instinctively she hugged him, simply happy to see an old friend and someone who might be able to help them out of the current situation. Webb was dressed in khaki pants and a white dress shirt, as if he had just come from a boardroom meeting or a preppie party. He was six feet tall with dark brown hair. Strong but not athletic, Webb was one of those all-around good guys, she remembered.

"Didn't expect to see me here, did you?" Webb shouted.

Kiram and Mumbato emerged from the ditch and quickly came to Amanda's side, as if to protect her.

"Everything okay, Miss Amanda?" Kiram asked her.

Amanda turned toward Kiram and said, "Yes, this is a friend of mine. He's going to help us."

"That's right. It looks like you guys need to get out of here fast. Let's get on the airplane," Webb shouted. She looked over his shoulder at the buzzing aircraft and saw a black man looking through the open door and pumping his fist, the international symbol for, "Let's get the hell out of here."

"You're serious? What are you even doing here?" Amanda gasped. Then, hearing the fire rage, she motioned toward the airplane and said, "You're my hero."

"Let's go!" he shouted as he grabbed Amanda by the arm and began to run toward the airplane.

"Come on, guys!" Amanda called over her shoulder.

Kiram and Mumbato jogged toward the Sherpa. Kiram still carried the cooler in one hand while Amanda lugged the backpack on her shoulders. All of them ducked as they ran into the full blast of the Sherpa's prop wash prior to entering the rear cargo door, dropped onto the road like a tongue. Amanda skidded onto the metal floor and carefully lowered the backpack beside her. Kiram and Mumbato were running behind the now moving airplane. Kiram slid the cooler next to her as he and Mumbato raced behind the airplane.

Amanda saw the pilot wave his hand and shout, "Go! We must go!"

While Kiram and Mumbato each had one foot on the cargo compartment and one foot on the ground, the airplane increased its speed. She leaned over and grasped an arm of each of the boys, who were trying to hold on.

Leaning back, she felt both boys move toward her and land on the floor of the airplane. Her head hit the back of the pilot's seat, but at least she had all of her charges.

She lay there a moment, collecting her thoughts, when she noticed small holes suddenly appear in the side of the aircraft, sending one-inch-diameter lasers of sunlight spearing through the cargo bay.

When Mumbato grabbed his arm, which was bleeding, she realized someone was shooting at them.

The Sherpa bucked as it left the road and shot skyward, causing Amanda to slam into the rear of the aircraft. She had been attempting to tie a tourniquet on Mumbato's arm and nearly did a full tumble backward.

"Are you okay, Miss Amanda?" Mumbato asked, holding his bleeding arm.

"I'm fine," she said, straightening and moving her hair behind her ears. She took her kerchief and refastened it above Mumbato's left bicep, which had actually caught a piece of shrapnel from the skin of the airplane when a bullet had exploded through the aluminum.

"Me, too," Mumbato said. "I'm fine."

Amanda finished tying the knot, exhaled heavily, felt the plane surge again, and then looked at Kiram, whose eyes were staring straight ahead at the backs of the heads of the pilot and Webb Ewell. Amanda watched him as the warm air buffeted them through the open cargo door. His mahogany eyes seemed especially dilated, almost entirely black. His scalp and close-cropped hair were glistening with sweat; but somewhere in the madness, Kiram had found the time to put on a green and red soccer jersey. Probably when she had gone to get the supplies, Amanda figured. As she watched him, it seemed his countenance remained clear, almost mystic, as if he were staring into a different astral plane.

"You okay?" Amanda asked Kiram.

When she got no response, Amanda crawled toward Kiram at the same time that Webb leaned back from the copilot's seat and shouted, "You guys okay?"

Amanda looked up and nodded, giving him a weak thumbs-up sign.

"We need to go to Kenasha Airfield," she said. "That's our destination."

"Crazy, you know this airfield?" Webb said to the pilot.

"Yes, yes, I know. It's the airfield we were going to. About thirty miles southeast. No problem."

Amanda watched the interchange, noticing the worried look on the pilot's face that said, *I'm not telling you everything.* More importantly, she thought, *the pilot's name is Crazy? Really?*

She looked over her shoulder and saw the thick jungle beneath them. Two main tributaries fed into Lake Victoria from the south. These streams were bordered by dense jungle on either side. Though navigable, the forests were filled with lush undergrowth that made any travel a tough slog.

Amanda had little experience in the African outback beyond the occasional hiking adventure with the orphans. Those were usually tame events led by an experienced guide and a well-armed militia member or two. Though the wars were over, the wounds were still fresh and deep.

"We're going to crash!" Webb shouted.

Amanda looked up at the pilot, who was nervously playing with a control in between the two seats. The plane's aspect was angled forward, and she could see through the open starboard cargo door that the ground was rapidly approaching. The pilot let out a slew of African curse words that she recognized. Crazy glanced nervously to his right and left and then leaned forward to look over the dashboard through the windscreen, which could have used a good cleaning. As he turned his head in her direction, Amanda saw wide eyes filled with fear.

"What's going on, Crazy?" Webb asked nervously.

"We are out of gas," he said flatly, his voice belying his facial expressions.

"I thought you said…"

"I know what I said, but someone either shot a hole in the gas tank or we hit a rock on that road because we are—"

The propeller began sputtering and coughing.

"Shit," said the pilot.

"Do something, man," Webb hollered, anxiety clearly taking over.

Amanda's instincts kicked in.

"Kiram! Mumbato! Lie down on the floor and hold on to these," she said. She lifted a small metal D ring that was anchored into the floor of the aircraft. They were most often used for securing cargo to the floor of the aircraft so that freight would not shift or slide during flight. "Kiram, help Mumbato." Amanda then lay atop the two boys who were lying face down on the sheet metal floor of the aircraft. She hooked the snap link of a three-inch wide cargo strap into one of the D rings, pulled it across their stacked bodies, and snapped the other link into the floorboard. She cinched the strap tight across them, like a big seat belt. When it became hard to breath she quit pulling on the tightening strap. "Both of you, hold on tight," she said. She wedged the cooler and backpack into a small nook between the pilot's and copilot's seats, quickly laced straps from each through the D rings, and kept her hand pressed firmly on the backpack. The cooler was locked, insulated, and padded. Her rucksack was less so. She could feel the boys beneath her trembling. Neither had ever flown in an airplane.

"Jesus, man, we're going to die!" Webb shouted from the front seat. Amanda looked up and saw Webb pulling at his hair as if he were trying to figure out a tough math problem.

"Crazy, can you land this on the road?" Amanda shouted above Webb's screaming. She looked at Webb, and she flashed on him briefly at Columbia. He had always seemed to be...wherever she was. Perhaps he'd had a crush on her, but her love for Jake shut down any opening for a potential suitor. They had taken several biology and chemistry classes together, but Webb had gone in a different direction than medical studies, though not entirely.

"No bother me." Crazy was pushing and pulling on the controls of the aircraft. The engine had shut down, and they were in a deep glide. Amanda felt the plane losing altitude quickly, but not without some semblance of control.

She felt the wheels nip the first of the trees.

"Jesus!" Webb was clearly out of control. Amanda, for her part, stayed within herself, retreating to that place she had learned to go when she needed help the most. God had always been there for her. *I'm curious about this one, God,* she thought to herself.

The second strike on the aircraft was more forceful, and Amanda dared to peek. She saw the tops of trees above the airplane as she looked out of the open starboard cargo door. Not an altogether bad sign, she surmised. The closer to the ground the better.

"Watch out!" Webb screamed, though Amanda had already begun tuning him out. Their lives were with God now. Her work was too important for mankind, and she believed—she had to believe—that her accomplishments were divinely guided and that God would want her to continue. No, the HIV and Ebola programs would not die an unceremonious death in the African outback.

She felt a large object strike the aircraft, and despite her faith, fear dominated her mind. Her thoughts shifted from *Project Nightingale* and God to her husband and then her father.

"Help me, Daddy. Jake? God?" she whispered. Closing her eyes again, she clutched tightly to her backpack and the cooler. She pressed her face into Kiram's back as he turned and tried to look at her. He wanted eye contact, she could tell. So she leaned over and looked into his deep eyes, which stared back not in fear but with a clear expression, as if he knew everything was going to be okay.

"Good wins," he whispered to her. That was their common refrain and hope.

"Good wins," she said back, trying to sound as reassuring as he had.

She thought she heard Mumbato say, "Sometimes." But his head was turned, so she couldn't be sure given the chaos surrounding them at the moment. She hugged her boys, protecting what was left of her flock. She had nursed these two orphan boys back to health. And Mumbato was living proof that the cure worked.

So many had tried to develop a vaccine or cure. She and Dr. King had succeeded on both accounts.

Project Nightingale; Jake Devereaux, her new husband; Zachary Garrett, her father; God; Kiram; Mumbato; and her uncle, Matt, were all cycling through her mind as the aircraft crashed into the Kenasha Stream fifty miles east of Lake Victoria.

She had one last thought before the plane hit the dirt. She remembered, *Webb Ewell hadn't gone on to pursue a doctorate or further research. He didn't get a job in a medical practice.*

He had gone to work for a pharmaceutical company.

7

The Leopard believed he had shot a hole in at least one of the plane's gas tanks. He had aimed primarily at the wings using his Sig Sauer 101 Hunting Rifle with 4X scope. A couple of the .30-06 rounds had most likely entered the fuselage, but there was no avoiding that. Best case, he had not hit Amanda Garrett and they would force land on the same road.

Worst case, the airplane would crash, everyone in it would die, and the recipe would be destroyed in flames. The airplane had caught him by surprise. His plan had worked perfectly until the rogue aircraft had made a daring crash landing on the dirt road.

The Leopard picked his way through the jungle, found his jeep, and cranked the engine. Looking over his shoulder, he spied the billowing smoke from the orphanage. In less than twenty-four hours, he had wreaked significant havoc on this swath of land.

Nothing they haven't seen before, he said to himself. Yet something nagged at him. While he generally did not overreact to uncertainty, he was curious about the airplane that had saved the girl and the *Nightingale* formulas.

Had his organization betrayed him? Had two operatives been given the same mission? Had someone outsmarted him and used a more reliable technique? Rhazziq would do that, he figured.

The questions served as fuel for his ambition to complete the job. He believed that nobody was better than he was, which motivated him. Even if his own or another organization were after the cure, he would ultimately succeed.

Rhazziq had given The Leopard five hundred thousand U.S. dollars to accomplish this mission, with another one and a half million to follow when he delivered. If he did not meet success, he would keep the five hundred thousand, yet ultimately there would be a price on his own head, and he would never be able to rest for fear of someone like him picking him off from a mile away with a sniper shot.

For the last year, he had watched with interest the establishment of the Islamic State and thought that his expertise would prove useful to the highest bidder. He was ambivalent about the establishment of the caliphate but saw opportunity in the chaos. He would pursue those opportunities to quench his killing thirst and reap financial benefit as the Islamic State stretched from Europe and the western shores of Africa to the far reaches of Indonesia.

After serving as a sniper in Rwanda, he had deserted from the French Army and become a rogue gun for hire around the world, conducting assassinations, fighting with foreign armies, and participating in insurgencies, such as those in the Balkans, Sierra Leone, and Afghanistan. He had made the mistake of returning to France, where he had been apprehended at a former girlfriend's apartment in the southern coastal town of Toulon. While The Leopard could fly a helicopter or small airplane, he had chosen to arrive in Toulon by boat at night. Unfortunately, the ship's captain had been working as a bounty hunter for the French government for many years and had wasted no time in turning him in.

The captain had been the first man The Leopard had killed upon his escape.

And on this particular mission, when an interested party had offered two million dollars to him, well, there was never a doubt as to what he would do.

With the money in mind, The Leopard sped his jeep along a trail on the west side of the stream that ran in between his position and the road from which the airplane had departed. He believed that he would find the aircraft about ten miles south of his location. He knew of a crossing about two miles up the road.

His patience wearing thin, he would find the airplane and Amanda Garrett.

8

U.S. Army Colonel Zach Garrett and his CIA operative brother, Matt, jogged toward the Gulfstream G5 jet waiting in the corrugated metal hangar.

They had been in Zach's Special Forces headquarters in Djibouti reviewing the CIA report of the assassination of Islamic State senior leader Hawan Quizmahel when Amanda had called from Mwanza declaring *Broken Needle*.

Both Matt and Zach had decided to make the trip to Tanzania. Zach's two primary commando warfighters, Hobart and Van Dreeves, still in the process of traveling to Djibouti, were not yet available. Frankly, there was never any question whether the two of them would go, whether their two Special Forces operative friends had been on hand or not.

As they ran to the hangar, each of them checked their Berretta nine-millimeter pistols. They also had two silenced M4 rifles slung across their backs. They were dressed in midnight black jumpsuits that zippered from the collar down to the crotch.

They walked up the ramp to the G5 that was waiting at the newly paved airfield in the Joint Task Force-Djibouti basecamp. The huge hangar doors slowly opened as the two brothers climbed the steps of the jet.

Zach made a point to meet both pilots based upon a previous experience Matt had had with a pilot who had turned out to be a part of a terrorist sleeper cell in the U.S. Air Force. These men were CIA pilots, and Zach was accordingly satisfied that there was to be no hijacking of this particular aircraft today.

"Shotgun," Zach called.

"Hey, my airplane, bro."

"Tough shit," Zach said as he sat in the big leather chair in the forward cabin and put his feet up on the facing chair. This move relegated Matt, the younger brother to begin with, either to the bench chair along the side or to the multiple leather chairs in the aft cabin.

"Fine," Matt said. He sat on the bench, dropped his ruck on the floor, and lay on the full-length padded bench.

"We need to get moving," Zach urged.

As he saw the crew chief begin to raise the steps that also served as the entry to the airplane, Kristyana Cixi came running up to the Gulfstream.

"Hang on, guys, you need to see this before you take off," she said. Trying to catch her breath, she was holding out a piece of paper to the crew chief, who suspiciously stared at Kristyana until Zach told him to hand him the paper. Kristyana was a petite Indonesian-American woman who had graduated first in her West Point class before becoming a Rhodes Scholar and State Department analyst. Her interest in serving in Djibouti coincided with an interest in Matt Garrett.

"I'm coming with you," she said. Kristyana waited for the crew chief to lower the steps to full extension before climbing the ladder. She was carrying her own duffel over her shoulder. As soon as the crew chief snapped the door shut, the airplane was rolling off the runway and lifting into the sky.

Zach looked at the paper and then at Matt.

"What?" Matt asked.

"Listen to this bullshit," Zach said and began to read.

Al Rhazziq Media: Dar es Salaam: Today: Tanzanian authorities are searching for Amanda Garrett, an American woman who is believed to have murdered a scientist who was working closely with Islamic State sources on the development of a vaccine for HIV, the virus that causes AIDS, and the Ebola virus, which is killing thousands of Africans along the west coast. This woman is also believed to have raided an orphanage, burned the village, captured the cure, and has now taken at least two orphanage personnel hostage in the jungle. Amanda Garrett is the daughter of American Army Colonel Zachary Garrett and the niece of Central Intelligence Agency spy Matthew Garrett.

The Tanzanian government official we spoke with, who asked to remain anonymous, said that they were quickly investigating the possibility of an American conspiracy to steal the HIV and Ebola cures from the Islamic State.

"You've got to be shittin' me," Matt said. "Amanda's been working that project from day one. Who's doing this to her? To *Nightingale*? That's *our* program. We handpicked her."

Zachary continued to stare at a printout of an Internet story from MSNBC. The lead photo was of his daughter, Amanda, tossing a burning piece of wood onto the porch of a building. In the picture, he could make out the faintest hint of a sign next to the screen door. The sign was a simple red cross. The paint was faded but clearly distinguishable.

"Oh, man," Zach muttered.

"Someone set her up," Matt said flatly.

"The plan was always to torch the lab if someone came after them," Zach said absently.

"I know. Let me make a phone call back to Langley to see if I can't get some insight on this one," Matt said.

"Roger. After that, I need to call the rear team in Stuttgart to let them know where we're going. *Nightingale* is on our top tier list of NEO plans," Zach said. He was referring to the Noncombatant Evacuation Operation list, which his brother's organization was responsible for monitoring and potentially executing. *Nightingale* was the name Matt had allowed Amanda to select for the program she oversaw. The NEO list typically included all of the U.S. embassies within the region as well as other high-profile facilities and programs. Even if Amanda were not involved in this crisis, Zach would have some level of responsibility in either planning or performing the evacuation given his new military duties.

"It would be nice to get Hobart and Van Dreeves on their way down here," Matt said.

"Already in motion," Zach said.

Kristyana came forward as the airplane's wheels snapped shut beneath the airplane.

"Just got an update. Amanda is out of the village with the recipe and has Kiram and Mumbato from the orphanage with her," she said.

"Where we getting that from?" Matt asked.

"Amanda sent us a text message," Kristyana replied, showing Matt and Zach her satellite cell phone display. *Moving. K, M w/ me.*

"That's my girl," Zach said.

"It was a group text. Check your phones. Anyway, they're both big, strong kids, and they love Amanda," Kristyana said.

"Don't we all," Zach said.

Zach and Matt checked their phones, and Zach nodded as he reassured himself by seeing the two simple, abbreviated sentences. He turned his head and looked out of the Gulfstream window. He spied the rugged expanse of southern Ethiopia gliding beneath them. He thought he could make out the winding etching of the White Nile on the west side of the plane and the steep ravines of the Rift Valley on the east side. Everything he saw reminded him of Amanda. Her love for Africa. Her compassion. Her courage. He stared at the river and thought that, like a primary artery of the body, the Nile was one of the world's most vital ecosystems helping this forlorn land and its people hang on, however tenuously. And so was Amanda. He welled with love and pride as he thought about her principled courage to help fight disease in Africa.

They droned on in silence for the majority of the flight, Zach figuring they were all three lost in thoughts about Amanda.

Kilimanjaro Airport was an asphalt runway that stretched like a long, bony finger from north to south. As they approached the runway, Zach could see the terrain rising abruptly off the sea floor toward Mount Kilimanjaro and the Great Rift Valley. The G5 landed with a smooth glide, rolled to a taxiway, and quickly dove inside an open hangar. Zach looked through his window and asked, "Okay, where's the Black Hawk?"

The crew chief lowered the stairwell, and they disembarked with their equipment in tow.

"Coming," Matt said, pointing to an aircraft with spinning blades.

Then he asked, "Kristyana, anything from Amanda?"

"Nothing," Kristyana said, checking her satellite phone. Muting the screen, she continued, "I've texted her twice and called her twice. Goes straight to voice mail. No reply on the text messages."

"Maybe there's no reception there," Zach said wistfully.

"It's satellite. There's always reception," Kristyana said.

An MH-60 Black Hawk helicopter piloted by Task Force 160 Night Stalker pilots ferried toward them along the ramp. They stepped outside of the hangar, and the searing Tanzanian sun baked them on the white concrete apron. Shimmering waves of heat emanated upward from the runway in the distance. Zach could make out a low forest on the opposite side of the landing strip. Soon the incessant chopping of the Black Hawk rotor blades broke his concentration.

"Try Amanda once more before we get on the Hawk," Zach said.

"Flying time to the airfield is about an hour and a half; it'll be quicker if we pour on the coals," Matt interrupted.

They grabbed their gear, looking like a small team of insurgents ready to do some damage. Ever since Matt had rescued Zachary from an Iraqi terrorist in a Chinese aircraft carrier posing as a merchant ship, the brothers had been nearly inseparable despite high-paced careers. Kristyana's own role as an intelligence officer had proved useful to the two brothers, who had a knack for marching to the sound of the guns.

Zach watched Kristyana check her M4 carbine by pulling the charging handle back, then looking inside the chamber. With no magazine in the well yet, she had no danger of locking and loading a round. She rode the charging handle forward and pulled the trigger. Then she grabbed a thirty-round magazine from her backpack and slapped it into the magazine well. She was ready. Zach was impressed.

He and Matt were performing similar function checks on their assorted weaponry when the MH-60 stopped about fifty meters away. The port crew chief leapt from the open door, jumped onto the tarmac, disconnected his communications cable from his crew helmet, and jogged toward Col. Garrett.

"We're ready when you are, sir! One MH-6 in support!" An MH-6 helicopter, known as a *Little Bird*, zipped toward their position.

"Okay, good to go. We've got a wing man," Zach said.

The crew chief gave them a thumbs-up.

Once in the helicopter, Zach, Matt, and Kristyana dumped their gear and donned headsets.

"Who we got up front?" Zach asked.

"Sir, this is Mr. Rogers. Mike Rogers. We've flown together before, sir."

"Roger that. It's a beautiful day in the neighborhood. I remember."

Rogers chuckled into the microphone. "Roger that, sir. And my copilot today is Captain Ben Strawbridge. He's our company commander."

"Okay, Mike, Ben, we're moving to the grid coordinate we passed to you before we departed from Djibouti, but we have cause to believe that we might be looking elsewhere. Bottom line, my daughter is being chased by a terrorist. She's in charge of a sensitive, specially compartmented project, and she has in her possession something more valuable than a nuclear weapon."

"Hey, sir, give me a hard one," Rogers chirped from the front in typical pilot bravado.

"Let's just get there as quickly as we can. We haven't been able to raise her on her satellite phone, so I'm concerned for two reasons. First, she's my daughter. Second, she's got all of the *Nightingale* materials with her."

After a pause, Rogers came back. "Whoa. That's serious shit, sir. We are the primary NEO aircraft for *Nightingale*."

"Serious shit. Now let's get going," Zach said. He registered that the pilots would be familiar with the terrain because they would have rehearsed the evacuation of the orphanage based upon their responsibilities.

Before Zach could finish his sentence, he felt the aircraft lift prominently into the sky, turn ninety degrees, and then tilt forward as Rogers pushed the nose over toward 150 knots.

"Little Bird's going to have a hard time keeping up, Zach," Matt said.

"He'll find us. Important thing is to get there and intercept whoever is chasing Amanda and her team."

Zach looked at his younger brother, Matt, who had rescued him twice from certain doom. As they sped across the dusty Tanzanian terrain, he felt lucky to be alive with his brother by his side. Raised on a farm, the two brothers had promised to die for one another if necessary. In their line of work, that promise had been put to the test more than once, and neither had wavered, making their trust inviolable.

Zach had no sense of foreboding even though they could possibly be heading into a firefight. Yet he stayed positive. They would land at rally point two and secure Amanda and her precious cargo before it expired.

Kristyana interrupted his introspection when she started rapidly fumbling with the push-to-talk button on her internal communications system.

"Guys, we've got a problem."

The two brothers looked at her with concern as the helicopter pushed past 150 knots. Zach saw her press her transmit button and ask, "Mister Rogers, where are we refueling?"

Rogers quickly responded, "Arusha airfield. Then Shinyanga. Then we'll finish the leg out to Mwanza, ma'am."

"Thank you."

She turned to Matt and Zach. "I just got a State Department text with a document attached that explains a Paul Inkota escaped from the International Criminal Tribunal prison in Arusha. The prison is next to the airfield where we're refueling. I have limited details, but I know this man's reputation. During the Rwandan genocide, he went by the code name 'Cheetah' and was personally responsible for killing thousands of his countrymen."

"How's this connected?" Matt asked.

"I'm not sure. But it's more than a coincidence," Kristyana said.

"Don't believe in those," Zach added.

"Wait. The attachment says he teamed with a French sniper when the French Army allowed the killers to escape."

"Huh?" Zach asked.

"There's a French sniper called The Leopard who provided safe passage for the attacking Hutu tribe. If you can believe it, the French government provided troops to allow the Hutus to escape. The Cheetah, as he's called, is a hardline Hutu who is reported to have linked up with The Leopard in Rwanda. Both are war criminals. The report suggests that they both went above and beyond the call to get a few more days of killing under their belts. The French government convicted and imprisoned The Leopard, but…holy shit."

"What?"

"The Leopard escaped from a French prison in Toulon two months ago."

"They both escaped?" Zach asked.

"How did they escape?" Matt continued.

"All I've got is on The Cheetah. Just says a group took him in a jeep and that several guards are dead in Arusha. And a Russian helicopter was seen leaving the airfield heading west, toward Mwanza. And," Kristyana added, "his last name is not original. His village elder changed it to Inkota when he was a teenager. It means: *sword*. That's how he kills."

"Find out more about this Leopard guy. If The Cheetah is just free, then maybe the French asshole is the one after Amanda," Zach said.

9

Zhor Rhazziq stared at the Atlantic Ocean. He would not be denied the medicine. His report from The Leopard was disappointing not because of the money he might lose to a failed operation—he had more money than he could spend in two lifetimes—but because the elusive cures would be another day away, at least. Already he was receiving reports of tens of thousands of Africans lining up at medical clinics for medicinal salvation from the diseases that plagued them. Once they were offered a new lease on life, they would be forever enslaved to him, Zhor Rhazziq, the leader of the Islamic State, the caliphate.

He was enough of a businessman to know that he had needed a backup plan. Where The Leopard represented finesse, The Cheetah was brute force. Finesse had not worked, and so he'd made a call to his squad of Somali Shebab, Islamic terrorists, who had been encamped in Arusha. They had devised a plan to release The Cheetah, the most prized of all Rwandan war criminals. Rhazziq tried to avoid emotion, but The Leopard's failure to deliver within twenty-four hours grated on him.

As he watched the sun begin to settle into the Atlantic Ocean, his phone buzzed.

"Yes?" he answered.

"I am free," The Cheetah said. Even his voice from halfway across the continent sent a chill down Rhazziq's spine. Rhazziq had unleashed the fiercest killer in the world, whose energy could either capture his prize or annihilate it.

"Take the Russian helicopter to Mwanza and find the recipe," Rhazziq directed. "When you have it, I will have another waiting for you."

"The Shebab have briefed me on the mission. I understand."

Not only was The Cheetah a brutal killer, he was technically a genius with an IQ above 160. Rhazziq had paid for his lawyers through a shell company, much the way he had arranged the operation to free The Leopard. The lawyers in Arusha had given The Cheetah multiple IQ tests, all of which he had easily surpassed.

"Kill who you have to, but do not harm the medical container or its contents."

"I said I understand."

Rhazziq's hair stood on the back of his neck. He ran a hand through his thick, gelled mane and closed his eyes as he pressed End on his phone.

The saltwater mingled with the ocean breeze, stinging his nostrils and eyes. While the mission to capture the cures was vitally important, it was only half of the plan.

He placed a second call to someone who answered on the first ring.

"Yes?" a female voice answered. Rhazziq stirred at even the one word she uttered.

"Status?"

"On course."

"Roger."

Both parties hung up. While he didn't believe his communications were on the radar of the United States National Security Agency, he had to be careful. Rhazziq had his own network of secure satellites that powered his African, Arabian, and European media empires. But he knew the power of the United States to infiltrate the technological domain of warfare. While the Chinese were the best at cyber war, the United States was getting better. So it was best to keep his communications short.

Rhazziq leaned against the rail of his marble deck that hung over the sandstone bluffs diving into the Atlantic Ocean. Staring at the sun sinking low in the sky, he considered all of the operations he had in place. The Leopard. The Cheetah. Nina, the woman he had just called. His combatant commanders in Syria and Iraq. He was still confident that everything was on track, even with the minor setback.

The keys to success were twofold. First, engender mass adherence to the cause, which the cures would achieve. Second, synchronize operations to destroy the Allied airbases and armies attacking the Islamic State soldiers.

He did not like the mildly hawkish move that President Barkum had made by deploying Special Forces and bomber aircraft to the region to fight ISIS and save what, Iraq? And now his informants told him there was a battalion of 82nd Airborne Division paratroopers flying toward Syria or Iraq. Rhazziq chuckled as the sea spread before him like a fluttering turquoise blanket.

Rhazziq had a plan for the president. He believed he could persuade the man to step away from the brink of total combat.

Once the president blinked, Rhazziq would plant a flag in the ground and proclaim himself the leader of the entire Islamic State.

10

Tanzania

Amanda Garrett moved her right leg and then her left. *Okay*, she thought, *my legs move. Now the arms.* She lifted each arm and inspected them, confirming in her mind that her vision seemed to be in good shape also. She might be ambulatory. The heart-shaped gold locket was still hanging around her neck. Her smashed iPhone was still inside her breast pocket, and her iridium satellite phone rattled inside the Velcro pocket of her cargo pants.

She took inventory of the objects most important to her. The locket was a gift her father had given her on her sixteenth birthday. The iPhone had been her primary means of communication. It looked inoperable. The satellite phone, of course, was her backup lifeline, and she prayed that it would work.

Further emerging from her fog, she turned her attention toward her gear. She inspected the rucksack, which had lodged against the copilot's seat. The contents were surprisingly intact, and her D ring tie-down had held.

The cooler lid was dented, but thankfully the cargo strap she had routed through the other D ring had kept everything secure. Lifting a canvas cover that allowed her to see inside the cooler without breaking the refrigerating seal, she noted that the contents appeared okay as well.

Next, she checked on Kiram and Mumbato, both of whom appeared to have been thrown from the airplane, as they were lying outside just above the stream on a grassy bank. She began to exit the aircraft when she saw Kiram move his head in both directions.

As she stepped to the edge of the airplane, she saw that the pilot had been killed. A tree branch had skewered him. His lifeless body hung awkwardly to the side, as if he were napping. His last act had been to save them, Amanda thought.

"Kiram," she whispered against the gurgling noises of the stream and the random calls of animals in the jungle.

Kiram turned slowly and waved his hand as if to say, "Be quiet."

That was when she noticed that Mumbato was moving also. Indeed, his focus was in the opposite direction. She was confused. What were they doing?

"Webb, you okay?" she asked. Her friend seemed unconscious but appeared to have at least buckled his seat belt.

She was startled to see Kiram standing outside the damaged aircraft. His face was bloodied, but he seemed okay. He was also holding an AK-47 rifle.

"Where'd you get that?" She pointed at the weapon.

"It was in the airplane. When we crashed, the box broke open. One for Mumbato and you, also."

"I don't like weapons, Kiram. You know that."

"We need weapons in the jungle, Miss Amanda. Bad people, bad animals, bad place."

Amanda considered his comment. She had been firmly opposed to having armed civilians come into the orphanage. She relied entirely on the constabulary, the Askari, which was her plan. Let everyone do their job the way society intended. But she understood that her view was a minority one that she would, on occasion, have to subordinate to the greater good, namely survival.

"I'll make an exception, but you don't even know how to use that thing," she said.

Kiram looked down at the ground uncomfortably, as if embarrassed.

"What?" she demanded.

"Kiram was using Russian weapons before Miss Amanda came to our village," he said, not making eye contact.

Amanda was momentarily shocked. She had never looked back or explored the nefarious history of her orphans. She was Little Miss Positive, always energized and forward looking. It had never occurred to her that Kiram or Mumbato might have been warrior children.

Suddenly she understood that they had not been thrown from the airplane; rather, they had immediately gone into defensive posture to protect her and what they knew she was transporting.

"Okay. Keep the weapons, but they're not for me," she said.

"Pilot dead. Nervous guy will be okay," Kiram said, pointing to Webb, who was moaning.

"Can we bury the pilot?" she asked.

"No time. We come back," Kiram replied.

They both turned their heads as each heard the faint rumble of a gasoline engine in the distance. One of the beauties of the African jungle and plain was that a man-made object could be heard from afar, depending on the winds and the immediate environment.

"Let's pull him from the airplane and put some rocks over him, Kiram. Now," Amanda said, regaining some of her authority over the boy.

Kiram hesitated, looked at her with his brown eyes, squinted, and then said, "Yes, ma'am." He tapped Mumbato to give him a hand, and they went about pulling the tree branch from the chest of Crazy, which took longer than anticipated.

Amanda stepped carefully to the ground, finding that the airplane had tilted toward the starboard side, making the drop into the stream much shorter than she would have anticipated. She grabbed her rucksack and slung it over her shoulder as she also snatched the cooler. Weighed down, she reached the far bank and dumped her ruck and the cooler. She more thoroughly checked the cooler's contents, which were securely packed and undamaged. Then she returned to check on Webb.

Cutting her way back through the stream, she cupped some water and splashed it on Webb's face. After no response, she did so again, this time to a coughing and gagging response.

"You okay?" she asked.

"What the fu—"

"Anything broken?" she interrupted.

"Hard to tell," he said, trying to determine exactly what had happened.

"We crashed," she said. "You survived. Crazy didn't."

Webb turned toward the pilot and saw the boys sliding the tree branch from his abdomen. Amanda saw the vomit coming and stepped out of the way as Webb puked through the broken window of the Sherpa.

"Toughen up, Webb. You did great saving us, but we're still in some deep stuff. We have to get moving."

"Cut me some slack, Amanda." After some more coughing and spitting, he wiped his face.

She softened her tone. True, she thought, they would probably be dead now had it not been for Webb. "Come on," she said, helping him toward the door. "We need to check you out and then get the hell out of here. We're a target."

She opened the door and helped him down into the stream. He shivered as the water saturated his pants. Perhaps he was going into shock, Amanda thought. Her mind raced ahead and wondered if he would become a liability on their trek back to rally point two, wherever that might be from here.

The boys had removed Crazy's body from the fuselage, and she saw that Mumbato had the dead pilot slung across his back as if carrying a freshly killed deer.

"We need to move, Miss Amanda," Kiram said, his voice full of authority. "Hear that?"

She listened for a moment, the echoing howls of vicious Serengeti dogs closing in on them like a submarine's radar pings.

"Dogs. They will attack us if we don't move," Kiram said. He waved his hand at the ridge above them. "Then they follow."

Amanda sensed even more that he knew the jungle and he knew combat. The most formative years of a child's life were between two and seven, Amanda knew, and she had no idea what either of these children had seen or been asked to do at those ages.

By their dispositions, she figured they had seen death, and likely had killed as well.

Amanda pointed Webb in what she believed to be a southeasterly direction based upon the angle of the diminishing sun to her back. She let Kiram lead on point with Mumbato in the rear.

With the sun about to fall on this difficult day, Amanda Garrett silently prayed to God that her father would be able to find her.

And that they would be able to save the *Nightingale* program.

Then she heard the vehicle motor on a cliffside road just above them and said, "Move, now!"

11

Zach stared out of the windscreen of the Black Hawk helicopter, wondering about the safety of his only child.

"Hey, sir," Mike Rogers said through the MH-60 intercom system.

"What's up, Mike?" Zach replied.

"We're getting word from Kilimanjaro air traffic control that we are to turn around and go to Dar es Salaam."

"Gotta be about Amanda," Matt said.

"Or this Cheetah guy. Keep going to Shinyanga to refuel, and then we'll bounce to rally point two," Zach ordered. In so doing, he had just taken them off the grid. Their presence in Tanzania was now officially in violation of the African Union charter. *Big effing deal*, Zach thought.

He looked at his map studying their trajectory from Kilimanjaro Airport, past Arusha to Shinyanga, where Matt had two assets pre-positioned with a fuel tanker full of JP8 jet fuel as part of the evacuation plan for *Nightingale*.

"Roger, sir. Just wanted you to know," Rogers said. Zach thought he could see a hint of a smile on the corner of his mouth.

"We've got the fuel on standby," Zach said. "Just got word they are expecting us. Amanda's about to be public enemy number one in the world. This is bad shit. Kristyana, we've got to get with State and have them keep the Tanzanian military off our backs for twenty-four to forty-eight hours."

"I'll do what I can," she said, retrieving her satellite phone.

Kristyana punched in a series of numbers, waited briefly, and then began speaking loudly in order to be heard above the din of the prop wash.

"Andy, this is Kristyana Cixi," she said to Andy Romero, the operations watch officer in Foggy Bottom's Foreign Service office in Washington, D.C.

Zach knew that Romero was a seasoned veteran and would help as much as possible. Romero had just completed a seven-year run serving in provincial reconstruction teams in Iraq, Afghanistan, and Kosovo. His rank was the equivalent of a brigadier general in the Army, and his superb performance had landed him the job of managing the operations center.

"I'm connecting you to our internal communications system so Matt and Zach Garrett can hear you," Kristyana said.

"The Hardy Boys. This is indeed a privilege."

"Have you seen the Islamic State release on Amanda Garrett?"

"You mean Al Rhazziq Media's release?" Romero asked.

"Yeah, same thing," Kristyana corrected. "It's all bullshit."

"Looks pretty bad from here. All the major networks have picked it up, and they keep showing that picture of Amanda chunking a burning log into the laboratory. President Kiwimi has already called and wants her arrested and tried in Tanzania. And I have to tell you there are several African nations that are checking in with the Secretary of State for two reasons. First, they want to know why they weren't in the know about this program. Second, they are livid that a rogue med school student allegedly destroyed the program. Domestically, all the usual suspects are going apeshit. I'm not so much worried about that. I think the real issue now is the Islamic State. They were probably banking on getting that vaccine for a cash cow and to win friends and influence people around the world. Provide some legitimacy to their transnational existence."

"Okay, slow down," Kristyana interrupted. As Zach listened, the helicopter banked hard to the left and dove to twenty meters above the savannah. Beneath them he saw zebras, elephants, and impalas picking their way through the plain. "You've got to tell President Kiwimi that there's no way in hell we're giving up Amanda to Tanzanian authorities. She was destroying that lab to protect its information from terrorists Tanzania doesn't want to fight. She kept whoever was attacking the village from recovering remnants of a specially compartmented program and possibly using the formula for the wrong reasons. Tanzania should be lauding her as a hero."

"That's not what it looks like on television. Also, there are some constabularies who are saying she was the last person to see Dr. King alive. Tanzanian authorities are all over this thing," Romero said.

"So, they think she killed King, torched the village, and destroyed the program?"

"Or, she took the vaccine recipe to market it herself and claim the patent for financial purposes. Gotta be worth billions, don't you think?"

"No question," Kristyana said. "But Amanda didn't want a dime for that project. She was working for the orphanage for peanuts and in medical school, for crying out loud."

"I'm just saying. Young girl, she realizes the potential financial rewards here, and she snaps. It's a scenario some are considering, to include President Barkum."

Zach looked at Kristyana in disbelief. He shook his head and muttered, "No good deed goes unpunished."

The Black Hawk yanked upward, and Zach noticed that they were moving across a dense forest of trees nurtured by the delta that fed the Serengeti Plain.

"Okay, we can consider it, but it's a waste of time. Amanda's clean, and worse, she's in danger. I need you to keep Tanzania off this thing for the next couple of days," Kristyana said with force.

"Couple of days? I'll be lucky to get a couple of hours. We'll have to get the secretary involved, and you know how she hates that."

"She'll hate dealing with me even worse if she fails to act on this. Amanda's a brave young woman who has been putting it all on the line to find this cure and vaccine. We owe her this, at least," Zach interrupted.

"I'll see what I can do. Be back in touch shortly. We've got the *Nightingale* team coming in," Romero said.

Coming in? Now? Zach was incensed. Romero was better than this. This thing was at least six hours old. The entire team should be in and providing reach-back analysis, preparing to move forward if necessary and set up an intermediate staging base in Dar es Salaam or somewhere even closer. *Bullshit,* he thought. He watched Kristyana hang up the phone and put its sound selector switch on vibrate. The pilots maneuvered the helicopter onto an asphalt runway overrun with weeds and foreign objects and debris, which the rotor shot in all directions like a small explosion. Nonetheless, Matt's refueling team topped off the Black Hawk and Little Bird aircraft in record time. They took off again, the MH-6 attack helicopter in their wake, struggling to maintain the same velocity.

After about forty-five minutes of flying, Zach said into his headset microphone, "Okay, the village is up on our one o'clock."

Mike Rogers said, "Roger. I'll put it out your right side and do a circle. There are still some places burning, but mostly charred buildings there."

"Kristyana, take some pictures with the digital," Zach said. He leaned over and opened the door of the aircraft so that she could get an unobstructed view. The pilot put the aircraft into a slow turn that gave Kristyana the ability to unhook her shoulder straps and loosen her lap belt, allowing her to lean outside of the helicopter for the best pictures. Matt hooked a monkey harness into her cargo vest by connecting the snap link into a small D ring on the back. Her cargo vest was triple-stitched and had wire mesh running in a thin band just below her breasts inside a Velcro sleeve. The D ring was woven into this mesh and could hold two thousand pounds of tensile strength.

Kristyana surveyed the damage, and Zach saw her shake her head. He shook his in agreement. So much promise wasted.

"Okay, now work your way toward the airfield about thirty miles southeast of here," Zach commanded the pilot. "And stay on this road. We might intercept Amanda or The Cheetah." He pointed at the dirt route of egress that led to the southeast and rally point number two.

As they roared to 150 knots, Zach looked at Matt and said, "What do you think?"

"Not sure what's going on. We need to put a few pieces of the puzzle together quickly or we're going to be shooting behind the flock the entire way."

"We've never hit anything that way," Zach said absently with a shake of his head.

They watched Kristyana remove her headset and put the satellite phone up to her ear, cupping it to decrease the sound of the rotors near the earpiece. She plugged the phone into the internal system so that all could hear.

"Roger," she said.

"Kristyana, Romero here. Okay, SecState is going to call Kiwimi, but she said no guarantees. She's going to try to get you forty-eight hours but thinks you'll be lucky to get twelve before the Tanzanian Army is crawling all over that place. Islamic State communications channels are going apeshit also. Lots of Moroccan chatter in the same area where that doctor, Quizmahel, was killed by a Marine sniper rifle," Romero said.

"Starting to smell like a frame job to me, Romes," Kristyana said.

"Remember, guilty until proven innocent, and maybe even after that," Romero countered.

"Okay, work it and get back with me ASAP," she said. "Get that entire team stood up, and let's start moving. This is huge."

She disconnected. "You guys heard," she told them. "SecState is going to call Kiwimi and tell him forty-eight hours is what we need."

"Hopefully all we'll need is the next few hours, but it's always good to have that buffer," Matt said through the intercom system.

Zach's stony gaze out of the window said everything he was feeling. His daughter was suspect number one in the crosshairs of the Islamic State, several African governments, and perhaps even a few other countries and non-state actors. The true issue, as Zach saw it, was, where was the tipping point? While Matt's loyalty to Amanda was never in doubt, his agency's track record for commitment to field operatives was suspect. If CNN, Fox News, Al Rhazziq, Al Jazeera, and BBC were already carrying this as a lead story, would the lie ossify and become the unvarnished truth? And could they rescue Amanda, secure the remnants of the program, and then extract her and themselves from the country without destroying relations or, worse, getting into major combat?

"Okay, here we go," Zach said. "Right there. There's the airfield. Fifty or so people are milling around the shack on the west side of the strip."

"Don't see any white females," Matt said, his voice flat as a worn stone.

Zach remained silent.

Mike Rogers hovered over the dirt runway, the MH-60 rotors spitting dirt and small rocks in a 360-degree pattern. The refugees from the Mwanza orphanage huddled against the small wooden shack for protection against the sand blasting. Rogers took the helicopter farther down the airfield to diminish the menacing dust storm he was creating.

With a slight jolt and jiggle, he put all three wheels on the ground.

"Don't shut her down, Mike," Zach said as he, Matt, and Kristyana jumped onto the dirt runway and stayed low until they were outside the range of the whipping helicopter blades.

They ran toward the huddled black children and one older woman, perhaps in her mid-twenties.

"Speak English?" Zach asked the woman. He saw about ten children with frightened eyes holding on to her legs. She had a broad face with a soft nose and high forehead. Her black hair was cut short, almost military style. Her lips were plump, and when she spoke, Zach could see that her teeth were only half there. Though she did speak English.

"You scared my children with that machine," she admonished.

"We're sorry. We're looking for Amanda Garrett," Zach said. "I'm her father."

The expression on the woman's face changed immediately from suspicious to familiar.

"God bless you, sir. You raised a wonderful girl. Miss Amanda left after we did. She should still be on the road," she said.

"What's your name?" Kristyana interjected.

"Sharifa," she said, turning toward the Asian woman.

"Hello, Sharifa, how long ago did you get here?" Kristyana continued, easing in front of Zach, who knew her subtle message was, "I'm a woman, she's a woman. Let me deal with her."

"We got here about two hours ago," Sharifa said. "We left as soon as the bad man started burning the village."

Good, Zach thought. Here's a live witness who can go on television and talk about what really happened. He made a mental checklist to make sure that happened quickly.

"Get some iPhone video of her saying that," Zach directed. It wasn't much, but it could help.

He watched Matt step away from the crowd of children. The runway was an unmaintained dirt strip surrounded by a barbed wire fence that was partially intact. Zach's guess was that the farmers had stolen most of the wire to fence off their own fields. Low scrub brush intermittently grew in clumps of brown, tinged green at the tips for as far as his eyes could see. Shimmering heat waves radiated off the sandy soil, and he was sure the temperature would reach one hundred degrees.

"Matt, why don't we get some water and chow to these folks," Zach said.

"Sure thing." Matt pushed the talk button on a Motorola personal mobile radio and issued orders to the crew chief to bring three cases of water and four cases of MREs, meals ready to eat, to the shack. Zach also heard him tell Mike Rogers to be prepared to call the Tanzanian government to send humanitarian aid to the airfield after they left.

"Two hours," Kristyana was saying to Sharifa. "How far behind you was Amanda? Who was she traveling with?"

"She shouldn't have been more than thirty to forty-five minutes behind us, but obviously I'm wrong. She was with Kiram and Mumbato. They're strong boys, but Amanda"—Sharifa smiled for the first time—"can take care of herself."

As they stood there talking to Sharifa, two boys came running up from the west edge of the airfield.

"Are they yours?" Matt said, placing his hand on his Berretta.

"Yes, mine, so put your guns away," Sharifa demanded.

Two boys, looking about twelve to fourteen years old, stopped in front of Sharifa.

"Miss Sharifa," the boy with no shirt said between rapid breaths. "Jurumu thinks he saw a plane crash."

"What? We didn't see no plane," Sharifa challenged.

"No. But we did," Jurumu said. "We were behind you."

The boy who'd spoken first elbowed Jurumu in the ribs as if to indicate that he was not supposed to share certain information. Sharifa's sternly raised eyebrow confirmed that Jurumu's confession just might result in recriminations.

"We saw a white airplane with open doors fall into the swamp. It was a long way away, but we saw it," Jurumu said.

Zach listened to the conversation. He believed the kid. Airplanes sometimes crashed in the African plains, their occupants never to be heard from again. Whether the information was relevant was another question altogether.

"Yeah," the other boy continued, deciding that now that they had made Sharifa aware of their separation from the group, he might as well offer up the real explanation. "We jumped into the ditch at the crossroads. We were going to wait for Miss Amanda to help."

"Okay, but you should have asked me for permission. It is dangerous out here," Sharifa chastised.

Both boys looked downward.

"There's more to the story," Kristyana said. "Why did you come back and not link up with them?"

Jurumu looked up, his eyes as wide as Okami tea saucers.

"We watched this airplane land, and we think we saw Miss Amanda get on it with Kiram and Mumbato."

Zach felt his stomach drop. He looked at Matt and gave him the rally up signal, twirling his hand in the air.

"We're going to need these two boys," he said to Sharifa. "They'll need to show us where this happened."

"No. I can't let the children fly in your machine," Sharifa said, pulling the boys close to her, their heads beneath her large chest.

"We can do it without them," Kristyana said. Then, turning to the boys, she said, "Where is this intersection?"

"Easy, the only trees between here and the village are at the intersection. Just follow the road."

Zach led the way to the helicopter. Before they could buckle their seat belts, Mike Rogers had the helicopter airborne.

"Heard most of it through your open microphones, sir," he said to the team.

"Get there," Zach said. "Find the wreck. We're losing daylight fast."

12

The Leopard drove his jeep along the western road that followed the stream. He could see faint wisps of smoke coming from about four miles away. Perhaps it was an illusion, or maybe even it was a family cooking a pig or dog. But his gut told him that it was the crashed airplane.

He would drive about four hundred meters, stop his jeep as close as possible to the heavy vegetation that bordered either side of the stream, disembark the jeep, and wade onto the rocky shore. He would look in each direction with his binoculars and even use his ARM-Sleeve to scan the riverbed with a Al Rhazziq Media satellite. He applied a finger to the touch screen and slid the now-famous picture of Amanda Garrett to the side as he called up the satellite feed. Hell, he thought, he should have made sure he got some royalties out of that photo.

The satellite download took a second, but soon he zeroed in on a white object less than a half mile away from his current location. With night approaching, he shut down the high-tech gadget and moved toward his prey.

As he stalked, he thought about how twenty-five years ago he had ably mixed the roughhewn days of his Parisian *banlieue* youth with a few years at the Sorbonne studying philosophy. He had operated on the outskirts of the capital city with a group called the Gang of Barbarians, whose brutality had mostly targeted Jewish people. Again, not really adhering to any philosophy, it had been nice to fit in and be able to inflict violence. Since then his life had been a maelstrom, violence at its core.

He looked to his right, where the sun was a flaming semicircle slicing into the African plain. Night was at hand.

He made a quick dash into the jungle to attempt one last look at this section of the stream. He had crossed the water about an hour before and had driven a mile in each direction, seeing nothing. He'd then reversed his direction, come back to the west side of the river, and continued to the south. His review of the satellite downlink told him that an approach would be best concealed from this azimuth.

As he picked his way through the dense foliage, darkness crept toward him. He moved near the sound of the bubbling stream, only meters to his front now.

Stepping from the underbrush, he clasped his Sig Sauer rifle in one hand and his machete in the other. Along the stream, the blackness of the jungle gave way to a grayish hue; light crept over the tops of the mahogany trees and into the cut of the river. He waded into the clear water, testing its depth with each step. Once knee deep, he looked north, the direction from which he had come. He could see nothing unusual in the gray cavern of light.

The Leopard carefully turned to his right, toward the south.

Instantly he noticed the white frame of an aircraft, its wings shorn, one hundred meters downstream. The satellite had been true, though the evening was dark enough that he had not noticed the airplane in his periphery when he'd first entered the water.

Now, his eyes locked on his quarry, he waded through the shallow stream toward the fuselage remnant.

The Book of Catalyst

13

Zanzibar, Tanzania

From his yacht, the *Intrepid*, Jonathan Beckwith watched the full-motion video provided by his satellite downlink from one of his dozens of orbiting satellites. On the large plasma screen, he watched Amanda Garrett, the two African boys, and an unknown white kid pick their way through the Serengeti. In much the same way he had monitored the document thief's actions two years ago, he followed this four-person crew.

He turned away from the video, knowing the race had just begun. He sat comfortably in the leather chair of the command center in his 127-foot Benetti Yacht powered by two Caterpillar engines that boasted 2,760 horsepower.

He swilled a half-filled glass of 1966 Louis XIV Cognac in his long, slender fingers, his nails perfectly manicured. Catching his reflection in a blank television screen, he sucked in his cheeks and smacked his lips. He admired his perfectly preened gray mane that rode in a soft wave over his ears and ended just above his collar. Parted on the right-hand side, just like JFK, his hair was what he called his best feature. Bone-white, really, his thick shock matched his often-bleached teeth. Set against a permanent bronze tan, his handsomeness was not so much captured in any single asset but in their collective portrayal.

Attractive men were everywhere, and he knew his wealth and power were what made him project his handsomeness with such authority. He was magnetic. Perhaps when he'd bought his first radio station at the age of eighteen, he could have predicted he would one day be sitting on this sailing yacht with electronic, carbon fiber sails that automatically deployed and set their own tack and trim.

That radio station had evolved into a television station and then, given his knack for leveraging assets and keeping his money in the game, the minor media footprint he had established had begun to expand like a South California wildfire. He'd rapidly built the corporate infrastructure to accommodate the requirements of the Internal Revenue Service and the exponential demand for his unique brand of content: websites that followed television and radio. His best move had been hiring some young-gun Internet geniuses about fifteen years before to parlay his legacy web systems into future cash-flow machines.

Beckwith had started his own finance channel that was broadcast worldwide and outperformed Bloomberg, CNN Finance, Fox Business, and CNBC. He'd hired young, hip prognosticators who were plugged into the tech and venture capital worlds, could smell the prevailing winds before they began blowing, and would provide him with useful analysis the way a seasoned military intelligence analyst advised a commander. He was constantly shifting his team to analyze and acquire what he believed would be the next big idea. Accordingly, he was able to visualize emerging markets in the same fashion Napoleon's *coup d'oeil* had helped him win the Austerlitz campaign. *At a glance*. Beckwith saw, he understood, and he acted. No hesitation.

And for Beckwith, it was *always* about the money or the sport. No exceptions.

As Beckwith stared into the caramel pool of cognac, he looked up at his carbon fiber sails as they adjusted his position in the Indian Ocean. *Alternative energy*, he thought to himself. Not those red herrings of ethanol or solar, but something truly transforming. Wind power was okay, but expensive and often impractical. Solar seemed to be able to provide steady power in certain locales, but it was a niche market, at best. Oil and coal were going away; at least they needed to. Not particularly wedded to patriotism, he had no overarching altruistic goal to rid the world of Muslim extremism. No, he was somewhat of a financial slut. He smiled at the thought.

He had some ideas but needed to chew on them a bit before acting on them. While the United States had put a moratorium on the best source of energy the world would ever see, nuclear power, his multinational corporation had not. His primary challenge, and he loved a good challenge, was to be able to transport this energy worldwide.

He was visualizing autonomous vehicles powered by nuclear energy cells the size of car batteries. Watching his carbon fiber sails, he understood that he would be able to use transformative materials to contain the radiation to the extent that it would be harmful, which he doubted. Vehicle accidents might break open a nuclear cell, but his tests had shown the radiation would be nothing more than a dental x-ray. Gas stations would also become highly regulated nuclear cell recharging stations. This idea was so bold, so transformational, he had to smile.

He stepped from the command center and walked to the fore of the ship. He stood at the far stanchion looking over the azure sea beneath and beyond. He thought briefly about standing on the rail and spreading his arms, shouting, "I'm king of the world!"

But it had already been done. And Jonathan Beckwith was an original.

Which was how he'd come up with the idea that currently intrigued him and against which he was applying most of his excess research and development funds. His play money.

"Satellites and Bluetooth," he whispered. "Who would have thunk it?"

He exited the command center and stepped past the bridge of his yacht as he considered his robust satellite dish array. *Could he really do this?*

He descended a small ladder and entered a new room on his yacht. This was a twenty-foot-by-twenty-foot room. He shivered as he closed the door behind him. Each wall of the room was stuffed with state-of-the-art electronic equipment to include computers, monitors, electronic jamming devices, receivers, and radar. The equipment ran twenty-four hours per day and pulled a significant amount of power, which created a heat problem. Beckwith, once he had embarked on this course, had had the room retrofitted with air conditioning to prevent short-circuiting of his hardware. The room was like a refrigerator.

In the middle of the room was Styve Rachman, the Internet genius who, two years before, had plucked the Aktar email containing the Book of Catalyst. From that point forward, Rachman had been promoted to work in Beckwith Media headquarters and then ultimately as the primary communications operator for the travel team.

When Beckwith had first offered the promotion, Rachman had replied, "Whatever. It beats sitting in a basement and eating Little Debbie bars." Plus, the half-million-dollar salary had seemed incentive enough.

This evening, Rachman was wearing a hoodie sweatshirt, flannel pajama bottoms, and unlaced hiking boots. His fingers crawled across the keyboard that was connected to several large monitors with binary code scrolling across the screen. He had dyed his hair an orange and yellow mixture that escaped from the hoodie in tangled, random knots, and now he sported two earrings in each ear. None in the nose, thank God, Beckwith thought. Rachman's sweatshirt had the word *Peace* written on it in five different languages. *Salam* (Arabic), *Paix* (French), *Paz* (Spanish), *Dan* (Chinese), and *Peace* (English). The words were splashed across the black hoodie in pastel colors of pink, chartreuse, mauve, bright yellow, and light blue.

Beckwith shook his head and smiled. "Hey, whack job," he asked, "what have you figured out?" Of course, Rachman didn't respond as he was probably cranking to Dr. Dre or some other artist Beckwith didn't know. Beckwith pulled down the hood and saw the earbuds plugged deeply into Rachman's head. The young man immediately pulled the earbuds out and spun around in his chair.

"Hey, boss." Rachman flashed newly whitened teeth at him. Freckles scattered across the bridge of his nose belying the man's twenty-five years.

"What are you listening to, Snoop Doggy?"

Rachman laughed. "Snoop Dogg," he corrected. "And no. Jethro Tull's 'Skating Away on the Thin Ice of a New Day.' Classic. Always motivates me. Very deep."

"Great. Now what have we got?"

Rachman punched a bunch of buttons on the computer and said, "It's really pretty easy and not that time intensive. I've developed a protocol where I can send a signal to each satellite, essentially going into the satellite's operating system through a hole in the security. Each company's satellite constellation has different vulnerabilities, but I found that once you figure out one in the constellation, they are all the same. I've discreetly probed and entered each constellation you've asked about. There will be no problem loading the Bluetooth software."

"And the master satellites?"

"Man, you own those. They are easy." Rachman laughed. "Just steer those babies where you want them to go. No problemo."

"You're sure?"

"Book of Catalyst?" Rachman said in a teasing voice, which was his code for, "I'm a genius, so trust me."

"Okay, we'll probably want to go hot in the next twenty-four hours based on what I'm seeing on the news. This whole Garrett thing is pretty interesting," Beckwith said.

"Man, she's smoking hot," Rachman said, looking at a closeup shot of Amanda Garrett on the full-motion video display in his refrigerated room.

"Her husband's an Army paratrooper." Beckwith eyed their movement on the screen.

Rachman frowned as if he'd really been on the verge of landing Amanda Garrett and the opportunity had just been snatched from his grasp.

"Man, that sucks," he said, scratching his chin. "How do you know all this shit?"

By now the screen savers on all three large screen monitors had activated. Each one looked similar to Rachman's shirt with funky sayings or words scrolling across the screen. One was simply the same words as his shirt, *peace* written in different languages. Another had sayings such as *Love not War*, and another had the famous Saturday Night Live skit quote from Hans and Franz made famous by Dana Carvey and Kevin Nealon, *Listen to me now and hear me forever.*

"We're in the information business," Beckwith chuckled. "Okay, Hans and Franz? Seriously?"

"Hey, Carvey and Nealon are my favorite even if it is your generation. Besides, you lock me down here, and I get bored, okay?" Rachman laughed defensively.

Beckwith smiled and shook his head. As he climbed the ladder out of the The Cooler, as they called the room, he shook his head.

Beckwith walked to the rear of the vessel and looked over the chrome stanchion. The calm waters reflected the golden hues of the setting sun. He pulled the secure satellite phone from his pocket and dialed his good friend Jack Venzetti, or Jack Johnson, owner of Jack Johnson Laboratories. JJL was on the verge of delivering a drug that would delay the onset of AIDS in patients with HIV, perhaps forever. Beckwith had invested in the lab and was a member of their board of directors.

Beckwith was not an impatient man and considered himself a professional, but he needed an update. Certainly he expected goods to be delivered in accordance with an established timeline. He understood that there was little in-transit visibility, as his logisticians called it, on this particular operation. That was to be expected on a mission that was taking place across vast stretches of a country, if not a continent.

"Jackie V," he said into his satellite phone. "Did I wake you?"

Johnson's voice was gruff, as if he was either drinking or emerging from a deep sleep. Then again, it was evening in the Indian Ocean, Beckwith had just watched a beautiful sunset, which made it about noon in Suffolk, Virginia.

"Beck, what do you need?" Johnson asked.

"Just wondering about our endeavor."

"I'll call you when I've got something," Johnson said. "He just got there today."

"I was hoping for more than that," Beckwith said, his voice smooth. His criticism was not in his tone; rather, it was implied.

"He's a young guy. He knows this girl. He'll get the job done," Johnson said.

Beckwith remembered the full-motion video of the four fugitives crossing the Serengeti. Could the white kid be Johnson's guy?

"Let's hope he's good," Beckwith said and hung up.

His partnership with Jack Venzetti Johnson had been born thirty-five years earlier at Fordham University. Venzetti had met his match in Beckwith, an equally enterprising entrepreneur who not only had a radio station but also competed with him in the bookmaking department. Beckwith had beaten Jack Venzetti in a million-dollar bet on the Army-Navy game. Venzetti, abandoned by his Mafia connections after the loss, hadn't been able to pay the entire tab. As part of his payment, Venzetti had turned over to Beckwith the deed for a defunct aspirin-making facility. Over time, Beckwith had enslaved and then mentored Venzetti from hapless ex-Mafia kid on the run to a rising star in the pharmaceutical business.

Beckwith had told him, "Lose the name. Get something normal, like Johnson." So Jack Venzetti had become Jack Johnson, and Beckwith had created a legitimate drug-making enterprise in the process with his indentured servant as its leader.

Standing on the bow of his ship, Beckwith looked out at the blue-green sea that spread before him like a fluttering sheet in the wind and thought about that day. He had taken that opportunity and parlayed it all into what he was doing right now. Everything else he had achieved would appear meaningless next to this. Immediately after Rachman had identified the Book of Catalyst email, he'd had his private contractors kill Aktar and, later, Akunsada in Egypt. His severe disappointment had been that the men had not returned with the original document.

Yet the copies had served him well, and with the help of interpreters and cultural anthropologists, all sworn to secrecy on binding nondisclosure statements, he finally understood the meaning of the fabled Book of Catalyst.

Standing there, stiff wind pushing against his face, the air was pungent with the smell of the sea. Questions ran through his mind. *What is it that everyone seeks? What is it that captures the imagination of all of mankind?* He visualized the four-person party racing across the Serengeti Plain toward the Olduvai Gorge with a cooler full of Ebola and HIV cures and vaccines.

His hands formed a temple under his chin, and he whispered into the wind, "To live forever."

And he believed the Book of Catalyst and Amanda Garrett would soon show him how to achieve that goal.

14

Beckwith walked into the yacht's salon on the second deck, where he nodded at Father Roddy McCallan, an Irish Priest, and former University of Southern California running back Roosevelt Rivers, a best-selling author on evolution. The salon could have been a living room in any stately mansion on land. It was filled with white leather sofas that sat empty along the outer edges of the room. In the middle was a teak table with four comfortable leather chairs.

He looked at the barely open door to the guest suite on the same level. His current lover, Nina Grace, had accompanied him on this cruise. With red hair, a mild Irish accent, and a triathlete's body, Nina had just about worn him out. He imagined she was in the adjoining suite and really didn't care if she overheard the conversation he had been having for days with his guests.

"Where did we last stop, Padre?"

"You were going to tell us your secret, Jonathan. The reason you brought us on this boat."

"Yacht," Beckwith corrected. "And the secret will keep for now. Please continue."

Father McCallan nodded. "Okay, then, Jonathan, as we were saying, the Garden of Eden, as we all know, comes right out of Genesis, the most disputed book of all the Biblical texts."

"Why is Genesis the most disputed book?" Rivers asked. Rivers had graduated from the University of Southern California magnum cum laude with degrees in chemistry and sociology. He had parlayed the two seemingly disparate fields into a Masters and PhD in anthropology focusing on the evolution of mankind. He had been on the cover of *Newsweek* magazine with the banner "Modern Day Darwin" beneath his smooth black face. Dr. Roosevelt Rivers was an imposing figure. He had also played second-string running back to the Heisman trophy winner that season and had gained over seven hundred yards. Seeing playing time in every contest, Rivers had never sought an NFL career and had indeed turned down some offers to play. By the time he was drafted in the nineteenth round by the Detroit Lions, he'd been finishing the graduate school admission test.

McCallan was a compact pale man with a few wisps of gray hair on the top of his head and a halo of white just above the ears and along the collar. He was an internationally renowned expert on the Bible and creationism. Rivers was his contrast. Black and large, Rivers had given up on religion many years ago. Beckwith had intentionally hired these two for this cruise.

"We could start with the historical inaccuracies, but we've trod that turf, Rosy," McCallan said to Rivers. "Regardless, four rivers supposedly flowed into and through the Garden of Eden. The Bible mentions specifically the Tigris and Euphrates and then refers to two others that cannot be found." He sat at the teak table with the inlaid nautical map of the world as his armrest. His elbows pressing down on somewhere along the Pacific Rim, he gestured his soft hands descriptively beneath a smooth and cherubic face.

"Bringing into question the entire foundation of this notion of a garden from which all mankind sprang," countered Roosevelt Rivers, his deep bass voice sounding like James Earl Jones.

"Let me lay out the facts, Rosy, and then we can debate." Without pausing, McCallan continued. "There has been much speculation about the remaining two rivers, the Gihon and the Pishon. Some claim that these rivers were renamed over time and that the actual Garden of Biblical reference is in the northwest corner of Iran or southeast corner of Turkey."

"But you disagree," Beckwith said. A statement of fact, not a question.

"I do. And here's why." McCallan leaned over the map, Rivers to his right and Beckwith to his front at the other end of the table. Beckwith could feel a slight listing of the boat, as if another ship had passed recently, its wake caroming off the massive hull of the *Intrepid*. A series of gold Rolex clocks, handmade specifically for Beckwith, hung on the far wall. The first clock was the present time, wherever he might be. It read 8:16 p.m. The second clock was Greenwich Mean Time. It read 5:16 p.m. The third clock was Eastern Standard Time, the location of most of his business activities, and of course, Wall Street. It read 12:16 p.m. And the fourth and final clock was Pacific Standard Time. It read 9:16 a.m. With precision, they all changed to seventeen past the hour.

"There are doubtless few places on the Earth that could claim to house the Garden of Eden," McCallan continued, "though many have. Iran, Turkey, Iraq, Israel, Syria, Jordan, Egypt, and Armenia have all claimed that they are the wellspring of the four rivers and that they alone can prove that the Garden of Eden was, and is, in their borders. By the way, they all claim they found Noah's Ark also."

"Further evidence that the Garden of Eden is mythology," Rivers smiled.

"Let me ask you, Rosy, is two plus two four?"

"Of course," Rivers scoffed.

"Then how about eight minus four? What does that equal?" McCallan continued.

"Four, of course," Roosevelt said, curiously.

"Well, gee, how about twenty minus sixteen?"

"Fo— What are you doing?"

"I'm just wondering how so many different combinations can claim to have the same answer, mathematically speaking, of course."

Rivers stared at McCallan, unsmiling. Beckwith leaned back and said, "Well, Rosy, I'm not even going to ask you about one hundred minus ninety-six."

"That's enough. Point made, to an extent. All of those equations *do* lead to the same answer, which is correct and provable." His deep, baritone voice echoed with defensiveness.

"The point is, dear friend, that just because there are many different explanations for the same answer many sources have determined—that the Garden of Eden is theirs—doesn't make the answer moot. Perhaps, using your logic, it further proves it?"

"Go ahead."

"I think I can account for the multiple claims," McCallan said. "Biblical texts were written mostly on papyrus, a water reed found along the Nile and made into parchment. But papyrus is brittle and does not survive the elements. So essentially, all of the Biblical texts were recreations of what people either knew or thought was written based upon piecing together small pieces of papyrus."

"So the Old Testament truly is just history rewritten?" Rivers challenged.

"Not just the Old Testament, or just the texts that ended up there, anyway. Vellum, a much more durable parchment, was used before Christ's birth, and so some fifteen percent of the Old Testament survived."

"Fifteen percent?" Rivers asked.

"As opposed to almost all of the New Testament, written on papyrus, being destroyed, fifteen percent is pretty good," McCallan said.

"But it's still fifteen percent."

"Well, it's all a matter of perspective. The scriptures were spoken and recorded many times before they were recorded in writing. The Hebrew palimpsests are the best example. There were multiple fragments found of these scriptures. Then you have the Masoretic text, which provided huge volumes of information regarding the scriptures."

"What about Genesis?"

"Well, there are multiple versions, all incomplete. For example, the sixth-century Vienna Genesis contains letters written in molten silver on vellum, though it is lacking many chapters. Even the Vatican's own Genesis is incomplete. It is a fourth-century document and lacks the first twenty-eight chapters. My point is that all of these books were damaged or mis-handled in some way. Religion was not such an easy topic back then." McCallan chuckled.

"So people went back and made it up?" Rivers asked, more interested now than antagonistic. Beckwith watched with amusement as this discus-sion led directly where he had wanted it to go.

"Well, 'made it up' is incorrect, as thousands of scholars and religious leaders have endeavored for centuries to get it right. I think they have.

Though there were many books that were not canonized; they were not included in the Bible as we know it today."

"What are you saying, Padre?" Rivers asked. "Seems to me that you're making my argument. It's all just sort of made up."

"No. Quite the opposite. This is something that you should be interested in, actually," McCallan said. "While a devout theologian, I cannot ignore the historical facts that are put before me every day."

"Which facts?" Rivers asked, curious.

"As I read about Mary Leakey's find of the oldest bipedal human footprints in the Olduvai Gorge and the oldest human remains up and down the Great Rift Valley, it seems to me that there is an opportunity here to take your significant research on evolution and couple it with some of the seams in the canonization process of Biblical books."

"What's Leakey got to do with this? True, she found the human footprints in lava flows in the Olduvai, as well as some of the oldest known tools. The carbon dating has been superb based upon the preservation caused by the four lava flows that have crossed one another over time. The evidence is irrefutable that human life originated there, or at least very close to there."

"Exactly my point," McCallan said. "Four lava flows. Keep that in mind."

"But Genesis refers to Jordan, Israel, and all of Mesopotamia. What's the connection?"

"You know how in the United States you have a Herculean effort ongoing to make your history books less Eurocentric and more, shall we say, worldly? To include Afrocentric works and perspectives?"

"Of course. The white men were writing history. That's no surprise." Like a combination falling into place, Rivers's face seemed to register exactly McCallan's point.

After a pause, McCallan said, "See what I mean? There were many books not included in the final version of the King James Bible. Even today, the Catholic and King James versions differ based upon differences of opinion over what is called the Apocryphal books such as

Maccabees, Baruch, Judith, and so on. These books address history, legend, prophesy, or ethics, and we Catholics believe them to be canonized."

"You're saying that the books of the Bible were selected by a group of men who wanted to impose a certain set of beliefs," Rivers said.

"Partially. Of the hundreds of religious and spiritual texts written throughout time, very few were seen by the 'selection committee,' as you call it, as 'of God' or 'from God,' which is the standard."

"But that's so subjective," Rivers scoffed.

"In some cases, yes, I agree. And it was especially subjective in dealing with anything from south of the Sahara."

Rivers paused. Beckwith knew that Rivers had followed his own personal journey from believer to agnostic evolutionist.

"The original threat wasn't Eve, then, but sub-Saharan Africa?"

McCallan nodded. "The black man, the African, the Nubian, whatever we want to call him, has been completely misrepresented over time. If you think racial divisions today are bad, try going back five thousand years into ancient Egypt or other early societies where light-skinned and dark-skinned people lived in proximity."

"You don't have to lecture me on that one, Padre," Rivers said. "So, bottom line, you're arguing that some African texts were not included in your Bible?"

McCallan pointed a finger at him.

"Exactly."

"To counter the threat of people knowing about the origin of life? To steal credit from the black man? To give us no credence?"

"Yet evolution shows you have all the credence in the world. As we all know, you were the first. But what is misunderstood is that the gatekeepers, who saw themselves as immortal, or of God, had agendas. This, we cannot deny. And they saw anything that challenged their belief, or perhaps hope, as a severe threat."

Rivers nodded. "The mortal threat."

Beckwith watched Rivers shudder and smiled. *The first.*

McCallan set his steady gaze on Rivers and continued.

"Can you find me a more neglected people in the world? No, I don't think so," McCallan asked and answered. "Did Jesus not say that the meek shall inherit the earth? Who is meeker than the citizens of the African continent? Perhaps no one."

"That doesn't prove anything," Rivers scoffed. Beckwith's dossier on Rivers indicated the man had been raised a devout Baptist but had abandoned religion and was now agnostic, moving toward atheism. As his books *Monkey to Man, The Reality of the Spiritual World,* and *Science vs. Creation: Why Can't We All Just Get Along?* sold millions of copies, he had been courted by all of the talk shows. Just like with the NFL draft, though, Rivers had eschewed the limelight, though he did modestly pursue the opportunities created in order to deliver his message: *There is a spirit life, yet the Bible cannot possibly be accurate.*

"Of course not, Doctor. I know that you are going to put forth the standard arguments that deny the scriptures, especially Genesis."

"Well, I am. Noah lived to be nine hundred years old? Please."

"Nine hundred and fifty, to be exact. Tell me, Rosy, how long ago did you get on this boat?"

Rivers thought for a moment.

"I don't know, about five weeks ago?" It was a question.

"But you're not sure. The notion of time is elusive. We've been on this vessel nearly seven weeks. You were off by twelve days."

"So I'm bad at math."

"Indeed, we all are. If you are off by twelve days every two months, that's seventy-two days in a year. If you live to be eighty years old, a reasonable age by anyone's standards, and miscalculate by seventy-two days a year, that's five thousand seven hundred and sixty days, or just over fifteen years."

"Okay, so I'll give Noah ninety five not nine hundred and fifty. You're still off by a multiple of ten," Rivers said, smugly satisfied.

McCallan continued on, confident.

"Well, that was just a hypothetical example. You guessed wrong, and you live in a world with state-of-the-art GPS, cell phones, calendars, and so on. They can give you time to the millisecond synchronized with Greenwich Mean Time, the world standard. If you were back in Old Testament days, do you think that there would be wildly different estimations of time and, ultimately, age?"

"Sure, but all you're claiming is that no one knew for sure how old anyone was at the time. And still, a day is a day. The sun comes up and the sun goes down," Rivers countered.

"If you are navigating using dead reckoning, and you set your compass just one degree off, what happens?"

"You miss your mark by one degree," Rivers said, tiring quickly of McCallan's questions.

"No, the farther you walk, you exponentially increase the degree of error. One degree perhaps at one hundred meters, ten degrees at a kilometer, and perhaps twenty at ten kilometers. It's all mathematical and provable. The farther away you get from your point of origin, the more an error in your azimuth will impact your course."

"Interesting, but so what?"

"So we can agree that you don't have to make a literal interpretation of the math of Genesis?"

"Let's just say there is margin for error, though I don't agree that it's by a factor of ten."

"Fine. If you have moved off your initial negotiating position of 'Genesis is wrong, therefore God does not exist' and have migrated to 'Genesis can be wrong simply because of math issues,' then we are getting somewhere."

Rivers did not respond. Beckwith smiled, enjoying listening to the repartee.

"Cat got your tongue, Rosy?" Beckwith taunted.

Beckwith, for his part, had had his epiphany nearly two years ago when he had been hot air ballooning solo over Mount Kilimanjaro and the blast valve on his burner had malfunctioned. Standing in his Kevlar gondola, he had looked up with amusement through the throat of the envelope and thought, *I'm screwed.*

He had taken off from Dar es Salaam on a beautiful Tanzanian day, leaving the *Intrepid* moored offshore with his concerned crew. Lifting into the sky, he had precisely managed the helium and propane flows of his Rozière hybrid balloon and caught the prevailing winds. Tanzania has two sets of trade winds, those from the northeast and those from the southeast. This particular morning they had been blowing from the southeast toward the mountain.

He'd ridden the updraft from the coastal lowlands to the plateau along the Pangani River toward the nineteen-thousand-foot-high volcano. Beckwith had known that beyond Kilimanjaro was the Serengeti Plain, the largest wildlife preserve in the world and nearly ten thousand feet above sea level. As he'd lapped the military crest of the volcano, he'd caught a huge rush of air that pushed him near one hundred miles per hour to the southwest beyond the mountain base.

He had crashed in a deep crevice, his gondola striking the face while the deflating envelope flipped onto the ground above. The crags and low scrub brush had created enough friction and resistance as the weight of the Kevlar basket had followed gravity and had actually served to lower Beckwith gently to the base of the gorge.

The Olduvai Gorge, he would later learn.

He had not known how long he had been unconscious, but he'd awoken to two young boys feeding him water. When he'd opened his eyes, he'd seen his blood everywhere. He'd heard the boys talking but could not understand them. Fading in and out of consciousness, he had watched them take a black paste and mix it with water from army canteens into a silver canteen cup.

One boy had been mixing the paste in the tin cup while the other had been trying to stop his bleeding. He'd noticed the boy working the paste reach into a black saddlebag and grab what appeared to be large berries. He'd immediately thought they might be feeding him poppy resin, but had never heard of poppy being produced in Tanzania or Kenya.

He'd kept hearing the term *Mwanza*. Then, he'd had no idea what the words meant, but today he knew that they'd been referring to the Mwanza orphanage on the border of the Serengeti Plain and the Lake Victoria water basin. He'd awoken at the orphanage hours later feeling relatively well for having just survived a hot air balloon crash. The two boys had fashioned a makeshift litter and had dragged him several miles back to the orphanage.

In fact, later his primary physician would tell him, "Jonathan, I've told you many times you've escaped death, but as I read the labs on your blood work, you've got remnants of deoxygenated blood in your tissue mass indicative of a ruptured aorta. With the volume that I've found, there's no way you should have survived. Did you have a blood transfusion?"

"Not that I know of," Beckwith had said. Beckwith knew what his physician was saying. He had been dead.

And those boys had brought him back to life.

He looked at the large HD screen showing the satellite camera following the two boys who had saved his life, Amanda Garrett, and who he thought looked like Webb Ewell from Jack Johnson Labs.

"Isn't that right, Jonathan?" McCallan said. Beckwith was brought back to reality by McCallan's Irish lilt.

"Can you repeat the question, Padre? I was lost somewhere else momentarily."

McCallan and Rivers both chuckled and looked at the television screen, nodding their understanding.

"Beckwith, for some reason we are having these debates for your pleasure. You are paying us too well to ignore us," Rivers said with a wide, toothy grin, bleached teeth the perfect negative to his dark skin.

"My question, Jonathan, was, is evolution happening now?"

Beckwith smiled. He knew the answer, which was no. Amazingly, with all of the science and facts, there was no evolutionary process ongoing. There were thousands of distinct species, but no scientist had been able to document "evolution," as it were, over the last several thousand years.

"Scientifically, it's hard to prove," Beckwith replied. "Which, of course, leaves the question, how could we say that we evolved from monkeys or chimpanzees if there is no evolutionary process today?"

McCallan pointed at Rivers and said, "Exactly. And even more, why did we all of a sudden stop evolving? Did we max out, reach our limit?"

"Well, Dr. Orgel was the leading scientist on evolution, and it's too bad we can't have him here," Rivers said, dodging the difficult question. Rivers was speaking of the world-renowned scientist Dr. Leslie Orgel, who had believed and taught the Darwinian concept of continuous evolution. He had spent a lifetime trying to prove it, but had come up empty-handed.

"Come on, Rosy, you're the best in the field. I wanted you here for a reason!" Beckwith was emphatic.

After a pause, McCallan egged him on. "There are, in fact, no transitional species that have been found in all of the research in the world. There are a couple of highly questionable finds such as the winged dinosaur or the walking fish, which really never occurred. Compare that to the millions of distinct archaeological finds out there. It is either one thing or another. There has been nothing to demonstrate true evolution."

"You're discounting the very chimpanzees and apes that we began talking about, Padre," Rivers said, a bit of defiance creeping back into his voice. "They are evolutionary. It is provable. The chimpanzee has something like ninety-seven percent of our same DNA."

"But the chimpanzee is the chimpanzee and will forever remain such. Why do we continue our never-ending search for the missing link? Even your own Dr. Orgel, a committed evolutionist if there ever was one, said, and I quote, 'And so, at first glance, one might have to conclude that life could never, in fact, have originated by chemical means.' He's one of yours, for God's sakes."

"Seems like he's got a good point, Rosy," Beckwith said.

"Orgel defected and 'found' religion in the end. I think he was in the gap," Rivers said thoughtfully. "He spent an entire life not believing in God and focusing on evolution. Then as he approached his own death, he got scared. He didn't have a fallback. He just believed that, hey, we get one shot and that's it. There's nothing else—and that nothing lasts forever. In the end, that scared the shit out of him."

"*That's* a rationalization," McCallan shot back. "With bullshit like that, don't ever come at me again on the whole faith thing."

"Orgel's collapse at the end is true, though."

"Dear God. Orgel even said, 'There is no known way by which life could have arisen naturally.' Even Miller's experiments failed!" McCallan was on a roll. Beckwith enjoyed the banter. Stanley Miller was a professor who had performed experiments on gaseous combinations that, at first glance, gave evidence that RNA could be created from scratch. Ultimately, though, his tests could not be replicated. They were fool's gold.

"Okay, so now that we've sorted out *that*," Beckwith said, "I want to get back to the exclusion of validated African stories from the Old Testament."

Beckwith smiled.

"Have you ever heard of the Book of Catalyst?"

McCallan's red face drained to a pallid white. "Of course. I'm one of the few."

Beckwith stared at McCallan with a cocky grin.

"My God, Jonathan, is *that* your secret?"

Beckwith nodded, looked at the large-screen television, and said, "Even better. I've found the Book of Catalyst itself. And our fugitives are going to lead us straight to the Tree of Life."

15

Amanda Garrett took a knee as she watched Mumbato and Kiram stop and hold their hands up, each making a fist, the symbol to halt. They were darkened figures etched against the barely distinguishable crags of a steep ravine they had been following eastward. She touched Webb lightly on the arm, and he went to one knee with her.

Amanda looked at Webb in the dim moonlight. He was battered but okay. Still wearing his white pinpoint oxford shirt and long khaki pants, he looked like a tourist.

Having been on the move for three or four hours, they rested in a deep gorge on a path lit by the moon. The onset of evening had brought cooler, mid-seventies temperatures that made traveling on foot easier. Amanda felt her knees ache as she leaned against the rocky banks of the culvert riddled with tall grass and Kigelia and umbrella thorn trees. She was not sure of their precise location; however, she knew they had not traveled by air for more than thirty minutes away from the burning orphanage. But how fast had they been flying, and in what direction? She ran her hand over the small cooler that held the frozen ingredients of the recipe. They needed to find a power source soon, as she suspected her battery power was diminishing rapidly.

Kiram came to her quietly. Each member of the team was on lookout, scanning different sectors of their immediate vicinity.

"Miss Amanda," Kiram said, holding his AK-47 like a soldier might, his trigger finger riding parallel to the magazine, ready to move in a nanosecond to the hair-string trigger.

"Yes, Kiram," Amanda said stiffly, her small protest against the weapons. She had been on a nonviolence kick for the past five years with the orphanage and thought she was making progress. She was still processing how to react to the availability of the weapons and their obvious need for protection. Practically speaking, she considered, they would be fools to take another step in the darkened gorge without the weapons as they navigated the Serengeti Plain. She knew and had accepted the need for violence and strategy, had even employed it in the past, yet she had been so overwhelmed by the prior brutality visited upon the children she supervised that she'd enacted a no-violence policy in the orphanage. Now she knew her survival depended upon summoning her father's warrior instincts.

"Animals. Serengeti dogs follow. Pack of about fifteen. They started out smaller, maybe seven, but as they watched how slowly we go, they went back for more," Kiram said.

Amanda watched her star pupil talk in near fluent English.

"These are the wild dogs you have told me about?" she asked. "They're smart, hungry, and operate in packs, right?"

"True," Kiram said. "Like I told you at the crash. They follow." He licked his dry lips. So far they had been simply drinking from the stream that fell across the rocky gulley that fed into the steep gorge. "There are two parts of the pack to our back, and they are guarding our escape from this hole. The other two have moved forward to the mouth, where this valley opens into the bigger valley."

Amanda considered the comment. The wild dogs of the Serengeti Plain were carnivores as fierce as any lion or cheetah and quite frequently fought and won against those predators. An eerie sense of foreboding crept over her now that she realized the predicament Kiram had just described. They were surrounded, out-fooled by a pack of dogs.

"Where is the alpha dog, Kiram?"

"Main dog is on right, ahead of us up above on the ledge."

"Can you shoot that thing with any authority? I mean really aim it and hit something?"

Kiram smiled a hardened grin, worlds removed from the innocent smile he had flashed Amanda this morning when he had scored the soccer goal.

The African experience, she surmised in small moments like these, was one of too much maturity at the wrong time, feeding the wrong wolf, as the Indian myth went. In every person, there were two wolves: one was the wolf of goodness, humility, and loyalty, while the other wolf was filled with rage, resentment, hatefulness, and bitter anger. Amanda remembered telling the story to Kiram, who had asked at the end, "Which wolf wins?"

"The one you feed," she had said.

Here she was asking him to feed the fighting wolf. Rather than analyze her decision, she simply wanted them to survive this austere place and its menagerie of inhospitable inhabitants.

"I can shoot, Miss Amanda. That does not make me bad," Kiram said, emphatically, reading her thoughts. His dark face glowed with sweat against the rising half-moon. Eyes large and white, they conveyed both compassion and ferocity. Simmering just beneath the irises, Amanda figured, were memories of wars fought as a child and visions of family members hacked to death. What would it be like to have no family to call your own, no one who loved you, she wondered? What must it have been like for Kiram and Mumbato and the others to flee men with machetes chopping everything in their paths?

"I never said you were bad, Kiram," Amanda replied.

"It's all over your face, Amanda," Webb contributed as he kept a careful hand on a low-hanging branch of an African umbrella thorn tree.

"I'm not that transparent, am I?" Amanda whispered. It was true, she knew. Her face expressed everything.

"Respect me and my ability to use this weapon," Kiram said flatly. He was no longer the carefree orphan. He was a man in the wild with charges who required his care.

"I respect you, Kiram," she said.

Sounds of insects filled the air like cicadas. An occasional bark echoed down the canyon.

"They are speaking. The dogs," Kiram said. "We must do something now or they will attack us. Here, take this knife. It will protect you and the white boy."

Amanda looked at the hunter's knife with its long, eight-inch curved blade reflecting yellow in the moonlight.

"I don't need this," Amanda protested.

"Miss Amanda, please do not argue," Kiram emphasized.

She handled the knife, hesitated, and said, "Okay, my thought is you shoot the alpha first. What do you recommend?"

"The main dog is protected by two others. I can kill them, but whoever killed Dr. King and attacked our village will hear my shots."

Amanda nodded. "Kill the alpha, and then we will move to a defensive position until sunrise."

Kiram stepped carefully toward Mumbato and whispered something in Swahili.

"What are they talking about?" Webb asked nervously. Amanda saw that he was absorbing what was happening but that he might be out of his element.

"He's giving Mumbato the plan. Mumbato will watch from that small rock outcropping up there," she said, pointing above them about twenty meters. "Kiram needs to go another twenty meters or so to get a good shot in the darkness. He's saying he needs to get close."

They watched Kiram and Mumbato clasp hand-to-forearm in the warrior's grip. The two boys scaled the moderate cliff on all fours. She watched Mumbato lie down on the rock and aim in the direction from which they had traveled. The sun had been at their backs as they followed the protective cover of the dry streambed, so Amanda knew that they had been moving in an easterly direction. Kiram moved on his hands and knees in the opposite direction of Mumbato, but soon he was out of Amanda's sight, her field of vision blocked by the rock ledge directly above.

The action unfolded more quickly than she expected. She heard three rapid pops from what she presumed was Kiram's AK-47, followed by howling. Quickly, she turned her head when two loud reports echoed over their heads. Mumbato's gun, she thought. Crouching in a defensive stance, she saw a flash before her eyes and realized that one of the dogs was leaping through the air from the ledge and flying directly at her. She watched the bare teeth and ferocious sneer of the wild animal. Its savage eyes reminded her of a rabid raccoon she had seen as a young child. The dog's moist breath blasted her face with a morbid scent that hinted of decaying teeth. She instinctively threw her hand in front of her face, and miraculously the dog missed her, going high, over her head.

She turned, defensive and ready for a counterattack. The dog skidded on the slick rocks but was able to turn around and spin its claws against the magma outcropping. Lunging toward Amanda, the dog was airborne again, its legs outstretched.

Amanda lifted the knife and stepped to the side, pulling the smooth edge upward as if hitting a tennis backhand. The knife sliced through the dog's throat until it got caught on the left shoulder bone. She twisted her shoulders, like a golfer's follow-through, and the knife came free of the dog's neck. Amanda felt the warm blood ooze across her hands as the animal yelped and snapped. Like a bluefish released from a lure bouncing in the bottom of a boat with barefooted anglers, the wild dog continued to click its teeth, its mouth inching toward Amanda.

Reflexively, Amanda drove the knife into the chest cavity of the dog and wrenched it sideways until she could retrieve the blade. The dog convulsed and then lay motionless.

Kiram came running down the cliff with Mumbato in tow.

"Quick, Amanda, the dogs are running away, but Mumbato heard a motor. We must go."

Amanda slid the knife across the matted fur of the dog, wiping the blade.

"Now, we must move!" Kiram whispered emphatically.

Amanda, still on one knee, looked at Kiram and nodded. She picked up the cooler and said, "Webb, get that backpack. Let's go. Kiram, lead the way."

Carefully, they picked their way down the crevice until they found reasonably level ground across which they traveled with increasing speed through the haunting night. Amanda recalled the dog's sneer and hadn't had time to think about how Webb had cowered against the canyon wall during her confrontation with the predator. Webb's demonstration in the airplane had not been an act. He was scared, Amanda thought, perhaps even a coward.

They walked quickly for what seemed like another two hours. Amanda followed Kiram, while Mumbato was always the last in trail. Webb followed Amanda closely.

Adrenaline surged through her body. Sweat soaked her clothes. They reached a flat spot that seemed well defended on all sides by high rocks.

Perhaps sensing a break from the long trek, Webb excused himself, telling Amanda he needed to "use the bathroom."

"Good luck with that," she said, wiping a loose tendril of honey-blond hair from her eye. Amanda knelt to rest in the small valley, the hard rock uncomfortable against her bare knee. She looked over her shoulder as Webb disappeared around the rock formation to their nine o'clock. The boys turned around to see why she had stopped. They each took a knee to rest after moving closer to her. Feeling safe, she surveyed her situation in the diminishing moonlight. Recovering from the shock of being attacked, Amanda was surprised at how quickly and thoroughly her survival instinct had kicked in.

I killed that wild dog as if…I had done it before, Amanda thought.

The sky cast a golden mixture of starlight and moonlight that painted a yellow hue against everything, like a weak spotlight at a Broadway show. Jessi Alexander's "This World is Crazy" began to play in Amanda's mind as it had so many times before during periods of distress. "*If you fall, my arms are open wide; when your night is dark, I'll light your way…*"

How appropriate, she thought. Kneeling here in the deep ravines that ambled away from the flat Serengeti toward Mount Kilimanjaro, there were times that she had been falling but had remained steady. The black night covered them like a shroud. She had to be careful. Both the backpack and the cooler carried not only the formula for Ebola and HIV cures and vaccines but also live viruses. Falling and breaking things was not an option.

The serums were stored in crushed Styrofoam. The tubes containing actual live HIV and Ebola were sealed tightly. Of course, if they did not find a cool place to store all of it or recharge the batteries, everything would expire in the next twenty-four hours. While, unfortunately, there was plenty of the virus to be found here on the African continent, isolating HIV or Ebola was a labor-intensive process. She wondered, though, how long the vaccines and cures would last without the proper temperature.

That fear made her remember their initial success. The biggest shock to Amanda had been when their first set of positive-to-negative conversions had come in. She had experimented with Dr. King's formula just a bit by using the village doctor's black paste, which Kiram and Mumbato had told her had medicinal properties. Though too old and weakened from the hardships of the Serengeti, the village doctor always walked with a mahogany staff that he had carved and shaped over the years. Amanda remembered that day two years ago that the elder had turned to her and said, "This paste. Only boys, Kiram and Mumbato, know the location. When mixed with right ingredients, has cured sickness here. Very special, but secret not to be revealed." He had pointed a long, bony finger at her face and repeated, "*Nguvu Roho.*"

Amanda knew that *Nguvu Roho* meant *powerful ghost*. Powerful ghosts or not, she was going to protect the cures and the vaccines. The only problem was that she was not privy to the exact source of the black paste. Kiram and Mumbato were the only two who would go retrieve the healing nectar. Once they were out of this dilemma, she would talk to the boys, and they would go to the source together.

As if on cue, Kiram knelt next to her and began whispering.

"We are still being followed. Still hear motor moving toward us. We will move farther east, toward Kilimanjaro, but down into the valley."

"But Kiram, how close can he be? We've been walking for hours," Amanda said.

"Mumbato has good ear," he said, pushing his hand against his right ear. Amanda knew Mumbato's hearing was exceptional. "He hears gasoline engine slowly moving in our direction. We take you to cave. Can hide there. About an hour from here."

She looked at her protégé, proud that he had the leadership skills to be a point man, but fearful at how easily he slipped from budding medical student to fierce child warrior navigating the African highlands in the Great Rift Valley.

"Okay, let's round everyone up and get moving. We don't have much time with the medicine," she said.

"Then we move now," Kiram replied, knowing how important the project was. "We move to *Mahali*, private place where no one can find us."

They exchanged a long stare in the still night. Tall savannah grasses swayed with the gentle breeze that pushed softly across the valley floor beneath them.

"Where's white boy?" Kiram asked.

Amanda thought about Webb for the first time since she had been talking with Kiram.

"He went around the rock wall to go to the bathroom," Amanda said. She turned and scampered down about twenty meters of steep ravine and placed her hand on the enormous rock outcropping behind which she had seen Webb disappear. Rounding the corner carefully, she saw him sitting against the rock, his hand doing something near his crotch.

"Webb, what are you doing?"

He immediately fumbled with his iPhone, which he dropped, as he was apparently zipping up his pants.

"Is that an iPhone?" Amanda asked.

"Yeah, I'm using the flashlight function so I don't piss on a viper or anything." He bent over and retrieved his phone.

"Urine never hurt anything," she said.

Amanda looked at the face of the phone, which glowed with green and blue text.

Webb noticed and said, "Just reading some texts from my girl-friend. You know, this is the type of situation where anything could happen." He had a sad tone in his voice, as if warning they could be killed at any moment.

"Well, she's a lucky girl," Amanda said, helping him up. "We're moving out now. Someone's following us, so you probably shouldn't leave the group again."

Webb nodded. Amanda grabbed him by the shoulder, her face inches from his.

"I'm serious, something *can* happen to you out here. We need to stick together."

16

Col. Zachary Garrett stepped carefully from the MH-60 Black Hawk helicopter. Through night vision goggles and satellite assistance, they had found the crashed Sherpa airplane.

Matt and Kristyana remained on the helicopter as it lifted away, the Black Hawk's rotors blowing rocks and dust onto Zachary as he knelt in a small crag and protectively closed his eyes. Once the noisy machine merged with the night, Zachary pulled open a small assault pack and plucked out an infrared beacon. He slipped his night vision goggles on and conducted an operations check, noting that the beacon flashed every three seconds or so. Perfect.

He walked carefully about fifty meters from his touchdown point and snapped the lightweight signaling device onto a small sage bush. The piece of plastic didn't weigh more than a couple of ounces, the battery being the heaviest component. He flipped the on switch and saw it was flashing. Lifting his goggles away from his eyes, he saw nothing. Only someone wearing night vision equipment could detect the infrared pulse.

Returning to the uneven terrain near the stream and the crash site, he scanned through an open gap in the trees. He could make out the fuselage of the aircraft, but that was all. There was no activity near the crash site. Perhaps everyone had survived.

He heard the slightest fluttering of silk and then the soft footfall of two paratroopers landing fifty meters from him and close to the guiding beacon, a paratrooper's lighthouse. Through his goggles, he watched as Van Dreeves and Hobart, his two most trusted operatives, pulled in their parachutes while simultaneously charging their weapons and adjusting their night vision goggles.

Zachary sent them one infrared blip from his goggles. Hobart or Van Dreeves returned his near recognition signal with two quick infrared bursts. Soon they linked up at Zachary's position.

"Any word?" Hobart asked.

"Plane's over there. It crashed. No sign of life."

They moved quietly through the tall grass and followed the low ground to the streambed. Wading across the pooling water, they soon were stepping up the small bank where the Sherpa had come to rest.

With Zachary in the lead, Hobart and Van Dreeves fanned out to both sides, looking to the periphery and rear for any danger. As they approached the airplane, Zachary felt his heart pounding in his chest, driven by the fear that he might find his daughter dead in the wreckage.

Through his night vision goggles, he could see no signs of life anywhere. Not even a stray predator looking for carrion. That was a good sign, as dead bodies would have attracted scavengers. The tall African acacia trees on either side of the stream bowed slightly with the breeze as he reached toward the open door of the fuselage. The silver moon cast a weak pallor upon the scene as if it were a secondary stage and the main event was occurring elsewhere.

As the three operators approached the aircraft, they stopped. Hobart and Van Dreeves were silent, understanding that the colonel was contemplating the potential loss of his daughter.

"Okay," Zachary said. "Let's check this out."

Hobart entered the port side of the cargo compartment while Van Dreeves moved carefully to the starboard side. Zach entered through the passenger seat in the cockpit.

"Nothing in the cargo hold," Van Dreeves called out.

"This side, either," Hobart said.

"Cockpit's clear, but there's a lot of blood on the pilot's side. Any blood back there?"

"Got some in the right rear," Van Dreeves said. "Seems pooled in one place."

Zachary stepped down from the cockpit and joined Van Dreeves, who was shining a white lens flashlight on a two-foot-square section of the flooring. The circle of light also made evident some scattered gauze and strips of cloth.

"Someone was doing first aid," Zachary said.

"Check this shit out," Hobart remarked. He had joined his two teammates on the starboard side. They were violating their own rules in that no one was securing the team, but Zach felt the fight was elsewhere, and so they were all looking inward toward the aircraft.

Zachary lifted his head when he heard a branch break on the far side of the stream.

"What you got, Hobes?" Zach asked.

"Watch." Hobart shined his white lens flashlight along the exterior of the rear of the fuselage. "Look inside."

"I'll be damned. They were shot down," Zach said, noticing the white rays of light poking through the skin of the aircraft like lasers.

"Roger that."

"Van Dreeves, you and Hobes go secure about ten meters out in either direction. I'll finish the site exploitation. You guys tell me which way you think they went, because either someone came and got them or they walked out on their own," Zach said.

Both men moved as Zach used his flashlight to more closely inspect the fuselage. He found some picked-over ammunition and a couple of broken AK-47s. He wasn't sure what to make of that other than the pilot may have been running guns on the side and the crash had opened the container. He leaned through the space between the two cockpit seats and saw beneath the oval of light large black stains that suggested to him that someone had died, most likely the pilot. Certain that Amanda had not been flying the plane, his hope gained traction.

Finding nothing more of use, he jumped out of the port side, found Hobart on one knee, and said, "What do you think?"

"Lots of footprints going this way," Hobart said, pointing to the east. "And a dead African dude under these rocks here."

Zach looked at the shallow grave and small pile of rocks.

"Amanda would have had him buried. It looked to me on the plane as if the pilot bought it, so this makes sense. Van Dreeves, come on over." He pressed a detent button on his sleeve that activated the small microphone in his ear.

"Roger," Van Dreeves replied.

As Van Dreeves joined them, Zach was pulling out his compass and Global Positioning System. He stood and said to his men, "We'll follow the tracks as far as we can and then take a general azimuth based upon axis of travel. We have to assume they were moving with a purpose, a destination, perhaps rally point two if they got oriented."

"Maybe," Hobart said doubtfully. "Plane crash. Everyone shook up. Don't know, man."

"Remember the text I sent you before you jumped in? Two African boys were with them. I'm guessing the boys know their way around."

All three of the combat veterans looked at the cliff above them when they heard the motors of trucks driving. Spotlights crisscrossed in search of something, perhaps them.

Then a machine gun opened fire.

17

Jonathan Beckwith, Father Roddy McCallan, and Dr. Roosevelt Rivers watched the foursome stumble along the goat trails into ravines and over ridgelines. Beckwith turned to his two experts and nodded at the screen.

"They're getting close. Watch. The boys are slowing down over every ridge."

"Dogs aren't following them anymore," Rivers said.

"That was some reality TV for you," Beckwith said.

"Gentlemen, we need to focus. The implications of the Book of Catalyst are huge," McCallan began. He stood, walked to the refrigerator, pulled a bottle of Pellegrino from the top shelf, and walked a few steps to the bar and grabbed a bottle of his namesake's Scotch whiskey, Macallan 24.

"This must be huge shit." Rivers smiled. "Padre drinking his own stuff."

"I wish it were mine," McCallan said. "It's made by a different family with a taste for how to make this stuff." He swilled the single malt in the crystal tumbler and then gulped it down without a grimace.

Beckwith remained serious.

"Right now I have a four-man team atop Mount Kilimanjaro. Two years ago on a ballooning expedition, I spotted what I thought was an oval shape that was worth exploring. They just sent me these pictures back."

Beckwith spread an array of photos across the world map inlaid on the teak table. Four bearded men in various climbing garments with ropes and pitons hanging from their chests could be seen holding assorted items. Then there was one picture taken from about two hundred meters away. The photo clearly showed an oval of wood barely distinguishable from the black lava that had entombed it.

"Noah's Ark?" McCallan asked.

Beckwith nodded his head. "Noah's Ark. The wood matches. Cypress. I know they say gopher wood, but the common interpretation of that is cypress. My guys carbon-dated it. Ten thousand years. This is the first piece of the puzzle, which is my point about the non-African bent to the Bible and the Koran, which both tell the story of Noah's Ark being somewhere in Mesopotamia. Now look at this."

Putting the photos away, Beckwith laid six Xeroxed pages on the table. The drawings and Swahili writing were the dominant script that ran along the pages horizontally. Above the Swahili, someone had translated the text into English.

McCallan tossed down a shot of whiskey and spread his hands across the table.

"My God, you're serious."

"Will someone please tell me what the hell is going on?" Rivers said, standing. He was a foot taller than McCallan and physically imposing. His gleaming black head shined beneath the fluorescent lights of the galley.

"Rosy, what we are saying is that we're pretty sure we've found Noah's Ark—"

"I thought someone found that in Turkey on Mount Arafat," Rivers said.

"Ararat," Beckwith corrected. "Which is the Biblical location of the Ark. But there have been claims that the Ark has been found in Syria, India, and even brother Ripley, of *Believe-it-or-Not!* fame, said he found the anchor in Tunisia. As Padre has been pointing out, the Bible contains some historical inaccuracies based upon the type of paper available."

"So what about this Book of Catalyst thing?"

McCallan took over. "Well, as we said earlier, some speculate that The Book of Catalyst is an alternative to the Book of Genesis. The very small group that even knows about the Book of Catalyst believes it was never canonized because it named the Olduvai Gorge, in so many words, as the Garden of Eden, where, of course, men were black," he said to Rivers.

"We've discussed this," Rivers said.

"There are many books that never made it into the Bible. But none were as controversial as the Book of Catalyst. It references rivers flowing atop one another, the Great African Rift, and the Red Sea dividing the Tree of Life from the Tree of Knowledge and Good and Evil. Over time, the document became more urban legend, and soon people began believing it never existed."

"So racism began with God?" Rivers asked.

"No. God, if you believe the Book of Catalyst or the Book of Genesis, created you. I don't know enough about it to say for sure, but the Book of Catalyst clearly states that the Garden of Eden ran the entire length of the Rift, which essentially spans from Tanzania to Lebanon. The Tree of Knowledge was in Palestine while the Tree of Life was in the Olduvai."

"How's someone in Tanzania eat an apple in Lebanon?"

"Catalyst supposedly explains that, but the conventional wisdom of those who know about this book, and like I said, there are very few, is that God created man in the Olduvai, which has the Tree of Life. Remember, Donald Johanson found Lucy, the first human remains, in the Rift. He proved her existence back to three point one million years. From the Rift, life spread up the Nile and across the Sinai, and eventually man discovered the Tree of Knowledge in Jordan, which was his undoing. This accounts for the hundreds of years that Genesis says that people lived. The Tree of Life was feeding the people before they found the Tree of Knowledge. At some point, Catalyst and Genesis merge."

"At first you want me to believe that Jesus is man's savior. Now you want me to believe that there are good apples and bad apples and the bad apples won?"

"Catalyst accounts for the fact that Satan set up camp and God sent Jesus to the one location he needed him most. If you're a military commander and you're in a tough fight, where do you send your best leader?"

"Where you need to win," Rivers said.

"Exactly. Meanwhile, Tanzania has been relatively peaceful compared to the chaos of the Israeli-Palestinian issue, the Iraq War, you pick the conflict on the east side of the Red Sea."

"What about Darfur, all the chaos here in Africa? It just doesn't get the press," Rivers countered.

"Catalyst accounts for this," McCallan said. He slid the pages across the table and stopped on the third page. "*God's original creation will wither, at first as servants to those who deem themselves superior, and then they will fight amongst themselves, the Tree of Life buried and full of decay yet still living.*"

"Okay, suppose I buy this," Rivers said. "Shouldn't people be ecstatic about it? If what you say is scientifically provable, you will have provided evidence of God's existence."

"Ah, therein lies the rub. The Book of Catalyst references prophets. And while not named specifically, in reflection, we see that it most likely references Jesus, followed by Mohammed, and a third will come at some time later, this year, I believe it says, to bring peace."

"A third prophet? This year?" Rivers asked.

"The third. This year," McCallan replied.

"If I were religious, I'd say that was sacrilege," Rivers said.

"I'm not saying I believe it," McCallan responded. "I'm explaining the text as I understand it."

McCallan stopped and looked at Beckwith. A long moment passed between the three men in the room.

"You're going after the Tree of Life?" McCallan inquired.

Beckwith nodded. "In the Olduvai."

Using a remote, he punched up a sixty-four-inch flat-screen television on the wall. As he played with the buttons, a grayish picture began showing full-motion video. Beckwith zoomed the satellite lens into a narrow field of view.

The image showed four people walking down a steep ravine, watchful, wary.

With more focus, he was able to zoom in on Amanda Garrett's face.

"She's invented the cure for HIV and Ebola. Two of her orphans get the key ingredient from the Olduvai. Those two orphans also saved my life when my balloon crashed into the gorge two years ago."

They watched in silence as Amanda, walking second in line in the column, moved her hand, touched the African boy to her front on the shoulder, said something, and continued moving. She turned and looked back at a white man. At the end of the column was a young African boy, also carrying an AK-47.

"There's also this. Al Jazeera started running these images today," Beckwith said, swiveling his leather chair to another flat screen of similar size. The talking head on the television was showing a picture of Amanda Garrett throwing a burning timber into a small building with a red cross on it. Then the image changed to a rifle with the words *American Sniper Rifle* beneath the picture.

Beckwith shut off the news program but left on the real-time video of Amanda moving to the Olduvai Gorge.

"And so, my friends, what we have is this: we think we've found Noah's Ark on Mount Kilimanjaro. The African boys will take Amanda to where they get this special medicine, and my money says that medicine is a derivative of the Tree of Life. It's that simple."

"My God, Jonathan," McCallan sputtered, now on his third Scotch.

"I can't believe what I'm hearing," Rivers said.

"The issue is that Garrett is being framed somehow. The Islamic State said that they had the vaccines and cures, when, in fact, Garrett had them all along. She's probably on a preplanned escape route. I'm certain she's got some folks chasing her, and the entire world will be looking for her in about twenty-four hours as the word spreads that she destroyed the Ebola and HIV cure facility."

"How do you know all of this?" Rivers asked, suspicious.

"I'm in the information business, Rosy," Beckwith said.

"Well, I'm in the ass-kicking business, but that doesn't mean I go around kicking ass," Rivers replied.

"You push on me, Rosy, you'll die in your sleep," Beckwith said.

"If you're going into the gorge, Jonathan, I'm going also," McCallan said, breaking the standoff.

Beckwith clicked his white teeth and broke away from his staring contest with Rivers. "That's the plan, Father. I would never go to the origin of life without the proper authority," Beckwith said. "And Rosy, just so you know, you're going, too. Your mission is to give me the balance that I need. Your PhD in anthropology and your utter disbelief in religion will counter the Padre here. Your job, and you will accept it, is to keep me honest."

"I understand that's a challenge," Rivers said.

"That's why I picked such a big asshole to do it," Beckwith said.

"All right, I'm in." Rivers said. "When do we go?"

"As soon as the boys take her there."

Beckwith looked up and saw Nina Grace walking toward them. She was dressed in a bikini that barely covered her most private areas.

"Just getting some more wine, boys," she said. Winking at Father McCallan, Nina purred, "Doing okay there, Padre?" Then to Beckwith, "Coming to bed soon, I hope?"

And almost as soon as she had entered, she was gone.

18

In his Moroccan mansion overlooking the Atlantic Ocean, Zhor Rhazziq's phone buzzed with a text. He felt the vibration on the bed and picked up the device. Beyond his bed, he could see the white silk curtains flutter from the ocean trade winds.

Making progress. Book of Catalyst.

He had left the phone in bed with him, pretending that she was there. He smiled as he saw that it was her and replied quickly. Still, he tried to keep his response sterile.

What about?

Her response was immediate.

Tree of Life. Olduvai Gorge. Not sure??

He paused, considering what to say. Could he indicate that he knew what she was talking about? Despite her hypnotic pull, Rhazziq decided to play coy and responded as such.

?

There was a pause, and he began to wonder if she was doubting him, but then came the follow-up text.

Get scholar… Any news on your end?

This time, he chose to update her on the big picture.

Media frenzy over shooting and vaccine theft. Going well on this end.

Better shut down. Kisses.

Back at you.

As he pressed the delete button on his private text messages in his Wickr account, he looked at the sea.

While he trusted Nina Grace, he could not share his grand strategy, the Greatest Mind Game of All Time, with her. For now, he would keep her in the dark about The Book of Catalyst, which was why he had responded with a question mark.

Otherwise, he trusted her sufficiently to confide in her much of the rest of his plan. For two years, they had been lovers. While a devout Muslim, he enjoyed the occasional cocktail and, of course, could not resist the temptations of a beautiful woman. Rhazziq had reconciled his taste for the finer things in life with his Islamic faith through a more moderate interpretation of the Koran. Naturally, one could argue that he was simply being selective, he acknowledged. But that wouldn't change anything. Where the militant aspects of Islam suited his needs, he pursued those. Privately, however, alcohol and women were two vices he could not refuse, and he was able to compartmentalize these errant behaviors in his mind.

Nina Grace, for her part, was a vice on steroids. He smiled at the thought. He'd had his ample sources research her background and had been most intrigued by her Irish paramilitary background. He had determined that she was a rebel with too much money and time on her hands.

This, of course, was perfect for him. She was gorgeous, good in bed, and totally submissive to him. She had found her niche, apparently, and had parlayed her rebellious energy into a total focus on helping him achieve his goal of expanding his media empire in order to create a foundation for the Islamic caliphate. Rhazziq had tested Nina on a smaller operation in Morocco, where her mission had been to go to the U.S. Embassy, file some paperwork, flirt with one of the defense attachés, and then bring him something of value.

She had visited the embassy three times during her planning phase and decided upon the perfect time to conduct her espionage. Rhazziq had tinged with jealousy when she had pulled her black stockings up her slender legs and then let her midnight cocktail dress fall loosely around her knees.

Returning four hours later, her hair a bit mussed, she had grinned as she'd dumped onto the table a thumb drive that contained information about a military operation called Silent Lamb, which would focus on information dissemination in the Northern Tier of Africa.

"This is good, my dear," Rhazziq had whispered into her ear. "You are ready for Beckwith."

Nina had surprised him when she'd said, "I want the caliphate as much as you, darling. I'm honored to do my part and will martyr myself if necessary."

Rhazziq looked at his phone, the message gone. Beautiful Nina.

His mind immediately began calculating the stakes of his ongoing gambit to spread his media influence into farther reaches of Africa and onto the southern shores of Europe. He had already brokered profitable deals in Spain, Portugal, southern France, and isolated pockets of Germany to cater to the expanding Muslim communities in those countries. Likewise, he owned the most popular local and satellite stations in all of northern Africa, from Morocco to Egypt. He had some inroads in Pakistan and Afghanistan and had seen recent gains in Iraq.

He had ordered his stations to give maximum play to the Amanda Garrett story, but not to the exclusion of the American sniper rifle that police had located on top of an apartment complex in downtown Marrakesh. The two stories combined spoke to an American conspiracy on the African continent to deny the cure to the suffering. Already his relentless news stories had sparked outrage across the Northern Tier of Africa.

He turned away from his phone, found his television remote control, and looked at his seventy-five-inch flat screen on the wall opposite the window. When the picture appeared, the new American president was answering a question in a news conference about the death of Dr. Quizmahel.

"While the American government had no role in the death of Quizmahel, we will investigate fully and work with our partner nations in Africa to determine who did. The United States does not support the assassination of anyone, but it could be argued that the world is a safer place now that Quizmahel is no longer in it."

From his bed, Rhazziq laughed. *Barkum's an idiot*, he thought. He sat up and began thinking of a way to clip and spin the quote to entice outrage in the Muslim world. He used his phone to record some thoughts. He decided to direct his stations to run just the portion that had the president saying, "The world is a safer place now that Quizmahel is no longer in it."

Next, he used his phone to call his director of operations and instructed him to use the quote. Then he said, "Also, throw this in there before Barkum's comment: 'The Americans rejoiced over the murder of well-known Muslim Doctor Hawan Quizmahel today when Moroccan authorities identified his body. Police were quickly on the scene and chased after the assassin, who fled so rapidly that he left behind an American sniper rifle and spent ammunition casing. Authorities are conducting forensic analysis as we speak.'

"Then, after the presidential quote, I want all stations and websites to either read or display the following text: 'Meanwhile, in Tanzania, an American medical student raided and scuttled the Islamic State Ebola and HIV vaccine program. In these images seen here, Amanda Garrett, a CIA spy operating undercover as an alleged orphanage missionary, is seen destroying the medical clinic where the Islamic State was finalizing its Ebola and HIV vaccine and cure programs. The Islamic State had been weeks away from delivering the medicine to millions of Africans. Tanzanian authorities are attempting to capture Amanda Garrett and are receiving the assistance of many African nations that are hanging in the balance on the hopes that Islamic State efforts to cure Ebola and HIV will materialize quickly before the diseases reach a tipping point.'"

He paused and continued to recite what he wanted on television and the websites.

"One has to ask if the murder of Dr. Quizmahel, moments after his announcement of the Ebola and HIV cures for all Africans, and Amanda Garrett's raid on the Tanzanian facility are related. Indeed, how could they not be? Amanda Garrett is the daughter of U.S. Army Colonel Zachary Garrett and the niece of known CIA spy Matt Garrett. She entered advanced training as a spy at an early age. Further, the Islamic State Ebola and HIV vaccines had been Dr. Quizmahel's lifelong project. Now American spies have destroyed the program. Indeed, they have created a reverse weapon of mass destruction, a metaphorical improvised explosive device, if you will. By destroying the vaccines, the Americans will ensure the deaths of millions of Africans and Muslims."

He played with the words the way an author worked his prose until he had touched all of the right chords. This felt right and good. He repeated the messages: American spies, Islamic State cures, Amanda Garrett on the run, and African unity in search of the cures.

To Rhazziq, this was all a game of chess. He had to make the insecure American president feel as if he had gone too far with his quote. By highlighting the sniper rifle, burning orphanage, and stolen cures, he would put the president on the defensive, which would make him more cautious. Ultimately this messaging would set the stage for the actual psychological operation. Every deception operation required a target. Rhazziq's was Barkum, and he was only beginning to mess with the American president's mind.

He ran a roughhewn hand across his light stubble. He would typically go a few days without shaving, giving his olive-skinned face a dark, menacing look. Yet when dressed in one of his silk Armani suits, he cut the figure of the penultimate businessman. His midnight hair was thick and wavy, combed straight back.

Rhazziq laid his head against the pillow and looked at the wall-mounted television as the masses in Cairo, Tripoli, Addis Ababa, Amman, and Baghdad rioted. They wanted the cure, and they hated America.

Phase one was working, and phase two, with Nina in place, was looking pretty good.

19

Matt Garrett gave Kristyana a thumbs-up when Zachary called in the code word confirming that Van Dreeves and Hobart had successfully parachuted into the makeshift drop zone on the edge of the Serengeti Plain.

They sat in the Specially Compartmented Information Facility (SCIF) in the U.S. Embassy to Tanzania in Dar es Salaam. Kristyana was working feverishly with the ambassador to call off the Tanzanian military and surrounding countries' forces. African leaders were reacting with rage as the media continued to show the images of Amanda Garrett burning the orphanage medical clinic, and "HIV and Ebola cure facility," as the press was now referring to the building Amanda had set ablaze.

The SCIF was a Spartan affair. They sat on either side of an old gray desk with two secure phones, one a red switch with direct lines to the secretary of state and several other ambassadors around the continent. Low-wattage fluorescent lights hung nakedly above them, casting a weak glow upon a large-scale map of Tanzania, which Matt knew was not much good for military planning. Clearly the defense attaché and his team had been spending too much time in the Dar es Salaam discos and not enough doing their damned job, he fumed.

The one decent piece of equipment in the room was one he had brought down from Djibouti. He had spent fifteen minutes setting up a satellite radio on the roof of the embassy so that he could communicate with Zach and the C-17 aircraft that had dropped Hobart and Van Dreeves from twenty thousand feet above ground level.

"They're in, and they think all but one survived the wreck," Matt said.

"Who was the one?"

"The pilot, Zach thinks. He kept his burst short," Matt said.

"Thank God," Kristyana muttered.

"Sucks for the pilot."

"You know what I mean."

"I do. Now where are we on the bullshit photograph of Amanda?"

"The African Union is convening in the morning. The word is that they are going to make Amanda public enemy number one. She will go to the top of their terrorist watch list. The U.S. ambassador to the A.U. is a political appointee, and she's utterly incompetent, not to mention the fact that she is on vacation in the Seychelles, where, I'm told, she spends quite a bit of her time," Kristyana said.

Matt ran his hand across his face in frustration.

"What the hell are we doing, Kristyana?"

She held her hands up. "Don't vent on me, Matt. You know the deal. Let's focus on the here and now."

They were still dressed in the same clothes they had worn on the trip down from Djibouti to Tanzania and then out into the Serengeti. Zach had made a quick decision to send Matt and Kristyana back to work the embassy and try to forestall disaster when he had learned that Hobart and Van Dreeves were airborne. Kristyana had been trying to contact Amanda on her satellite phone, but to no avail.

A U.S. Army major opened the vault door to the SCIF.

"We're busy, Major," Matt said flatly.

"Sir, I think you're going to want to see this," the major said, holding his ground. Matt summed him up: a bit chunky, his shaggy black hair a tad long, and he had the round, pockmarked face of a kid who ate paste in third grade.

"What have you got?" Matt said.

"Read this," the major said, a bit of attitude in his voice.

Matt eyed the major but took the piece of paper from the officer's outstretched hand.

Making progress. Book of Catalyst.

What about?

Tree of Life. Olduvai Gorge. Not sure??

?

Get scholar… Any news on your end?

Media frenzy over shooting and vaccine theft. Going well on this end.

Better shut down. Kisses.

Back at you.

"What is this?" Matt asked.

"You're probably not cleared for sources?"

Matt stood, towering over the officer and taking a step toward him.

"My brother and niece are in the middle of the Seren-freaking-geti Plain being chased by some real assholes. Drop the attitude or I will knock you out right now. Got it?"

"Matt…" Kristyana began but then stopped when Matt refused to turn toward her.

"So let's start this over. What is this?" Matt demanded, remaining in the major's space.

The major deflated and took a step back.

"I apologize, sir. This is an intercept our station chief got from Langley. It went down about an hour ago. They say it is a conversation between or through two servers, one in Morocco and the other in or near Zanzibar."

"Keep going."

"The Book of Catalyst is interesting, sir. I was the intel officer for a "MITT" team in Nineveh Province in Iraq 2012-2013. One of our Iraqi intelligence units got a tip and raided a house near the old museum there. We thought there was an IED maker in the house, but all they came back with was a ton of historical documents."

"MITT team?" Kristyana asked.

"Military Transition Team," the major responded. "All of the combat brigades were out by 2011, but we still had advisory and training teams, called transition teams, helping the Iraqi Army."

"Get to the point, Major," Matt directed.

"My point is, sir, that the Iraqi military guys gave us the documents and our documentation exploitation guys found these pages that they said were thousands of years old. Turns out the guy who used to live there was a history professor, and he had hidden these documents behind a false wall. Dude and his wife were killed in 2013, and no one knew those documents existed until our expert search guys went through that house looking for IED stuff. I was there. Dead bodies were still in the house. Place smelled like death."

"The documents?" Matt redirected the major back to the point.

"Right. The weird thing was that we had to have someone who could read and write Swahili do the translation. Being an African foreign area officer with experience in Kenya and Tanzania, I skimmed the documents quickly. It started out by saying it was the Book of Catalyst. We thought it was just some bullshit and it *was* totally irrelevant to our mission, so we just locked it up with everything else."

"I'm still not getting you. Your document exploitation team tells you this thing is thousands of years old, but you shitcan it?"

"No, sir. Didn't shitcan it. It's in storage with the unit chaplain who rotated back to Fort Stewart, Georgia. Once the translation came back, it had heavy religious overtones, sounded to me like the Book of Genesis, only different. It said essentially that God created life in what is present-day Tanzania and that the Garden of Eden runs the full length of the Great African Rift."

"How do we know it isn't bogus?" Kristyana asked, standing now also.

"We don't. But what bothered everyone is that it was on vellum, a type of paper used before the Egyptian papyrus," the major said. "What's really bullshit, though, if you'll pardon the expression, is that the chaplain is hanging on to this thing like it's a war trophy when, in fact, if it's real, it is pretty significant."

"That's an understatement," Matt said. "So tie this together for me." Though he thought he already knew what it was all about. Someone had found it or intercepted it, somehow, and they were interested in confirming its validity, he believed.

"The fact that the Book of Catalyst is mentioned in the same conversation as the Tree of Life and Olduvai Gorge is what I remember about the document." The major nodded at the intelligence report in Matt's hand. "What is inconsistent is the reference to a shooting and the vaccine theft."

"I can help out there," Matt said, then sat on the edge of the gray desk. He offered the major a seat, which he took. "The shooting has to be in reference to the killing of Quizmahel in Morocco, and of course, the vaccine theft and media frenzy are related to Amanda Garrett, my niece. The real question is, how do all of those issues come together in one conversation?"

"Let me pull what I've got on the shooting," the major offered. "I remember reading the traffic but just now connected it. Thanks. I've got my intel team in the next SCIF over. I've ordered them to twenty-four-hours ops, twelve on, twelve off. You need any help on your operation, let me know."

"Thanks. Your name?"

"Jeff. Major Jeff Dunwoody."

"Great work, Jeff. Also, why don't you give me the name of the chaplain who's got this document?"

"He might have left the unit. Was a few years ago, but his name is Lieutenant Colonel Vincent Irons. Southern Baptist."

"Okay, we'll compare notes in a few hours. Meanwhile, I'll get my team working on the document and figuring out this chat message. Please ask the chief of station to come see me when he gets a chance," Matt said, more pleasant than he had been.

"Yes, sir. I'll get right on it." Jeff Dunwoody departed and closed the SCIF door behind him.

Matt looked at Kristyana, who was shaking her head.

"You have to be that hard on everyone?" she asked.

"I'm focused," Matt said.

"Well, so was he, so lighten up. I know we've got some pressure on us right now, but these people are on our team."

"We need to get you to the States. Take the G5."

"The chaplain?"

"Roger."

Matt stood, walked over to the map, and pointed at it.

"They're right there," he said, pointing to a spot midway between Lake Victoria and Mount Kilimanjaro. "Zach thinks they headed almost due east. He's following some tracks."

Kristyana joined him at the map and pointed.

"Due east goes directly to the Olduvai Gorge."

The Olduvai Gorge

20

Tanzania

"This way, Miss Amanda," Kiram said.

They wound their way down a snake-like trail that included several switchbacks across the granite rocks defining this portion of Tanzania. Amanda knew that the Great Rift Valley had been created by the separation or collision of three tectonic plates: The Arabian, the African, and the Indian plates all converged and diverged on a path from lower Tanzania through Kenya, Ethiopia, Egypt, across the Red Sea, and directly into Jordan, fizzling out somewhere in southern Syria.

Mount Kilimanjaro and several active volcanoes dotted the Great Rift Valley reflecting a timeless march in response to ever-shifting geography. After the attack by the wild dogs, Amanda and her team had emerged from that dry riverbed and plunged into a series of brutal climbs over steep ridges as they entered the outermost reaches of the Great African Rift.

As she followed Kiram, her mind wandered in the darkness as they ambled along a rare flat piece of terrain. She thought about her husband, Jake. She was concerned that she had not heard from him before the plane crash had destroyed her phones. Normally, he was quick to respond. She reasoned that he was probably on a training mission somewhere, maybe even a training jump. She was proud that Jake had become a paratrooper in the 82nd Airborne Division. She thought of a sunset in Piñon Canyon, Colorado, on their honeymoon. The sun had lowered slowly that peaceful evening. Her head had rested on Jake's strong shoulder. Neither of them had said much. The flaming ball had dived beneath the horizon and had painted the gorges orange and purple, the ledges crawling away from them like a never-ending road. The Tanzanian terrain was similar, and she now ached for her husband's presence. She needed to feel his love to know that everything was going to be okay.

Now, the moon cast a faint silvery glow across the rocky path, creating shadows that looked like more obstacles. The ad hoc team picked their way slowly down the trail. Kiram was in the lead as point man. Mumbato was following as rear security. Amanda was still mildly disturbed by the way in which these boys had converted to warrior children so quickly. But then again, hadn't she just savagely killed a wild dog in her own defense? She had felt a primal fury as the fight-or-flight response had rocketed through her body. What was she capable of, she wondered? She had killed a dog; could she kill a man? And what had happened to her nonviolence credo? She couldn't have just said, "Nice doggy," and petted it behind the ears so that it wasn't so vicious. No, she'd had to kill or be killed.

At that moment, Amanda knew that it was truly survival of the fittest in the African outback. She *was* her father's daughter, she thought, as she watched Kiram take a knee.

"Where are we going?" she whispered.

"Safe place," Kiram said. He did not turn his head toward Amanda. He continued to scan the horizon and then made a small cackling sound like an animal might. A hyena, Amanda thought immediately.

Shortly, she heard the same sound coming from the rear of the formation. Kiram was communicating with Mumbato without giving up the security of the column.

Quickly, Kiram was up and moving. "Now, we must move. Now," he hastened. "You hide in cave. We protect."

Amanda, too tired to protest, said, "Here, take this. Leave it for him." She reached into her backpack and retrieved a smaller pack from inside, commonly known as an assault pack. Her father had given her the rucksack just for a contingency like this. The assault pack held backup supplies and Styrofoam-enclosed vials of the cure and virus packed in dry ice. She understood that they could get separated and wanted at least one of them to survive with the recipe. Or, she figured, Kiram could use it as an offering, to make the attackers go away. The vials were incomplete, missing the magical black paste.

Kiram looked at her in the darkness, his face glistening with sweat. "I understand," he said as he slipped the small assault pack over his shoulders. Their strategy now was to let the attackers have a few vials of the partial cure, hoping it would provide them a buffer to escape.

Amanda nodded. "Good."

The brief stop and Kiram's sweaty face had also reminded her that none of them had the proper attire for surviving at six thousand feet above sea level. She was still wearing her cargo shorts with white T-shirt and khaki Humvee vest. Her Timberline hiking boots were holding up okay, but she was cold. The cloudless nights allowed all of the day's heat to radiate through the atmosphere, making the temperature extremes severe. As the adrenaline from the dog attack waned, she realized that unless they got moving, they would need to build a fire.

She turned to signal to Webb, who was following her, that they needed to start moving. He nodded and got to his feet. Amanda thought she could see Mumbato's stealthy profile lying across a rock, facing to their rear.

"So is this a first date?" Webb asked, sidling next to Amanda in the darkness.

She felt his warmth against her shoulder and couldn't deny she welcomed the contact.

"Since when did you start dating married women, Webb?" She was not standoffish but wanted to draw the line clearly. She figured, though, that Webb had just been trying to lighten the mood.

"Let me help you with that rucksack," Webb said.

Amanda looked at her college classmate and wondered, *Can I trust him?* She knew that they would be dead or captured by now if it weren't for Webb. But still, why was he here? It had to be something to do with his job, yet she hadn't really had the inclination to speak to him. But she couldn't carry everything into the cave, so she let Webb slide the heavy rucksack onto his back as she lifted the much lighter medical cooler.

After a few moments of more switchbacks, Kiram slung his AK-47 across his back and pulled at a large rock about the size of a home air conditioner. He slid the boulder with ease along the sandy soil toward the downhill side of what she could now see was a small cave opening.

"Flashlight?" Kiram asked Amanda.

She pulled a small Maglite from her vest and handed it to Kiram, who leaned over and stuck his arm into the small opening. Amanda looked over his shoulder as he shined the light into the cave. She saw nothing out of the ordinary, perhaps a few beetles crawling around.

"Snakes?" Amanda asked.

"No time to worry, Miss Amanda. Yes, there will be snakes, but it is nighttime, and they will be less aggressive. Take flashlight and go about fifty meters, then the cave will get wide. Stay there and wait. You will see. Only Mumbato and I know about this place."

She steeled her nerves, took the flashlight, and began sliding feetfirst into the cave, dragging her cooler above her head. She felt the coolness surround her body, yet it was somehow comforting, as if it would be consistent and might even be warmer the deeper she crawled. The tunnel angled about thirty degrees downward, so crawling backwards was not a physical challenge. The mental challenge, she thought to herself, was a different story. With every step, she could step onto the head of a viper, or into the mouth of a wild dog, she thought. She shook her head, attempting to rid her mind of such negative thoughts. Kiram had gotten them this far, and he would not be leading them into this cave if it weren't safer than what was behind them. Her foot slipped but quickly regained leverage on the downward climb. She gingerly kept the cooler above her head, balancing its weight against the friction of the granite and quartz upon which they were descending. She felt dirt fall in her face and realized that Webb was entering the cave and making the downward trek. She could visualize her two brave Nubian warriors feeding the scared white boy into the cave and then following.

Or not.

Her exhausted mind tested the boundaries of her trust in Kiram and Mumbato. Where did this cave really go? Sure, she had worked with them for five years now, but she had never been with them to this place. Who had influenced these boys back in their formative years? What intentions did their spirits truly hold?

"Crazy thoughts," she whispered to herself about the time she felt her foot find level terrain. She carefully placed both feet on the firm ground, gingerly lifted the cooler, and then placed it at her feet after she had shone the light in a quick 360-degree fashion. She was indeed at the bottom of what seemed to be a craggy cylinder or tube that now gave way to a large open area. Instead of the gray or tan rock across which they had been traversing outside, she now seemed to be inside an almost purely black cavern.

"Lava flow," she whispered in amazement. "Kiram and Mumbato have been coming to a lava flow." Talking to herself, she took a few tentative steps away from the base of the tube. Shining the flashlight up, to the left and right, and down, she saw a series of alternately jagged and smooth layers of magma from ground level to the top of the cave, which was about sixty feet high. As if she were standing in the foyer, the cave seemed to angle in two directions, each about forty-five degrees from her current position, putting her at the base of a triangle.

Soon, Webb came sliding down the hardened magma onto the floor of the cave. He stumbled and fell, grabbing at Amanda, whom he accidentally pulled down onto the floor with him. She saw her backpack slap onto the base of the cave.

"Careful!" Amanda said. She realized Webb had removed the backpack from his shoulders prior to the descent and that it had tumbled the remaining few meters with him.

"Sorry," Webb said, getting to one knee.

Distracted, Amanda looked up and heard the two boys talking loudly. Then she heard the rock slide across the opening of the cave, sealing them inside.

Then silence.

Amanda turned to Webb, who was standing close to her as if there was protection in proximity. Webb placed the backpack on the floor of the cave near where she had put the cooler.

"Did the boys say anything to you?" she asked.

"No, they just fed us into this hole," Webb responded. He looked around, hands still in his pockets. "Chilly."

She shined the flashlight toward the top of the tube they had descended. The cone of light unfortunately had no one moving through it. Amanda stared at the stillness and felt a pang of fear. Kiram and Mumbato had not followed.

"What are you thinking?" Webb asked.

She dropped her chin before turning her head toward Webb. "I'm thinking we can trust them," Amanda said. "Meanwhile, we need to check on the medical equipment. You dropped the rucksack."

She knelt next to the cooler and checked its external digital display. It was better than she'd thought.

"We've got several hours left on this cooler," Amanda said. "Webb, open that backpack for me, please. Be careful. There's live virus in there. Make sure nothing broke when you fell on me."

"Yes, ma'am," he said, feigning a salute. Webb loosened the secure straps and began digging through the contents of the backpack. Almost immediately, he retracted his hand and yelped, "Son of a bitch!"

He held his hand up, and she saw a shard of glass dangling from a finger, a clear liquid running from the glass into the newly formed cut. Amanda simultaneously shined the flashlight and placed her free hand over her mouth as she watched Webb yank the sliver from his skin, blood running down his arm in small rivulets.

"Here, use this," Amanda said, handing him an alcohol wipe she carried in her vest pocket. She quickly put on the latex gloves she also carried in her vest. Tearing open the vacuum-sealed pouch, she lifted Webb's wrist and dabbed at the blood as she nervously looked in the container.

"What?" Webb asked.

"Nothing," Amanda said. "Here, hold your hand out like this." She straightened his arm, then removed a small Band-Aid from another pocket and placed it over the minor wound. "Keep pressure on it."

The black cave seemed to echo the halting sense of unease in Amanda's voice.

"What?" he said more forcefully this time.

"I'm—I'm hoping that the virus had died with transport," she whispered.

"What virus? I thought this was a cure. If anything, I've just been inoculated from the Ebola or HIV virus, right?" Webb's voice rose in pitch toward the end of the sentence as if his recognition couldn't quite keep pace with the words he was speaking.

"I'm required to carry live Ebola and HIV to develop the cure and the vaccine. I keep six bottles of each virus ready for mixture so that I can rapidly make the vaccine. When you slid down the magma and landed on the bag, you must have cracked something. It's very fragile."

"Cracked something!" Webb screamed.

"Webb, relax," Amanda said, reaching out and placing her hands on his shoulders. She was face-to-face with him and could see his lips trembling as if he was cold.

"Jesus Christ! You want me to shut up and I just got infected with HIV or worse—Ebola!—and didn't even get the luxury of getting laid?"

"Please, Webb, I know it's scary, but please try to relax," Amanda pleaded.

Amanda was carefully rummaging around the rucksack, shining the light on the jumbled contents inside its insulated compartment. Clearly, she thought, the rough slide down the cave opening had disgorged the tubes, bottles, and syringes from their Styrofoam lodgings and into this mangled mess she now saw. She saw the other five bottles and four unbroken wax-filled test tubes. The broken tube was labeled *HIV*. If the brief exposure to the air had killed the virus, Webb had nothing to worry about. If the virus was still alive, she would have to inoculate him immediately.

"Webb, I can give you the cure if you wish. It looks like I've got some left that might work," Amanda said, now pawing through the cooler, which was intact.

"Might! What is this bullshit?"

"It's the best I can do. Might. Has. It *has* worked and probably will. All of my cases have been either African children or adults. You're clearly not one of those, and we haven't had a chance to test the serum on different populations. But you need to be quiet, because if you keep screaming, the people who want these recipes and serums will find us."

"Sorry," Webb said. He shuddered. "It's just that I'm scared, okay, Amanda?"

"I understand," Amanda said in her most consoling voice. "If I give you this now, you may never feel the effects of the virus, if you were infected. You will be the first white patient to receive the cure. Think of the book rights and movie contracts." She smiled as she flicked the syringe and pushed a small amount of the dark serum through the needle. "I'm just going to roll up your sleeve, dear."

"Dear? I've had a massive crush on you for years, and I have to get infected with HIV for you to call me dear?"

Amanda looked at Webb, uncomfortable.

"Webb, I'm sorry, I never knew," she said clumsily.

"Never knew? I carried your books, helped you study, washed your laundry…"

"You never washed my laundry," Amanda said, smiling.

"Not that you know of," Webb replied, regaining some of his composure.

"That's creepy. I thought I was missing some panties," Amanda joked.

"I'm in love with you, Amanda Garrett," Webb said, a slight sweat breaking out on his brow.

"You won't be after I give you this shot," Amanda said, leaning over him with the needle.

Amanda had the needle in his bare arm just above the triceps before he could respond. The serum had a signature characteristic. It hurt. Going into the body, the serum was thick, and it burned. The paste that Kiram and Mumbato brought back from that undisclosed location had a searing quality.

"Oh my God!"

"Still love me?"

Webb fell into Amanda's arms as she extracted the needle. He had fainted. Careful to avoid blood, Amanda manipulated Webb's leaden body toward a magma wall, where she propped him on his side.

As she stood, she heard the muffled sound of rifle fire from above.

21

The Leopard determined Amanda Garrett and her posse were within range. The black night settled upon him like the arm of an old friend around his shoulders. He stood on the hood of his jeep, holding his night vision goggles to his eyes. He was perhaps at the highest point on the Serengeti Plain within a few kilometers and could see miles in all directions. To the east, he knew that the system of valleys that created the Great African Rift began just beyond the escarpment, which fell into a series of bony, descending ridges, like crisscrossed fingers, which ultimately gave way to the Olduvai Gorge.

Why would they be going in that direction? he wondered. *Perhaps it is the only safe way. Or the only way they know.*

He looked down at his ARM-Sleeve, expecting a message from Zhor Rhazziq, but there was none. The Leopard understood the importance of obtaining the Ebola and HIV cures. Legions of Africans would immediately be forever beholden to the Islamic State and its requirements. They would literally owe their life to the good Muslims, who would en masse distribute this elixir as the caliphate solidified. What would follow would be the infrastructure for an enduring army and war. The fighters would arrive first. Mineral-rich countries in Africa would galvanize to support the Islamic State with resources to fuel epic conflict with the West. Yes, as a mercenary, he would reap the rewards of the oncoming conflagration.

He turned to the west, the direction from which he had come, and checked again for the helicopter. About four hours ago, he had heard the American UH-60 flying somewhere overhead but had not seen it. Like the wind, it was gone. Upon hearing the audible signature of the machine, The Leopard had found a small depression surrounded by the tall cereal grass so prevalent in this area. For thirty minutes, he had not moved. He had shut off his vehicle engine, knowing that thermal imagery would identify him quickly. Now, with his engine cooled, he was eager to assess his situation. So he had moved to high ground.

He had lost valuable time but was reassured that he could discern the four people walking single file off the Serengeti and down the escarpment as if they were leaving a stage. One by one, they disappeared over the ridge.

They were a kilometer away, maybe two. They were carrying a box—the drugs, he assumed—it appeared, and one of them had a backpack. If that box was not what he expected, then he would catch them and kill them all but the girl until she confessed to the location of the cure or divulged its recipe. Then he would kill her, too. The delay had been a minor setback, he reassured himself. His plan had been a good one, for he had no way of telling exactly where the cure was stored. But the crafty woman had hidden the real potion in a storm cellar instead of an exposed clinic.

So he had flushed his quarry, she was on the run, and he was the big game hunter.

He felt his ARM-Sleeve vibrate against his forearm. He watched the text scroll across the screen:

Book of Catalyst. Olduvai Gorge. If close, add'l mission. Standby.

He stared at the display screen, then typed:

Roger. Close. Continuing original mission until given new mission.

Continue. Additional instructions shortly.

The Leopard pressed the dim function of his ARM-Sleeve, jumped down from the hood of his vehicle, sat in the driver's seat, and was soon bouncing across the Serengeti Plain, where he would dismount at the point where Amanda Garrett and her team had gone over the ridge. He reached the steep drop-off within minutes and retrieved his hunting rifle from his truck.

As he began to tread onto the trail his quarry had followed, a hulking figure stepped from behind a rock.

A high-pitched metallic screech pierced his eardrums. It was the sound of blades sliding against one another, like sharp knives in preparation for cutting meat at a dinner table. His neck hair stood on end.

"Hello, Leopard," The Cheetah said. "Ready to kill again?"

22

With Webb passed out from the inoculation, Amanda retrieved the knife from the side of the rucksack and crawled to the top of the cave. She quietly pushed the heavy rock downhill, the direction she had noticed Kiram had chosen. She summoned every ounce of her former high school and collegiate swimming stamina and shoved until the boulder moved enough to let her slide out. The gunfire had raised her concern about Kiram and Mumbato, and she couldn't stand feeling useless. Webb was unconscious, and so she went to check on her boys.

She looked in every direction but saw nothing. Convinced that the best option was to stay near the cave opening, she chose a spot a few meters away on higher ground that gave her an unobstructed view in every direction.

Finally, she saw them. The two boys were nearly indistinguishable from the terrain. She watched as Kiram directed Mumbato toward a high rock that was a hundred meters back, toward the direction from which they had traveled. And, she presumed, from which the pursuer would be coming. His plan most likely was to attract the pursuer and then have him give chase, allowing Mumbato a shot from the rear. She felt her palms sweat as she anticipated the duel that was about to happen, but she was optimistic that the chase would come to an end right here, right now. Then they could continue to safety.

Mumbato moved silently below the ridgeline until he was situated in a good defensive position behind some rocks. She looked at Kiram, now moving toward the trail. He handled his AK-47 the way a Samurai would wield a katana. She saw Kiram aiming the weapon and observed that the wood buttstock melded perfectly with his face.

Kiram stood in the middle of the path, where the hovering moon cast a weak glow that would highlight his presence to their pursuer. She could hear Mumbato shifting and aligning his aim amidst the faint whisper of the wind sliding over the escarpment they had all traveled down together. Kiram was thirty meters below the opening of the lava tube and still had the assault pack she had given him.

She knew that they both believed that the time had come for some tactics. If the attacker got some of the sample, perhaps he would go away and leave them alone. The fact that they had chosen to make a stand here told her something. It was a destination that the two boys knew would provide protection. This had to be the location from which they had been retrieving the black paste. It occurred to her that the cave below her position where Webb rested was actually a lava tube.

She heard a cackling sound, like hyenas, and realized it was Kiram and Mumbato communicating. She saw Kiram turn his head at the sound of heavy footsteps moving too quickly and clumsily along the path. The pursuer's momentum had carried him too far for his own good, she thought. Kiram made an audible movement, one she determined was intended to lure the attacker's attention. The footfalls stopped momentarily, which must have been Kiram's cue to scuffle along the trail as if he were a rabbit seeking the bush.

Two shots zipped past her, followed by the muffled report of a silenced weapon. She heard the chambering of the round and the metallic functioning of the weapon, probably a pistol or small carbine. The still night carried even sounds that were designed for silence. Moreover, she could hear the sound of the bullet churning past her. She clawed into the dirt and rock, spreading reeds of grass to keep her view of the action. The attacker had probably noticed Kiram's assault pack and felt that this was the opportunity he had been seeking; he could kill Kiram and still secure his intended prize.

She watched Kiram hustle in serpentine fashion along the trail making sure he remained silhouetted, but not obviously so. Mumbato's job must have been to watch over the developing situation and to intervene if it did not go as planned.

Once he was one hundred meters past the entrance to the lava tube, Kiram stopped briefly, using a rock outcropping for protection. She listened intently to the sound of the oncoming footsteps. Sweat streamed down her face. Her heart pounded loudly against her chest. Her mind raced. *What was their strategy?*

Once the attacker was within fifty meters, Kiram coughed and stepped clumsily onto the trail, spraying a couple of bursts of the AK-47 errantly into the brush.

His actions were met with the immediate return of shots from a silenced weapon, to which he responded by screaming loudly, as if hit. Amanda gasped and gripped her knife. She watched as Kiram dropped the assault pack into the middle of the trail, rolled on the ground, and slid down a steep embankment. He appeared to be bobsledding on sand.

Her vantage allowed her to see that Kiram had reached the bottom of the ravine and rolled to his left, sighting up his weapon in case the attacker pursued him and not the assault pack, she presumed. She wondered, *Would he kill the man? What if there was more than one? Would this man take the bait?* Their pursuer had to be working for someone who would continue to come after them if he was not satisfied.

She watched Kiram lie still against the rock as he aimed his rifle. The man walked within ten meters of her as she hid behind the rocks above the lava tube opening. Their attacker's size was a surprise to her. He was a giant. Carrying a long rifle in one hand and a pistol in his other, he moved cautiously. Adjacent to her position, he stopped and sniffed the air like an animal might. He did a 360-degree scan before he moved forward along the trail, toward Kiram's waiting assault pack.

She let out a breath as he passed. After a moment, she heard the zipper being ripped open on the assault pack. She heard the sounds of the plastic bag rustling beneath clumsy hands.

After a few minutes, she saw him close the assault pack and head back toward her. The man passed close to her again, but this time he continued without stopping. She could see that he had the assault pack on his back. She gave the attacker another fifteen minutes and then began to crawl back toward the lava tube when she saw Kiram move. He made a sharp barking sound like the dogs they had killed earlier. A few minutes later, she saw Mumbato carefully picking his way down the trail to avoid alerting the pursuer.

She watched the two boys clasp arms, the Roman warrior's grip, and then turn to move to the rear entrance. They were twenty meters away from her position when she felt a presence behind her.

Then she heard the screeching of metal on metal. As she turned, she saw silhouetted against the starlit night a hulking beast brandishing two swords, arms outstretched like a gymnast. His voice was a dissonant bass chord amidst the gentle symphony of the Serengeti.

"I killed children smaller than you in Rwanda. I am The Cheetah."

23

Zach Garrett approached the vehicle carefully as Hobart and Van Dreeves focused elsewhere. The machine-gun fire they had heard at the aircraft crash location had been random fire from what they believed to be the Tanzanian Army, which must now be searching for his daughter. They'd been able to escape on foot and move rapidly without detection.

"Looks like an old Range Rover jeep," Zach said. His voice was transmitted to his two operators through the earbuds they were all wearing.

"Looks secure," Hobart responded.

Night had fallen like a soft blanket on the Serengeti Plain. They walked in thigh-high cereal grass that grew sparsely in this dry patch. Through his night vision goggles, Zach could see the horizon drop off the escarpment into a valley. Beyond that, the terrain rose in jagged waves as if cut by a plow, pushing the rocks up and the soil down. At six thousand feet above sea level, the night became cool much more quickly than it had in Djibouti, which was sea level. The polypro moisture-wicking T-shirt he was wearing kept him warm by pulling the sweat away from his body and transferring it to his outer tactical vest. Earlier, he had replaced his sunglass-shaded eye protection with the clear lenses, and he had ensured they all had tested their infrared aiming devices for their rifles.

"Okay, this is his vehicle. Blood in the back, some maps in the front here that show the orphanage and where he killed King. You got any footprints in this dust?"

"Wait one," Van Dreeves responded.

Zach lifted his goggle monocle and flipped it back on his head harness as he pulled a small Maglite from his vest pocket. Using the red lens, he scanned the contents of the jeep. He found some loose ammunition for a pistol, the maps, and a cradle for a GPS device. Importantly, he found no sign of Amanda or any of the others.

The pursuer was still in pursuit.

"Boss, we've got some prints moving east. Looks like Bigfoot," Van Dreeves said through the radio system.

"Okay, let's thermite this thing and move out," Zach said.

"You sure you want the audible signature?" Hobart asked.

"Well, I don't want it to work. Maybe just disable it," he said, thinking.

"Roger, no problem."

Zach moved toward Van Dreeves and flipped his goggle down. Immediately he saw that Van Dreeves had locked his infrared flashlight into the on position and was scanning a set of boot prints that initially clustered around the vehicle and then moved distinctly east.

"Okay. It's one guy, not a bunch of hostages; that's my first impression," Zach said.

"Roger."

Hobart approached from the rear, tapped Zach on the shoulder, and said, "That thing's not going anywhere. Engine is disabled."

"Okay, let's go," Zach said.

The three men stood and fanned out as Van Dreeves tracked the boot prints. Zach could see a small cut in the escarpment about a half mile away. It was an indistinguishable dark notch against the blackened backdrop of the rising terrain. He sensed that he was close to Amanda.

Trying to hold at bay the paternal emotions that wanted to rage, he kept his soldier's focus as they walked. Everything that had happened over the past few years had so dramatically changed his world. Amanda had gone from estranged daughter believing he was dead to loving child and friend. His relationship with his girlfriend, Riley, had blossomed to the point where they were discussing marriage. His career as a selfless servant to the nation, which every soldier truly is, was most likely about to end. Tough decisions were ahead.

But right now all that mattered was the automatic weapons fire they heard in the distance.

Zach began sprinting toward the sounds as Van Dreeves and Hobart followed suit.

Over the horizon, from the jagged set of wave-like formations in the distance, came two hulking helicopters spitting cannon fire in their direction.

"What the hell?" Hobart said. All three of them rolled onto the ground and narrowly avoided the surprise attack.

"Who is that? And where are *our* Little Birds?"

"Sir, that's got to be the Tanzanian military, and our attack aircraft are back in Shinyanga refueling," Hobart said. "They were holding there until we called."

"Well, call them. Let's move before another run comes in," Zach said. They rose and moved quickly into a small wadi that ran perpendicular to their direction of movement. Though it would take them off course, the terrain would provide them necessary cover. After moving about two hundred meters, they stopped and took up defensive positions.

"Oh, man," Van Dreeves said.

"What?"

"They're offloading infantry to come get us," Van Dreeves said.

"Or Amanda," Zach added.

"Can we declare them hostile?" Hobart asked.

"They just tried to kill us, Hobes. I think we're cleared hot here," Zach said.

"Okay, because I've got a shot," Hobart said.

"Take it."

24

Zhor Rhazziq was in his study, walls lined with books written in many different languages. Sitting in his Corinthian leather office chair, his back was to the twelve-foot French doors that opened to the Atlantic Ocean. He pressed a button on a standard-sized remote, pointing it at a small television screen with the label *Tandberg* beneath the thirty-six-inch visual display. He ran a well-manicured hand over his black stubble that made him look more like a playboy than a devout Muslim, which he most certainly considered himself.

He turned away from one satellite feed where he was watching The Leopard secure his prize and now was beginning a video teleconference with the operational commander in Al-Qaim, Iraq, just south of the Syrian border, a full continent away from the action in Tanzania. Rhazziq was also including others in this call. He was conducting a commander's battlefield update, something he did rarely. Two developments, though, had necessitated this conference, which would be conducted over secure satellite connection using the vast array of technology employed by his media conglomerate. Mostly, his men were wearing the ARM-Sleeves and were able to simply look at the high-tech wearable devices on their forearms and talk.

Looking back at him on the screen were two men dressed in black combat jumpsuits and red-and-white-checkered *keffiyehs*. The scarves did not completely cover their faces, and the men appeared to Rhazziq to be battle weary.

Rhazziq's commanders frequently moved nightly. Regularly changing locations of their headquarters by even one building often saved their lives in a tepid U.S. bombing campaign that none of them considered effective.

The Islamic State controlled the Iraq-Syria border from Al-Qaim to the Turkish border, where they also paid off the remotely based Turkish customs officials to allow passage of black market gasoline.

Soon other commanders joined the conference, their pictures appearing on the screen, each time making the previous image a smaller rectangle.

The first development was the completion of the caliphate strategy. Rhazziq had drafted the white paper, as he called it, run it by his senior leadership peers in Raqqah, Syria, and then set about getting the logistics into place.

His rationale was that because American forces had withdrawn from Iraq and were about to withdraw from Afghanistan, the American intelligence apparatus was significantly weakened. Because of recent attacks from the Islamic State, the Americans were struggling to reassert their intelligence operations in Iraq and Afghanistan. This part of his plan was essential: Islamic State attacks must continue to keep the Americans and their intelligence apparatus focused on the Middle East, Iraq and Afghanistan in particular.

His strategy was to keep the Americans fixed using an economy of force in Iraq, Syria, and Afghanistan while shifting the recruitment of foreign fighters to key nodes in Africa. Let the Islamic State drain U.S. resources from the next fight: Africa. Rhazziq's strategy would be full spectrum. There would be combat operations, but the gambit would be one of capturing the hearts and minds, classic insurgency doctrine, Maoist even.

The first step, capturing the Ebola and HIV cures that were being developed in Tanzania by the CIA, was happening now. His electronic warfare capabilities had intercepted enough email traffic from the village outside Mwanza to have him send a single operative, his Leopard, to the location and steal the recipe. He had just watched The Leopard pick up a small pack from a trail and head back toward his vehicle. Comfortable that the formula would soon be his, he thought of his dead friend, Quizmahel, whom he believed would approve of how things had progressed since his martyrdom this morning. Coupled with Amanda Garrett's boneheaded move to burn her own aid center, captured perfectly on ARM-Sleeve high-definition digital image, his information campaign was also off to a great start.

Rhazziq laughed when he thought of the Americans who had attacked the Taliban in Afghanistan and had dethroned Saddam Hussein in Iraq, curing two of Iran's greatest ills in the region. Like a chess novice, the American government had made two moves that took their own pieces off the board! They'd had Iran pinned at least by Hussein in the west. Now, all of the American focus was on Iraq, Iran, Syria, Turkey, and Afghanistan, opening a corridor for the next move of the Islamic Jihad that was gaining momentum in establishing a caliphate from Morocco to Pakistan.

Rhazziq shook his head and chuckled again. It was almost too easy. The Americans had established their African Command with a headquarters in *Europe*! They had such little confidence in their endeavor that they hadn't dared to place the new outfit's headquarters on the continent. The Benghazi disaster was just a symptom of this remote, hands-off approach by the Americans. Other than a small base in Africa's poorest nation, Djibouti, the Americans had little presence in Africa.

The second step was aimed at the American president himself. Jamal Barkum was in his first term. As the second African-American elected president, Barkum had demonstrated an eagerness to settle disputes with the Islamic world. The American media had also characterized Barkum as having a messiah complex.

We shall certainly find out, Rhazziq thought to himself.

"*Salaam alaikum*," he said into the secure videoconference.

A few seconds later, he saw the time-delayed head nods and some utterances of "*Alaikum salaam.*" *Hello and peace.*

Rhazziq spoke. "My great warriors, we are set to begin our massive undertaking. Each of you has a task. To our brothers in Syria, Iraq, and Afghanistan, you must increase the attacks on the infidels using homemade bombs. To my friends in Cairo, Tripoli, Amman, Damascus, Beirut, Riyadh, Algiers, and Addis, complete your organizations and begin your demonstrations, effective immediately. Your goal is to mobilize the people against the Americans because they have killed our friend Quizmahel, who invented the cures for Ebola and HIV. They have destroyed the laboratory where the cures were made. The Americans want the Africans to suffer. You may use violence to attack embassies or Americans, but be careful. We want the people on our side, so only you know best the limitations of each of your populations. Our purpose is to turn all Africans against the United States, incite them to join our ranks, and then quickly train them and move them into martyrdom activities. It will be a classic pincer movement with our brothers in Afghanistan, Syria, and Iraq attacking simultaneously as the Northern Tier of Africa unleashes its hordes on the infidels. Are there any questions?"

Rhazziq saw on the screen that one of the many video boxes showed men looking at their ARM-Sleeves and listening intently.

One man's voice came through Rhazziq's speakers. It was Abdullah bin al-Lib from Amman, Jordan. A Jordanian by birth, Abdullah had never accepted his country's modernization efforts. In Rhazziq's mind, Jordan was more cosmopolitan than almost all other Muslim countries but had failed the Palestinians. He knew Abdullah felt the same way. As long as that issue remained unsolved, Abdullah should never accept peace as an option, Rhazziq believed.

"What about the Jews?" Abdullah asked.

"The Jews," Rhazziq said, "will be isolated in their own prison. America will lose what little legitimacy they have in this part of the world. In eastern Jordan, it is your job is to incite chaos amongst the Iraqi refugees and cause the Jordanian military to react. Faqir, your job in the West Bank is to attack every Israeli outpost. Finally, al Dhuri, in Gaza you will lead your thousands of new African recruits into Rafa."

The Israeli geopolitical position in the world was as tenuous as one could possibly be. Ravenous enemies surrounded them from all sides except the east, where the Mediterranean Sea protected their least assailable flank. The Iraq war had displaced nearly a million refugees into the eastern reaches of Jordan, draining a particularly strong U.S. ally. The idea now was to lock Israel in mortal struggle while simultaneously inciting violence from Morocco to Pakistan. The Americans would be placed on the horns of a dilemma: *Do we get into yet another ground war in the Middle East, or do we continue to bomb from the air as the Islamic State takes shape and hardens?*

"This is a bold chess move, my friends. Already you can see the televisions replaying the scene of the American woman destroying the clinic. People are already angry with the Americans. Europe is too weak to do anything, and now we will weaken all takfirs who seek to block our progress." Takfirs were unbelievers, and Rhazziq had no tolerance for them.

"An indirect approach?" Abdullah asked. It was more of a comment than a question.

"Exactly. Strengthen the Islamic State as we weaken the Americans, isolate the Jews, and then take the next step."

"What is that next step?"

Rhazziq stared at the camera. He would not reveal the ultimate plan. He had learned the hard way that operations were most successful when information was passed to only those who needed to know.

"I will inform you of future operations as the time comes. It involves the greatest psychological operation of all time. But for now, attack the Americans with the thousands of recruits you will get from this campaign. Attack them everywhere. Iraq, Kuwait, Egypt, Jordan, all across the caliphate," Rhazziq replied. His passion was obvious. "We have already reached our time limit. Once we have fully destabilized organized governments in the region, we will have millions more martyrs for the jihad and will be closer to establishing the caliphate. Each of you may expect to be formally recognized as commanders of your areas when we destroy the Americans. Then, we take the fight to a weakened American homeland. On their soil, not ours!"

He watched the others touch their ARM-Sleeves, which went blank. When they were all black, he shut off his own device.

Rhazziq stood and looked at his electronic map of Iraq. Not only could he follow every man in his forces who was wearing his ARM-Sleeve, he had also found a way to tap into the Blue Force Tracker information that the U.S. military used to monitor their troop locations. On his digital plasma display, he could see the new U.S. forward operating base in Northwest Iraq that housed the clandestine Special Forces teams that were assisting the bombing campaigns against the Islamic State. The Americans had reoccupied an airfield and base to the west of Al-Qaim on the Syrian border. He had received reports that American commandos would soon be parachuting into the base. That would be his first target.

Rhazziq smiled. His plan was a good one and seemed to be working so far.

He walked to his balcony and leaned against the marble rail. Dark clouds gathered offshore in the night. Lightning flashed and thunder rumbled across the sea. Waves crashed beneath the bluff upon which his mansion sat. Rain began to spit down from the sky.

He raised his arms, holding them wide against the sky, and shouted, "You're next, Barkum!"

25

Tanzania

Amanda stared into the eyes of her would-be assassin. His countenance held no mercy. He was an executioner, a killing machine. His large frame blocked the moon and starlight like a giant, sinister shadow.

His body was covered only in a pair of dusty camouflage pants. Barefoot and bare chested, he flexed his powerful frame in preparation for the downward strike. It was a move she sensed that he had performed thousands of times and one she would not stop.

But she could try. Sensing where the blades would cross, she dove to the ground as the sword rushed past her body. She felt the breeze from the wide blades swooshing past her body. Sparks leapt in front of her face as the metal struck the magma onto which she had leapt. Her moment was now. She had to move quickly. The man would take less than a second to strike again.

Amanda rolled toward him to grab a filthy leg, then pulled at the man's heel as she landed a kick into his groin. She felt something give, and the man lost his balance.

A shot rang out, followed by two more. Bullets snapped past her head, one sparking off the lava rock.

She heard the swords scrape against the rocks. The man was moving to one knee, fury in his eyes. He flexed his arms and pectoral muscles the way a cobra flares its hood before a strike.

She heard another shot and saw the man stop and look at his chest where a small blossom of blood appeared. One shot would not stop this man, Amanda thought. She heard another shot and saw the man look down again.

Her attacker tumbled backward and rolled down the hill, swords clanging along the way.

Kiram and Mumbato stood over her.

"What are you doing outside the cave?" Kiram admonished. "Are you okay, Miss Amanda?"

"I'm okay. I was checking on you two," she said.

"Quick, back in the hole," Kiram said.

Mumbato had glanced at her, then looked outward as if the other man might return.

Kiram helped her to her feet and guided her down the cliff to the cave entrance.

"Go in here. Stay with white boy."

"Where are you going? Aren't you coming into the cave, too?"

"Yes, but first we need to check on man who attacked you. Very bad man. Called The Cheetah."

"Yes, that's what he said, but you shot him," Amanda said.

"Man not go away, Miss Amanda. Very bad man from Rwanda. Now please."

Amanda and Kiram rolled the rock uphill. Mumbato came running toward them, saying, "He is still alive. We must chase him away."

"You know how to close. We will come in another way," Kiram said.

She watched the two boys chase after The Cheetah and wondered if she would ever see them again.

26

"You're kidding me, right?" President Jamal Barkum asked his national security team.

"No, sir. Afraid not," Vice-President Camille Dillon replied.

They were sitting in the Oval Office with the secretary of state, secretary of defense, and the director of the CIA. Muted sunlight splashed across the stately room in opaque rectangles. Anti-blast improvements on the windows had filtered the light, giving the room a yellowish hue. The desk, the sofas and chairs, and the paintings on the wall had been essentially unchanged from the previous administration. President Jamal Barkum thought to himself that halfway into his first term, his national security team should not be descending upon him like so many barkers at a carnival. He could sense the circus callers wrapping their arms around him and turning him in one direction, then another: *Mr. President, focus your attention here,* then *No, focus it here or, better yet, there.* He had barely made a dent in his domestic agenda. How could he focus anywhere? But here he was, and there was a big pile of rotting foreign policy garbage stinking up the Oval Office.

"Okay, run it by me again," the president said.

The director of the CIA, a retired Army general named Stan Carlisle, said, "Sir, I've been in communication with Matt Garrett, one of my freelancers, who is with Sandy's gal down in Tanzania." Sandy was Sandra Bianchi, the secretary of state. An Ohio congresswoman, she had been President Barkum's first pick based upon their long-standing friendship and his belief that she would actually listen to partner nations as opposed to trying to ram a democratic ideology down their throats. Bianchi was a social anthropologist who had taught at Ohio State after working some field projects abroad, primarily in Africa and the Middle East.

"That's Kristyana Cixi," Bianchi said.

The president nodded at her and motioned for Carlisle to continue.

"She's an Army intelligence analyst on loan to the State Department and is on her way back here from Tanzania as we speak."

"So what we know right now is that Amanda Garrett, Matt's niece, was working on *Project Nightingale*, which was our clandestine Ebola and HIV vaccine and cure project in Mwanza, Tanzania. We had authorization to test both on orphans and each was working."

"Who gave the authorization?" Barkum asked.

Carlisle said, "I did, with the consent of my counsel. HIV has been a huge issue on the continent, Ebola has been increasing, and we needed to do something about it. I ran it by the legal folks, and they didn't say no."

Barkum shook his head. "That's not a good answer, General."

"Well, it is the truth, Mr. President."

Barkum listened intently as the CIA director spoke, mulling what he would have done. On one hand, you could take the bureaucratic stance and cover your ass, he thought, which would mean do nothing. On the other hand, you could say, "These children are dying anyway; we're trying to do something to help, so let's do it." He had run on a platform of "Government is Your Friend," and this general was trying to help the most neglected of all crawl out of despondency. He measured his next words.

"I understand what you did. I would like a review of the program as soon as possible. In the meantime, don't change anything."

"That would be pretty hard to do anyway, sir," Carlisle said. He was a hulking man. A former paratrooper with the 82nd Airborne Division, he had commanded troops at all levels from platoon to Army, hundreds of thousands of soldiers, airmen, marines, and sailors. He had thick gray hair and a tanned ruddy complexion that hinted at some Native American blood in his lineage. He leaned forward and began speaking again.

"The contingency plan if the lab was compromised was to destroy it. Amanda did exactly what we told her to do. She's got with her several vials of the vaccines and cures that had been working, as well as some of the viruses. At least that was the plan. She kept a go-bag in a sealed container there. Our word is that she got the bag and left on a plane that then crashed."

"Crashed?" the president asked.

"Yes, sir. Right now her father, Col. Zach Garrett, is on the ground with two other operatives looking for her. They reported the plane was shot down, so we know someone is trying to steal the formula. They called into Zach's brother and one of my guys, Matt Garrett, that it looks like they survived. The pilot of the airplane might have been killed. They found one dead African buried in a shallow grave. Matt tells us that they weren't kidnapped, at least not yet."

"Why would this be happening?" the vice-president asked. Vice-President Camille Dillon, a former senator from Florida, was dressed in a conservative, navy pinstriped pantsuit. Her brown hair was clipped just above her collar.

"Ma'am, we think it is related to the Islamic State's announcement that *they* found a cure to HIV and Ebola. We believe that what really happened is that someone in Islamic State circles somehow found out about our program and timed their announcement with what they thought would be an easy snatch of the formulas. They have a team, maybe one guy, we're not sure, that has killed Dr. Arthur King and destroyed his lab. Of course, Al Rhazziq and Al Jazeera, the two primary Arab networks, are saying that Amanda killed King and torched the lab."

"Hold that thought for a second. Why are we calling it the Islamic State?" the president asked.

"Because that's what they're calling it," Carlisle said.

"That's not a good reason. Not all Muslims are part of this movement," President Barkum replied.

A stony silence fell over the room until Carlisle moved past the issue.

"There's also been text and email chatter about a non-canonized Biblical text called the Book of Catalyst," Carlisle said. "We're not sure what to make of it."

"What is this about a book?" the president asked. A portion of his mind was searching for a frame of reference onto which he could latch. He had little interest in foreign policy beyond how his administration could stop the madness so that he could move forward with his domestic agenda.

"The Book of Catalyst," Carlisle said. "Bottom line, we're not sure. But," he said quickly before his response could be mistaken, "we think the Book of Catalyst is being propped up as an alternative version of the Book of Genesis, an African version that essentially argues that the cradle of civilization is a place called the Olduvai Gorge in Tanzania. There's a huge Wikipedia page that's been updated multiple times in the last several months. Before all of this occurred."

The president leaned forward, his crisp silk suit rustling like the fluttering of wings. "Tell me more."

"I can pick it up from here, Stan," Secretary Bianchi said. She turned to the president. "In 1978, Mary Leakey found the oldest set of bipedal footprints in a lava flow about thirty miles south of the Olduvai Gorge. Just about every African nation claims to have the oldest human remains: Ethiopia's got Lucy, Eritrea's got the baby, et cetera. But Olduvai's got the oldest footprints, the oldest tools, and arguably the oldest human remains. The Book of Catalyst is a little-known, controversial text that was written thousands of years before the birth of Christ. The bottom line is that it was last seen in Addis Ababa, Ethiopia. Few people realize that the Ark of the Covenant was once stored there. Several African Old Testament books were either destroyed or believed to be destroyed by Pharaoh Ramses II. What little recorded history there is of this asserts that the Nubian pharaohs had already built the Ark of the Covenant and were moving it toward Jerusalem when the Assyrians surrounded the city."

Sandy Bianchi paused. The daughter of an Italian immigrant father and a mother with Pakistani lineage, her face captured the most perfect lines of each ethnicity, creating a striking countenance and beautiful brown eyes that glowed copper when she was focused. Barkum could tell that his friend was carefully considering her next words.

"You know, Mr. President, ignoring black history is not a new phenomenon. We may be catching up with our history books, but think about a time before computers and typewriters or even a printing press. The Egyptians called the Nubians and their Biblical texts 'the Mortal Threat.'"

"Mortal Threat?"

"Yes. Mortality versus immortality is a timeless struggle, and those who believed themselves to be divine, generally Europeans and Middle Easterners, saw sub-Saharan Africa as a threat to their immortality," Bianchi answered.

"I get that racism isn't a new thing," the president said. "But you're also telling me that there is an alternative version of how life began from a creationist point of view and it meshes with what the anthropologists say? That God created life in sub-Saharan Africa?"

"That's what I'm saying," she said. "Ever hear of Occam's Razor?"

"Of course," the president replied. Then a chill shot up his spine at the first thing that came to his mind. He said, "The simplest solution is usually true. Instead of creation and evolution being in competition, they are in concert?"

"Jesus," the vice-president whispered.

"Well, maybe not," Barkum replied, then tried a slight smile.

The secretary continued, leaning forward, her pearl necklace hanging loose above her white blouse and navy blazer. "The bipedal prints Leakey and her husband discovered in the Olduvai Gorge are more properly referred to as the Laetoli footprints. Volcanic ash and light rainfall apparently covered them and preserved them thousands of years ago."

"Couldn't they be some kind of animal?" the vice-president asked, perhaps not in her most politically correct tone.

"They are distinctly human," she said. "There is an arch, and there is no mobile big toe, such as those of apes. And they are bipedal."

The group sat silently for a moment. The president figured they were each contemplating what the discussion might mean. On a surface level, it was boring anthropology and theology. But the notion was earth-shattering. If the creationist argument could be coupled with the evolutionist argument, they could perhaps answer the most pressing question of all time. *Where did we come from? Are we products of mere bacterial evolution or did God truly create us?*

President Barkum's mind tossed these notions around. He was, if nothing else, a religious man who believed he had a higher calling than most. He did not see himself as clergy. No, he saw himself as above that, nearly divine. The pomp and circumstance of his inaugurations had led critics to label him with a messiah complex. So be it, he thought. I am on a mission from God.

"We're talking about the possible destruction of the underpinnings of our nation's entire Judeo-Christian foundation, right? If what you are implying is true, that this Book of Catalyst shows that the Garden of Eden was in Tanzania, then this information will create chaos."

"From a national security standpoint, it would be a nightmare," Carlisle said.

"What do we do with the information?" Vice-President Dillon asked.

"A better question is, who else has this information? We have to contain this thing until we can sort it out for real. Plus, I'd like a world-renowned theologian to become a temporary member of the national security team here until we sort this out." The president was now focused on national security and foreign policy more than ever before. "But it has to be someone we can trust."

The message was clear. Don't let anyone into the inner circle who was not on the president's side politically.

"I'll call Ireland's prime minister and see if he can loan us Father McCallan. There's no better expert," Sandy Bianchi said.

"Okay, but be discreet. Tell him I just want to explore some faith-based initiatives," Barkum said. "So what else do we need to do?"

CIA Director Carlisle looked at the president. "Sir, I think we've got two courses of action developing here," Carlisle began. "The first is the rescue of an American citizen and her safe return. We have to do whatever we can to get Amanda Garrett back alive with whomever she has with her."

"Agreed, but shouldn't that be with African Command?" the president asked. African Command was the fledgling headquarters based in Stuttgart, Germany with a forward base in Djibouti. Their mission was more of an information operation with a purpose of increasing American influence and countering the Islamic State's effort to establish their caliphate across the Northern Tier of Africa. After the Benghazi debacle, the previous president had fired the African Command's commander, who had defied orders by attempting to deploy quick reaction forces into the fray to save the ambassador from a terrorist attack.

"Col. Zach Garrett is in charge of all African Command Special Forces, so he'll be reporting through General Kaine, the new commander, to the secretary of defense."

"That's right," said Secretary of Defense Phil Bateman. A retired Navy admiral and three-term congressman from Louisiana, Bateman had been the president's first pick for secretary of defense. Both Cajun and Southern Baptist, Bateman had little foreign policy experience. Barkum had heard the retired admiral once say, "Never miss an opportunity to keep your mouth shut." He had also heard his secretary of defense say, "God will let you know when to speak," and wondered what the man was thinking about the information he had just received. But he doubted he was going to share it. "And we can't forget we've got paratroopers about to land in Iraq."

"Keep that contained, Phil," the president said. He looked back toward Carlisle and said, "Okay, the other course of action?"

CIA Director Carlisle continued, "The vaccines and cures are clearly the centerpiece of an Islamic State campaign to influence the people of Africa against the United States, to lessen our influence in the region. There would be huge geopolitical implications if the Islamic State were to convince the world—as they have been trying—that we destroyed that vaccine and set

Africa on fire, so to speak. We need to come clean on *Project Nightingale* and get you on television stating exactly what we were doing there."

The president mulled this over. He had to admit that their enemies were brilliant in their execution of a chess move on the world game board. If the United States could be widely perceived as destroying an HIV or Ebola vaccine and cure on his watch, the emotions would not only roil in Africa but would ignite tender racial relationships in the United States. The president would do everything he could to keep insurgency on a global scale from becoming his legacy.

"Okay, I'll do it. We need an aggressive information campaign here, though. I don't want just one statement and that's it. Where does the Book of Catalyst fit into the rebels' strategy?"

An uncomfortable pause reflected the tension in the room. While everyone was looking at Carlisle, the president was staring at Secretary of State Bianchi, who had offered up lead on this topic earlier in the discussion. She got the message.

"We're not sure if the book fits at all," she said. "It could be an entirely different issue. While the intercepts that Stan's guys have received argue that something is occurring with the Book of Catalyst, it's too early to tell." She looked at Carlisle.

"Thanks, Sandy," Carlisle said, picking up on her cue. "I, on the other hand, do think the book is involved somehow. But I agree that we need to get some religious scholars in here to tell us what this really means. See if we can find some copies of it or get the text that these people are talking about. My questions would be: a) Is it authentic? b) What does it say? and c) What are the implications if it is real?"

"I can already tell you that the book argues that God created life in Africa and that Genesis is an interpretation, whereas Catalyst is an actual account," Sandy Bianchi said.

The president summarized. "So, what you are telling me is that we've found a cure for HIV and Ebola, but it may either be destroyed or captured by those who oppose us to be used for information purposes," the president said. He held up a fist and lifted his thumb as he ticked off his first point. "We have a young American woman being chased by at least one fighter as she tries to protect what might be left of these cures, provided she didn't torch the program herself." He lifted his index finger, which made a pistol of sorts with his hand. "And now we have an alleged missing book from the Bible that specifically predates Genesis and the Old Testament and states that God created life in the Olduvai Gorge? Do I have that right?" He lifted a third finger, staring at the nodding heads around the room.

"Where is Amanda Garrett right now?" the president asked.

Carlisle began speaking again, "Last ping we did on her satellite phone put her about two miles west of the Olduvai Gorge, heading east. The phone is not operational for outbound calls, but we're still able to ping her simcard and geolocate her."

"Okay. Dismissed," the president said. He watched the team file out as he sat at his desk. He opened his iPad and touched his finger to the security camera function. He watched Vice-President Camille Dillon steer Secretary of Defense Phil Bateman to the side. Using his earbuds, he listened to her conspiratorial whisper.

"Phil, you and I are both deeply religious. I need some options here. If this is real, we may have to destroy it; both the book and the Olduvai Gorge."

Secretary of Defense Bateman, his face ashen, nodded at the vice-president, looked up at the security camera, and turned back into the Oval Office.

"Mr. President," Bateman said.

Barkum removed the earbuds and smiled up at the secretary of defense.

"Yes, Mr. Secretary?"

"That battalion of paratroopers you ordered to protect the Special Forces base in northwestern Iraq is about to jump. It's four p.m. here, which makes it midnight there. You can watch it in the basement if you'd like."

"I trust that all will go well. Thank you," the president said.

Bateman did an about-face and walked out of the office as Barkum replayed the video of his vice-president and secretary of defense. After the break-in of the White House last October, the Secret Service had installed extra cameras everywhere in the White House and had provided the president omnipotent access.

Destroy the Olduvai Gorge and this mysterious book? Not a bad idea, he thought, but better to give them some rope and keep his distance from the rogue notion.

27

Iraq-Syria Border

Somewhere over the Iraq-Syria border, Amanda's husband, Jake Devereaux, shoved his static line at the left door safety and stepped into the 140-knot slipstream of the C-17 aircraft. They had taken off from Pope Air Force Base, conducted two in-flight refueling missions over the Atlantic Ocean and the Mediterranean Sea, and were now dropping at five hundred feet above ground level.

He felt the testicle-crushing snap of his parachute opening above him, a sensation no paratrooper ever complained about but all hated. Better dealing with some bruised testicles than having no canopy overhead and burning a smoking hole into the ground in some godforsaken place.

He watched the darkened shapes of his fellow paratroopers floating to the ground. He tugged on his risers and checked his canopy; all good. His rucksack was heavy but comfortably situated in front of said testicles to protect them against small arms fire. Good, he thought, before realizing he was giving way too much thought to his testicles. Perhaps he was focused on his family jewels because he hadn't talked or texted with Amanda in a few days and they were both eager to start a family together.

The ground was rushing toward him more quickly, and he was about one hundred feet from landing. His mind drifted for a moment to wonder in which direction Al-Qaim might be and how close the Air Force had actually put them to the Syrian border. He would find out soon enough, though, and he came back to the task at hand.

He pulled the quick release on his lowering line and held it for a few more seconds, a technique he had found useful in managing his landing. About fifty feet from the ground, he picked out his landing spot, released his rucksack, and immediately felt the tug of his gear to his left as the ruck-sack drew the line taut. He pulled on his right set of risers to counteract the pull of the equipment and the slight wind drift.

Keeping his feet and knees pressed firmly together, he maintained a focus on the horizon to avoid ground rush, the temptation to reach out with his feet as the ground approached, which usually resulted in injury. Conducting a proper parachute-landing fall required no thought or skill other than to avoid thinking or doing. *Keep your body in a tight ball and roll with it*, Jake told himself.

The soft sand greeted him with a welcoming embrace. He rolled slightly and thought, as always, *that wasn't so bad*. He quickly released his parachute to keep it from inflating on the ground and dragging him. He stayed in the prone position and pulled on his lowering line, dragging his rucksack to his location. Opening his weapons case, he removed his M4 carbine and slapped a magazine into the well. He chambered a round and made certain the safety selector switch was set to safe. He removed his knife from his ankle sheath and cut the lowering line near the ruck, placed the knife back in the sheath, and put his radio into operation.

He spoke softly into his MBITR, Multi-Band Individual Tactical Radio, saying, "White seven, this is white six, radio check, over."

White seven was his platoon Sergeant First Class Willie Mack, a career paratrooper who, with this jump, was on his seventh combat tour in the last seven years. Granted, a few of them had been three- or six-month deals, but he stood just as good a chance at being killed in those as he had in the fifteen-month tours, he had told Jake once.

Mack's job was to roll up the entire platoon of thirty-five men toward Jake, who was to remain stationary and put a small infrared beacon on his radio antenna, which he did.

Jake popped his night vision goggles onto his helmet and flipped them down over his eyes. He noticed a jagged line running through the middle and realized that the lens must have cracked when his rucksack struck the ground. *That sucks*, he thought to himself. He could still see, but his view was distorted.

"White six, this is white seven. Moving in your direction. Is marker set?"

"Roger. Marker is set," Jake replied.

As the adrenaline rushed from his body, his first thought was, *cooler than I expected.* He'd known they were jumping into a higher elevation, around three thousand feet, but still, he'd figured the desert was the desert: namely, hot. He was okay, though, with his polypro silk-weight underwear and Army combat uniform. If needed, he had some warmer clothing, called snivel gear, in his rucksack.

There were six other C-17 airplanes, all dropping the rest of his battalion. In his corner of the world, though, all he really cared about were his thirty-six guys, including himself. His mission was to move about two miles to the confluence of three dry riverbeds that were suspected by intelligence to be used by the enemy to smuggle fighters, supplies, and bomb-making materials.

And for that moment, all alone in the Iraq countryside, Jake felt at one with the world. A sense of pride and purpose washed over him. It was a feeling that had to be greater than winning the Heisman trophy or throwing a touchdown pass to win a big game. No, he was in charge of his men, had been given an important mission, and was at the cutting edge of national security. *This is exactly what I signed up for*, he thought to himself.

"Salerno." The whisper was barely recognizable

Jake recognized the voice, but with the crack in his lens had missed the darkened figure of Willie Mack.

"Sicily," he replied with the proper password.

He saw his platoon quickly forming around him in darkened shapes. They created a triangular patrol base about fifty meters across in each direction. Mack and Jake huddled briefly.

"What's up, sir? You were supposed to challenge me," Mack said.

"My goggles are cracked. I missed you," Jake replied. "Anyway, I'm ready. I've got the azimuth and the grid. We're not far."

"Let me get you some new goggles from one of the men," Mack said and began moving. Jake grabbed him and countered, "No. I wouldn't be able to live with myself if something happened to the man who uses these."

"Pardon me, but that's bullshit, sir. We need you to keep *us* alive," Mack said, removing his arm from Jake's grasp.

"We'll sort it out when we get there, Willie. We need to get moving," Jake whispered in his no bullshit tone. Willie Mack may have had seven combat tours under his belt, but Jake was the leader, and the two men understood that clearly.

"Your call, sir. Okay, I'll count everyone out and pull up the rear," Mack said.

"Good. Right now the captain says no sign of enemy activity. I want to get to our battle position and start scraping out a few holes in case they have indirect fire."

"Wilco," Mack said and moved to the leading edge of the triangular patrol base. Jake grabbed Private Robert Roberts, otherwise known as R-squared, who carried the radio on which he could communicate with the company commander, a captain.

"C'mon, Squared, let's move," Jake said. "Follow me."

Jake walked slowly to the tip of the triangle and watched as the platoon sergeant counted out the first squad, which was charged with navigating to the objective area.

"You got the azimuth and grid set?" Jake asked the squad leader, Staff Sergeant Manny Alvarez.

"Got it, sir. We're moving," Alvarez replied.

Jake had picked Alvarez's squad to lead the movement precisely because of his abilities to navigate foreign terrain.

Jake and R-squared tucked into the tight V-shaped wedge that the lead squad formed and began moving down an incline toward the objective. The night was no longer cool as the adrenaline and movement warmed him considerably, and he was again thankful that he had not worn too much gear. His rucksack was heavy but not unreasonably so.

The black night was weakly illuminated by a slight moon and a brilliant array of stars. As the ground fell away beneath him, he could see jagged terrain to his front through his cracked monocle. The compass addition to his goggles indicated they were moving two hundred and sixty-three degrees, almost due west.

By Jake's calculations, they should be at the objective area in less than two hours without any interruptions. That would make it midnight Iraq time and give his men about five hours to prepare their positions. He and Willie Mack had designed an L-shaped ambush at the neck where all three ravines came together. They would use one squad to form each of the legs of the L while keeping the third squad in reserve to counterattack and finish off the enemy.

Jake was focused on his first combat mission ever as enemy tracer fire suddenly lit up the sky to their front.

Timeless Footprints

28

Fourteen hours later, President Barkum looked at Secretary of State Sandy Bianchi, who was standing next to an attractive Asian woman and a young African-American man dressed in a monk's robe. It was six a.m., and Bianchi had awakened him citing an emergency.

"Sir, this is Kristyana Cixi. She just arrived at Andrews Air Force Base, and we drove her here immediately. She was on the ground in Tanzania."

The president shook her hand.

"And this is Pastor Isaiah Jones. He teaches at Georgetown's Theology Department and has a theology PhD from Harvard."

Barkum gave her a look that meant, *So where the hell is McCallan?*

"Isaiah is the world's leading expert on African scriptures," Bianchi said.

"Be that what they are," Jones muttered.

Great, Barkum thought, *a man with attitude.*

The president had the group sit along the sofas and chairs so they could have a conversation. He trusted Bianchi, but Pastor Jones looked like he was under thirty years old, and his face held the hateful scorn of so many of his own friends from his youth. Men he had come to believe were so trapped by their rightful disgust of the past treatment of African-Americans that they were never able to move forward. *Did Jones have a security clearance? Was he trustworthy? Would he blab to the media?* Barkum determined he would have a word with Bianchi afterward but would entertain them for a few minutes now.

"So, Sandy, to what do I owe this wake-up call?"

"Sir, Pastor Jones has signed a non-disclosure statement. Ever since 9-11, he has worked closely with the Georgetown National Security Studies program and has a top-secret clearance for special compartmented information. He understands what's at stake here based upon a brief outline I discussed with him after I read him on." He trusted Bianchi knew her friend well and had covered the bases he would be most concerned about.

Barkum visibly relaxed but asked, "So how many people do we have read onto the Catalyst Project?"

The secretary of state had labeled the project immediately after the meeting with the president yesterday.

"You, the vice-president, CIA director, SecDef, me, Kristyana here, Matt Garrett in Dar es Salaam, and a major who works in the embassy there."

"A major?" Barkum asked.

Bianchi turned to Kristyana, who relayed the story about the Army intelligence officer's find in Nineveh province and how an Army chaplain now had the original documents in Virginia Beach, Virginia. Apparently the chaplain had been reassigned from the Third Infantry Division to a small post called Fort Story that fronted both the Chesapeake Bay and Atlantic Ocean.

"The plan, sir, is for me to meet with the chaplain and ask him to turn over the documents," Kristyana said.

"Can't we just declare them Eminent domain?" Barkum asked.

"My God, Mr. President, we are talking about the original account of how God created life! This book predates Genesis," Jones said. The young man leaned forward, hands on his knees as if he were going to propel himself upward. "Who are you, or any of us, to declare this document Eminent domain?"

The room was silent for a moment.

Barkum smiled. "I like your style, Pastor Jones," he said. It was true. Barkum had changed his mind about Jones. "But what do you suggest?"

"Well, I certainly think we should obtain these documents, safeguard them, and then have an international team of scientists and theologians come in and verify their authenticity. On one hand, what we are talking about is shaking the faith of over half the world's people. On the other hand, once they get over that, God will be a verifiable reality for them.

They will have reason to believe, and their faith, once shaken, will be restored anew," Jones said. He stood and began pacing the Oval Office.

"What about the implications for my administration?"

"Excuse me, sir, but this is bigger than your administration," Jones said. "No disrespect intended, but if you hear the story, then you'll understand why."

Barkum's blood began to simmer, but he nodded at Jones to continue.

"The Book of Catalyst was first drawn on acacia tree bark, then was transferred onto vellum, allegedly verbatim. Vellum is nothing other than animal hide. All of your history books will tell you that Africans thousands of years ago couldn't write, had no language, and so on. But if you study hieroglyphics, it's all right there. History does not start in Luxor or Karnak in Egypt as everyone would have you believe. No, history started in the Olduvai Gorge and was amply recorded in the Sudanese pyramid near Meroe, Sudan, on the Nile. Egyptian King Psantek II destroyed the acacia writings, but he didn't know about the vellum recordings or the story captured inside the pyramid."

Jones looked at the president as if to say, "Do I have your attention now?"

The president sighed. "Okay, I'm impressed. Keep going."

Jones turned to Secretary Bianchi and Kristyana Cixi, who were watching the one-sided duel with slack-jawed awe.

"What was my response to you when you asked me if I had heard of the Book of Catalyst?"

Bianchi coughed into her fist and said, "You squinted at me as if I was telling your secret, not mine."

Jones pointed at her. "Exactly. I've heard of the Book for a long time. The Sudanese have been working on a project to piece it all back together. They have found several of the pieces of the interior wall of the tomb where the Book of Catalyst was recorded."

"Where were the vellum documents?"

"In the Ark of the Covenant," Jones said flatly.

"How can that be? The Ark wasn't built until—"

"If you accept Genesis," Jones interrupted. "If you accept Catalyst, then you can make the argument that Genesis is an extraction of Catalyst. Kings destroy the black man's history not knowing they are destroying the evidence of God."

Barkum gasped inaudibly. He had never heard anyone say it quite like that before.

"Where the Old Testament gets it right is in Book of II Kings where the Assyrians had Jerusalem surrounded around 701 B.C. and Nubian Pharaoh Shabaka drove the Assyrians away. The book doesn't tell you that; rather, all it says is that Sennacherib up and left, went back to Syria. But Shabaka was on the move across the Sinai, and he wasn't going to Jerusalem because he thought it was a cool place to go but because the scriptures had spoken to him. He knew the importance and he carried the Ark of the Covenant there."

"You know this?" the president asked.

"It's history," Jones replied. "Listen, Stoneking, Wilson, and Cann did some groundbreaking work in the late '80s with mitochondrial DNA and confirmed that humans are a distinct species. There is no evolution. They traced the DNA of mothers, and they scientifically determined that Eve was created about one hundred fifty thousand years ago."

"Scientifically determined?" the president asked.

"Check it out yourself. They prove that there are 133 variants of humans today. They reverse engineered the DNA back to a single variant. Think of it as a tree with 133 branches that all stem from the same trunk."

"My God," Kristyana whispered.

"That trunk is Eve. And she was created in the Olduvai Gorge. Which is the Garden of Eden."

Jones gave them no time to consider the import of what he was saying as he continued. "The Old Testament is essentially true. Instead of the Garden of Eden being in Tanzania as in the Book of Catalyst, it is recorded as being somewhere in Iraq or Iran or Turkey or Jordan. Scholars to this day disagree. Why? Because the Book of Catalyst talks about the four rivers flowing atop one another. They are lava flows from Mount Kilimanjaro, not the Tigris and

Euphrates. Unfortunately for brothers like us," Jones said, pointing his finger at the president and then himself, "our stuff gets erased."

Barkum tapped his chin, listening intently to the passionate pastor. Part of his mind was considering the country's perception of him essentially hiring a young African-American theologian with attitude to advise him on an unheard of book that unhinges the Bible. He was also considering the domestic and national security implications.

Jones was staring in reverence at a painting of Martin Luther King, Jr. that Barkum had hung in the oval office. King was seated in a Victorian chair with his right hand pensively propped under his chin.

"You know where the good Dr. King got it wrong, Mr. President?"

Taken aback, Barkum said, "No, please tell me."

Instead, Jones whirled around and strode toward Barkum.

"I know you think I have an attitude, but I also have a PhD in theology from Harvard University and another PhD in African studies from the University of Addis in Ethiopia. I'm thirty-one years old, and I spent the last ten years of my life walking the Great African Rift from Tanzania to Jordan." He smiled and said, "And no, I didn't part the Red Sea and walk across, though I thought about it."

"Isaiah, I don't doubt your—"

"Just listen, please. I voted for you, so if nothing else, entertain me as a constituent. Anyway, the way I know about the Book of Catalyst is that the idea and the stories are very alive in sub-Saharan Africa." Jones continued pacing, becoming more demonstrative as he talked.

Barkum noticed that two secret service agents had stepped inside the office and were positioning themselves to gain the best advantage should Jones turn out to be a nut case. Barkum turned his head slowly when Jones wasn't looking and moved his fingers in a brushing motion indicating for them to leave the room. He knew they would be just outside the door and would be able to react before Jones could do anything nefarious.

"The Book of Catalyst was held in Sudan, Ethiopia, and ultimately in Jerusalem. The story Kristyana tells makes sense. Over time, it was just another archive written in an unintelligible language, so it was buried in the back of some museum in Iraq. The one good thing to come out of that war may be the discovery of these documents, if indeed they bear out to be true and accurate."

"But what about the national security implications? We need to keep this under wraps until we can sort it out," Barkum said.

"How in the world do you keep God under wraps?" Jones boomed in his preacher's voice, bringing the secret service agents back into the room. Barkum could tell they weren't going anywhere even if he ordered them out. Jones didn't seem to notice or care.

"I ask you, Mr. President, do you believe in God?" Jones leaned over the sofa, his hands pressing down on the fabric so hard that they were making indentations. "*Do you?*"

"You have no right to come into my office and demand anything from me," Barkum said, standing. He faced Jones from across the blue davenport. "What you are not considering is the national security second- and third-order effects. What will happen to America and our Judeo-Christian foundation when people learn that the Bible is missing a few pages?"

"The only relevant question here is whether or not the leader of the free world is more concerned about managing reaction to God's word or ensuring that the inhabitants of Earth know that they are part of God's plan. And the only way you can arrive at that answer is by looking inward, sir, and answering my question, *do you believe in God?*"

The two secret service agents were on either side of Jones now, nearly touching him.

"Pastor Jones, I do believe in God. But I also believe in my responsibility to this country. There is a way to do what you suggest and to prepare the country for receiving this information if it turns out to be true."

"Do you think for a minute that it is a coincidence that you are the leader of the free world as this information becomes available? God is trusting you to do the right thing!"

"As are my people, the American people."

"Your people? I'm here to tell you, the *world* is your people!" Jones had thrown his hands into the air, generating a sharp reaction from the agents, who grabbed each arm and held him. Sandy Bianchi and Kristyana Cixi were standing off to the side watching the face-off between Barkum and Jones. Immediately, more agents entered the room and ushered the two women into the hallway. Barkum noticed their departure in his periphery.

"What do you mean by that?" Barkum asked. He waved his hands at the agents, and they released Jones's arms but remained close.

"Did you not say at every campaign stop that 'our footprints are timeless'?" Jones asked in a more moderate tone. The agents had done nothing to dissuade his passion.

"Of course. I was picking up on Dr. King's marching theme. Our footprints are indeed timeless. We have traveled far and cannot rest," Barkum responded, catching himself before he slipped into his well-practiced stump speech.

Jones sighed, the air audibly escaping from his lungs.

"The Book of Catalyst refers to the Laetoli Footprints, the ones Leakey found. If what I learned in Sudan is correct, the Book says that, in the Arabic year 1436, a man with timeless footprints will steer the world away from catastrophe."

"So, that's a long time ago, Pastor," the president said.

"Sir, 1436 on the Arabic calendar is 2015 in the Judeo-Christian calendar, and you are that man."

29

Tanzania

A full twenty-four hours had passed, and Amanda believed Webb was looking much worse. His face was gaunt, he had developed a sudden rash, and his breathing was labored. He had the look of a rabid dog nearing the end of the hydrophobia cycle.

Kiram and Mumbato sat at a fire about thirty meters away in the lava tube. They had returned yesterday a couple of hours after The Cheetah had narrowly missed killing her. Entering through a different access point to the tunnel, Kiram and Mumbato had appeared exhausted. But they had outmaneuvered The Cheetah for the moment.

She looked at Webb, sweating. "How are you feeling?" she asked. She sat next to him in the dank cavern and placed a hand against his forehead. He felt cool to the touch.

Webb turned his eyes toward Amanda without turning his head.

"Like shit," he said. "Weak. Like something's eating me alive."

Amanda sighed. She did not have the heart to tell Webb that the samples she'd had to keep of Ebola and HIV had been the most virulent strains so that she could develop the best possible antibodies. Weaker strains could be partially defeated, but the viruses were so adaptable that they could mutate and survive, ultimately defeating the cures. If there was an upside, it was that HIV and not Ebola had apparently infected him. Ebola would be deadly to all of them quickly, especially in this cave.

Instead of relaying that news, she said, "We've treated almost one hundred HIV patients, and all but one have recovered fully, and all nine of the Ebola patients we've treated have recovered. We've also vaccinated hundreds with no evidence of sickness from either virus."

"So you really did it?" he asked. His voice was raspy, full of gravel.

"Did what?"

"Made a cure for HIV."

Amanda hesitated. She understood that she had signed her life away with the Central Intelligence Agency when she had agreed to participate in *Project Nightingale* in Tanzania. She was not allowed to discuss *Nightingale* with anyone other than Dr. King, her father, or her uncle, Matt. Though it seemed rather ridiculous that she would keep the information from Webb after he had stuck himself with a vial of the most potent live HIV known to man.

Amanda looked across the dark cave and saw the two boys huddled together arguing quietly and out of earshot. Upon their return they had brought some wood for building a fire.

"Yes," she whispered. "But you can't tell anyone. It's classified."

"Government?"

Amanda didn't respond to his question.

"You need some rest," she said, patting his head. "I'm going to talk to Kiram for a minute."

"Wait. Don't leave me."

After Webb had told her that he loved her, she'd had mixed emotions. Her love for Jake was impenetrable. She did not question her ability to stay loyal to him. Her confusion stemmed from the dilemma of how she should proceed with Webb. Here they were in the middle of Tanzania with two orphans, and they were running for their lives. Webb was possibly infected with HIV. She was not certain about his loyalties to his job or motivation with the formula. She wanted to be a comfort to him but not lead him on in any way. To be direct might be to seem ungrateful. To be comforting might give him false hope.

Amanda looked at his weak eyes and the way he opened them despite the obvious pain. He wanted her close. Suddenly she was struck by the fact that she had not contacted Jake in the last two days. The satellite phone had been damaged in the plane crash, yet she had seen Webb using his iPhone.

"Okay, I'll trade you." She joshed him with her shoulder. "Let me borrow your iPhone to send a note to Jake, and I'll hang out with you."

Webb managed a weak smile. "Sucker's dead. Plus, couldn't get any reception in here if you tried." Webb started giggling, as if he were going delirious. It was a high-pitched *hehehehe*.

Then he started babbling. "I hacked your email, you know. In college. Password was JakeD24. Pissed me off that you used your boyfriend's football number as part of your password. Hehehehehe."

"What?" Amanda pushed away from Webb. That *was* her password then and remained so today. She had nothing to hide, but her daily missives with her husband were sacrosanct.

Kiram approached them from the long axis of the lava tube. Amanda had noticed that the two boys would disappear and return from the tunnel, appearing almost ghost-like as they reemerged from the blackness.

Amanda watched Kiram look at Webb, who was leaning against the blackened wall of the lava cave. Webb's face was sallow, and his eyes glowed red in the small fire they had built. In the cave, the walls were rippled like black corrugated metal.

"He's sick," Kiram said, looking at Amanda.

"We should let him die," Amanda said.

Kiram looked at Amanda. "Why you say that?"

"He's been stalking me. That's how he got here. I just figured it out."

"What you mean, stalking?"

"He's been reading my emails and figured out where I was. Though traveling halfway around the world to corner me seems a bit extreme."

Kiram nodded. "Well, he is sick. Do you want him to live?"

"I gave him a shot, the cure," she replied, shaking her head. "He'll be okay."

Kiram studied Amanda and then turned his eyes back to Webb.

"You gave without me?" Kiram asked.

"Yes. You were up fighting the Cheetah guy."

Kiram thought for a moment, then said, "But he's still sick. The cure did not work for him."

Amanda looked at him and asked, "How can you be so sure? It's only been a day."

"Give him your test," Kiram said, referring to Amanda's portable saliva Western blot test. "Unless you want him to die. Then let him die."

Amanda looked at Webb and back at Kiram. She crossed her arms and shook her head.

"I only have a few of those oral tests. I'd rather wait."

"Miss Amanda, you've been trusting me to help you all this time. Trust me, please," he pleaded.

Amanda dropped her arms by her sides. She was clearly tired and unnerved but holding strong.

"Okay, you win," she said. She reached into her duffle bag and pulled out an Oral Sure test kit. She squeezed some antibacterial cleanser on her hands and sanitized them as best she could before snapping on some latex gloves. Removing the cotton swab, she leaned over Webb and said, "Open up, asshole. I'm just going to take a sample here."

Webb's eyes, but not his face, moved to find Amanda. They were vacant, a stare she had seen so many times in so many orphans plagued with especially virulent forms of HIV. She lightly held his jaw, and he opened his mouth while Amanda quickly swabbed the inside cheek. She removed the stick and slid it into the plastic container, which she snapped shut with an audible click.

"We wait twenty minutes now, but only rarely do antibodies show up this quickly," she said to Kiram.

"They will show," he said.

Amanda looked up at Kiram and then down at Webb. For the first time, Amanda noticed Webb's iPhone light flashing in his shirt pocket.

"I'll wait with him and come get you when the test is done, Kiram," she said.

Kiram nodded and walked across the floor of the tube, where, thousands of years ago, the molten lava had been hotter on the bottom than on the top and this tunnel had formed. The smooth, rounded waves of hardened magma glistened silver and black in the warming glow of the fire.

Once Kiram had disappeared on the other side of the fire, Amanda lifted Webb's iPhone from his shirt pocket.

"Hey," he protested, but weakly.

"Shut up," she said.

As the screen appeared, she saw the remnants of a text message, which she read with horror.

She dropped the iPhone onto the hard lava, its crash sounding like a weapon falling on concrete.

She stood and backed away from Webb as she saw his eyes rolling up into his head.

"My God," she whispered. "Is that why you're here?"

Webb passed out, the cracked phone next to him like a guilty accomplice.

Amanda turned and walked to the far side of the tunnel and knelt next to Kiram, who was building a second fire. When he finished, he sat next to Amanda and held his hands toward the fire.

"I don't know what to think," she said. She was unaccustomed to sharing personal feelings or even concerns with the orphanage children, but Kiram and Mumbato had proven their mettle over the past few days.

"Someone named Jack Johnson has asked him to steal the formula. Someone named Jonathan Beckwith is asking for it. That's all in his damn phone," Amanda said.

Mumbato shrugged. "He not get it. He got virus instead."

Amanda refrained from saying *good*. She would never wish illness on anyone, but it was a challenge to keep her emotions in check. Webb had betrayed her.

"Karma," she said instead.

"He is decent man given bad direction," Mumbato said from across the fire.

Kiram stared at the boy he had known for years. Amanda knew that he considered Mumbato a brother.

"Bad man with bad mission," Kiram countered.

Mumbato stared at him with the same ferocity he had the day Kiram had kicked the soccer ball into the jungle.

"Not always right, you," Mumbato said.

"Guys, let's not argue," Amanda said. "His iPhone said he was to destroy the vaccine or take it. That it was worth billions of dollars. While wealth is a difficult incentive to turn down, I still feel betrayed by Webb."

"Vaccine is worth only the lives it saves," Kiram said.

"Saved my life," Mumbato muttered. "So it means something to me."

The fire highlighted their faces in flickering images like a slow-motion liquid strobe light. First Mumbato's hardened facial features and seemingly permanent scowl would show, but then the flame would drift toward Kiram's clear countenance. The fire jumped to another piece of wood, framing Amanda's worried eyes.

"They are all worth something," Kiram said. He did not mean to sound as if he was arguing with Mumbato, but Mumbato certainly took it that way.

"Why do you always say something different? I'm wrong?" Mumbato asked, clumsily trying to debate with Kiram.

"I am not doing that. I am saying they are all worth saving. You are special as any child we have saved," Kiram said.

"Hey, you guys make a good team, and you're both awesome, so cut it out," Amanda intervened.

Mumbato grunted and stood. He walked the thirty meters to the other side of the lava cave, where Webb was lying beneath two silver space blankets that Amanda had kept in her ready bag. They had built two fires, and Mumbato sat next to Webb, stoking the dying embers.

"Why do you have to be mean to Mumbato, Kiram?"

"Not mean. Maybe tough, but not mean. Africa tough world."

"I understand, but he loves you."

Kiram looked at Mumbato, who was out of earshot, and said, "Mumbato loves himself. He is a survivor."

"Where would you be without him?" she asked. "Where would any of us be?"

"Question is not real," Kiram said. "Where would we be without the sun or moon?"

"You're in one hell of a mood," she snapped.

"Tired," Kiram said.

"Then get some rest. We'll check the results and give him a new shot when you wake up."

Kiram studied Amanda and said, "You are good person, Miss Amanda. You help save our people. Your heart is good heart." He tapped his bare chest as he spoke. "But do not let your heart always rule your mind. You are scientist, doctor, when it comes to medicine. Use that part of you with people, and you will know the right thing to do."

"What, are you a philosopher now?"

Kiram smiled thinly.

"No, sleepy. I will rest."

Amanda watched Kiram lie on the hard magma floor and decided she would do the same. The warmth of the fire and the tension of the last thirty-six hours made her mind swoon, and she was soon asleep. As she drifted, Kiram's words floated in her mind like a leaf in the wind.

You will know the right thing to do.

30

The two Navy SEALs turned on their flashers as they sped through the east gate of Fort Story in Virginia Beach, Virginia.

Kristyana eyed the driver and his companion from the backseat of the up-armored Suburban as they peeled around a tight bend, raced between the two lighthouses, and hooked a right toward the beach. The senior-ranking SEAL kept calling the driver "Smooth Dog," to which the driver would smile and just reply, "Roger."

"Take this right, Smooth Dog," the ensign directed. Soon, Smooth Dog parked the car in front of a newly constructed home that over-looked the Chesapeake Bay. In front of the two-story dwelling was a small sign that read:

LTC Vincent Irons, Chaplain.

"Pretty sweet assignment," Kristyana whispered as she looked at the red brick home with tan siding.

"Ma'am, you've got thirty minutes, and then Smoothie and I are coming in," the dark-haired ensign said to her from the passenger seat. He spoke from behind Oakley sunglasses.

"Relax, wild man. It'll be fine," she said as she put a shoulder into the heavy door.

Kristyana walked up the driveway past a black Chevrolet Suburban and hunter-green BMW 525i, both with *We Support Military Families* stickers on the bumpers.

As she knocked on the door, she heard the rapid footsteps of young children. Soon, the door opened, and she was staring down at two black-haired twins who she guessed were about five years old. Their mother scooped them up quickly and ushered them away as she opened the door farther, saying, "You must be Miss Cixi. Please come in. I'm Barb."

"Thank you," Kristyana said as she stepped across the threshold. She was wearing a navy pantsuit with light pinstripes. She had chosen a conservative white blouse with a pilgrim collar in case the chaplain was on the ultra-conservative end of the spectrum. She'd found little information about him in the agency files other than his military records, which she had read thoroughly. Irons had received above average to superior ratings throughout his career. Reading his file, Kristyana had thought he sounded like an honest man who cherished his family and enjoyed serving in the military.

"I'm Vince Irons," a tall man said from behind her. He had caught Kristyana off guard as he'd come in through the front door.

"Oh, hello. Kristyana Cixi," she said, spinning around to greet him. "Didn't expect you from that direction." She sized him up quickly. He was extraordinarily handsome, over six feet tall with thick black hair combed from the left side, and muscular, like a body builder.

"Didn't mean to scare you," he said.

"No, just surprised me," Kristyana replied. And she was surprised. This man could be on the cover of *GQ* magazine.

"You're staring," he said, flashing his own movie star smile at her.

"Sorry. You're just not what I expected."

"Right. All chaplains or men of the cloth have to be bald perverts?"

Kristyana blushed. So much for the pilgrim collar. She felt like ripping the itchy thing away and just being herself.

"I apologize. I didn't mean to imply that, Colonel," she said.

"He gets it all the time," Barb said. "He knows he's a hunk. I know he's a hunk. Heck, that's why I married him. That, and I figured I stood a better chance of getting to Heaven being married to a preacher." Kristyana noticed that she was a stark beauty herself. Brown hair, brown eyes, and smooth features, she was lean and had the sinewy frame of a runner.

Kristyana smiled. Interesting couple.

"Hi, again, Barb Irons. Sometimes they call me Barb Wire. Depends on my mood."

They shook hands and Kristyana said, "I'm sure."

Barb led her into the living room, where she had laid out three glasses of tea. Apparently she had locked up the children somewhere, because the house had turned quiet. Kristyana noticed the absence of traditional military plaques and mementos and instead saw that the Irons had displayed an assortment of artwork and sculptures that ranged from replicas, she presumed, of Henry Moore's *Knife Edge* to Donatello's *St. Mark*.

"The Dying Gaul?" Kristyana asked. She was certain that the artwork on their mantel was a small marble rendition of the *Dying Gaul*, a nude Celtic warrior dying on the battlefield.

"Impressive," the chaplain said. "We like the image of a nobleman awaiting God's hand."

Where Kristyana had come to expect a simple man or couple, she had found a cultured family that seemed to have some range or depth. When she considered the two vehicles in the driveway and the obvious taste for expensive art, an alarm rang in her head. *What have they done with the Book of Catalyst?* She realized her task might be a bit more difficult than she'd originally assumed.

"Let's have a seat, dear. It's not every day we get a high-level visitor from the State Department," Barb said.

"Much less to be ordered not to tell your base commander about such a visit," Vince Irons added.

"Or anyone, for that matter," Barb said with a hint of disappointment.

"I appreciate your discretion," Kristyana remarked as she sat down and took a sip of her tea.

"How can we be of service?" the chaplain said, sitting down across from Kristyana and leaning forward with his elbows on his knees. Barb sat to Kristyana's left on the sofa. She had the distinct feeling that she was being guarded as in man-on-man basketball. Barb made her think of a Stepford wife, and the chaplain's cheerfulness belied an undercurrent of tension. She would let her instincts guide her approach. Her mission was to obtain the original Book of Catalyst that this man was reported to possess. If he still had it.

Kristyana sipped her tea and held the sweating glass in her cupped hands.

"You were in Iraq in 2012 and 2013, correct, Colonel?"

"That's right. I was the chaplain for the military transition team in Nineveh Province near Mosul. Nifty acronym of 'MITT' teams is what you'll hear most people call them."

"I'm told that your document exploitation team found a significant historical document," Kristyana said bluntly. Amanda Garrett was on the run, and no one had any idea how or if this document might be involved in the Islamic State's plans.

The husband and wife exchanged awkward glances.

"So that's what this is about?" the chaplain asked.

"You know, Colonel, that war trophies are unauthorized, and what you have in your possession may be the ultimate war trophy," Kristyana said, a hint of threat in her voice.

"They gave me the document, and I had no idea what it was. I did bring it back with me and had it appraised," he said honestly.

"And?" Kristyana asked, expecting a shoe to fall from the ceiling.

"They told me it was priceless, that I had won the lottery," he said.

"Who are 'they'?"

"I went up to Catholic University in Washington, D.C. The university has a pretty good religious text examination department."

"Did these people make any copies of it?"

"No. They didn't want to damage it. They said the light from the Xerox machine might harm the parchment."

"Who specifically examined it? You keep saying 'they.' Who are 'they'?"

"Well, really just one individual. His name is Isaiah Jones."

Kristyana felt a thrum when the chaplain mentioned the preacher who had just been in the Oval Office with her. She kept her reaction muted.

"And where is this document now?"

"Vince?" Barb said. Her voice was cautionary, as if warning him away from danger.

"I was approached by a wealthy individual who said he would pay handsomely for the document."

"How much?"

"One million dollars," the chaplain said. Barb gasped as he spoke, but apparently the chaplain was an honest man.

"How did he know you had it?"

"Have it," Irons corrected.

"You didn't take the one million?"

"You're kidding, right? That would have been illegal not to mention sacrilegious. I'm a man of the cloth, and my integrity is inviolate," Irons said.

Kristyana saw the set jaw and hardened eyes and knew the man had struggled with the decision, if indeed he was telling the truth.

"So, where do you keep it?"

"It's in my safe," Irons said. "Where it will stay."

"Chaplain, the president of the United States sent me down here to get those documents so that he can have them examined. I have an airplane waiting for me at Oceana Naval Air Station just down the road. If I don't have the documents within thirty minutes of my arrival here, a Navy SEAL team has instructions to come to your house and arrest you," Kristyana said. She looked at Barb Wire and said, "And anyone else who might try to resist."

"It's not yours to take," Irons protested.

"Neither is it yours. Did you risk your life by entering that building, taking fire, and killing the bad guys?" She hated to make that point, because he had served in combat, but she was certain that he had not participated in the raid that had led to the capture of the historical documents.

"No," he whispered, guilt finally gaining balance on pride.

"The documents are the property of the United States government until such time that we can determine where they belong," Kristyana said, her patience wearing thin.

After a long pause, the handsome preacher looked at Kristyana and said, "Okay, I'll get it."

"Wait," Barb said, reaching her arm out to hold back her husband. "We don't have them anymore." She was staring intently into her husband's eyes as if to communicate some unspoken word or signal. The chaplain gave his wife a confused look in return.

"Okay, I'll call the SEALs and they can do a house search," Kristyana replied. She stood and brushed off her pantsuit. "I was really hoping to avoid this."

As she walked toward the door, Barb said, "You don't understand. It was a million dollars."

"Barb!" Kristyana heard the chaplain exclaim behind her.

Kristyana spun on her heel and leveled her eyes on Barb Irons.

"You're telling me that you sold the Book of Catalyst?" Kristyana asked.

"It's not possible," the chaplain said. "She didn't have the combination." He scrambled into the home's study, where he removed an original oil painting of a pinto horse looking over its shoulder in the forest. Maybe a Bev Doolittle, Kristyana thought, but that would be way above their price range.

Unless they had sold the Book of Catalyst. Vince Irons spun the dial of the safe and opened the heavy metal door.

"Half of it is gone," he said. Confusion crawled across his face like the ray of a rising sun.

"Half?" Kristyana and Barb asked at the same time for different reasons.

Irons turned and walked over to his cigar humidor.

"Several months ago, I thought these pages were especially brittle, and I was trying to rehabilitate them in here." He slid the bottom drawer open, shoved several cigars away, and pulled out a large Ziploc baggie with what appeared to Kristyana to contain three or four pieces of old wax paper.

"Oh, shit," Barb muttered. "I am so screwed."

"Talk to us, Barb. What happened?" her husband demanded.

"A few months ago, a man came by the house, Vince. It was when you were on that two-day TDY," Barb said. Kristyana knew that TDY was military parlance for temporary duty, which usually involved an excursion away from home.

Barb hustled into the den, grabbed a card, and showed it to Kristyana.

"This is the guy who has the documents. At least half," she said, pointing at the card. Kristyana held it in her hand and read the lettering:

Joseph P. Grimes.

"Who's he?" she asked.

"I don't know. He showed up with one million dollars and said he wanted the documents. I made the deal," Barb said to Kristyana. She then turned to her husband and said in a less-than-theatrical voice, "I'm sorry, honey."

Kristyana immediately believed that they both knew about the deal and that the wife was protecting the husband, who would be subject to the Uniform Code of Military Justice, an arbitrary and less-than-fair disciplinary system. But that wasn't her concern. Her job was to get the documents, not to administer punishment, if warranted.

"Okay, I'll take those," Kristyana said as she reached for the envelope Irons had pulled from the humidor.

"Fine," he sighed as he handed them to her.

"I need to know more about Grimes," she said, turning to Barb.

Her face flushed, and Kristyana immediately wondered, *Is that all you gave him?*

"My two friends can help you remember," she said, noticing that the two Navy SEALs had arrived through the front door.

"Yes, we can," the ensign said.

"What is this, some kind of joke?" Irons said. He moved closer to his wife.

"I don't need to know what you did with Grimes, Barb. All I need to know is where he is," Kristyana said.

"He works at Jack Johnson Labs, you bitch. Now get out of my house! All of you!" Barb Irons shouted.

Kristyana checked the documents, looked at the shocked chaplain, and then said to Barb, "You better be telling the truth, or we will be back for you and your husband sooner than you think."

She turned and said to the SEALs, "Let's go, Smooth Dog. We're going to Jack Johnson Laboratories."

31

Ensign Morris got out of the Suburban to open the door for Kristyana as they stopped in front of the beautiful brick colonial façade of Jack Johnson Laboratories. Kristyana had done a fair amount of homework in the forty-five-minute drive from Fort Story to JJL in Suffolk, Virginia. Stepping from the vehicle, Kristyana could see directly through the high glass doors and entryway all the way to where the historic James River met the Chesapeake Bay.

"Nice digs," she said to Morris. "What's up with the name Smooth Dog?"

"He's always bird-dogging hot chicks," Morris replied. "So you want us in there with you?"

"Better wait out here. I'll text you if I need help," Kristyana said. She pulled out her iPhone and traded numbers with Morris and Smooth Dog.

She pocketed her phone and walked into the grand foyer of Jack Johnson Laboratories. Less than a full forty-eight hours had transpired since Amanda's original call to her father, and she had been in Tanzania, the White House, and now Hampton Roads, Virginia. Things were moving quickly, and her adrenaline was keeping her awake, though she had slept briefly on the fourteen-hour flight from Tanzania to Washington, D.C.

She showed her credentials to the receptionist, but instead of being escorted directly to Grimes, she was ushered to the office of Jenny Cartwright, the young public affairs specialist. Jenny lasted about one minute with Kristyana, whose hard edge began to surface.

"How can we help you today, Miss Cixi?" Cartwright asked, smiling. She was holding a brochure full of JJL propaganda.

"Listen, I'm a federal agent and I need to see Grimes now," Kristyana said. "If not, I've got a team and a search warrant for this entire building."

Cartwright buckled immediately.

"I don't know a Mr. Grimes, ma'am, but I can certainly put you in touch with our legal department."

"Either get me Grimes or the CEO. I'm not wasting any more time with you," Kristyana said and flashed her credentials again.

She was ushered up to the CEO's office, where Jack Johnson emerged from the double oak doors as if Kristyana was a long lost friend whom he had been expecting. Kristyana noticed his crisp blue Zegna suit and thick, gelled gray hair combed straight back across his head. Though he was perfectly groomed and styled, something about him seemed off, as if he belonged in the barrio and not in this well-appointed office.

"Ms. Cixi, how can I help you? I understand you've got some questions," Johnson said.

"That's right. I'm looking for Joe Grimes. You sent him to meet with Barb Irons out at Fort Story to purchase some documents," she said, looking directly into his eyes, studying his reaction.

And she knew she had him. He flushed red, averted his eyes, and then came back to her with the gregarious smile and flashing teeth.

"I don't have any idea what you are talking about. We have no Grimes who works here that I am aware of. I certainly didn't send anyone to…Fort Story, you say?"

"You're lying, Jack," Kristyana said. She knew Jenny Cartwright was still in the back of the office. Kristyana had been led to a chair near his desk, which she hadn't taken, and she was faced off against Johnson with the glass walls offering her a beautiful view of the James River and Chesapeake Bay, though to the right she could see the hulking cranes of Newport News Shipyard. "I've got a team of Navy SEALs waiting outside who are bored and very eager to come in here, shut this place down, and begin a floor-to-floor search. Before they get done with the first floor, the *Virginian Pilot* will have five reporters crawling all over this place asking questions about investigations. And I'm sure they will wonder about your HIV drug cocktail and how you've sewed up the generic rights. That would make a great story, don't you think?"

Johnson's face turned white, and he dismissed Cartwright, who scampered through the CEO's door like an admonished puppy.

"What is it that you really want?" he asked, turning toward her. "Are you one of Beckwith's geeks?"

Several thoughts ran through Kristyana's mind in the few seconds before she replied. *Beckwith? Media mogul Jonathan Beckwith?*

"I am who I say I am," she said.

"Who's that, Popeye?" Johnson laughed.

Kristyana pulled out her cell phone and pressed the ensign's number. When he answered, she said, "Send two men to the fifth floor now. CEO's office. Be prepared to make a federal arrest."

She punched the off button and looked at Johnson.

"I don't have time for your bullshit," she said. "You may not know me or who I am, but I know who you are. Your real last name is Venzetti, as in the same Venzettis of organized crime fame from New York. You took a dive on an Army-Navy football game and came out the black sheep of your family. Since then, you've broken from the family, had a few lucky breaks, and you now run a giant aspirin-making company that has bet it all on an HIV cocktail that is snaking its way through the FDA. The first thought on your mind every morning and last at night is, you get this one wrong and you're toast. Am I about right?"

During her ride in the Suburban, she had received a full dossier on Johnson. Her tactic from the beginning was to go in high and hot, as she did not believe a Joe Grimes existed, or if he did exist, then he certainly wasn't on the JJL payroll. So, in that instance, Johnson had been telling the truth. But she saw the lie in his eyes when she had ambushed him with the name. So there was some fire near the smoke, she determined, and now she had her two SEAL buddies coming into the office of the CEO of a Fortune 500 company in Hampton Roads, Virginia. With a young ensign and a driver named Smooth Dog, she was not sure what she had started, but all she had to do was think of the predicament that young Amanda Garrett was in and her adrenaline urged her forward.

"You're bullshitting about the SEALs, right?" Johnson asked.

"No, actually," Kristyana said, crossing her arms across her chest and flicking her finger at some lint on her blue blazer. "Where are the documents?"

Again, he quickly blanched and slightly averted his eyes.

"What documents?" There was a stutter in his voice now. She heard the commotion in the receptionist's area outside of Johnson's office about the time the doors slammed open.

Ensign Morris was retrieving a pair of handcuffs from his vest pocket as a man followed the two SEALs into the office. Smooth Dog immediately turned and pushed the man out of the office and closed the doors.

"Christ!" Johnson yelled.

"I need those documents now," Kristyana said. "By the way, there's more where these guys came from."

Picking up on her cue, Ensign Morris whispered into his sleeve loud enough for all to hear, "Prepare teams two and three now."

Kristyana raised an eyebrow at Johnson, who deflated like a punctured life raft.

"The documents you bought from Chaplain Irons? They are federal property, and I need them now." She felt that she could get the documents without using the words *Eminent domain* but was prepared to do so.

Johnson walked to his safe, spun the dial, and opened the heavy door.

"These aren't mine," he said, retrieving a plastic bag from the vault.

"Well, whose are they?" she asked. Kristyana quickly took the documents from Johnson before he changed his mind.

"Not for me to say," he said.

But she already knew.

Jonathan Beckwith.

32

President Barkum listened as Isaiah Jones continued to stress that Barkum was the chosen one.

In the Oval Office, Jones spread the transcription across the coffee table in front of the sofa. Muted splashes of light cut yellow trapezoids across the room as the morning sun inched across the sky.

"These documents might be at least thirty thousand years old, if not older. The carbon dating and DNA testing done by my document examination teams indicate that this is some type of mammal skin, probably a series of genet hides," Jones said.

"So this is a transcription of an original, correct?"

"Maybe. Maybe not. My guess is that this is *the* original. Regardless, to have something in writing from thirty thousand years ago blows away the notion that man did not start recording history until 3500 B.C. What this proves is that *our* ancestors had language and writing capabilities beyond everyone's imagination."

Jones emphasized the word *our* when he was speaking to Barkum, even though CIA Director Stan Carlisle and Secretary of State Sandy Bianchi were in the room along with Secretary of Defense Bateman and National Security Advisor Gail Chapman.

"Isn't the point that these would be all of our ancestors?" Barkum asked.

Jones paused. "Of course," he said. "But *our* history is the only one that has been erased by the Egyptians, Romans, Greeks, and Persians. The Egyptian Pharaohs actively sought to destroy Nubian history all the way up the Nile. How this document survived, we'll never know, but it survived. It is verifiable."

"But what distinguishes this from Genesis?" Barkum asked. "Genesis is another book that talks about the creation of life. Why would this one be more acceptable?"

"Precisely because it was written closer to the time that man was created. Its prophecies are accurate. It gives the dimensions of the Ark of the Covenant. It talks about the Great Rift Valley, specifically the Olduvai Gorge, as the Garden of Eden," Jones said. His passion was evident as he spoke rapidly, his hands sweeping across the carefully protected documents.

"But I thought the Garden of Eden was verifiable in Iraq," Bateman said. "Anthropologists there have staked their careers on it."

"Just as ones before them have staked their careers on the 'verifiable' proof that the Garden of Eden is in Iran, or Turkey, or Jordan, or Egypt. No one has been able to conclusively prove where the Garden of Eden once was because of the thousands of years of climatic change and terrestrial movement. Earthquakes, floods, wet seasons, dry seasons, tectonic plate shifts, and dramatically different weather patterns have all combined to make what was once there, not there, and vice versa. But now the truth has been unearthed, so to speak. As Secretary Bianchi said, Occam's Razor applies here. The simplest answer is correct. Evolution and creationism no longer have to be in conflict. They are one and the same."

Jones was walking wildly about the room now. He was dressed in a more subdued outfit, this being his third visit to the White House in the last two days. He was wearing a tan corduroy sport coat and brown slacks with a khaki-colored cotton shirt, without a tie. He looked as professorial as any thirty-one-year-old theologian could possibly look.

"There is no question that Nubian history has been almost completely destroyed," Jones continued. "Charles Bonnet's digs near Kerma in the Sudan proved that Nubians once ruled all of Egypt, which, at that time, was considered the modern world." Jones paused. "And now, you have the document right here in front of you that says, and I read: *The black man's footprints are timeless, and he is beckoned to lead not only his people but all people to liberate the world. The path will fit his stride and he will march toward peace.*

"Again, sir, that is you."

"How do we know that these pages are authentic?" Bianchi asked. "I get back to the president's question about the difference between this and Genesis. I understand the contention that this was written closer to the time you say creation happened, but what makes this more verifiable?"

"Right here," Jones said, pointing at the last document. "In the year 1436, he will step forward for all to know. And there's a part that is just impossible to read other than the translators were able to pull out an R, a K, and an M. We think that's the name of the leader Catalyst identifies. You fill in the rest."

"Fourteen thirty-six was, like, six hundred years ago, Isaiah," Secretary of Defense Bateman said. "We're a bit late."

"Sandy, you know Islamic calendars right?" Barkum asked, remembering that the secret service had ushered Bianchi and Cixi out of the room just before Jones had told him this earlier.

Bianchi began to speak, then flushed red. "Oh my God," she said, looking at her friend Jamal Barkum, the president.

"The Arabic year for 2015 is 1436. You add an AH, anno Hegirae, to symbolize that the calendar began after the first Hijra, Mohammad's migration to Medina in what we know to be 622 A.D. The difference is that the Islamic calendar has eleven less days than the Christian calendar. Over time, that makes up the difference in days. Oh my God, Mr. President, it must be you."

Jamal Barkum stood listening to his national security team and his new religious advisor. The world was in flames from Ebola scares and ISIS attacks, and now the Islamic State was manipulating *Project Nightingale* to their advantage. He thought about the alleged religious text in front of him, sitting on his coffee table. He was having a difficult time grasping what his friend, Sandy Bianchi, and this theologian, Isaiah Jones, were trying to tell him.

That he was chosen by God to lead the world.

Slowly, a feeling of divine power began to seep through him. He knelt in front of the low table holding the documents. Reaching his hand toward the one that supposedly had the three letters from his name, he began to shake. A bright light shone through the Oval Office, penetrating the opaque blast-proof windows as if those would not be needed anymore.

He placed his hand upon the thirty-thousand-year-old documents and felt the energy surge through him; and he *knew* this would be his destiny.

He was heaven sent, and they would tell the world.

He would do exactly as the Book of Catalyst promised.

He would bring peace.

As Pastor Isaiah Jones departed the White House, he smiled. A kid from Detroit, Michigan had just convinced the President that he was the chosen one.

And he was a million dollars richer.

He hadn't bothered telling the president that the concluding line of the Book of Catalyst read: *her pierced heart will save Him and because of this she will enter Heaven.*

Once the President knelt before the Book of Catalyst in the Oval Office, Jones had stopped his sales pitch. Better not to overdo it. He believed he had struck the correct balance.

He waited until he was an hour away from Washington, DC, near Fredericksburg, when he pulled into a Starbucks. He opened his laptop, turned on his email client, and opened a cut out email account.

He typed:

He believes.

Then he saved that message in the draft folder and continued driving south.

Zhor Rhazziq couldn't sleep and decided to check his email. With so much happening throughout the Middle East and in the United States, he was operating on multiple time zones.

He set his MacBook Air on one leg as he sat in his windowsill, the crisp Atlantic breeze stinging his face. First, he went through several work emails, which were the usual complaints from employees and customers or offers from other businesses wanting to merge. He couldn't care less about any of that at the moment. He was on the cusp of the greatest psychological operation campaign ever developed, which made him think of and open the dummy account. He smiled when he saw a new draft message.

He believes.

Rhazziq laughed out loud. "Holy shit, he believes. It's working!" he shouted to no one in particular. His voice sang out over the crashing waves of the Atlantic Ocean.

33

Vice-President Camille Dillon crossed her legs and leaned back into the white sofa in her office. She leveled her best gaze at Secretary of Defense Phil Bateman.

"You have to do this," she said.

"Do you know what you're asking me to do, Madam Vice-President?" Bateman said.

She nodded for him to sit down in her office in the Old Executive Office Building adjacent to the White House. The ornate room was decorated with a few Remington bronze statues and many pictures of the vice-president with famous people. Those who would meet with her in this office would often comment later that she was both masculine and proud of herself. In truth, though, being a powerful female politician was a tough trick to perform. She had to have balls, but it helped if she was pretty. She had to be a good decision maker, but she couldn't be a bitch. She had to be a good listener, but she couldn't be weepy and indecisive.

So Vice-President Dillon had decided, *what the hell, I'll put whatever I want in here*. And so she had. She had determined that she would define herself as a tough woman who was proud of her past accomplishments. But that wasn't enough. Getting toasted in the primary when she'd had all of the momentum before the race began was humiliating. Now, she thought, she might have her inroad to the presidency.

The president is actually buying into this Book of Catalyst bullshit, she thought. She wouldn't be surprised if he had paid someone to dig this up or create it. In fact, she had some investigators taking a discreet look at that possibility.

"If Barkum goes public with this thing, Congress will have no other option but to impeach him," she said to Bateman.

On one hand, I could let him hang himself, she considered. *On the other hand, my responsibilities to the American people are to protect their national security. The only way to keep this whole Catalyst idea from unhinging the Judeo-Christian underpinnings of our nation,* she thought, *is to destroy the Book of Catalyst and to destroy the Olduvai Gorge.*

While world events were not perfect by any stretch, she could not imagine a worse scenario than one in which the president of the free world declared that because the Bible had a few typos and the research was a little shoddy, the people should believe in some other thing claimed to have been written on some rat hide thirty thousand years ago.

"Think about it, Phil," Dillon said. "We go to the same church. We believe in the same God. We are people of faith. What do you think will happen if this thing goes public?"

"Shit storm. We have to stop him," he said.

"Stop him? You heard him and that crazy pastor in there. They believe their own bullshit."

Bateman rubbed his chin. He was a thin African-American man with graying hair. His time in the Louisiana bayous and years in the Navy had weathered his face. The vice-president considered that perhaps he'd been too quick to accept the Secretary of Defense posting, but then again, he was a good public servant. She had picked him for this discussion because they shared the same faith and he always seemed to make decisions that served the greater good.

"But to put a bomb on the Olduvai Gorge just so we can destroy whatever evidence is there? That's an act of war."

"We'll use a stealth bomber at fifty thousand feet and drop a couple of JDAMS. We'll put out some press leaks that the Islamic State was sniffing around there with IED materials and that they bombed the Olduvai. Use your psychological operations guys and get creative. C'mon, Phil, work with me here."

Bateman stared at the vice-president. "I'm not used to conspiracies, Madam Vice-President."

"This is not a conspiracy, Phil. This is saving the free world and saving the God that you and I believe in."

If there was anything that would motivate Phil Bateman, it was religion. She knew that he had been an officer on the board of the Officer Christian Fellowship group since he'd been a young lieutenant.

"But what about the people who will be under those bombs? Our people that we put in harm's way?" he asked.

"We'll send them messages to get out of the way, if they can. If not, we have to believe that it was God's will. Besides, if Amanda Garrett really did steal this cure to get the Nobel Prize or to make a billion dollars, then we will have delivered justice for her heinous crimes."

"I need to think about this," he stammered. Clearly uncomfortable with the clandestine mission, Bateman was beginning to sweat. Dillon went in for the close.

"There is no time. I need a B-2 in Qatar to accomplish this mission within the next twelve hours. They will execute at my command," Dillon said.

"Are you going to mention this to the president?" he asked.

"Let me handle that," she replied. "Now let's get going."

Bateman nodded, though clearly reluctant, and departed.

Vice-President Dillon leaned against the windowsill and stared at the Washington Monument sticking into the sky like a middle finger. *Yeah, that's right,* she thought. *Book of Catalyst, my ass.*

34

The president watched the television as JoAngela Jackson was reporting live from downtown Amman, Jordan. In the background, there were thousands of rioters and looters ransacking the previously immaculate business district.

"I have to tell you, Mark," said the anchor to her counterpoint in Atlanta, "this is the worst I've ever seen it. There are machine guns firing over the crowd, as the standard nonlethal methods did not work. The rioters have set cars and buildings on fire and are making their way to the American Embassy chanting the usual 'Death to America' and a new slogan—'Death to Amanda Garrett.' She is public enemy number one in this portion of the Middle East, as the Palestinians have converged on the capital from one side while the Iraqi refugees living in camps along Jordan's east border have descended on the capital as well. It's frightening, and I'm afraid it's only beginning."

The television cut to Mark Barnes, the anchor in Atlanta, who said, "JoAngela, thank you for that report. Please stay safe. Now we go to Nancy Harwood in Cairo."

The screen cut to a short blond woman shouting into her microphone and looking nervous. Two firebombs exploded in the background, which was a street teeming with angry young men and women with scornful looks on their faces.

"Mark, they don't pay me enough to be standing here right now. The Islamic State has absolutely converged on Cairo, and this ancient city is in flames, literally. Many have thrown Molotov cocktails on the pyramids, which you know are just outside the city here, very close. The secretary of state has ordered all non-combatants out of Cairo, where, as you know, there are thousands of American citizens. There is no word right now from the president of Egypt, but we are expecting him to deploy the military to defend critical sites around Cairo, one of the most populated cities in the world. Anger here is palpable, with American flags being torched and the chants of 'Hang Garrett' and 'Death to America' being shouted everywhere."

The screen was back to Mark Barnes, who said, "Nancy, I think you'd better follow the secretary of state's order." With a well-practiced grimace, he said, "And now we go to Frank Crest in Rabat, Morocco, where things are not much better."

"That's right, Mark," said another anchor when his image appeared. "As you know, Morocco has struggled some with the virus that causes AIDS. To further worsen the situation, Ebola is creeping up the west coast from Liberia and Sierra Leone. As you can imagine, the average citizen is angry that an American is alleged to have destroyed this program. I've been talking to one young man here whose brother was infected with Ebola a few weeks ago—"

"Death to American Garrett! Death to all Americans!" the man said.

"Okay, Mishab, tell us what your family has gone through," Frank Crest said, a furrowed look of concern on his face. In the background, young men were running through the streets, some carrying Molotov cocktails and AK-47s.

"Ebola cure was coming. Islamic State announced the cure, and America destroyed it to keep Muslims under thumb! Death to Americans!"

The television quickly flipped to Mark Barnes, who was sitting coolly in his anchor chair in Atlanta. "I think we're getting an idea of the anti-American sentiment, already strong in the region, which has erupted, and I use the word carefully, across Africa. Let's go to Sarah Dunnagin in Addis Ababa, Ethiopia."

"Hi, Mark," Sarah said. She was adjusting an earpiece beneath her dark brown hair. "As you know, I'm just a school teacher who does the occasional CNN report for the network, and I have to tell you that during my three years teaching here, I have never seen anything like this."

Sarah was standing on the balcony of a hotel with the camera panning across the streets, which were filled with tens of thousands of chanting Ethiopians.

"The AIDS virus has been especially brutal in this country, and no one can understand the reports. Why would Amanda Garrett, a med school student, be working undercover for the CIA in an effort to destroy the Ebola and HIV vaccine programs? I have one source, to remain unnamed, that has told me that Jack Johnson Laboratories is about to release its Fabulous Five HIV cocktail that provides better quality of life to AIDS victims. Yet a vaccine or cure would render the Fabulous Five obsolete before it ever got out of the pipeline. And I do have a report, Mark, that a member of Jack Johnson Laboratories was involved in this caper."

The anchor shuddered at an explosion in the distance.

"Listen, Sarah, that's great information, which we will pursue. You need to stay safe there in Addis, and we will be back with you later."

"Thanks, Mark," she said before her image disappeared.

The screen shifted again. "And now we're in Baghdad with our longtime correspondent Anna Savage."

A worried redhead appeared on the screen.

"Mark, the unrest from Morocco to Ethiopia to Egypt to Syria and Jordan is extremely unsettling for Iraq. While we've had a rise in violence tonight, commanders here believe that the bow wave, as they call it, will hit in the next few days. The reports of a med school student who has destroyed Africa's greatest hope, and quite frankly the world's greatest hope, of ridding itself of Ebola and HIV, has absolutely stunned those in charge here. Many say that they know Colonel Zachary Garrett, the father of Amanda Garrett, and are convinced that the Islamic State is behind this report and the destruction of the medical laboratory. One officer said to me, and I quote, 'There's no way in hell that Amanda Garrett did this. Her husband and father are Army officers. Her entire family is fulfilling a service to their nation, Amanda included. What this is all about is our screwed up information operations capabilities and our broken public affairs capabilities. Islamic terrorists leave us holding our jockstraps every time in this domain.' For obvious reasons, this general did not want to be seen on television or associated with that quote, but his point, Mark, is that this war is beyond the borders of any battlefield. And as we've seen with the beheadings, this war is being fought in the media. So the question commanders here have is, how much of this is the Islamic State manipulating the media? Mark, the big concern is that these riots will translate into a flood of foreign fighters right at the time President Jamal Barkum claims he is not going to get into a ground war against the Islamic State. Quite a dilemma for the president tonight. Back to you."

"Thanks, Anna, for that insightful analysis."

President Barkum clicked off the television and turned to his wife, Cynthia.

"The world is exploding," he said, looking at her. They were retired in the East Wing, and she was lounging on a chaise with her head resting gently on a pillow. He was massaging her feet.

"So are my feet, chosen one." She smiled. "I've been standing all morning at the Annual Women's Basket Weaving Association Convention, or something like that."

"So, what do you think of what Isaiah Jones is telling us?"

"Well, if you can save the world the way you massage feet, then I'd definitely say you are the chosen one. Aside from that, you're just my husband."

"Can I get you to be serious for one second?" the president asked.

Cynthia sighed. "Darling, I've been serious all day, all month, all year, ever since I met you. It's been all about you." She was toying with her heart-shaped broach made of diamonds, rubies, and sapphires. Her mother had given it to her to wear for the inauguration two years ago. The heart was forged platinum with half-carat gems alternating in a red, white, and blue pattern.

"That's not fair," he said.

"It's fair," she countermanded. She studied the broach again and placed it on her nightstand. "But I don't mean it in a negative way. Honey, I chose you. You chose me. And in my corner of the world, that's all that matters; that and our three beautiful children."

"But if you believe in God and the scriptures, what do you think this means?" he asked.

"You know I'm getting this family to church every Sunday. You know what my beliefs are, Jamal." She shifted on the chaise lounge and pulled her feet away so that she could sit up. Her long, brown legs looked sexy and smooth, and Jamal eyed them as her bathrobe fell away.

"Is the chosen one having sinful thoughts?" she asked.

Barkum smiled. "Not yet, but I could be convinced."

Cynthia Barkum was beautiful and slender, as her television roles had required. A quick burst through Ford Modeling Agency as a teenager had landed her some semi-significant television roles, mostly playing high school kids or college students in situation comedies. After graduating from New York University, she'd been studying for a role about a young black woman who challenges a state legislature to change its immigration rules. There, she'd met Senator Jamal Barkum. Ever since, she had been his primary advisor and confidant.

She ignored his comment and said, "So, you know, I made a speech today, and I told the story of the day you were to speak at Howard University's commencement and said to me, 'Honey, did you think in your wildest dreams that I would ever be speaking at such an esteemed university as Howard University?' And then I told the crowd that I said, 'Baby, you aren't in my wildest dreams.' That got a chuckle."

He laughed and caressed her leg at the calf muscle and kneaded it.

"It'd be pretty wild if I am the chosen one," he said.

"You really want to talk about this, don't you?"

"I can see you don't believe it," he said.

"Baby, I believe in you. I believe in God. Do I believe that you have been chosen by God to lead the world because a thirty-thousand-year-old documents talks about a black man marching through time?"

"This year, 2015," he reminded her. "It's not like I asked for it, but there it is."

She slid across the chaise next to her husband of twenty-four years and kissed him.

"You have been elected by the people of the greatest nation on Earth, and the foundation of our beliefs is based upon Judeo-Christian faith. If you announce to the world that Genesis is a bunch of make-believe, you will not only lose your constituency but you will throw the world into further turmoil." She turned her head toward the television as she finished her comment.

He heard her, but he could not let go of the notion that he was the chosen one.

"I've thought of that, Cynthia. And maybe initially it would. But what about the notion that the Book of Catalyst proves the existence of God?"

"Baby, it doesn't prove anything other than people back then could read and write on animal skins."

"So, your advice would be to log it away as an interesting development but not to announce it to the world?"

"You know me well, Jamal Barkum. You know that old saying, 'never believe your own press releases'?" she asked.

"But the date and the campaign themes and the commonality between what we've been saying and doing, it just all fits," he said.

"It fits if you want it to fit. I admit that the date is freaky and the letters match, but still," she said, shaking her head. "It's just too wild to consider. I mean, the fact that you are president isn't good enough? You need to be Jesus, too?"

"I didn't invite this, Cynthia," Barkum countered.

"I know you didn't, baby, but if you accept it, what then?" She wrinkled her forehead the best she could with the recent Botox shot still holding firm.

"I have to consider it as part of our destiny," Barkum said. He looked at his wife. She was worried, and her eyes drooped at the corners, weighted by doubt and concern.

"*Our* destiny? This book say anything about the chosen one's wife? Do I get special powers, too?"

For the first time, he felt his anger surge, and he let it show. "Get serious, Cynthia, please!"

She flinched at his voice but came back quickly. She stiffened her back and put her hands out to either side to emphasize the point she was about to make. Her face was expressive: eyes wide, lips pursed, and teeth flashing. She spoke rapidly, the thoughts tumbling into one another as they rolled off her tongue.

"Oh, I'm serious, Jamal. This is my way of dealing with it. What if it is true? What does that mean for me and the kids? You don't think you'll be become a target, more than you already are? What am I supposed to do? I have supported you ever since we got married. I have been there for you one hundred percent of the time. You are the president of the United States, and now you are telling me you're a Biblical savior? Cut me some slack, please. Am I supposed to get pregnant or something, you know, without you doing anything?"

Barkum reached out to his wife, whose emotions were revealed at the slightest hint of stress, perhaps an indicator of how close to the surface they truly were. Her nerves, every day, screamed that her husband was going to be shot or that some lunatic was going to kidnap their sons or daughter.

"Now that wouldn't be any fun, would it?" he said, nuzzling his face into Cynthia's now wet cheeks.

"Shut up," she said, smiling. "You wanted to be serious. And I'm just telling you if this whole Jesus gig is real, don't leave me behind."

"I would never," he said.

They both stared at the television as more news reports showed violence spreading across the Northern Tier of Africa like a wildfire.

35

"Matt, Kristyana here," she said into the cell phone.

"Whatcha got?" Matt asked. He was standing in the SCIF staring at the map, waiting on a radio call from his brother.

"I just went over everything with my people at State. You ever hear of Jonathan Beckwith?" she asked.

"The TV guy?" Matt responded.

"Well, yes. He's more than television, though. He's everywhere there's media: TV, radio, Internet, satellites, etc."

"What about him?"

"He's the one who paid for this Book of Catalyst. I had no idea there's a huge market in precious religious documents. People accept the Bible as if it has always been leather-bound, but there are dozens of books and documents that are missing or could have been included. No one knows for sure where the Book of Catalyst came from ultimately, but now some pastor named Isaiah Jones is advising the president on its significance. He says it's real."

"Do we have anything on Jones?"

"Not yet, but I've got people building me a file. He spent some time in Africa finishing his theology studies. The history professor who had these documents is another story. He and his wife were killed in 2013."

"Okay. What else?" Matt asked.

"As we pull the string on this thing, it appears the history professor sent an email to Raul Akunsada, an Egyptologist in Cairo."

"Let me guess, Akunsada met an untimely death also?"

"Bingo. The day after Aktar, the history teacher."

"So how did Beckwith get it?"

"He got copies. We've got the originals, if, in fact, they're real. The best we can tell is that Aktar probably scanned the documents and emailed them to Akunsada. Beckwith must have his own version of Carnivore for his own reasons."

Carnivore was the National Security Administration email-scanning algorithm that vetted millions of emails and texts hourly for threats against the country or leadership.

"So he intercepts the document and then kills the only two people who know about it, but couldn't find the actual document until recently?"

"Makes sense, though there's no proof. All of Aktar's email files operated using a Beckwith satellite and—"

"Have been erased. Oh, man," Matt said.

"So get this," Kristyana continued.

"Do I hear optimism?"

"Yes. Two things. First, Mohammed Aktar was a document thief of some renown. In black market circles, he was on the short list."

"Okay. And?"

"While Aktar's Beckwith Media emails have been erased and his hard drive stolen by the masked gunmen, he'd also had a cloud account with Al Rhazziq Media."

"Have we tapped it?"

"Not yet, but we're trying. There's a team on it."

"I'm wondering if Rhazziq knew Aktar. What's the second thing?"

"Well, guess where Beckwith's yacht, the *Intrepid*, is right now."

Matt walked over to the window of the U.S. Embassy in Dar es Salaam. He looked through the thick, yellow-tinted, blast-proof material that gave him a distorted view of the neighborhood's rooftops and satellite dishes, which gave way to the flat, pristine surface of the Indian Ocean.

"Where?" he asked.

He could tell that when she heard the inflection in his voice, she visualized him staring at the sea. "You guessed it," she said.

"Where are you?" he asked.

"About to go into the National Security Council meeting," she said.

"Don't tell them what I'm about to do."

"Be careful, Matt. If Beckwith is pulling the strings here, he's going to be security conscious. This is a bad dude."

"We've got to stop him, though. He might be the reason Amanda is being plastered all over the world as a pariah."

"Might be," she said. "But Zhor Rhazziq has something up his sleeve. Thousands of foreign fighters are moving into Syria as we speak. His network is alive with chatter."

"Well, I'll do my part down here. Keep me posted on the rest."

Matt hung up and called Zach on the satellite phone.

"Status?"

"We've been fighting the Tanzanian Army for about a day now and lost contact with the trail of this guy," said Zach. "Amanda and her crew are nowhere in sight. It's like they vanished."

"I arranged a Merlin airplane with SAFIRE night-and-day thermal and infrared optics for you. The contractor had to fly it over from North Carolina, but they're here and will be ready in a few hours. It's got full capability. The only issue is that it's manned and can only stay on station for about five hours."

"That's five hours more than I've got now. Also, I'm running low on ammo. Can you get us any?"

"I'll work it. Maybe the Merlin can drop you some. You know, Zach, the entire Muslim world along the Northern Tier of Africa is going nuts about Amanda and this Ebola and HIV thing. Al Rhazziq Media especially, on behalf of ISIS we think, has really spun this hard."

"Well, the only way to get the truth out there is to find Amanda and get those cures into the public," said Zach.

"Roger. Another development that's come up, and we're not sure how it relates, is that Jonathan Beckwith is somehow involved in this thing. His boat is offshore. I'm taking a couple of the SEALs from the embassy protection detail, and we're going to scope that thing out tonight."

"You and your boats, man. Be careful," Zach said.

Zach was referring to the time Matt had ventured into the Chesapeake Bay with his best friend, Blake Sessoms, in search of a Chinese merchant ship that had crudely but effectively been converted into an aircraft carrier. Zach had been held captive on the ship. Matt, with Peyton O'Hara's help, had rescued him and saved the United States from an attack by unmanned Predators rigged with nuclear devices.

"Just my karma, man," said Matt. "Don't sweat it. And find Amanda, bro."

"Don't need to motivate me there."

"Roger. The major in the intel section here will monitor you. He's got the word to get this Merlin over you and talk you through what they're seeing. If Tanzania hadn't gone into lockdown, I'd fly the remote viewing station out to you, too."

"We can probably try to get the downlink on the sat phone, Matt. Just make sure I get the phone number of the guys in the airplane."

"Yeah, roger," Matt said. "Okay, I've got to pull this mission together for tonight. Good luck."

"Be safe."

Matt hung up the phone with his brother and dialed the embassy protection detail on the landline. A team of Navy SEALs had been assigned to secure the U.S. ambassador to Tanzania and his family based upon the ambassador's previous assignment in Pakistan and his aggressive strikes on Al-Qaeda in Waziristan Province.

"This is Bob," Matt heard on the other end of the phone.

"Yeah, 'Bob,' this is Matt Garrett. I need to talk to you and two of your men in the next thirty minutes."

"The Matt Garrett? The one who saved the free world? Would it be possible to get your autograph, sir?"

"Screw off and get up here, Les," Matt said.

"Roger. I like it when you call. Always leads to action."

In thirty minutes, Les Buckingham and two of his larger men were standing in the secure information facility inside the embassy with Matt.

Matt pointed at the map and turned on the Merlin ground control station.

"I just got this Merlin in, and I'm sending it out to help Zach find Amanda. Told the crew to load up some ammo, too. They're running low. I told the pilots to be on the lookout for a huge yacht but not to go searching on their run in to a remote refueling site we've got. They got lucky, saw the yacht, and are doing a few orbits, which we are recording," Matt said.

As if on cue, the visual image of the *Intrepid* went blank, and Matt knew that the Merlin crew had stored their full-motion video gear. He pressed a button, and an image reappeared from digital storage showing Beckwith's yacht.

"This is our target. It may be hostile but we're not sure. You can see right here, and here, that there are circular pods that could house anything from telescopes to cannons," Matt said, pointing at the locations of the two Bofors guns.

"See that, Matt?" Les asked, pointing at small black specks to the right of each pod. "Those are links from belt-fed ammunition."

Matt looked at Les, who stood six feet and carried the broad shoulders of a Naval Academy swim team captain. His sandy hair and blue eyes were true to the southern California boy he was.

"Okay, like I said, it's hostile," Matt said. "We have to be careful. We have a workable RB-15?"

"We've got a Zodiac and can be ready in about an hour. Have to get our weapons and make sure the ambassador has full protection from the rest of the detail. Then we can go. I'm assuming he doesn't need to know about this?"

Matt thought a moment. The ambassador probably would applaud their efforts, but the mission was so time-sensitive he could not risk delay. "Roger, not yet."

"Meet you at the Suburban in an hour," Les said. The three SEALs departed, and Matt picked up his combat gear and the satellite phone.

36

Tanzania

Jonathan Beckwith stood behind Styve Rachman as the Internet miner pulled open another Little Debbie peanut bar and wolfed it down. Orbiting satellites cut parabolic circles across the three forty-eight-inch monitors in front of the men.

"Okay, genius, let's do it," Beckwith said.

Rachman stood at the keyboard and typed in the command:

Enable pairing.

Then he clicked on the words:

Always connect.

Once he received the digital display that the Bluetooth was armed, he typed:

Attack.

Beckwith watched the monitor to his left that showed the master satellite, which was one of his own fifteen satellites, as it turned and aimed its Bluetooth portal at the parabolic line directly next to it. Coming over the horizon, Beckwith saw an icon for an Al Rhazziq satellite and cheered, "Might as well start out with the big guys."

As the two satellites passed within a mile of each other in extraterrestrial orbit, Beckwith satellite number one fired an electronic message from the Bluetooth sender. The target was the Bluetooth receiving unit, the Rhazziq satellite, on which Rachman had maliciously but passively installed the reception code. This was no different than connecting a phone to a car via Bluetooth, Rachman had told Beckwith.

Rachman had explained to Beckwith that this technique was a common practice of Bluetooth geeks known as Bluebugging. "Essentially the master, your satellite, transmits to the slaves, the receiving satellites, and creates a grouping of Bluetooth-enabled devices. On Earth, it would typically involve about ten computers. Here we're talking about mastery of very specific components of hundreds of actively orbiting commercial satellites that perform television broadcasting, 4G web-enabled phone functionality such as video, chat, and texting, and online streaming video. Once the piconet is established, one person can control the content of the entire network."

"The content?" Beckwith had asked.

"Yes, the content. For a brief period of time, we can broadcast from a single point and push content across every satellite in the piconet, which will interrupt programming of televisions, websites, text messages, you name it. Anything that would normally travel through any of these satellites gets replaced by your message."

It had all started over a year ago after Beckwith's ballooning accident and when he had finally had the six Swahili documents fully transcribed. Beckwith had come to Rachman asking about the possibility of controlling the content of all of the commercial satellites in orbit for a few minutes.

Rachman had nervously stuffed down a Little Debbie, shaken his head, and said, "Dude."

Beckwith had taken that as a no.

"Think about it," Beckwith had said. "A one-million-dollar bonus is involved."

To which, Rachman had said, "Dude." That time it had sounded like a yes.

Rachman had updated him each time he made progress, from experimenting with Wi-Fi and a variety of other options to settling on the Bluetooth technology as a foundation. While typically a class one Bluetooth could send and receive in a hundred-meter arc on the spectrum in the 2.45 GHz range, Rachman had calculated that, in space, it would have no interference and be able to travel at much greater distances, particularly if he installed Hyper Gain REO5U 2.4 GHz antennae on the new satellites that Beckwith would have to launch. In short, Rachman had created a way to have enough power to push the signal through outer space and to dominate the target satellite.

Beckwith had happily launched the new satellites with the updated technology. Still, it was an experiment, and Beckwith had wondered if it would work. The receiving satellites were easy enough to hack from Earth, Rachman had told him, which meant that they should be easier from outer space. Beckwith knew that, fifteen years ago, a British student had gained control of a U.K. defense satellite just for kicks by sending a low-powered microwave signal from Earth. Beckwith's plan was to have his new satellite constellation serve as multiple masters to the two hundred commercial satellites he intended to control for no more than ten minutes.

By maliciously installing a passive, unrecognizable Trojan on each of the satellites over the course of their voyage from New York City to Zanzibar Island, Rachman had essentially created his own Bluetooth network. The fifteen master satellites were programmed with massively powerful antennae that would send the recognition code to the Trojan, causing the ill-intended code to open the Bluetooth reception program. On the heels of the Trojan opening code were the Bluetooth connection message and confirmation digits. Simply put, the receiving satellites were now ready to be manipulated. Beckwith would be able to broadcast content through these satellites until the companies' personnel on Earth figured out what was happening and how to stop it.

By then, Beckwith would have communicated his message. Beckwith smiled as Rachman diligently went about the business of getting all fifteen satellites turned in the right orbit so that they could pass within a mile of their ten to fifteen respective target satellites, Bluebug them, and then be prepared to receive content.

That source would be the *Intrepid* and her powerful satellite antenna fed by Jonathan Beckwith in the Olduvai Gorge.

He tapped Rachman on the shoulders as the high-pitched whine of the helicopter outside of the computer room on the *Intrepid* told him it was time to go.

Beckwith stepped out of the cooler and fit his goggles to his eyes, pulling the strap tight. He walked over to the helicopter, its blades spinning in harmony, and sat on the outboard bench of his very own MD-530-F that he had purchased from Hughes aircraft and later modified.

He had ordered the pilot to prepare an hour ago, immediately after he had told Rachman to Bluebug the satellites. The two-man crew had rolled the aircraft out of its hold near the forward portion of the deck and made quick work of snapping the six blades into place.

Beckwith had ordered the helicopter with every reasonable option possible without overloading the aircraft while still allowing it to operate at high altitudes. The outboard benches on each side, forward looking infrared system (FLIR), and searchlight were three key modifications that he had tacked on. A South African arms dealer had added the two M134 Miniguns. Hughes had balked at installing the entire system, though they had agreed to rig the helicopter with an A kit, essentially the wiring system for the guns. It was much like having a house wired for ceiling fans but installing them himself, Beckwith thought.

The whine of the Allison 250-C30 engine surged through his headset as he watched Roosevelt Rivers nervously sit behind him on the outboard bench and snap his harness into the frame of the aircraft. They were on the port side, while Father McCallan and Nina snapped in on the starboard side.

Soon the whipping rotor blades were a constant whir above them. Mac Charles, the pilot, who sported a thin goatee and wore tight-fitting Under Armour shirts and pants, gave Beckwith a thumbs-up sign. Beckwith returned the signal with a verbal, "Let's go."

To be sure, all four of them could have ridden in the back webbed seats of the aircraft, but Beckwith was having none of that. Their communications relay equipment and their supplies took up much of the passenger bay.

The helicopter lifted with ease like a dragonfly alighting from a lakeshore reed. Mac Charles dipped the aircraft so that it was a mere ten meters above the Indian Ocean, then tilted the rotors to gain about one hundred knots of airspeed. Soon they were buzzing across the calm waters beneath them as the final orange and purple hues of daylight were squeezed into night. Beckwith looked over his shoulder into the cockpit of the aircraft as Mac Charles snapped on his night vision goggles.

From their position just north of Zanzibar Island, they were traveling approximately three hundred miles to the Olduvai Gorge area. With the addition of an inboard auxiliary fuel tank, they had the range to make it there but would require a refuel to get back to the ship. The plan was for the pilots to hit an airfield at Manyara on the way back, refuel, and wait for further instructions. Beckwith envisioned that they would be on the ground at least twenty-four hours, if not longer.

Slicing between Zanzibar and Pemba Islands, Beckwith could see the rippled sandbars. The tide was moving out, perhaps at complete ebb, as they began to cross over land. The light aircraft sped along the contours of Earth, first over sparsely populated swampy lowlands near Crecida, a small fishing village. Beckwith could feel them continue to climb as the palm trees and thick jungle forest typical of a windward tropical climate gave way to a plateau that was sparsely populated with acacia trees and scrub brush. The slipstream beat against his face, but adrenaline prevented him from feeling anything but the sheer pleasure of the ride. He was a billionaire, and this was his carnival.

The long ride gave him the opportunity to think through his plan, which he knew he would have to modify once on the ground. That there was an unexpected stranger in the mix, perhaps Webb Ewell, complicated things a bit. Having had his intercepted version of the Book of Catalyst completely translated, he was focused on two items. First, his guess of Jamal Barkum being the chosen one seemed to be right.

Accordingly, Beckwith had contributed substantial sums of money to Barkum's presidential reelection campaign. He had donated so much money that Barkum had joked, "So, Jonathan, if I win again, which country do you want to be ambassador of?"

To which, Beckwith had chuckled and said, "I'm not willing to take a pay cut, Jamal, but thanks for the offer. Just keep me in mind once you figure it all out." Barkum had not appeared to understand Beckwith's comment but had replied that he would indeed.

His second concern had centered on whether the Ebola and HIV vaccines and cures were really the stuff of Biblical fruits. The two boys with Amanda now had saved him. His balloon had crashed that year between Kilimanjaro and the Olduvai Gorge. His very own doctor had told him that he had been dead. He believed that those boys had brought him back to life with a paste that they were using in the cure and vaccine. If he could find the source of the paste, he could determine how much could be harvested. Once he knew that, he would be able to have it tested and perhaps replicated. Sure, the Ebola and HIV vaccines and cures were going to be a huge step forward for the millions who were suffering with the diseases or were most at risk of contracting them. The vaccine would change the world by protecting millions against a malicious disease. Still, he thought there were other possibilities. If, indeed, the Garden of Eden was in the Olduvai Gorge and if this paste, or fruit, was from the Tree of Life, well, that added a whole new perspective on things.

He was taking the ultimate believer, Father McCallan, and the ultimate doubter, Roosevelt Rivers, into the place where he believed God had created human life and would broadcast it simultaneously on all of the commercial satellites in orbit.

After two hours, Mac Charles cut the speed of the helicopter to about fifty knots. They were passing over a large sisal field, the tops of the rope plant looking akin to knife-like pineapple leaves.

"Boss, we're coming into the grid now," Mac Charles said through the wireless headset.

"Roger. Team, are we up?"

Beckwith's face was reddened from the two-plus-hour flight on the outboard benches of the helicopter. He smiled at Rivers to his left and looked through the helicopter's cargo compartment at Father McCallan on Nina's left, toward the pilot. Nina appeared as though she had enjoyed the ride, but through the green shade of the night vision goggles, McCallan appeared nauseous.

He turned and watched the helicopter approach the ground slowly, the pilot obviously searching for a level spot in the rocky gorge. Nearly barren of trees, the terrain did possess hazards to the crew such as large boulders, virtually invisible crags, and high scrub brush that could ding the rotor blades. As they began to touch down, a huge cloud of dust encircled them.

Once he felt the helicopter settle onto firm terrain, Jonathan Beckwith grabbed Roosevelt Rivers and stepped off the platform. He looked over his shoulder and saw Nina guiding McCallan. He reached into the cargo compartment and lifted two duffel bags of equipment and supplies he had packed. He tossed the duffels next to Rivers and knelt.

"Take a knee!" he screamed to Rivers, who did exactly as instructed.

Beckwith moved next to Rivers, placing an arm around him as the helicopter's blades began their thrust pushing the aircraft back into the sky. Then, in an instant, the ear-shattering noise of the whining blades was replaced by silence.

Beckwith waited for the dust cloud to dissipate and saw Nina lying on top of McCallan, perhaps keeping him from getting back on the helicopter.

He stood and yelled across to Nina and McCallan, "Let's move!"

The Leopard finished communicating with Rhazziq's contact on Beckwith's helicopter and shut down his ARM-Sleeve as he ran toward the billowing dust cloud, which was the perfect screen for his movement.

Once he entered the cloud, he narrowly avoided the tail rotor but managed to keep far enough away to avoid injury. He saw two people, a woman and a man, tumbling from the starboard bench seat. He locked eyes briefly with the woman and continued his dash. Carrying his cargo, he did a headfirst slide onto the outboard seat attempting to not jostle the aircraft, which was difficult given his size.

He put the small assault pack with the miracle cures on the floor of the cargo compartment and snapped it in place with a climber's snap-link. All he needed was for the aircraft to get moving, and then he would take control. He had flown bin Laden's helicopter in Afghanistan and was a commercial fixed wing pilot as well. Though not rated in this small aircraft, The Leopard had received the aircraft specifications from Rhazziq, which he'd downloaded on his ARM-Sleeve and studied prior to tonight's mission. While he was angry that Rhazziq had put The Cheetah on the hunt for the cures, things had worked out. The Cheetah had served as a diversion, allowing him to escape and receive follow-up instructions from Rhazziq.

He would kill the pilot and then hit the autopilot button so that he could remove the body from the small cockpit.

The helicopter lifted off, and The Leopard held on to the outboard bench as if he were a surfer duck-diving a large wave.

As the dust cleared, he saw The Cheetah limping along a trail on the opposite side of the ridge. The man was holding two swords and staring at the people who had just disembarked the aircraft.

He saw The Cheetah lift his swords as the helicopter moved through the black night.

37

Amanda stood, hearing what sounded like an aircraft outside.

"God, let that be my dad," she said. There was a hint of hope in her voice. She had been strong in helping keep the team together, but a full day of helicopter sounds and gunfire had repeatedly elevated her hopes and then dimmed them. They did not dare give up the security of their hide position, lest they be captured. She could only imagine what some might do to her if they believed that she had either stolen or destroyed the virus. Their hope had been that once the pursuer got some of it, he would back off. But that had not been the case.

"What does the test say?" Kiram asked.

"It says that HIV is in his bloodstream."

"Let me take him and give him another shot," he said.

Amanda studied her protégé. His black face seemed to darken in the confines of their hideout. She looked deeply into his eyes as if to explore his soul to determine his intentions. She had seen a different side of Kiram in the last two days. He was more mentally assertive and physically aggressive. Perhaps those traits had been there all along and she had missed them.

"He is here to steal the recipe, Kiram," Amanda protested.

"So we let him die? Do you know the intentions of truck drivers we have cured? The children?"

"It just really pisses me off," she said. "He stalked me, then came here to steal the medicine. That's wrong on so many levels I don't know where to begin."

"Begin with your compassion. He is no threat to us here, Amanda. It will take him days to gain his strength back. In a way, he saved us with the airplane. We now owe it to him to try to save him. The virus is powerful, so he needs another shot," Kiram whispered.

Amanda nodded. "Okay. We'll do it together, but you know we've never done two shots on anyone," she said.

Kiram looked at Mumbato, who nodded.

"Follow me," Kiram said.

Kiram and Mumbato lifted Webb and carried him as if he were an injured football player being escorted off the field. Amanda strapped on her rucksack and grasped the medical cooler. She clicked on a flashlight when she saw that they were venturing deeper into the lava tube. As she waved the powerful flashlight, she saw rolled lava on the ground and jagged edges along the top of the cave. The spear of light stabbed about twenty meters to their front, but then the darkness defeated it. At times the tube would narrow so that she felt as if she needed to duck, and at other times it would widen to where she could not see the walls or ceiling at all. They made turns to the left and right, ascended and descended, but mostly walked level. Her thoughts wandered from the helicopters and gunfire to Webb's fate.

She also wondered about the fate of *Project Nightingale* and the text message from someone named Jack Johnson to destroy the formula. Why, she wondered, would anyone want to erase the hopes and dreams of so many millions of people who simply wanted to carve out a meager existence? They wanted to live decent lives and be productive members of whatever society to which they belonged. Seeing the text had startled her. At this rate, with thousands becoming infected every month by Ebola or HIV and tens of millions already infected, how long would it be before they reached a tipping point and this culture would suffocate under its own weight?

"It feels like we've been walking for a mile," Amanda whispered.

"Almost there," Kiram said.

They turned and the surface became flatter. At times the rolled, hardened lava had caused them to slip and fall, and now, Amanda felt more confident on more level terrain.

"Here," Kiram said and stopped.

Amanda felt immediately that where they had stopped was warmer. In their earlier resting spot, the temperatures had dived to the low forties, and they had built the fires to stay warm. Now, she felt the evaporating chill replaced by a steady, almost radiating warmth.

She shined the light on the floor and saw the residue of footprints, dust, and the black paste.

"This is where you get it?" she asked.

The light shone off the black walls onto Kiram's face. He seemed luminescent, as if a peace had washed over him. Kiram's eyes drifted over the walls of the cavern.

"There," he said.

Amanda followed the light beam and studied where it terminated against the black and gray magma. She could discern shapes like spider webs, but then she walked closer and saw that the impression had been incorrect. The shapes were more like tree branches and leaves…and fruit.

She had read of entire forests preserved in lava flows where the heat of the lava was enough to propel the flow but would cool quickly when met by the water-nourished forest. The trees never burned and appeared preserved, as if in ice.

The outline of an entire tree stood before her. It appeared to be a small fruit tree, perhaps an orange tree or even an apple tree. Like a bas-relief, the tree was in some places embedded in the lava flow and in other places protruding from the magma. She could see small, hollowed-out sections where hanging fruit might have been. As she moved closer, she could see that the cupped areas bore the scars of digging and scraping.

"This is your paste?"

Kiram swept his hand as if to indicate the entire tube and said, "*Mungu.*"

Amanda looked at him, knowing the Swahili word for God. Then she shined the light next to the tree and began walking quickly as she saw another tree and then many others until it seemed that she was in an orchard.

An orchard of apple trees.

Amanda looked at Kiram and then back at the bas-relief of apple trees that lined the lava flow, then back at Kiram.

"This is what you've been bringing me?" She touched the black paste where a fruit would have grown however many thousands of years ago that these trees had lived.

Kiram nodded. "This is the medicine."

Mumbato was on one knee watching in the direction from which they had come. Webb was lying on the floor of the tube, sweating.

"These are trees. How did they not burn when the lava came through?" Amanda asked herself. "And how did the fruit survive all these years?"

Kiram and Mumbato looked at her expectantly. Amanda continued talking as she recalled a visit once to Mammoth Crater in California when she once had gone hiking with some friends from college.

"It's a lava tube," she said, explaining as much to herself as she was to the boys. It was as if she were talking herself through the logic of it all. "The tree's moisture cools the lava, and a small fight of sorts ensues. Obviously these trees won, cooled the lava around them, and survived. I saw one in California a long time ago. It looked something like this, but I had no idea this was around here."

"We need to move. He's starting to convert," Kiram said, pointing at Webb, whose beads of sweat were racing down his face.

Distracted, Amanda looked at Kiram. "It's way too soon to seroconvert, Kiram. The virus has been in him less than forty-eight hours. It's not possible."

"Please, don't argue. I know," he said, touching his chest. "Trust me, I know."

Amanda nodded and haltingly said, "Okay, Kiram, relax. I trust you."

Kiram reached up with a knife and scraped some of the black paste from a cylindrical-shaped depression in the lava. "Get your needle and the serum."

But she had already done so. She snapped on some latex gloves and screwed the lid off a vial of serum and held it out to Kiram, who stuck the tip of his knife onto the mouth of the small jar and scraped the black paste onto the edge. With his finger, he gently pushed the paste into the already dark liquid. She replaced the cap, having done this with him a hundred times in the village, and then vigorously shook the jar. She poked the needle through the small hole and extracted a half syringe of serum, her thumb pulling back on the plunger.

Kiram knelt next to Webb and lifted him. Amanda could see that Webb was weak in Kiram's arms and felt guilty for arguing with Kiram, no matter what Webb's intentions were. He began his soft chant into Webb's ear, holding him by the shoulders as if hugging him.

Amanda took it as a bad sign that Webb didn't even flinch when she poked the needle into his arm and began pumping the searing liquid through his system. She emptied the syringe and retracted the needle from his arm, wiping it again with an alcohol swab. She was careful to avoid touching the trickle of blood running down his arm. She thought of Likika and where she might be. Amanda prayed the girl was healing and safe. On the move, Amanda had scraped and skinned her hands, and she knew that Webb was highly contagious.

She stood and put the needle back into its Styrofoam container, which she resealed with tape. Normally she would dispose of the needle, and it seemed wrong to discard it here. Amanda placed all of the medical supplies into her backpack and then walked away. She always left Kiram alone with her patients after she was done.

She heard his lullaby and the Swahili words he muttered every time as she stared at the apple trees embedded in the lava tube.

Mumbato's words, however, shattered her mental retreat, as they had done only a few days before at the soccer game when he had come running out of the jungle shouting.

This time he was more controlled.

"Noise coming. Move now," Mumbato said to Kiram.

Kiram looked up at Mumbato and said, "I know."

38

The B-2 Stealth Bomber rolled quietly along the secret airfield in Qatar and silently lifted into the air, its black wingspan as invisible against the dark night as its elusive signature was against radar.

Captain Ralph Loring looked at his copilot and smiled. "Real mission, baby."

Lieutenant Molly Brooks forced a smile as she kept her eyes on the instruments. Takeoff was the most dangerous time for the hulking aircraft. At over a billion dollars a copy, the B-2 was a complex marvel. It evaded radar, could drop either conventional bombs or nuclear bombs, and had a range of six thousand miles. Pilots would routinely zap a cheeseburger in the microwave behind the cockpit, wolf it down, release about fifteen one-thousand-pound bombs from forty thousand feet above ground level, and return to base.

"Not sure I understand the mission, sir," Molly said. "We're bombing a cave in Tanzania? Isn't that where Amanda Garrett supposedly stole these Ebola and HIV cures?"

"Yeah, I was thinking about that, but ours is not to question why…it's to do and die. Something like that," he smiled.

Molly was all business. She was the bombardier on this mission and would be responsible for releasing fifteen Joint Direct Attack Munitions (JDAM). The JDAM-102 was a Global-Positioning-System-guided bomb that rarely missed its target. It had been used effectively initially in the Kosovo air war and especially in Operations Enduring and Iraqi Freedom. Now, the Islamic State was feeling its punch, as well.

"I was thinking we'd be dropping bombs on the ISIS foreign fighters we've been hearing about moving through Jordan and Syria," she said.

"Probably got some other bubbas doing that one. We're just punching the clock here, Molly. Go with the flow."

Molly, just out of flight school, wasn't about to question her mission commander, but she had been riveted in her room at night while watching the news about Amanda Garrett.

As they reached altitude over the Persian Gulf, Captain Loring looked at Molly and said, "I'm taking a nap. You fly this pig for a while and let me know when we get to kill something."

Molly watched Loring as he crawled out of his cockpit seat and stretched out on a five-dollar lawn chair he had purchased at the Base Exchange.

Amanda Garrett's about my age, Molly thought to herself. *How scared she must be.*

39

Tanzania

Zhor Rhazziq had used his brand new HondaJet to fly from Rabat to Kilimanjaro. There he had met The Leopard, who had landed Beckwith's
helicopter on the opposite side of the airfield. After taxiing to the helicopter, he dismounted his jet and walked to Beckwith's machine. When he
looked into the helicopter, he found The Leopard asleep.

He slapped him in the face and said, "The formula?"

The Leopard coughed and rolled over. He had been injured in a fight,
perhaps for control of the aircraft. If The Leopard did not recover or had
failed, Rhazziq would need to find The Cheetah, wherever he might be.

"The medicine?" Rhazziq asked again.

The Leopard coughed again and seemed to realize he was being asked
for something.

"Here," he said, pointing at the assault pack secured by a D ring in
the helicopter.

Rhazziq pulled open the assault pack and then cut the tape securing
the Styrofoam packing material. Inside, he found dry ice and four vials,
all labeled HIV/Ebola. He caressed the vials, running his fingers across
them lightly.

He held the bubble-wrapped vials to the light in the back of his helicopter and was surprised that the serum was so clear. He hoped that a lack of
refrigeration had not begun to spoil the concoction. On that thought, he
would place the four vials in the refrigerator he kept in the passenger compartment of his jet.

After he gave himself a shot.

"You did well," Rhazziq said. "We have one last mission."

The Leopard was by now awake and sitting up.

"Son of a bitch hit me hard, but I hit him harder," he said, stroking the back of his head.

"Perhaps I sent you on one mission too many," Rhazziq said, smiling.

"No such thing. What is next?"

"That's what I like to hear. Right now there is something happening in the Olduvai Gorge, and I want to know firsthand what is happening."

"Firsthand?" The Leopard asked.

"Well, secondhand. Through you, as usual."

"So, you want me to go to the Olduvai and do what? I just came from there." The Leopard leaned forward. His back had been resting against the padded seat with his butt sitting on the plush carpet. He had dumped the pilot's dead body somewhere over the Serengeti.

"Take a sniper rifle and kill Amanda Garrett. You will be a hero."

Rhazziq wiped down and then handed The Leopard an M24 American military sniper rifle commonly used in Special Forces and conventional unit reconnaissance platoons.

"You've got ammunition, a night scope, and a laser aiming device. Leave the rifle behind for the Tanzanian military to find."

"And then?"

"And then we pick you up," Rhazziq said, knowing The Leopard was no fool, though. Unless conditions were perfect, he would have to fend for himself.

"I'll take another firearm," The Leopard said. "Just in case you're a few minutes late."

"Good plan."

They went over the plan. One of Rhazziq's two HondaJet pilots would fly the helicopter and drop The Leopard about a kilometer away from the spot of the last sighting of Amanda Garrett. The helicopter would go to ten thousand feet above ground level and turn on its thermal and infrared sensors. The other pilot would fly Rhazziq in the jet, from which he would communicate with The Leopard via secure chat and provide direction once

The Leopard had a visual identification of Amanda Garrett. Rhazziq would also put his signals intercept devices in both voice and digital intercept mode. If he got an intercept, he would be able to geo-locate the device and the person using it.

"I'm ready."

"Before you go, I want you to see something." Rhazziq pulled up his own ARM-Sleeve and pressed a button. After three European-style dial tones, the screen showed a bearded man, the Jordanian about to attack Al-Qaim, and several others milling around behind him.

"Yes, Rhazziq," the Jordanian said.

"We have the formula," Rhazziq said. He showed one vial for dramatic effect. "Our man here, our Leopard, has secured it for our broad purposes. I give you this message as motivation."

The hardened Jordanian looked at the screen and said, "Motivation it is. Leopard, you are a brave warrior, and we will attempt to do your courage justice as we create the Islamic State."

The Leopard said nothing.

Rhazziq and the Jordanian said, "*Inshallah*," and Rhazziq shut down his ARM-Sleeve.

Rhazziq had provided a rare cross-compartmental look at an operation. Typically only those performing specific acts knew the details of their mission. Now, he had cross-fertilized the information amongst his most trusted advisors and operatives.

The helicopter blades began to spin as Rhazziq's pilot fired up the engine.

The Leopard turned to Rhazziq and said, "I delivered. I'll take my money now."

He handed The Leopard a bag with one and a half million dollars in it. "I am a man of my word. You get another million when you kill Amanda Garrett."

The Leopard took the bag, looked inside, and said, "I will."

"And," Rhazziq shouted, "kill Nina Grace. She's not who she says she is."

40

Washington, D.C.

Events were moving much too quickly for Jamal Barkum.

The director of the CIA and secretary of defense sat in the Oval Office and briefed him on the significant migration of foreign fighters from the Northern Tier of Africa into the eastern reaches of Jordan and Syria. This buildup along the Iraq border threatened to disrupt the plans he had for that region. He had only wanted to use airpower and indigenous forces. That seemed impossible now.

The Special Forces soldiers at the airfield near Al-Qaim, Iraq, were in particular danger. Their mission was to call in airstrikes, but enemy fighters were massing, perhaps to attack the base.

Secretary of Defense Bateman had recommended that the entire 82nd Airborne Division, fifteen thousand soldiers, jump in to help protect the base near the tri-border area where Jordan, Syria, and Iraq all joined. He had argued for an aerial and artillery display that would pound the enemy into submission.

Barkum had argued, "But, Phil, if I've pulled out the troops from Iraq and am pulling troops out of Afghanistan, why would I be putting more in?"

"Sir, we need the manpower on the ground if we want to accomplish our objective to defeat ISIS," Bateman countered. "And Mr. President, I prayed hard over making this recommendation to you in light of current events." He had placed his hand atop the president's, saying, "And I prayed for you."

"I already authorized eight hundred, and we're not doing fifteen thousand. This is not a war against Islam. These are rogue bands of fighters who know how to cut off heads and use computers," Barkum said with finality. "That doesn't require the 82nd Airborne Division."

CIA Director Carlisle came to Bateman's defense. "Sir, as a former paratrooper, I can tell you that every single soldier at Fort Bragg and around the country wants to be there with that one battalion you authorized."

"Don't gang up on me, guys. I've made my decision. The Book of Catalyst says we are to bring peace this year, then that's what we will do."

"Surely you're not basing foreign policy decisions on a random, unverified document, sir?" CIA Director Carlisle challenged.

"Don't push me, Stan. Even the Bible says we should pursue peace. So don't go there with me."

"Sir, you went there. You believe the document is real and that it refers to you. That's a national security risk," Carlisle said flatly.

"What are you saying? You leading a coup?"

"I, like you, swore to uphold and defend the Constitution of the United States, not some piece of animal skin that may or may not have any bearing on humanity. You have a duty to the American people, Mr. President."

"Don't you dare take that tone with me. You want to talk to me about duty? You played your part in these wars that have unhinged the world. Do *your* damned duty, Director Carlisle!"

"We are hearing that Secretary Bianchi wants you to go public with the document," Bateman interjected.

"Surely you won't do that!" Carlisle said.

The three men were standing in front of the president's desk in a triangle. The two former military men bore on the president until he slipped his hand under the desk and pressed a button.

Quickly, two secret service agents and his secretary came into the office. It was time for another appointment.

Bateman and Carlisle departed, Carlisle locking eyes with the president as he left.

It was true. Barkum *was* receiving intense pressure from one of his most trusted advisors, Secretary of State Bianchi, to go public with the Book of Catalyst. Her logic was precisely that the find was so significant that public awareness of it could create at least a pause in the fighting.

Likewise, she argued that if he sat on it for too long, he would be accused of contributing to a conspiracy.

Thankfully, his wife, Cynthia, was, as usual, his biggest supporter and best confidant. With a rare moment now to himself in the office, he turned on the news. It was midday, and the television networks had deployed scores of reporters across the Northern Tier of Africa and into the Middle East.

The cable and network news channels were rotating between Tripoli, Rabat, Algiers, Cairo, Addis Ababa, Khartoum, Amman, Damascus, and even Riyadh. Of course, Baghdad and Kabul were front and center, as well.

Protests were everywhere. The outrage had saturated so many countries so quickly that it almost seemed preplanned. On the television, he saw the angry faces of Muslim youth plastered across the monitor screaming unrecognizable expletives, but the sentences always contained the recognizable "America" or "USA."

Counterinsurgency was all about winning over that on-the-fence population. Barkum had to admit that his adversaries' use of the sniper rifle and blaming America for stealing the Ebola and HIV cures were strokes of genius on the world stage. Would the U.S. have had the nerve to shoot one of its own men—even if he was dying of cancer—as the Islamic State had done with Quizmahel? *Could we think this diabolically? Do we even have any tricks up our sleeve?*

Then he thought of the Book of Catalyst and how it might help their cause.

41

Tanzania

Zhor Rhazziq was in the back of his HondaJet circling at thirty thousand feet above the Serengeti when he received a satellite call.

"Rhazziq, are you there?"

Rhazziq punched a touchscreen and said, "Yes, Abdullah, I'm here. How is the mission in Al-Qaim?"

"We are in position. I have given instructions to attack at sunrise."

"How many men do you have, brother?"

"Almost six hundred. And I have passed on to all of my men that already you and your Leopard have scored a great victory for the Jihad. Do not worry, I did not tell them the specifics. But your efforts have born us good fruit, Rhazziq."

Rhazziq smiled.

"Are you confident in your objectives?"

"Yes. We are using three separate routes of ingress and will link up inside of Iraq. From there we have some brothers meeting us to escort us to Al-Qaim, where we will overrun the American base that the Special Forces are using."

"You will send video using your new sleeves, correct?"

"I am doing so now," Abdullah said, holding up his ARM-Sleeve. "All of the men are equipped with your device. You can watch live if you wish."

"*Inshallah*," Rhazziq replied.

"Are there others?" Abdullah asked.

"Many," Rhazziq replied. "After you lead ISIS against the Americans, others from across the Islamic State will follow you. You are the first from ISIS to conduct a ground attack on an American base."

"The first. Good," Abdullah said. "Anything further? I must move."

"I am glad you have issued the Al Rhazziq Media Sleeves I sent to our fighters."

Abdullah again held up his ARM-Sleeve and nodded. "We have trained them how to use it and will coordinate our attack through the three riverbeds onto the American base."

Rhazziq nodded from the seat of his comfortable HondaJet. "Good. The device is secure. Any communications that you receive are from me. Any communications your men receive are from you. Make sure they understand that no one can penetrate this network and that as they receive orders on the devices, they are to obey them or be shot. If you get a message to attack, then attack. If you get a message to stop, then stop. Am I clear?"

"I have explained everything to my men. We want to keep the momentum going, and they will take orders through the devices."

Rhazziq saw the murky picture of Abdullah fade in and out as the airplane banked and switched satellites.

"Victory," Rhazziq said, smiling into the camera on his own ARM-Sleeve.

"Victory," Abdullah said.

Rhazziq switched to the satellite he had covering the Al-Qaim area. Zooming in, Rhazziq panned the camera over the hundreds of men behind Abdullah. They were huddled in three different ravines. He could see hundreds of small lights, indicating that their ARM-Sleeves were switched on and working. Rhazziq had determined that this was the best way to flatten a military organization and make each fighter more lethal. If they were able to continuously receive instructions, they could fight to the very end.

Rhazziq watched Abdullah play the commander as he walked from the rear of the formation to the front, passing his men as he stepped. He saw Abdullah talking to his men, pointing at his wrist and their wrists. He visualized what he was saying. *Watch your ARM-Sleeves for instructions, men. We're moving now. Fight well.*

The camera showed men inspecting their weapons and preparing for combat. They were a haggard bunch wearing checkered kerchiefs over their faces to keep the sand away. Many wore sandals while some had running shoes or hiking boots. There was an assortment of denims and robes and everything in between. *Many of these men have been Westernized*, Rhazziq thought to himself.

He saw Abdullah step to the head of the column and begin moving toward the American base. Soon thereafter, two similar columns began moving through different dry riverbeds. Rhazziq looked at his digital map and monitored the progress.

Soon his forces would converge at one spot on the ground in Al-Qaim, Iraq.

42

Jamal Barkum had gathered his wife, Vice-President Camille Dillon, Secretary of State Sandy Bianchi, CIA Director Stan Carlisle, and Secretary of Defense Phil Bateman to decide whether or not to go public with the Book of Catalyst and the obvious implications that he, Jamal Barkum, had been prophesized as the chosen one in a thirty-thousand-year-old scripture.

The president slightly favored making the announcement. A practical man, he could think of no better way to alter the geopolitical landscape to his benefit in achieving his term objectives and to his party's advantage for the next election. Sure, the suggestion that he was the man who some African tribesman had prophesized would lead the world to peace would create a maelstrom. But weren't they already in a maelstrom?

The war with the Islamic State and ISIS threatened to go on forever. Gains in Afghanistan were meager, and he had followed the previous president's directive that the United States withdraw from that forbidden land, as well. The Islamic State's dark vision of the future was oddly gaining momentum in a world moving toward technological modernity at warp speed. It seemed to Barkum that the gravitational pull of wealth and advancement created an inversely proportional reaction in the opposite direction for many people. Those who were left behind and had little hope for advancement and those who saw little possibility of using the technology to their personal gain were particularly susceptible to the Islamic State's reach.

He had invited Carlisle and Bateman in particular so that they would be part of the decision. They would own it, and later they could say nothing publicly to deny it.

"This war with ISIS is a war of ideas more than anything else," Barkum said. "Even our enemy, the fighters, say the same thing."

"And that makes it true?" his wife, Cynthia, replied. Only she could talk to the president that way. Out of superstition or maybe just because she loved the piece, Cynthia wore her heart-shaped broach again. The diamond, ruby, and sapphire jewelry was situated above her left breast and radiated against her navy skirt suit.

"No, it makes it relevant. If our enemy believes it, then that's important," Barkum replied, establishing his dominant position in the room of family, friends, and advisors. He was, after all, the president. While those who had known him a long time, such as his wife and Sandy Bianchi, saw him as a more human figure, he did believe that his destiny was to bring peace to the world. In a way, the Book of Catalyst made sense to him. He had been groomed his entire life for this, and there were moments in which he had not been able to explain why the passion of politics burned so fervently in his gut, but now he got it. Here it was and this was why. The world was falling apart, and he had risen from relative obscurity to become the second black president of the United States. Was it coincidence that while he was in office, the Book of Catalyst was discovered? How many other ancient African writings were still missing or had been destroyed over the centuries? He remembered the difficult transition that a politically aware America had made in migrating from its Eurocentric history texts to those that were more inclusive. Who knew how many important texts had been subverted or destroyed by powerful Americans during that time? How easy was it for dynasties, pharaohs, kings, and religious scholars to simply destroy the history or religious texts of the first humans?

Apparently, fairly easy.

"Mr. President, I think you're on to something," Stan Carlisle said, apparently setting aside his emotions from earlier in the day. "The CIA is getting chatter and data that the Northern Tier of Africa is funneling hundreds of foreign fighters into Syria and Jordan to attack our classified base there. If we go public with the Book of Catalyst and the obvious implication that your power may be beyond the political confines of the United States, then we may have an opportunity to solve several problems at once."

Barkum looked at Carlisle, admiring his political pluck. *That's a change. He gets it*, Barkum thought. "I may be the chosen one or I may not be. Regardless, we can use this as a chess move. Their information operation to kill their own man with a sniper rifle and then chase Amanda Garrett out of *Project Nightingale* was a brilliant move on their part. What have we got? More paratroopers? How long can we do this? We have to get smart and quit being so damned predictable."

"Now, now," Cynthia sniped, "the third coming would never swear."

Barkum ignored his wife's comment and looked at Sandy Bianchi, who shrugged.

"Mr. President, you know I'm in favor of going public with this," Bianchi said. "If you don't, then we'll suffer the wrath of the people who will believe that you covered this up and denied them their right to know about a potentially life-altering document. I agree that even if it's not true, it can be used to good end. I mean, isn't that what the Book of Catalyst is all about? The Bible? The Koran? How to find peace, bring peace, believe in something larger than ourselves, to guide us?"

Barkum nodded in agreement.

"I mean no disrespect when I say this, sir, but don't you think it's a bit dangerous to believe, or even pretend to believe, that you are godly?" Secretary of Defense Bateman argued.

Barkum measured his response. He didn't want to crush the former admiral, but just two days ago, he had already acquiesced on the small airborne drop of eight hundred paratroopers into western Iraq to stem the tide of foreign fighters. Barkum still raged internally from the squabble with Carlisle and Bateman. At least Carlisle had the sense to agree with him now in this expanded circle. How could the United States keep fighting fire with fire? The enemy manufactured fighters out of thin air by floating an idea or creating misinformation while the United States plugged away in pedestrian fashion with brute force. *This little guy is kicking our ass*, he fumed.

"No disrespect taken, Phil. As you know, I listen to all ideas and thoughts, including those from our conversation earlier." This was implied as a threat to Bateman that he was on a short leash. "It's not so much that I believe I am godly but that we are being told that there is the possibility that I may have a divine mission. It's a minor distinction, but a distinction nonetheless. It is what it is. If this is my mission, then it's our mission. And if it's our mission, then we're going to do it the best way I know how."

"How?" Cynthia asked, this time with a tone of sincerity in her voice.

"By letting the people decide," Barkum said. "They elected me president, and the least we can do is level with them and the world. This document is not ours to conceal. Rather it is the world's to assess. I'm not naïve enough to say that this won't cause uproar, because it will. There will be believers, and there will be cynics. Can anyone in here truly suggest that we just sweep this under the rug? Pretend it didn't cross our path? Oh, I'm sorry, this Book of Catalyst thing, we in our infinite wisdom didn't think it was important," he mocked. "C'mon people, at the very least, we stop the Islamic State's momentum and change the nature of the discussion. We can take away the ISIS fighters' dark vision of the Koran and replace it with one of greater spiritual significance. The confluence of evolution theory and religious texts is too large of a discovery for anyone to ignore, including us. And whether we like it or not, people will want to decide for themselves what their spiritual beliefs are rather than having their government decide what religious texts they get to read."

"So that's it?" Cynthia asked.

"That's it. It's three to two in favor of doing this. I will go public tonight on national television. We found out a few days ago, and we are doing the responsible thing by turning this over to the people and letting them decide."

"You're making a mistake," Cynthia said. "But as your wife, I'll support you, as always." Barkum didn't fault her for voicing her strong opinion despite the audience. The consequences of the decision would be huge.

"That may be true, Cynthia," he said, "but it has come to me, and I must deal with it. No one else in here has that responsibility, and ultimately it's my decision." He placed his hand on Cynthia's knee. "If anyone wants out, let me know now, because once this goes public, I will expect your full support. And out means out. You leave the administration. Clearly I have the support, if not the vote, of my lovely wife, which is her prerogative. Phil, are you in?"

Bateman sighed and looked discreetly at Vice-President Dillon, who slowly nodded.

"Sir, we haven't even had an opportunity to think our way through the second- and third-order effects that will surely occur," Bateman said. "How do we secure the nation from the internal discord that this will create? Homeland security isn't even in this meeting. They don't even know about it, and you are about to unleash on the world that you think you're the chosen one. Plus, you know how strong my spiritual beliefs are, Mr. President. How can you ask us to do this? How can I support you?"

"Is that a no?"

"Christ Almighty," Bateman sighed. He caved. "When can I call Homeland and Northern Command to give them a heads up so they can start planning?"

"After I talk. No leaks. So, you're in? I need to hear it, Phil," Barkum said, pointing a finger at the secretary of defense.

"I'm in, Mr. President," Bateman replied, sighing heavily.

The president's index finger swiveled to Dillon, who gave him a thumbs-up sign, then to Carlisle, who nodded, and then to Bianchi, who did likewise. Each member said, "I'm in," as they gestured.

"Okay, tonight I go public. I want the document and the experts who analyzed it to be available immediately after my statement. I will write my own speech to be vetted by only Cynthia, my most trusted confidant. Any questions?"

Bateman wiggled, still uncomfortable and probably loaded with questions, but he shook his head.

"Okay, I'm shooting for seven p.m. The only thing I want released is that I am making a statement. No hints or clues about what it is." Barkum looked each of them in the eyes, locking in their loyalty. "Okay, there it is. That's my decision."

Cynthia turned to her husband once the rest had departed and said, "Jamal, I know that was a difficult decision, and I do support you. But you are going to create a firestorm. You know that, right?"

"I know, baby, but it's the right thing to do," he said. Barkum looked at his wife, taking in her large brown eyes, movie star looks, and straight black hair. "You know what my father always said, don't you?"

"If you're right…"

"Don't worry about it." They finished in unison.

His confidence in his decision was bolstered by the feeling of invincibility he had been experiencing ever since Isaiah Jones had pushed him to the point of believing that he could be the one referenced in the Book of Catalyst.

"Then why am I so worried?" she whispered, a tear streaking down her cheek.

Barkum looked at her and said, "Believe in me."

43

Jonathan Beckwith had led his team down the lava tube. Even with a ten-digit grid coordinate, it had taken them more than an hour to find the well-concealed entrance. Another thirty minutes and they had removed the stone that they had watched Kiram so easily roll into place.

Finally they were all down on the floor of the lava cave. The fire still smoldered, and Beckwith witnessed the flotsam of a temporary refuge. Medical gauze, some broken pieces of glass with a darker stain surrounding it, and wrappers of Army combat rations all littered the floor.

"We know what this means," Beckwith said.

He looked at his charges.

Roosevelt Rivers was holding up well. He wore a black jumpsuit with a tan safari vest, and his shaved black head gleamed with sweat against the dull orange hue of the fire. But he looked ready to walk another ten miles. Accordingly Beckwith had assigned the large man the responsibility of carrying the digital camera and the satellite uplink that would film live evidence that the Garden of Eden was where they were standing.

"Good to go, Rosy?" Beckwith asked. Rivers simply nodded and stepped toward the fire to make way for the others.

He watched Father McCallan stand from where he had been sitting and brush his pants. Beckwith had asked McCallan to wear his priest's collar for the obvious visual impact of having a religious notable on site. The idea that someone like McCallan would even be here spoke volumes about the legitimacy of the Book of Catalyst, in his view. But the good padre did not appear to be faring so well. The roller coaster helicopter ride had sucked some life out of him. Beckwith had assigned no particular tasks to

McCallan other than to observe and verify. It seemed even that would prove tough for him.

"Padre, we hanging?"

"What god-awful mess have you gotten us into, Jonathan?" McCallan managed.

"Well, it does look like we've got some litterbugs on our hands." Beckwith smiled. "But I think if we follow their trail, you'll see what I've been talking about."

"If this place is Biblical, then why do we need her behind us with a rifle?" McCallan harrumphed. He was pointing over his shoulder at Nina Grace, the redheaded Irish paramilitary refugee.

"I'm your best nightmare," she said, smiling.

Nina was dressed in a black jumpsuit similar to what Rivers was wearing. Her khaki vest was filled with 7.62 mm ammunition to feed her AK-74.

"Okay, shall we, team?" Beckwith said. He didn't wait for a response. Rather, he flipped on his high-powered Magnum flashlight and strode confidently past the fire and into the darkness of the lava tube. He led slowly at first, picking their way past the detritus and making mental calculations as to what Amanda and her team might have been doing. Was someone hurt, he wondered? Was that why they'd come here, to get the paste?

As they walked, he reminisced to himself about his short stay in the village at Mwanza, Tanzania, after his balloon accident. Each morning, he'd had coffee with Sharifa, and they had discussed everything from balloon flying to gardening. He had found her an eager listener as she'd been attempting to perfect her English and to learn about life beyond the Serengeti.

He had left Mwanza asking Sharifa to keep in touch with him, though he knew it would never happen. His only real interest was in the paste. Having had the Book of Catalyst deciphered, after that trip, his mind had begun to click like the tumblers of a lock turning into place to allow the hasp to open. The accident had cut short his exploration, but as had always been the case for him, one closed door had opened another.

As he led his team deeper in to the bowels of the earth, he was snapped back to reality by the sound of voices.

"Noise coming. Move now."

"I know."

Beckwith looked over his shoulder and held up his fist, indicating for them to stop. "Voices," he whispered to Rivers, who was directly behind him. "Quiet."

Rivers turned around and relayed the message to McCallan and Nina.

"Follow me," Beckwith said as he increased his stride, quickening his pace.

He led them around a corner where the lava tube narrowed and then abruptly opened wide into a cavern. He descended onto the level surface and shined his flashlight ahead, thinking he caught the faint glimpse of a light or a white shirt, but he wasn't sure.

"That's them," he said, barely able to constrain his voice. As he stepped to begin running, his flashlight cast a glow on the wall of the tube.

Father McCallan shouted, "Jesus Christ!"

Beckwith stopped, keeping the light trained on the apple tree it had captured in a circular lighted frame. He smiled and said, "Well, Padre, you might be right."

Beckwith walked up to the rounded wall and looked at the tree. He shined the light in each direction, both times giving him a brief visual of other trees. He turned around and shined the powerful light against the far wall. More trees.

He walked up to the near wall and stuck his hand into the soft paste where an apple had once been. Digging out some of the fruit, he sniffed it and then touched it to his tongue. It had the familiar acidic, burning taste of the potion the boys had given him after the balloon accident.

He turned to his charges and said, "This is the Tree of Life. We will eat from it, but first we must find a spot to run our satellite cable to. Also, we need to find Amanda Garrett and the boys. If I'm right, and it looks like I am, this isn't our only surprise."

He turned and looked at McCallan and Rivers, who were on their knees staring at the embedded orchard with wonderment. Nina had lowered her rifle, and the reflection of light indicated her reaction to be one of perplexed intensity.

If this is their response, he mused, *imagine what the world will think.*

44

Jamal Barkum rehearsed his lines in the privacy of the West Wing. Cynthia stood at the balcony with her arms crossed, listening as he spoke. The heart-shaped broach was pressing into the flesh of her right forearm as it lay against her chest.

"My fellow Americans…"

"Too Nixonian," she corrected.

"Friends…"

"Too Roman."

"Peeps, homies…"

"Too black," she said. Barkum saw the hint of a smile at the corner of her lips. At least he had cracked the veneer enough for her to listen.

"Ready now?" he asked. She uncrossed her arms and turned toward him, nodding.

"Fair enough," she replied.

He straightened his tie and lifted the piece of paper with handwritten notes.

"Good evening. Tonight I come to you to make a short statement about the possibility of a significant discovery that could have far-reaching religious ramifications for the millions of our nation's faithful and spiritual citizens. Three days ago, it was brought to my attention that, in the chaos after U.S. forces departed Iraq, a history professor uncovered a set of documents titled the Book of Catalyst from the Old Testament Palace in Nineveh, Iraq. This document was found in 2013 during a raid by American and Iraqi forces—"

"Change raid to search operation and American and Iraqi to coalition," she corrected.

"—during a search operation by coalition forces. The document has been verified by seven different religious scholars and five different authorities on ancient documents."

"Do we know that for sure?" Cynthia asked.

"Isaiah Jones said his Catholic University team has verified these documents."

"One man? Jones?"

"Several men. They just don't all get to come to the White House."

She continued to stare at him.

"May I continue?" And he did anyway. "These scholars determined that the document is written on thirty-thousand-year-old animal skin called vellum. The writing contains both drawings and characters similar to Egyptian hieroglyphics. The document is of African origin, most likely from the Olduvai Gorge area of Tanzania commonly known for Mary Leakey's 1978 find of the oldest bipedal footprints known to man."

He paused.

"This document has been determined to be an authentic alternative to the Book of Genesis. It discusses the Ark of the Covenant, Noah's Ark, and other Biblical occurrences, all of which occurred according to historical sources and are consistent with the Biblical scriptures and the Koran. The document also states that a black man, whose name includes the letters R, K, and M, will step forward and lead the world to peace. I am not claiming to be that man. But considering potential ramifications for faithful Americans, I did not think it within my rights to decide what the American people should and should not be able to evaluate for themselves. I am bringing this information to you, the people of the world, so that you can make your own decision about your beliefs and your life.

"I have also given this speech and this document much thought, and there is one thing I am sure of in its claims. Peace *is* achievable. Perhaps not immediately, but we can work together to live in peace. I promise to make these documents available to all who wish to verify, challenge, or dispute them. I believe that the additional scholars who will assess these documents will come to the same conclusions we have: that God exists and He created man. According to my own personal beliefs, for too long we have ignored the possibility that creationism and evolution may intersect. The Book of Catalyst may widen our perspective on some of the most difficult questions people of various faiths have struggled with for years, perhaps allowing us to turn in the direction of peace for the first time as a people of many faiths. I welcome you to read it, reflect, and come to your own conclusions about what you believe about the path to peace in this difficult world. Good night and peace."

Barkum lifted his eyes to find his wife crying. She was hugging herself, weeping, her head hung low.

"What if it's true?" she sobbed.

"Then it's cause to rejoice."

45

Amanda followed Kiram through the dark tunnel. Behind her, Mumbato carried Webb on his back with some difficulty as they caromed through the tube.

"This way," Kiram said loudly. "Run, they are coming."

They ascended a steep incline and suddenly popped out of the lava flow and into the cool, black night. Amanda saw the starlight and looked to her left and right. She watched Kiram assess his position. There was a slight valley to their left front, and immediately Kiram ran in that direction. She looked over her shoulder and saw Mumbato flipping Webb on the ground as he climbed out of the hole. She watched Kiram slow his pace to give Mumbato a chance to lift the feeble man on his shoulders again.

"Kiram, where are we going?" Amanda asked, now at full sprint. Her load was heavy as well. She was still carrying the supplies and what was left of the medical reserves.

"Please, Amanda, just follow me," he said, picking up the pace. She heard Mumbato scream, "Wait!" Amanda looked back and could see that Webb was becoming a greater burden on Mumbato's back.

They had stopped on a level piece of ground about one hundred meters from the mouth of the cave. She didn't know how far they had come from the original entrance, maybe five miles, but it had been difficult to discern underground. She knew that they had traveled a long way.

"Mumbato needs our help, Kiram," Amanda said, stopping next to him and breathing hard.

"We need to go. They can't find us here. Not at this spot."

Amanda gave no thought to Kiram's comment, but she did register that, for the first time, he seemed almost nervous.

"You okay?" she asked. Mumbato grimaced as he tried to lift Webb again.

"White boy heavy," he gasped.

"Okay," Amanda said. "We need to find some cover and defend our-selves." Then she remembered Webb's satellite phone. She had pocketed it after dropping it once she had seen Jack Johnson's direction to Webb to steal or destroy the serum. She removed her rucksack and rummaged through the pockets until she found the iPhone.

"C'mon," she said, powering on the small device. The light flashed green, and the blue line indicated one bar of battery power. "Okay, we're good."

"Amanda, we've got to move," Kiram said. Amanda assessed their posi-tion and agreed. They were standing on a rough patch of ground with some unevenness. Importantly, anyone in the opening to the cave could look down upon them with clear lines of fire.

She dialed her father's satellite phone from memory. On the second ring, she heard his voice.

"Hello?"

"Dad. We're out of the cave and still being chased!"

"Amanda, baby, you're okay?"

"Okay, okay, Dad, but he's right on our heels!" She was exasperated.

"Okay, I'm coming," he replied.

But there was something in his voice that told her he wasn't close.

"Dad?"

The muted muffle of automatic weapons fire in the background made her realize that her father must have a fight of his own. Was he in the tun-nel chasing the man who was after the recipes? Or was he somewhere else in an entirely different fight?

"Yeah, baby, I'm coming. Keep this phone on."

Then he was gone. Just like that. In the thirty-second phone call, she had heard the distinct report of mortar explosions and the rapid ping of machine gun fire. What was happening? Was the world falling apart? Or just her world?

To add emphasis, a bright light shone upon them from the tunnel. Then she heard the man's words.

"Please don't move," he said. "Stay right there. Especially you, Kiram."

46

Jonathan Beckwith emerged from the tunnel holding the bright light on Kiram as if he were training a laser designator on the young boy to direct a guided bomb strike.

"Stay right there. Especially you, Kiram," he said.

Filtering out of the tunnel were Rivers, McCallan, and Nina, whose weapon was eye level.

"Rosy, bring the camera," Beckwith said, motioning with his hand.

Beckwith looked skyward at the African firmament, a pinpricked black sheath full of swirling constellations. He saw a star fall across the sky as if to signify something, like a flag dropping at the finish of a race.

Two years ago, I stumbled across the Book of Catalyst, and here I am in the true Cradle of Civilization, he thought. *I have brought with me a doubter and a believer, and we just saw the Tree of Life, and now, we could be witnessing something even larger.* Beckwith's machinelike mind that had closed so many business deals to his advantage churned to remain objective, but the task was proving difficult.

Agnostic for many years, Beckwith's discovery, rather, his theft of the Book of Catalyst, had spurred within him a deep introspection that had then sparked in him a spiritual curiosity. It wasn't so much that he suddenly believed in a spiritual being, yet he was intrigued by the possibility. And he had always prided himself on being an open-minded man. How else could he have built the empire that was called Beckwith Media Enterprises today? As he watched Amanda Garrett and Kiram stand in his spotlight, he asked himself the question that mattered most: whose footprints were marching through time? Had he guessed right on Barkum? Now, he wasn't sure.

He walked forward carefully. The bright light shooting a powerful ray onto Kiram was incongruous with the black night. It seemed distorted, out of place as if it were a foreign thread in the perfect fabric of this moment.

"Switch to the night vision lens on the camera, Rosy," Beckwith ordered. He had given Rivers a thirty-minute class on how to operate the shoulder-mounted High Definition digital satellite camera with night optic lens. He heard Rivers flip a few switches and assumed he had begun recording. With that, he shut the flashlight off, allowing the moment to regain its perfection. As his own eyes regained their night vision, he saw that little had changed ahead of him, though he did hear a slight noise near the mouth of the cave behind him.

Amanda stood a few feet away from Kiram. Her hair fell in loose, greasy strings across her face. Her breathing was rapid from sprinting up the lava tube and then tumbling into the cool night air. She could feel her heart thumping through her T-shirt and safari vest.

She looked at Kiram, who was standing erect and staring back at Beckwith despite the bright light the man shined on him. It was as if Kiram was looking *through* the light. His countenance was clear, almost divine, as if nothing could hurt him.

Mumbato took a knee to rest. With Webb still on his back, the weight must have been unbearable. He rolled Webb onto the ground and fingered his rifle as he looked at Kiram.

What the hell is going on? Amanda asked herself. *Who are these people?*

Amanda looked at her two orphans. The night was cooling quickly, and she shivered as she wondered where her father might be and if he could rescue them from this standoff.

Beckwith watched Rivers focus solely on the boy. The camera was the important part.

But he imagined what Rivers might be thinking, recalling Father McCallan's proclamation that his people had been God's first creation. *The first!*

Suddenly Beckwith believed he'd had it all wrong. Kiram, not Jamal Barkum, was the chosen one.

They all remained transfixed on the young boy standing in the flat patch of crusted lava. Rivers was staring through the eyepiece of the camera, which was in its night optics mode. Beckwith could see that the boy was turned to his right, with his left shoulder facing them. His face and eyes were locked onto the camera. Amanda Garrett was next to him.

Beckwith watched as Rivers slowly walked toward the boy, camera on his shoulder. He could see a line of footprints stretching northward from where the boy was standing. Beckwith marveled. Could these be the Laetoli footprints?

Beckwith looked at the ground, noticing a blue reflection coming from the camera. With clarity, he suddenly realized that Rachman had included his favorite screensaver on the teleprompter, which scrolled across the front of the camera lens.

Salam, Paix, Paz, Dan, and Peace. Additionally, Rachman had added No War, *Non Guerre, Waqf Jihad.*

Beckwith watched as Kiram cocked his head and began to read.

47

Lieutenant Molly Brooks listened to Captain Ralph Loring as he said, "Kill chain, kill chain, kill chain."

There was silence, and then he repeated, "I confirm kill chain is a go, and we are one minute out from target at Olduvai Gorge."

Loring looked at her, and she nodded as if to anticipate his question. She was ready. There were fifteen JDAM precision-guided bombs ready to revolve through the bomb rack assembly and fly to designated targets. Five were to bomb a grid coordinate where a helicopter had recently landed. The satellite monitoring had shown that a small helicopter had landed in the area and then departed. And then about two hours later, another helicopter had landed in the same proximity. Five other bombs were programmed to attack a small grouping of individuals who were presently being monitored at the Olduvai Gorge. The remaining five were intended to fly to a plane crash location and destroy all evidence that a man named Crazy had ever flown a Sherpa into the Serengeti.

"Okay, here we go, Molly," Loring said. "Execute."

Molly closed her eyes and lifted the red safety sleeve that prevented premature release of weapons. She said a quick prayer to spare her from the wrath of the military justice system for what she had done when Loring was asleep. Her slim finger pushed the "release" button, and she knew intuitively that the rack was spinning hard and whipping JDAM bombs into the Tanzanian night sky. She could visualize their fins popping open and guiding their descent to their intended targets.

A devout Christian, Molly clasped her hands together and said a prayer. *Lord, please forgive me.*

Loring pressed a red button he had purchased from Staples and put on the cockpit console.

"That was easy."

48

Secretary of Defense Phil Bateman struggled with what he was about to do. He appreciated the fact that Barkum had selected him as the Secretary of Defense, but first and foremost, he was a Christian. The bombing run had commenced, but that was only a temporary remedy. He needed to ensure that this Book of Catalyst thing was permanently fixed. He thought about the ramifications and the example that he would be setting, but, again, his life had been about service, especially service to God.

Could he really do what needed to be done? He knew that he could not live with the fact that Barkum was going to announce to the world that there was an alternative to the Book of Genesis. He had pondered for the last few hours what to do about it and had decided that there was only one thing he could do.

Announcing that there was an alternative to Genesis was one thing. *But to declare that you are the second coming, or whatever that thing proclaimed?* It was pure nonsense.

He had gone home to think about the proper course of action. Never one to consider himself a zealot, he was, in fact, a deeply spiritual man.

"What would you do if someone were to step forward and say that he was born of God?" he had asked his wife.

Betty Bateman, devoutly religious herself, had said, "Well, aside from the general idea that we're all from God, I'd see what he was smoking."

"No, seriously," he countered. "If a prominent person were to announce on national television that he was the chosen one, what would you think?"

Betty, his wife of forty-seven years, looked at him with her deep brown eyes. She had maintained her figure all these years, and at a spry sixty-nine years old, she could still look hot with her platinum hair and long, slender legs.

"Are you trying to tell me something, or is this hypothetical?"

Her husband paused and said, "Both."

Betty's eyes drifted to the television that was playing in the background when the Fox News announcer indicated that there would be a presidential statement tonight on a topic unspecified by the administration at this time.

She pointed at the television and said, "You're kidding, right?"

Bateman shook his head, fearing that perhaps his house had been bugged during his confirmation hearings.

"Let's take a walk," he said.

They stepped onto the back deck of their McLean home and walked into the middle of a perfect fescue lawn.

"I'm swearing you to secrecy," he said. "But, yes, the president is going to come on television tonight and tell the world about something called the Book of Catalyst. Essentially it's an old document that they are arguing is an alternative to the Book of Genesis."

Betty placed her hand to her mouth. "How could they? The Bible tells us what is real and what is blasphemy. That's sacrilege if I ever heard it."

Phil stepped forward and hugged his wife.

"I know, darling. That's why I'm asking you what I should do."

"You have to stop him," she said. "However you can."

However I can, he thought.

Bateman stepped away from his wife and kissed her forehead. "I love you, Betty Blue."

She looked at him and, with knowing eyes, said, "Be strong."

Upon returning home, he had walked into his study, opened his desk drawer, and retrieved exactly what he would need.

Now, back at the White House, he watched the president go to the podium and wondered how he had gotten this far into the building. He was in his dream job and, with his next action, would assuredly throw all of that down the tubes in one fell swoop in just a moment.

He saw Cynthia Barkum in a blue dress with her heart-shaped broach above her left breast. It was an alternating mix of rubies, diamonds, and sapphires. Red, white, and blue, Bateman thought. How appropriate. Well, maybe the book was right about one thing, he considered.

Her pierced heart will save Him and because of this she will enter Heaven.

"I'm going to put an end to this right now," he said to himself.

49

Jamal Barkum clasped Cynthia's hand as he made his way to the podium in the White House pressroom. Out of the corner of his eye, he saw Secretary of Defense Phil Bateman looking nervous. He knew the man did not agree with what he was about to do but was glad to have his support.

The pressroom was packed with the usual crowd and many new reporters he had not seen before. He wondered if someone had leaked the topic.

In the hallway to his left, he saw two secret service agents, one of whom was holding a locked briefcase that he knew contained the original Book of Catalyst documents.

He heard his press secretary say, "No, I have no idea what this is about. The president has reserved the right to make his announcement."

"Don't you think we've had enough surprises?" came one voice.

"How's the fight against ISIS coming?" came another.

"Ladies and gentlemen, the president of the United States."

Jamal Barkum walked forward and stood at the podium.

"Good evening. Tonight I come to you to make a short statement about the possibility of a significant discovery that could have far-reaching religious ramifications for the millions of our nation's faithful and spiritual citizens. Three days ago, it was brought to my attention that in the chaos after U.S. forces departed Iraq, a history professor uncovered a set of documents titled the Book of Catalyst from the Old Testament Palace in Nineveh, Iraq. This document was found in 2013 during a search operation by coalition forces. Seven different religious scholars and five different authorities on ancient documents have verified the document.

"These scholars determined that the document is written on thirty-thousand-year-old animal skin called vellum. The writing contains both drawings and characters similar to Egyptian hieroglyphics. The document is of African origin, most likely from the Olduvai Gorge area of Tanzania commonly known for Mary Leakey's 1978 find of the oldest bipedal footprints known to man."

He paused and looked out over the crowd of stunned journalists, many with their mouths agape.

He continued to read the speech he had rehearsed with his wife. Nibbling at the back of his mind was the inconvenient fact that his Secret Service team had been unable to locate Pastor Isaiah Jones, who was supposed to be present tonight.

He finished his last line. "I welcome you to read it, reflect, and come to your own conclusions about what you believe about the path to peace in this difficult world. Good night and peace."

When he finished, there was silence. The president's words washed over the crowd like a nuclear bomb, figuratively blowing back their hair and sucking the life out of the room. It was only after the shockwave had dissipated that someone had the nerve to ask a question.

But it didn't matter.

The word was out all over the world. Twitter crashed. The cable news channels stopped regular programming for the breaking news.

"Barkum is God!" read one headline. "Chosen Barkum!" read another.

Barkum looked at his image in the television screen that hung above the back of the pressroom. He saw his image fade. It was replaced by a green-shaded night vision camera.

The camera was focused on an African boy standing in an ash-covered lava flow.

50

Tanzania

Matt Garrett and three Navy SEALs had quickly secured the *Intrepid* and its crew of ten.

He kicked open one last door and found a slender redheaded man staring at the television screens in a chilled room full of computers.

"Dude!" the man said as Matt aligned the sights of his M4 carbine on the man.

"Hands up where I can see them," Matt said.

"I'm not moving, man."

Matt assessed the room. Several computers and monitors were scattered around the refrigerated room that was about twenty feet square.

"Name?"

"Styve Rachman. I'm, like, a peace activist, man. Don't shoot me with that thing."

"Where's Beckwith?" Matt asked.

Rachman nodded at one of the screens.

"Seriously, dude, I hate weapons. You're, like, giving me hives here."

"Shut up," Matt said. He removed some flex cuffs and secured Rachman's hands behind his back.

"Man, you gotta watch this," Rachman said, fixated on the television screen.

Matt sat Rachman in a chair and wrapped some duct tape around him, then inspected the rest of the room. There were no other exits.

Only then did Matt look up at the screen.

He saw the president making a speech.

"What's happening?" Matt asked.

"President's telling us he's God, or something like that."

Matt wondered if Rachman was on drugs, but he seemed lucid.

Suddenly the picture faded and was replaced by the grainy green image of a young black man and a woman standing in the open plain.

"What the hell?" Matt said.

"That's my baby!" Rachman shouted. "It's freaking working!"

"What is this?" Matt said. "That's Amanda."

"Damn right. She's smoking hot."

"She's my niece. Tell me what's happening," Matt demanded.

"Damn. Everybody shuts me down on this chick."

"Now!" Matt shouted.

"My boss, Beckwith, sent me a text about ten minutes ago to begin transmission of the uplink to the fifteen Beckwith Media, Inc. satellites. Those fifteen are transmitting into the now open portals of two hundred we Bluejacked."

"Bluejacked?"

"Bluejacked. Some call it Bluebugged. Like Bluetooth but in outer space. Dominating satellites through discreet back doors."

"This is live everywhere?"

"Actually, no. I was only able to get about 168, but the other thirty-two were minor outlets. Stuff like C-Span. But we've got Al Jazeera, Al Rhazziq, CNN, Fox News, MSNBC, BBC, ChinaSat, India.net, and most of the other major satellites that feed the cable and satellite dishes around the world. Every streaming video, television program, and satellite phone call is right now being interrupted and replaced by this transmission for about three to ten minutes."

Matt stared in disbelief. There was Amanda, looking frightened but tough standing next to an African boy who looked confident and poised.

The camera panned around the scene in a full 360-degree circle. He recognized media mogul Jonathan Beckwith dressed in full safari gear. There was a stout pastor wearing a clerical collar standing behind Beckwith. On the ledge behind the two men, he saw a figure on one knee, aiming a rifle. She had red hair and a lithe body, and he did a double take. He'd thought he was looking at Peyton O'Hara, a deep-cover intelligence agent with whom he had once operated. Peyton had fallen off the radar for several years. Could she be back in action? He saw a white man lying on the ground at the feet of a young black man.

The camera came back to Amanda and the African young man, who was standing still and staring directly into the camera.

51

Amanda looked at Kiram's feet, perfectly sunken into the tuff, which encased the original bipedal footprints that Mary Leakey had found.

She guessed that he had been here before. His feet appeared to be an exact match for these footprints preserved in volcanic ash. She knew that about twenty meters away, this single file of two footprints suddenly branched into three sets of footprints. Leakey had found this and puzzled over it as well. *Why is Kiram standing in the prints? What is he doing?* she wondered.

She thought of Kiram as a healer. She had not been able to give him the education that he needed, but he had been learning the ways of medicine by assisting her every day. She felt as if that was his calling. And he seemed to be good at it.

She stared at the large black man who was nearing Kiram with the television camera, which had some words scrolling across the lens. Why was he getting so close?

She wondered what Kiram was seeing in his mind. Did he see beyond what was in front of him? She recalled his distant look on the airplane when they had been crashing and his stern gaze when he needed her to listen to him. Did he remember the children in Darfur, his brothers, fighting a meaningless war that would provide the victor empty results? Had he been standing on this spot before, she wondered? And did he know where the path led?

"Kiram, I'm Roosevelt Rivers," the man with the camera said. "You are Kiram, correct?"

"Peace," Kiram replied.

She watched the camera pan from Kiram's face to his feet, which were still set firmly in the bipedal footprints, and a perfect match as if they'd been made for him.

Or by him, she suddenly considered.

"Peace, that's right. We want peace," Rivers said. "You have an R, K, and M in your name. It's Kiram, right? Are you the chosen one?"

"*Paix*," Kiram said. Instead of answering, he was reading the scrolling message. She was transfixed as she watched him read the words slowly moving across the screen.

Kiram took a step in the direction of the next footprint, his stride matching perfectly so that his left foot fell into the concave track precisely.

"Don't go," Rivers said.

"*Dan*," Kiram read. "*Non guerre. Waqf Jihad. Hakuna vita.*"

"No war. Yes, I understand. No war."

"*Salam, paix, paz*," Kiram continued.

She watched Kiram take another step with his right foot, which fell perfectly into the next footprint.

Continuing to repeat the words that scrolled across the screen, Kiram took more steps. Amanda figured he was a warrior and that sometimes the best way out of a tough situation was not necessarily to fight your way out but to negotiate. These words seemed to be helping. Amanda looked around. Everyone was frozen in place, speechless.

Absently, Kiram stepped forward again with his leg not too far, not too close, and his bare foot fell into the track. Perfect fit for both stride and foot.

He looked back at Amanda, who was watching him with wide eyes. He gave her a look that she registered as danger. He was giving her a warning with his furrowed brow and shaking head.

As she looked up on the ridge, she saw the redheaded woman, and then she eyed the short, chubby man who was wearing a religious uniform. Who was Kiram trying to warn her about?

Her protégé continued his chant, "Peace, *paix, paz, dan, non guerre*, No War, *waqf Jihad, hakuna vita*."

Amanda saw the redheaded woman level her rifle at Kiram as he continued his measured steps in the ancient footprints.

52

Iraq

Zhor Rhazziq watched Commander Abdullah move to the front of the column along the Iraq-Syria border. From his HondaJet satellite feed, he could also see that the other two patrols were converging nicely on their target.

Rhazziq zoomed the lens and studied his commander's face. Apparently, the walk had not been easy. Perhaps his forty-nine-year-old body could not handle the uneven rocks and cool, windy nights as it once had. Nonetheless, the commander had made it and had led his men the entire way.

Watching the attack unfold, Rhazziq had to marvel at his own genius. First was the misinformation with the Ebola and HIV programs, which provided motivated fighters.

And now, it was pure brilliance to have tricked the American president into believing he was of divine origin so that he and his buffed-up ego would send only meager reinforcements, if any at all. Rhazziq's thousands would crush the few hundred Americans sparsely scattered around the base. Having the faux documents planted in the library in 2012 as the Americans were leaving Iraq was brilliant. With Barkum as the obvious heir apparent to the presidency, Rhazziq had developed his plan to have the president believe he was divine so that he could exploit what he expected would be passivity on the president's part. His plan had paid off so far.

Rhazziq watched through the satellite feed as a young Arab man came running down the wadi toward them. Abdullah raised his rifle but quickly lowered it. Rhazziq figured that the man was a scout with a report. He saw animated hand waving between the two men. The scout was pointing in the direction from which he had come.

Rhazziq called on his satellite radio.

"Abdullah, what is happening?"

"Americans are at the checkpoint," Abdullah said into his ARM-Sleeve with a hint of confusion. Whether it was confusion about the Americans or how Rhazziq had known to call at that moment, he wasn't sure.

"It must be the small paratrooper force Barkum authorized," Rhazziq said.

"My scout tells me he saw fifty soldiers."

"Fifty? You can make quick work of fifty, but it will ruin your surprise," Rhazziq said.

"I can converge with all three patrols onto the American position or fix them with one and use the other two to continue moving toward Al-Qaim. I prefer to fix and move. Use tactics and brains. Outsmart them."

"Good plan. Continue your mission," Rhazziq said. He took a sip of wine and watched as Abdullah looked at his Rhazziq wrist device and pressed the button to begin communicating with his troops.

Keeping the camera zoomed in tight, Rhazziq watched Abdullah press the touch screen several times. It didn't appear to be working. Perhaps the commander had broken his device during the long walk to their attack positions.

Suddenly, Rhazziq's view of Abdullah turned into a grainy video of Amanda Garrett and a young black man spotlighted like deer on the side of the road.

Lieutenant Jake Devereaux listened intently as his first squad leader made the report.

"There are about two hundred personnel with weapons moving from west to east near checkpoint seven."

Jake knew checkpoint seven was a small, dry riverbed that branched off the main convergence of the three. Why would they be going there? he wondered. Most likely because his own position had been compromised.

He needed to take a fresh look at his situation. *What would I do if I were the bad guys? If my objective was to get beyond this position and attack the airfield near Al-Qaim where the special ops guys are, then I'd leave a small detachment to divert my attention so that the bulk of my force could move around me.*

"Okay, Red Six, place mortar fire on the lead of the column and then engage with machine gun fire as they squirt," Jake ordered.

"Good call, sir," Sergeant First Class Willie Mack said. The seasoned platoon sergeant looked nervously over the terrain. Deep cuts in the desert floor offset by stretches of deceptively rising ridges played tricks on the eyes. It was difficult to gauge distances.

A moment later, the squad leader charged with rear security to the east made a report.

"Sir, we've got about five hundred insurgents lying low in a ditch over here. It looks like they are waiting to attack."

Jake turned to Mack and said, "Willie, it looks like we're surrounded."

"Have to fight our way out of it, sir. Call the company commander and let him know."

"You thinking Broken Arrow, Willie?" Jake asked.

"I'm not saying we need a distress signal just yet, but we're thirty guys surrounded by twenty times that much."

"We can get air support to kill the back half of the column while artillery gets the middle, and we finish off the front," Jake said.

"I like the way you think, sir," Mack said.

As Jake picked up the handset to make the calls, the first squad leader called in a spot report.

"Uh, sir, something weird is going on."

"Send it," Jake said.

"The enemy has laid down their weapons, and they are praying."

"That's all we need. I've got air support coming in five minutes."

Jake and Willie Mack walked to a protected position where they could look into the dry riverbed.

They saw hundreds of enemy fighters on their knees, praying. As they bowed their heads to the dirt their arms seemed lit by some technological device. The small lights moved slightly in a synchronized pattern as the fighters canted their supplications.

"Orders, sir?"

"Get the artillery and mortars ready. When we've got airplanes overhead, we'll synchronize an attack to kill all of them."

53

Tanzania

The Leopard had walked several miles, Rhazziq directing him from his HondaJet circling overhead.

He had performed the timeless hump of an infantryman dropped by the well-meaning aviator too far from his ultimate objective. Tonight's trek through the Great African Rift Valley had not been an easy one with the steep ravines, rocky surfaces, and winding trails. He was fortunate enough, however, to find pathways that coincided with the directions he was receiving from above.

Finally he had found the spot, a small knoll that deceptively rose above a flat, ashen plain. As he had watched Amanda Garrett and the two black boys emerge from the tunnel, he knew he had selected the perfect spot. He had taken a few minutes to ensure his concealment was sufficient, yet something told him that the first boy had somehow detected him, which was why the boy and the others had stopped.

It appeared to The Leopard that the girl was in a dilemma. Soon others came pouring from the lava tube, and he recognized that it was Rhazziq's main rival, Jonathan Beckwith. If Beckwith was anything like Rhazziq, the girl stood no chance. Of course, he wanted to finish the mission, as three million dollars was always better than two million.

The Leopard carefully adjusted his M24 sniper rifle and dialed the scope two notches. His finger on the trigger mechanism, he let out a slow, steady breath, one of his seven points of performance for firing an accurate sniper shot.

He moved the scope first to the big black man who was holding a camera and seemed to be saying something. Even though The Leopard was nearly eight hundred meters away, the magnification of the scope made it appear that The Leopard was right there with them, part of the conversation. Next the scope drifted to the face of Jonathan Beckwith, an oft target of his that Rhazziq had never followed through on giving him the mission to kill, always waiving him. Perhaps Rhazziq wanted a larger showdown with his rival? Though having studied the target folders enough, he could recognize the man. As he scanned with the high-powered scope, his view passed over the bald pate of what looked like a religious man and then the lead black boy again.

And then Amanda Garrett.

He placed the scope's crosshair directly on Amanda's heart and let out another shooter's sigh. Controlling his breathing was the key to willing the bullet to the very spot he wanted it to go.

"Not getting away this time, little girl," The Leopard whispered.

Zhor Rhazziq watched Nina Grace find a good firing position. She lay on a relatively flat piece of ground that was above the lava tube from which they had emerged.

He watched her handle the carbine with ease as she slid down her night vision goggles and turned on her PAQ-4C aiming light that emitted an invisible pulse of infrared light in line with the muzzle of the weapon. With her goggles, though, she could see the infrared spectrum.

Rhazziq sent her an urgent text message:

You are on TV. This is working against us. Kill the boy. Make it look like the Americans did it.

He knew that she was an American. His assistant had uncovered a photograph linking her to the American spy, Matt Garrett, from several years ago when an Iraqi general had coordinated a series of attacks on the U.S. homeland. He believed her name was Peyton O'Hara, not Nina Grace. Regardless, he continued to play her, as he knew she was playing him. All he really needed was for her to kill the boy. Could she do it? She had provided him invaluable intelligence form Beckwith's camp, but he assumed she was at her end game on this current assignment.

Knowing her like he did, he imagined she was wondering if the boy she was sighting through her goggles was really touched by God in some way. He now knew that since she had been sleeping with him, she had pretended to slowly convert to Islam and its practices, which didn't mean she was abandoning her mission or her roots. He also understood that there was a fine line between executing a mission and playing the role so well that she actually fell into his abyss forever.

Kill the boy.

Could she do it? He knew she could. But what was her ultimate mission? Why had she infiltrated his operation and then Beckwith's on his behalf? A triple agent? Surely not.

He watched her through a backup satellite his pilots had switched to when the Beckwith bluebugging attack had initiated. He saw her shift the weapon slightly to the right, adjust herself, and lie motionless.

Then she pulled the trigger.

54

Amanda Garrett suddenly realized what was happening. She saw the tall white man hanging back in the distance smiling while the tall black man moved forward with a camera that continuously panned up and down from Kiram's face to his feet.

She looked again at the footprints in which Kiram was walking. She had known about the Laetoli footprints and guessed that was what she was seeing. It made sense in terms of location. They were south and west of the Olduvai as they had traveled through the lava tube, and villagers had reminded her of the history and stories that sounded like legend in the area.

Apple trees? Footprints? What could it all mean?

Certainly she felt as if she were in the presence of something larger than herself. She toyed with the heart-shaped locket around her neck that had the facing pictures of herself and her father. She looked down at Webb, hidden behind a rock and actually looking well enough to ask, "What's going on?"

"Showdown," she whispered. "So stay down. Stay hidden."

Then it occurred to her that Webb was indeed looking better and feeling well enough to talk. Could it be, she wondered, that the serum only worked when Kiram was involved? She was too much of a pragmatist to have ever considered that notion before, but now she wondered.

Was there something special about Kiram, other than her obvious love for a child who had endured so much and seemed to be surviving in this land that took more than it gave?

She looked away from Webb and caught the glint of something out of the corner of her eye. Opening her eyes wide, she focused on the rock ledge above the lava tube, thinking she saw a scope of some sort…and a rifle.

Then she saw a movement from behind the tall white man. A shorter man with a bald head stepped forward and was raising something. He seemed to be wearing a priest's collar and black coat. What was that he was holding, a cross? Or a pistol?

The man holding the camera sensed her concern and spun toward the short man, who was lifting a pistol. The short white man aimed the pistol as he ran toward her and shouted, "Sacrilege!"

"Kiram, get behind me!" she said, leaping in front of Kiram, who was standing firmly in the Laetoli footprints. She felt her pendant forcefully snap at her neck and swing in the air when she heard the shot.

The lead bullet bore through her face and then her father's face as it caught the heart-shaped locket squarely in the middle. As it moved through the pendant, the bullet found Amanda's upper left chest area just below her clavicle. Catching no bone, the shot went clean through her chest, though the smashed lead tumbling through her skin caused serious damage. Worse, Amanda thought as she fell to her knees, was that the bullet punctured Kiram in the left pectoral.

Directly atop the heart.

As she went from her knees to her side, weakening by the second, Amanda registered a second shot. She heard a heavy whooshing sound as if several airplanes were flying low above the ground. From her heavy eyes, she saw what looked like giant spears falling from the sky and landing with enormous thuds into the rocky ground like ten-foot-tall lawn darts. The large javelins thudded into the ground and vibrated, making a noise that echoed through the silence.

As Amanda lay on the ground bleeding from the chest, it occurred to her that these were bombs and that they were raining all around her like arrows shot by archers.

Though there were no explosions.

55

The president saw Phil Bateman in his periphery. The Secretary of Defense stepped onto the stage in the Press Briefing Room even though most eyes were on the television images showing the unfolding events in Tanzania at the Olduvai Gorge. The president monitored Bateman's approach while appearing to watch the television.

When Bateman reached into his jacket pocket only feet from the president, all of the journalists swiveled their heads back toward the podium.

Barkum felt his wife, Cynthia, perhaps in her role as his only true defender, step closer to him as Bateman approached.

"Mr. President, I can no longer support this announcement or this administration. As a good Christian, it pains me to do this," Bateman said.

His hand rose, and two secret service agents were moving quickly toward him.

"I hereby tender my resignation to you in front of the world," Bateman said. He held out a piece of paper with his signature on it.

Barkum looked at Bateman and then at the document, after which he looked up at the television and smiled grimly.

"Nobody's watching us," Barkum said. "Though nice gesture."

Bateman looked up at the television about the same time Amanda Garrett leapt in front of the African boy and was struck with a bullet.

It appeared that the African kid, though, was unfazed, as he knelt down briefly and then kept walking.

As she lay on the ground bleeding from the chest, Amanda saw the scene unfold in slow motion. She'd dived in front of Kiram, and the bullet had struck her, spinning her to the ground. Then, everything seemed to accelerate.

Jonathan Beckwith shouted, "No!"

Five missiles whooshed into the ground as if they were on the receiving end of the Olympic javelin competition. The ground shook, and the unexploded ordnance kicked out huge rocks that created shrapnel despite the absence of explosions.

Amanda watched Kiram, who, despite his injury, appeared unfazed. She saw him look skyward from where the missiles had been delivered and then back down at his wound, blood seeping from his left pectoral area. He knelt as he cupped some of the black paste from the lava tube in his palm. Chaos all around him, he then laid down his rifle and turned toward Amanda, smearing the medicine on her wound while whispering softly into her ear the same Swahili chant that she had heard him sing to every Ebola- and HIV-infected child they had cured.

"I love you like a sister, Amanda. Thank you for saving me," Kiram said. Amanda watched as the camera came within inches of her and Kiram's faces.

Kiram stood and then continued to follow the footsteps.

Amanda saw the man named Rivers look over his shoulder in time to place the camera on Beckwith leaning over the chubby white man, who had fallen to his knees as if in prayer. His head hung low, and a pistol fell from his hand. Amanda saw blood seeping from the corner of his mouth and looked up at the redheaded woman, who was running down the crevice cursing herself. "Damnit, I got the shot but was too late," she said. "I didn't see McCallan pull his gun!"

"Sacrilege," McCallan muttered. He dropped face-first into the beginning steps of the footprints. Amanda had watched the priest shoot both her and Kiram.

Amanda's breathing was slight and raspy. She felt them all around her.

"Let's get her to a doctor right away," one man said. "Him, too." They must have been talking about Webb. *Who gives a shit about Webb?* she thought. He'd come here with evil intentions. Her mind was spinning as her blood pooled in the footprints. She heard a man say, "Where the hell is my pilot? Where is my helicopter?"

"Please don't hurt Kiram," Amanda whispered.

"Amanda, no one can hurt him. He's the chosen one," a man said.

She turned her head to see Rivers filming the back of Kiram's shirtless black body walking into the northern darkness. He carried his AK-47 in his right hand, his thumb and forefinger circling the weapon just above the magazine well.

As Rivers filmed, Amanda watched.

Kiram continued walking and disappeared into the night.

56

Tanzania

The Leopard saw the events unfold from his well-concealed position. Though he no longer had a shot at the black boy walking slowly to the north, he had the others directly in his sights. He determined he would save the attractive redhead for his last shot. Even better, he might try to take her alive.

With the crosshairs on the head of the black man carrying the camera, The Leopard squeezed the trigger and blew away a good portion of the man's skull. The man thudded into the ground, dropping the camera. The Leopard watched from his remote position as Beckwith and the redhead searched frantically for the shooter, him. They were torn between tending to the dead black man, returning fire on him, and seeking cover.

Because they did not immediately do the latter, The Leopard moved the sight's crosshairs to the media mogul, Jonathan Beckwith, who was crouched over two bodies. One of the bodies he was certain was Amanda Garrett, who appeared to have been shot in the heart by, of all people, the religious man. The Leopard understood the man's motives. The Bible was sacrosanct. The Book of Catalyst was fiction.

He pulled the trigger and was disappointed when Beckwith slapped at his neck as if he had just been stung by a bee. Though the media mogul had dropped his weapon and was on one knee, then all fours.

The red-haired woman looked in his direction, but it was too late for her. He fired his next bullet and caught her in the torso. She kicked backward and dropped her own rifle onto the ground.

He had no clear shot on Amanda Garrett but believed he could now move in for the close kill.

Amanda watched Mumbato lie perfectly still when the shooting started. When the firing stopped, he crawled to Amanda.

"Kiram give you paste. You'll be okay," he said.

"We have to catch this man who has been chasing us, Mumbato," she said. "He will figure out that the vaccine only works when Kiram gives it, and they won't stop until they find him. We need to kill whoever that sniper was."

"But you no like guns," Mumbato said, kneeling over her.

"No, but you do. And I have this." She showed him the knife with which she had killed the wild Serengeti dog.

"I understand."

"Mumbato, I want you to go about a hundred meters along this lava flow and find the best spot to take a shot at him when he comes after me. I'll be the bait."

Mumbato's eyes grew wide.

"I understand."

"Then shoot him dead before he shoots me. Okay?"

"Yes."

She watched Mumbato crawl the length of the lava ash in the direction that Kiram had disappeared. He stopped at a cliff and next to a series of boulders that looked like they could topple over the steep drop-off at any moment. Then he was gone from her view.

As she lay in the Laetoli footprints, perhaps the birthplace of all humans, she heard the redheaded woman moan something unintelligible. She said a quick prayer for all of those who had been shot. As her mind drifted into and out of consciousness, she wondered if she had the strength to perform first aid on the wounded victims who had pursued her. She decided against expending the effort in order to conserve her energy for when he came, because he was surely coming.

As she lay in the ash hardened from thousands of years of rain and heat, she registered that the surface was like concrete. God would have wanted to leave this clue, she considered. As she waited, she also thought about Jerusalem, perhaps until now the holiest of locations in the world. How was it the fulcrum of so much violence and hatred? Would that happen here? Were the emotions that accompanied religion so powerful that when two distinct beliefs came into conflict, the only means of resolving the matter was through violence?

Before she had a chance to consider much else, she heard The Cheetah's slicing blades in the distance and felt the presence of another large man above her.

"Help me," she muttered, looking up at the big man. He looked down at her and then at Webb, who was unconscious next to her.

"Help me," she repeated.

"Help is on the way, child," the man said as he lifted his rifle.

Amanda heard a shot. The tiny bullet, though, seemed to do little to deter her attacker. He stumbled backward and looked at the crimson stain growing larger on his outer tactical vest. He stepped forward again, and Amanda mustered what little energy she had saved for this precise moment to sweep her foot across his ankle at the time he was stepping onto the ash.

Surprised, the man flipped to the ground onto his back, the jagged edges of the Laetoli footprints cutting into his arms.

Amanda rolled to her knees and lifted the knife, driving it into his abdomen.

Mumbato came running from his firing position and stopped just as another man stood above her with two large swords. She recognized him as The Cheetah, one of the men Kiram and Mumbato had chased away a day ago.

She looked over her shoulder and was about to roll away when automatic machine gun fire riddled The Cheetah's body. For a moment, the hulking man just stood there, statuesque. Then he slowly fell backward.

Amanda returned her attention to the man who had been chasing her. She had both hands on the knife handle as she stabbed the man's chest cavity again. She held the knife with such force and pressure her arms flexed and cramped. In her mind, if she let go, she believed he might survive. No, this was not going to be a B horror flick in which she would wound this beast and then turn around, drop the knife at her feet, and hug Mumbato, only to be overtaken when he got up again. On that thought, the pacifist and aspiring doctor performed the most meaningful surgery of her life by hitching the knife a bit farther into the cartilage of the man's sternum.

"Die," she whispered. "Die, you son of a bitch."

The man's eyes were nearly lifeless, but she saw a slight smile cross his lips as his head lifted ever so slightly.

"Good wins," she said.

Then she heard a helicopter and prepared for more combat.

57

"Get me there now," Zach said to Chief Warrant Officer Mike Rogers. "Now!"

"Wilco, sir," Rogers replied.

Rogers, for his part, had just conducted a daring combat tactical landing of his MH-60 Black Hawk helicopter amidst intense fire from the Tanzanian military. He had powered up just enough to fly nap-of-the-earth toward the Global Positioning System location that the Merlin reconnaissance airplane had provided. In fact, they were looking at the Merlin's video downlink live aboard the improved ROVER console inside the MH-60.

Zach watched the grainy video feed of the Merlin airplane with horror as a sniper dropped everyone standing in the tight circle. Kiram had disappeared. Next to Amanda, Zach could see the rumpled body of a white man who he now figured to be Webb Ewell, the representative of Jack Johnson Laboratories they suspected to be with her. He saw Mumbato crawl next to Amanda and then scurry away.

The Black Hawk was doing nearly two hundred knots as it coursed across the valleys and peaks of the Great African Rift Valley. Zach watched the Merlin video feed in horror as the lone operative stood atop Amanda and lifted his rifle.

"How far, Mike?"

"Three minutes, sir."

Zach clenched his fists as he looked at the video.

Then he saw something unbelievable.

The screen went blank at the same time Mike Rogers said through the headset, "Sir, Merlin reported that there is a HondaJet flying at thirty thousand feet conducting reconnaissance of the same location we're looking at. The jet somehow fired on them, and they had to take evasive action."

"All I care about right now is getting to Amanda. Move it."

"Thirty seconds, sir."

They were flying with doors open. Zach snapped his monkey harness into the D ring on the floor of the MH-60 and leaned outside of the aircraft now flying at about 150 knots. Through his night vision goggles, he saw some commotion at the target site and was so filled with adrenaline that he screamed, "Amanda!" against the drowning din of the rotors and the slipstream.

As they circled, Zach saw the JDAM missiles sticking in the ground like chucked spears and told Rogers to hover, not land, as he did not want the kinetic energy from the rotor blades to trigger an explosion. As he fast roped down the thick nylon rope, part of his mind was wondering, *Who the hell ordered a JDAM strike on my daughter?* After he dropped to the ground from the rope, Van Dreeves and Hobart followed.

As he landed, he saw Amanda. She was lying next to a large man he did not recognize, her hand barely touching the butt of a hunting knife. It was clear to him that she had killed this man and then passed out.

"Amanda?" He knelt next to his daughter, anxiety gripping his throat like a garrote pulled from behind. Barely able to breathe, Zach placed his face near his daughter's dirty, stained yet cherubic cheeks. "Baby girl?"

He felt for a pulse and got a weak report in return.

"VD, Hobes, let's get her onto the helicopter. Send down the penetrator."

"We've got a scared kid hiding over there behind some rocks; looks like a cliff. He's got an AK-47 trained on us."

Zach looked up and guessed that it was either Kiram or Mumbato. He knew that they would be protecting Amanda, though he could make little sense of the death and destruction that was scattered around him. There were JDAM missiles stuck into the ground like lawn darts, at least two dead bodies and maybe more, and blood everywhere.

Van Dreeves, a Special Forces combat medic by trade, knelt next to Amanda, opened her khaki vest, and cut away the portion of her shirt just above her heart.

"Small entry wound. Looks like she's lost a lot of blood. There's some kind of black paste on the wound, like someone treated her." He spoke with clinical, detached precision.

"Hold up, wild man," Hobart said to Mumbato, who had taken a few steps away from the steep cliff behind him. The lava tube opening was to his left. "Arms in the air."

Mumbato lifted his rifle and said, "Me friend of Miss Amanda. I shoot bad man trying to destroy our village and steal the medicine."

"Weapons down, Hobes," Zachary said. "Amanda trusted these guys."

Hobart looked over his shoulder at his commander with a wary eye but complied with the order. Then Zach saw something that made him uneasy. It took a second for the minor piece of information to register, but it finally occurred to him that the young boy had a flashing green light shining from the pocket of his mesh soccer shorts. It was the same indicator any mobile device would show when it was operational and had no new messages. Had Mumbato been communicating with someone else? Or was he the loyal friend?

"Where's Kiram?" Zach asked. Amanda had spoken at length about Kiram's potential. He remembered meeting a younger Kiram a few years ago. The boy had once drawn an uncanny caricature of Zach. She had rarely mentioned Mumbato, though.

"Kiram go away with *Mungu*," Mumbato said, leveling his weapon on Zachary. "Who are you?"

"Drop the weapon, man, or I'll shoot you now," Hobart said.

Van Dreeves, working on Amanda, looked up and grabbed his pistol, clenching his surgical scissors in his teeth. Zachary was the only one who didn't have a weapon trained on Mumbato.

"I save Miss Amanda. Kiram ran away. You drop your weapons or I kill you. I need to know who you are."

"Amanda's breathing is getting shallow, Zach. We need to get her up in that aircraft."

Zach assessed the situation. Mumbato was playing a card of some sort. Did he want the formula? The backpack was lying on the ground next to Amanda.

If that was what he wanted, he could have taken it. Did he really wonder who they were and whether they had Amanda's best interests in mind?

"I am Amanda's father, and she needs medical attention right away. But you are making it harder. For every good angel, there's a bad one. Is that it?" Zach asked.

"Mumbato good," he spat. "I protect Amanda."

"Then let us help her. We don't want to hurt you, Mumbato, but we will if we have to do it to save Amanda."

"It's really now two against three," Webb Ewell said from one knee. All but forgotten, he had grabbed The Leopard's sniper rifle and pistol in Amanda's moment of waning consciousness after she had stabbed their pursuer.

"Amanda must have forgotten I took acting at Columbia. Oh, that's right. She didn't even notice me, did she? Well, Mumbato's tired of Kiram getting all the press, and I'm tired of being poor. So we're going to take this drug and go save the world. So drop your weapons right now or I put a bullet in Amanda's head," Webb said. "You may kill me and Mumbato, but Amanda will die in the process."

After a pause, Webb screamed, "Now!" To add emphasis to his sense of urgency, he fired a shot centimeters from Amanda's head, spraying hardened lava ash into Van Dreeves's face. Thankfully his ballistic eye protection caught the spatter.

"Do what he says," Zach said. "I can't risk it. We can't risk it. They want the vaccine, let them have it."

Zach watched Hobart kneel down and lay his M4 carbine on the ground with a watchful eye. Van Dreeves followed suit as he also knelt and put his carbine on the tuff.

"Okay, take the backpack and get out of here," Zach said.

"First back away," Webb said. He was swinging the long sniper rifle back and forth between the three of them. Zach could see it was a manual bolt action M24 sniper rifle. Webb was such a neophyte that he hadn't charged another bullet into the chamber. What an idiot. But that still left

Mumbato, who was an expert marksman with the AK-47 if the dead man next to Amanda was any indicator.

"Okay. We'll leave our weapons, but we're going to huddle around Amanda. You'll have to shoot me before I leave her side," Zach said. "Just take the formula. I know that's why you're here. You're from Jack Johnson Labs, and Johnson wanted you to destroy it. So take it and do that or become rich, who cares? There are people dying here, and we need to tend to them."

Zach looked around and saw Roosevelt Rivers's lifeless body. Beckwith looked like he might still be breathing, but unfortunately the deep-cover CIA agent Nina Grace aka Peyton O'Hara appeared to have already gone pale in death. In addition to Amanda, Zachary had hoped to rescue her in particular. *Never leave a fallen comrade.* She had done well.

Zach, Hobart, and Van Dreeves surrounded Amanda, her breathing becoming more labored by the second.

"Okay, now turn around and kneel," Webb Ewell said.

"You're kidding me, right?" Zachary said.

"Okay, just hold that pose then," Webb said, lifting the rifle. "I always wanted to nail your daughter, but killing you will do. And I might still get to have some fun."

With the rifle less than ten meters from Zachary's face, Webb Ewell pulled the trigger, and a shot rang out.

58

Zach heard the shots and knew they weren't directed at him. He looked up and saw the quick bursting muzzle flash of an assault rifle. He watched as Mumbato dropped his rifle and fell backward from the cliff.

As Zach had known, Webb's sniper rifle was not loaded, and Zach quickly turned and flipped his Duane Dieter Spec Ops knife from his outer tactical vest, popped it open with a flip of his wrist, and in the same continuous movement, landed the blade between the second and third ribs of Webb Ewell, just to the left of his breast bone. The tossed knife punctured Ewell's heart, and he was gone instantly.

Hobart and Van Dreeves had their weapons back in their hands shortly and were scanning for other intruders.

Where had the shots come from? They had been precisely aimed at Mumbato and perfectly timed. He did not spend a long time wondering. Amanda was Zachary's concern, and within two minutes, Mike Rogers brought the MH-60 above them again. The jungle penetrator lowered on the hoist cable, the rugged terrain being unsuitable for landing the aircraft and the JDAM missiles still posing an explosive threat.

Zachary carefully lifted his still-breathing daughter and hugged her. "It's okay, baby girl," he said. "We're good to go."

He placed the small seat beneath his buttocks and hugged Amanda, pulling her onto his lap. If she woke up, she would see him first. With a tug on the line, the crew chief rapidly hoisted them into the helicopter. Van Dreeves and Hobart were next. Hobart brought the medical cooler and rucksack with the vaccine and cure. Van Dreeves had a backpack loaded with cash.

"What about the others?" Hobart asked

"Get the redhead. She's CIA. Then, we've got to get Amanda back. Matt is on the way with a second helo team and some medics. He's about ten minutes out," Zach said.

"Roger," Hobart said.

Van Dreeves carried Nina Grace into the helicopter and actually found a pulse. He affixed her to a litter and checked on Amanda, who was on the adjacent litter already. He spent ten minutes cutting and pulling and removed a few pieces of bone fragment that might have migrated toward Amanda's heart.

As Van Dreeves clipped and cut, Zach paced hunched over in the back of the special operations aircraft. Matt's voice came to him through Zach's headset.

"Status?" Matt asked.

"McCallan and Rivers are dead. Beckwith might make it. The redhead is barely hanging on. No sign of Kiram, but Mumbato was shot by an unknown. Someone dropped JDAM bombs on the location, so you have to land offset."

"How's Amanda?"

"Still waiting," Zach said.

"Just FYI, bro. Amanda killed an Islamic State operative known as The Leopard. Bad dude. We've been looking for this French asshole for a long time. He's connected to Rhazziq."

"I just hope she survives this, Matt."

"In our prayers, bro. She'll make it. She's half you," Matt said.

Zach said, "Roger. Thanks. I'll let you know."

Van Dreeves pulled away and removed his latex gloves the way an obstetrician might after delivering a baby. "She's going to make it," he said to Zachary above the din of the whipping rotor blades. "Whatever that black paste shit is probably saved her life. Stopped her bleeding and did some other stuff I can't even explain."

Zachary moved in close to Amanda's head and pulled away a few strands of matted hair.

"We're good to go, Daddy," she said weakly.

The big, tough colonel felt a tear stream down his face—happy, proud, everything—and he didn't try to stop the rest as they came flooding forth.

59

It had been a full two months, and Amanda had not seen Kiram again. In fact, no one had. Sure, she knew there had been multiple sightings, like Elvis, but the fact remained that there was no positive identification.

She had watched the news with fascination. The world had gone crazy with "Kiramania." Millions of people were making the pilgrimage to the lava tube and the Laetoli footprints making the Muslim annual Haj look like a little league stroll in the desert. Dar es Salaam Airport had been overwhelmed, but the Tanzanian government had adjusted quickly to the chaos by coordinating with neighboring countries and using small aircraft to ferry into remote airfields the continuous stream of pilgrims seeking the truth about the origins of life. There were protests, true believers, and curious onlookers. For a long time, Tanzania would not be the remote, quiet place she'd known.

Scientists were analyzing the Book of Catalyst's assertion that the Great Rift Valley was the Garden of Eden. Climbing teams had ascended Mount Kilimanjaro and indeed had found an ark-shaped outline of gopher wood. The evidence was mounting…and fleeting. For every piece of "proof," there was an equally substantial counter piece of evidence.

Was it all a charade or the real deal? Just as some believed the lunar landings had been filmed on the Big Island of Hawaii, many believed that Beckwith's Bluejacking of Kiram at the footprints was nothing but a grand hoax. The news media was covering the event around the clock from on location in the Olduvai Gorge. There was an uncoordinated worldwide dragnet searching for Kiram that was grander than anything that had been put together to find Osama bin Laden. Satellites, cell phone interceptors, unmanned aerial vehicles, manned reconnaissance airplanes, and anything that could cover ground quickly and search were all participating in the search for Kiram.

It was like the gold rush of 1849, Amanda thought, with walks of life panning for Kiram, filtering everything through their sieves, and coming up empty. But not completely empty, because they had seen the video, and many believed. The endless replays of the "God-boy," as he had come to be referred to in the media, reminded humankind that there was hope. Perhaps this life they were living would lead to something besides a coffin and darkness.

Amanda had watched television constantly as she'd recovered. Religious scholars were in a dither, their creditability somewhat damaged by the constantly repeating image of Father McCallan pulling a pistol from his coat pocket and shooting the "God-boy." The man who had so many times explained to the masses the significance of certain religious findings had sought to deny the world what some considered to be a modern-day savior. Only time would tell. But the fact remained that McCallan hadn't wanted the texts to have a chance.

Recovering in her father's family home in Stanardsville, Virginia, Amanda looked at him from her bed. Her honey-blond hair was lying against the pillow spread symmetrically like an opened Japanese folding fan. Zach stood over her bed while Matt, Kristyana, and Riley Dwyer fiddled with the computer in the corner of the room. A large bay window looked over the Blue Ridge Mountains to the west, providing a heavenly sight if there ever was one.

"Dad, could it be true? That Kiram was sent by God?"

"Baby girl, who knows? It makes as much sense as anything. The entire world saw it, and the good news is that it has altered the dynamic a bit with the Islamist Extremists. The fighting has stopped for the time being in Syria, Iraq, Afghanistan, and Pakistan. This thing may have changed the world. You name it. Somehow it has touched the conflicts between India and Pakistan, China and Taiwan, North Korea and South Korea.

Just about every living person has seen what happened at the Olduvai between seeing it live on television and the countless replays on the Internet. You're famous, kid."

"Unbelievable," Amanda whispered.

Zach's girlfriend and Amanda's former psychologist, Riley Dwyer, sidled next to Zach and held his hand. "Hey, girlfriend."

"Hey yourself." Amanda smiled.

"So you're all happening and everything out there saving the world?" Riley's signature thick, kinked auburn hair was tied in a ponytail.

"Don't get goofy on me," Amanda said. "It hurts to laugh." She reached out with her hand and rubbed Riley's belly. "Brother or sister?"

"Secret," Riley smiled, a tear sneaking down her cheek.

Riley wiped her eye and turned away as Zach took over. "You know, it was pretty hard to ignore Kiram's message and the whole Book of Catalyst thing. I think the only thing that gives anyone any real hope of moving beyond this fight is something bigger than our brute force trying to beat the enemy's big idea."

The guest bedroom was really Zach's room that he'd had as a child, but he'd had Riley and Kristyana do a makeover for Amanda once she had been wounded. They had brightened up the room with pastels instead of the eclectic gatherings and colors of a boy's room. Instead of Mickey Mantle posters and race car sheets, she had a few Peggy Hopper paintings and a bright yellow comforter that showed a rising sun spreading across the folds. Oddly, to Zach, the room felt as though it was Amanda's now.

"What?" Amanda asked, looking at her father, who was staring at her.

"I'm just so happy right now I don't know what to do," he muttered.

"Well, me, too. It took some time, but we're back together just like the old days," she said.

"I'm proud of you, you know," Zach said.

"Why? I just took a bullet for God," she joked.

Zach laughed. "That's exactly right." He stifled his laughter to get serious for a moment.

"You know, over a billion people saw you take that bullet for Kiram, and then they watched him walk the footprints. The leading religious scholars have no idea what to make of it."

"Doesn't Revelation talk about a slain and humiliated Jesus bringing peace to the world?"

"It does," Zach confessed. "It also says that certain people will eat from the Tree of Life. Right now the Tanzanian Army, whose ass I kicked, by the way, is protecting the Olduvai from the millions of people who want to get into the lava tube. But they've sort of turned it into a tourist attraction overnight."

"What does the Book of Catalyst say?"

Zach looked around uncomfortably for a moment and said, "It says, *'Her pierced heart will save Him and because of this she will enter Heaven.'*"

Amanda looked at her father, a tear in her eye.

"Good thing my heart wasn't pierced," she said. Her left hand touched the scar above her heart.

Zach lifted his hand and opened his fingers. Inside his palm was her gold heart-shaped locket that had endured a direct bullet strike. He dropped it on her bed next to her hand.

Amanda's eyes followed the locket and the thin, braided gold chain to which it was attached. She clutched the locket in her hand and began crying.

"I think you've got a front row seat when you get there," Zach said. "Regardless of what any book says."

Amanda shook her head slowly while the tears flowed.

"I miss them so much, Daddy," she wept, speaking of the orphanage children. "And Mumbato, how could he be so bad?"

"They miss you, too, but Mumbato just made a bad decision. It's called free will. Just like Kiram made his choice to save you," Zach said.

Amanda looked up at him. "Good and evil?"

"Maybe. You knew them better than me."

"Good wins," she whispered.

"Well, good happens," Zach smiled. "You know that tall white guy? That was Jonathan Beckwith of Beckwith Media, Incorporated. He lived, but no one can find him.

"And Webb? How could he be so stupid as to take on you, Daddy?"

"Greed is a powerful motivator, honey. Never let it take hold. By the way, Matt and some SEALs raided Beckwith's boat and got the information on The Leopard, the man who was chasing you."

"Thanks, Matt," Amanda said.

"Yep, that was all your uncle," Matt said. "The SEALs were just along to learn." Kristyana grabbed his hand as she rolled her eyes.

"Your uncle did well," she said. "Honey, The Leopard was linked to Zhor Rhazziq, a media giant from Morocco. Unfortunately, Rhazziq has disappeared, too."

"That sucks," Amanda said. "Two media companies were chasing me?"

"Yes. And we know Rhazziq is pissed," Kristyana replied. "Which explains our friends staying here on the farm."

Though Amanda had not seen them, there was a small security detail constantly roaming the 120-acre farm in Virginia horse country.

"We discovered that Zhor Rhazziq had hired Mohammed Aktar, a document thief, to plant the so-called Book of Catalyst in the library before Barkum was elected, but once the election appeared to be a lock," Kristyana said. "Our enemy thinks long term. He knew that Barkum had a high opinion of himself, and he exploited that. We think Barkum believing that he was the second coming caused him to refuse to send more troops to protect our forces over there. The president's decision would have been real danger for Jake and his men if it hadn't been, oddly enough, for Beckwith and his Bluejacking or Bluebugging or whatever we're calling it. Even stranger was that Beckwith had hired the same guy to steal the document that Rhazziq had had plant it earlier. Rhazziq baited Beckwith and tricked Barkum."

"So it's not real? The Book of Catalyst?" Amanda asked.

"No one knows. The pastor who originally identified it as real, Isaiah Jones, was found dead last week. Bullet to the back of his head," Kristyana said. "But other religious scholars admit that there is something to the document. The entire debate on creationism and evolution has sparked anew," Kristyana said. "Especially the debate about sub-Saharan African texts."

Amanda saw her dad wanted to change the subject. "On a more positive note, Beckwith has decided to fund all of the orphanages, because, as it turns out, all those lab PhDs can't seem to figure out how to make the paste work," he said.

"I sort of figured that," she said, wiping a tear from her eye. "Webb was sick one day and then recovering dramatically the next, but only after Kiram helped me inject him."

Matt and Kristyana turned around and stepped aside to show the screen of Zach's laptop, showing a live streaming video image of her husband, Jake Devereaux, still on combat duty in Iraq.

Matt said, "It's a loose connection. You've got fifteen to thirty seconds tops."

"Hey, sweet girl," Jake said. His image was distorted, and Amanda could see other soldiers milling around in the background. His face was stained with mud and sweat. He removed his advanced combat helmet and smoothed his hair.

"Hi, love," she said. "You be safe."

"I'm so proud of you, Amanda."

"Love you," she said, repeating their daily reminder. "All ways and always."

The screen went blank. Amanda closed her eyes and said a short prayer for her husband.

Epilogue

Standing on a nondescript mountain somewhere in Africa, Kiram Omiga looked skyward and smiled. The brilliant array of swirling galaxies spun through his eyes, and he saw the world as if from above. He lifted his arms upward and felt an omnipotent power surge through him. In his mind's eye, he was soaring through the night.

He felt a cleanliness wash over him, shedding the detritus of a youth lived in too much pain and agony. But it was that process, the humiliation of a shattered childhood and even the inability to save his good friend Mumbato from the throes of evil, that had delivered Kiram to his present frame of mind. Though just one choice, Mumbato had made the wrong decision that had cast him away. Mumbato had teamed with the wrong man, betraying Kiram's trust and endangering Amanda, his only true friend.

So he had sighted his weapon and intentionally wounded his African brother, who had fallen backward into the abyss. While he did not know whether Mumbato was dead or alive, he sensed that he had survived. In fact, he hoped so. Kiram believed that Mumbato had exercised free will in the cave when he had chosen to ally with the white man to use the paste for financial gain. He knew that same free will could lead Mumbato to the right decisions in the future. He could reject evil and accept good.

"Good wins," he whispered into the black sheet of night, echoing the refrain that Amanda had taught him.

He closed his eyes and visualized Amanda in her bed surrounded by her family.

And he heard her prayer.

"Good wins," he whispered again.

"Sometimes," came a familiar voice from behind him.

Acknowledgements

As always, thanks to Scott Miller and Trident Media Group, the best agent and agency in the business. Scott continues to be the most supportive agent an author could ever have. The team of Nicole Ross, Emily Robson, Brianna Weber, and Sarah Bush at Trident made *Mortal Threat* a better book. Each deserves high praise as they work hard behind the scenes to support their authors. Amy Knupp did a superb job with the edits and any mistakes in the book, of course, are my own.

Thanks to Gary Goldstein, my editor at Kensington Books for his advice and stewardship. Also, thanks to Scott Manning, my publicist for suggesting that we publish *Mortal Threat* before *Foreign and Domestic* as a way of reconnecting with the many readers who enjoyed the previous *Threat* books.

Chris Corbett has been working behind the scenes to upgrade my website, www.ajtata.com, and has done a superb job. Please check it out for updates.

Kaitlin Murphy did her usual superb job reviewing Mortal Threat and Judy Peppler provided invaluable feedback as well. Thanks also to Dianna and Robert Wuagneux, *Threat* Series supporters from the onset. Dianna read the very first edition of *Mortal Threat* and provided pages of helpful notes.

Most of all, thanks to my family, Jodi, Brooke, and Zach for their support. Our family research trip to the Serengeti was, according to Brooke, "The best trip ever." Under the able direction of our guide Willy Kissanga and others at Thomson Safaris, we visited the Olduvai Gorge and walked much of the terrain where the story takes place.

TURN THE PAGE FOR AN EXCITING PREVIEW!

ABSOLUTELY FANTASTIC…PULSE-POUNDING."
—Brad Thor, #1 *New York Times* bestselling author

From the author of
Sudden Threat, Rogue Threat and *Hidden Threat*

One year ago, Captain Jake Mahegan led a Delta Force team into Afghanistan to capture an American traitor working for the Taliban. The mission ended in tragedy, his team infiltrated and decimated by a bomb. After killing an enemy prisoner, Mahegan was dismissed from service—dishonored. Now, back in the United States and haunted by the incident, Mahegan is determined to avenge the loss of his comrades. The military wants him to stand down. But when the turncoat who calls himself the American Taliban returns to domestic soil—leading an army of ghost prisoners—Mahegan is the only man who knows how to stop him.

Outside the law. Under the radar. Out for vengeance…

FOREIGN AND DOMESTIC
By
A. J. Tata

On sale March 2015
Wherever Pinnacle Books are sold.

Military Oath of Enlistment:

I do solemnly swear that I will support and defend the Constitution of the United States against all enemies, **foreign and domestic;**

PROLOGUE

The generals had labeled the mission: "Kill or Capture."

Though Captain Jake Mahegan refused to consider anything but capturing the target.

With one-hundred mph winds whipping across Mahegan's face, he was running through the checklist in his mind: insert, infiltrate, over-watch, assault, capture, collect, and extract.

Mahegan knew his men were fatigued from days of continuous operations. They couldn't afford any mistakes this morning. He felt the mix of emotions that came with knowing they were close to snaring the biggest prize since Bin Laden: The American Taliban, the one man who had posed the gravest threat to United States security since Army aviators and Navy SEALs had killed Osama. Concern for his troops gnawed at the adrenaline-honed edges of excitement. Mission focus was tempered with empathy for his men.

This morning's target was a bomb maker and security expert named Commander Hoxha, who would lead them to The American Taliban.

Mahegan and what remained of his unit were flying in on the wing seats of MH-6 Little Bird aircraft to raid Hoxha's compound. Doubling as both expert bomb maker and the primary protection arm for The American Taliban, Hoxha had weathered wars in the Balkans, Iraq, and Afghanistan. Mahegan's review of Hoxha's dossier told him this could be the toughest mission he'd ever faced.

No mistakes.

The generals gave Mahegan this mission because they were on a timeline for withdrawal and he was the best. From the start of his special operations career, his Delta Force peers had called him, "The Million Dollar Man." The other twenty-nine of the thirty candidates in his Delta selection class had washed out. Each selection session cost the Army one million dollars.

For a year, Mahegan's outfit was casualty-free with impressive scalp counts of sixty-nine Taliban and al-Qaeda commanders. The better and more consistently he'd performed, the more Mahegan's legend had begun to take on mythical status within the military.

But that had mysteriously changed two months ago. A twenty-man unit had been whittled to eleven men over the past eight weeks during which they had conducted twenty-two missions. The pace had been relentless and Mahegan knew his team was sucking gas.

The brass, however, had insisted on this early morning mission. They had told him that the President wanted The American Taliban captured before the final troops withdrew. His senior officers directed him to press ahead based on what they called "actionable intelligence." Translated to Mahegan and his men: They were on their third night with no sleep as they kept pressure on the enemy like a football team blitzing on every play with the added threat that their lives were at stake.

In the two helicopters, Mahegan's team whipped through canyons so tight the rotor blades appeared to be sparking off the granite spires of the Hindu Kush Mountains. Through his night-vision goggles, Mahegan could see the static electricity produced by the rotors painting a glowing trail, like a time-lapse photo. The helicopters, called Little Birds, were nothing more than a light wind through the valleys. Two canvas bench seats on either side were supporting him and his three teammates with a similarly configured one in trail.

As a backup extraction plan, Mahegan had his protégé, Sergeant Wesley Colgate, leading a two-vehicle convoy from the ground a couple of miles away. The lead vehicle carried Colgate and two more of their Delta Force teammates. In the trailing Humvee was a contract document and detainee exploitation team, known as Docex, from private military contractor Copperhead, Inc. Mahegan had fought Copperhead's inclusion, but the generals had insisted.

The Task Force 160th pilots skillfully flared the aircraft and touched down into the landing zone at a twenty-degree angle like dragonflies alighting on grass blades.

"Blue," Mahegan said into the mouthpiece connected to a satellite radio on his back, giving the code word for a successful offload in the landing zone. He expected no reply, and received none, as they were minimizing radio communications. The two helicopters lifted quietly out of the valley and returned to the base camp several miles away in Asadabad.

It was nearly 0400, about three hours before sunrise. As always, on every single mission it seemed, the fog settled into the valley as if the helicopters had it in tow. He considered Colgate and his two vehicles a few miles away. Moving quickly through the rocky landing zone, Mahegan found the path to their target area.

"Red," he said, as they passed the ridge to be used by the support team. He watched through his night-vision goggles as Tony "Al" Pucino and his three warriors from the trail helicopter silently chose their support-by-fire positions.

Moving toward the objective, Mahegan noted the jagged terrain and ran the remainder of the checklist through his mind: assault, capture, collect, and extract. Eyeing the darkened trail above the Kunar River a half mile to the west, he paused. His instincts were telling him it would be better to walk away from this objective than to have Colgate risk the bomb-laden path to the terrorists' compound.

Registering that thought, Mahegan knelt and adjusted his night-vision goggles. He spotted the enemy security forces milling around. They were not alert. To Mahegan, they looked like a bunch of green-shaded sleepy avatars. The offset landing zone had kept their infiltration undetected. They were good to go.

Mahegan gave the signal; they had rehearsed the assault briefly in the compound a few hours ago. From over fifty meters away, he put his silenced M4 carbine's infrared laser on the forehead of the guard nearest the door, pulsed it twice, which was the cue to the rest of the team, and then drilled him through the skull. He heard the muffled coughs of his teammates' weapons and saw the other guards fall to the ground, like marionettes with cut strings. Motioning to his assault team, he led them along a defile that emptied directly into the back gate of Commander Hoxha's adobe compound. With a shove of his massive frame against the wooden back door of the open compound, Mahegan breached the back wall just as the target was yanking his tactical vest up around his shoulders and reaching for his AK-74. Mahegan knew questioning Hoxha was key to the ultimate mission, so he shot him in the thigh, being careful to miss the femoral artery. Hoxha fell in the middle of the open courtyard between the gate and the back door. Several goats bleated and ran, bells around their necks clanging loudly.

"Target down," he said. "Status."

"Team One good," Pucino reported.

"Move to the objective. Help with SSE," Mahegan directed to Pucino. Not only had they come to capture Hoxha, but Sensitive Site Exploitation usually garnered the most valuable intelligence through analysis of SIM cards, computer hard drives, and maps.

He led the assault team into the courtyard and Patch, one of his tobacco-chewing teammates from Austin, Texas, strapped the terrorist's hands behind his back using plastic flex-cuffs. Two more men were already making a sweep through the compound, stuffing kit bags full of cell phones, computer hard drives, and generally anything that might be used to kill American forces or provide a clue as to The American Taliban's location. Mahegan's agenda included searching for something called an MVX-90, a top-secret American-made transmitter-receiver he believed had fallen into enemy possession.

Mahegan pulled out a picture and a red lens flashlight to confirm he'd shot the right man. He felt no particular emotion, but simply checked another box when he confirmed they indeed had Commander Hoxha, the leader of The American Taliban's security ring.

With the fog crawling into the narrow canyons, Mahegan confirmed his instinct to call off the Little Birds and Colgate's team. They were walking out.

With the terrorist flex-cuffed in front of him and the place smelling like burned goat shit, he radioed Colgate, "We are coming to you. Do not move. Acknowledge, over."

"Roger." He recognized Colgate's voice.

On the heels of Colgate's reply, Pucino radioed, "Team One at checkpoint alpha." This was good news to Mahegan. Pucino's team had completed their portion of the sensitive site exploitation and was now securing the road that provided for their egress toward Colgate's vehicles.

Mahegan checked off in his mind the myriad tasks to come. They were in the intelligence collection phase. He entered the adobe hut, saw his men zipping their kit bags, and then moved outside where Patch was guarding Hoxha.

He heard Hoxha speaking in Pashtun at about the same time he noticed a small light shining through the white pocket of his *payraan tumbaan*, the outer garment.

Mahegan thought, *Cell phone.*

He also thought, *Voice command.* Like an iPhone Siri.

"Patch, shut him up!"

He went for the cell phone in the outer garment, while Patch stuffed a rag in the prisoner's mouth, tying it off behind his head. Fumbling with the pockets, Mahegan grabbed the smartphone, but saw the device had made a call.

His first thought was that the adobe hut was rigged with explosives. He pushed the end button to stop the call and wondered if he had prevented whatever the phone was supposed to trigger. He smashed the phone into a nearby rock, knowing the SIM card would likely be undamaged and still valuable.

"Everyone inside, get out of the house! All outside, get down! Now!" he said to his men in a hoarse whisper. Mahegan landed on top of the bomb maker, crushing him beneath his 6'4", 230-pound frame. He saw Patch and two others digging into the dirt, wondering. Patch silently mouthed the letters, "WTF?"

A few seconds later, he heard an explosion beneath the house as the rest of his team came pouring out of the back door.

"There was a tunnel. Put a thermite in it," Sergeant O'Malley, from southeast Chicago, said.

"Roger," Mahegan replied. A thermite grenade would have only stunned anyone in the tunnel, but Mahegan didn't want to risk going back inside. Two minutes passed with no further activity.

Mahegan stood, pocketed the crushed smartphone, lifted the terrorist onto his back, and said to his team, "Follow me."

Colgate

About ten minutes before Mahegan said, "We are coming to you," Colgate was getting eager. He inched his way forward from the rally point along the raging waters of the Kunar River, assuming the worst when he noticed the weather would most likely prevent aircraft from conducting the extraction.

Colgate kept easing forward, pulling the contractors along behind him. The trail they were on was rocky, filled with potholes. It made the Rubicon Trail look like the Autobahn. His gloved hands gripped the steering wheel, sensing the tires on the Ground Mobility Vehicle pushing dirt into the raging waters fifty meters below as he crept toward his mentor.

He and Chayton Mahegan had been together in combat for two years now. To Colgate, Mahegan was a brave warrior, a throwback to his Native American heritage. Chayton and Mahegan were Iroquois names for "falcon" and "wolf," and Colgate had no doubt Mahegan possessed the ferocity of both predators.

He was proud to be one of Mahegan's Quiet Professionals. Colgate adhered to his boss's motto: "Keep your mouth shut and let your actions do the talking." After two months as Ranger buddies and then being one class apart in Delta selection, Colgate and Mahegan had bonded. Combat had made them closer, like brothers.

Colgate was a big man, a former college running back for Norfolk State University. He had almost made the big time. As a walk-on for the

Washington Redskins, he had been cut the last day and enlisted a few hours later. After basic training, he was assigned to the Rangers and graduated Ranger school with Mahegan as his Ranger buddy. They got the same Ranger tab tattoo on their left shoulders and Colgate later made sergeant.

Now, Colgate flexed his left arm, thinking about the Ranger tab tattoo. He inched the vehicles closer. Not all the way, but closer, expecting the call. He was Plan B. Then Mahegan called: "We are coming to you. Do not move. Acknowledge, over."

"Roger," Colgate replied. But on the single lane dirt road with a drop to the violent river beside him, he couldn't turn around. He was committed. He had to continue.

He heard a dull thud in the distance, like a grenade, and stopped momentarily. But he had to find somewhere to turn around, so he continued toward the objective. He leaned forward straining to see through his own goggles.

His gunner was getting nervous. "Colgate, I can't see jack, buddy," he said through the VIC-5 internal communications radio set. "No place to turn around. We better hold up."

But Colgate had state-of-the-art jammers that could detect buried mines and roadside bombs better than cats could find mice. He had passive finders and active jammers. He had a heads-up display and wide-angle night vision that made it seem he was watching high-definition TV as he drove. He could see thermal out to thirty meters in front of his vehicle and he was scanning every radio frequency every second with a jammer so powerful he figured they were sterilizing the men in every village they passed. To Colgate, this vehicle was like the Terminator on steroids. He was good to go and so he kept going. Besides, he couldn't even Y-turn where they were without tumbling into the river. He considered calling Mahegan to tell him he had already committed, but knew his friend was busy.

Then he heard Holmesly say, "Hey, man, big ass rock pile in the road!"

Never a good sign, the rock pile loomed large in the HD viewer. Colgate slowed his vehicle and noticed through his goggles that they had crossed an infrared beam. He knew it was too late and muttered, "Oh shit."

Then he heard his radio come to life. It was Mahegan's voice. "Colgate—"

Mahegan

As Mahegan led his team single file down the road away from the village they had just raided, he stopped. He heard the GMVs moving not too far away, which was not good, not part of the plan.

He pressed his radio transmit button and said, "Colgate—"

A fireball erupted through the night mist. The billowing flame hung in the distance, a demonic mask sneering at Mahegan and his men. Shrapnel sizzled through the air with a torturous wail. Mahegan felt the pain of burning metal embedded into his left deltoid.

The shockwave knocked all eight of them down, plus the terrorist Mahegan was carrying. Hoxha, bound and gagged, was getting up to one knee. The fireball had momentarily destroyed Mahegan's night vision, but he could see enough that the prisoner was standing, squaring off with him. Mahegan calculated Hoxha's options. Run toward the wreckage? Jump into the river rapids with hands bound? Scale the cliffs to the east? Or move back toward his compound?

The fireball receded but still flickered brightly about one hundred meters away. The shadows of the jagged rocks were black ghosts dancing in ritual celebration of more foreign blood spilled in this impossible land.

Mahegan ignored the burning and bleeding in his left deltoid as he fumbled for the weapon hanging from a D-ring on his outer tactical vest. A secondary explosion sent another fireball into the sky, probably the ammunition from Colgate's GMV, he thought. The second blast gave the terrorist more time, but Mahegan still had him in his field of vision. Instead of choosing the three options away from him, Hoxha ran directly at him.

Hoxha faked one way as if he were a football running back and then attempted to get past Mahegan. Mahegan thought about Colgate and the casualties his team had suffered over the last two months. Then a flywheel broke free in his mind.

"Impulsive and aggressive," the Delta Force psychiatrist had said.

Mahegan figured, this time, the man was correct.

He cocked his elbow with his right hand on the telescoping stock of his M4 carbine and his left hand on the hand guard and weapon's accessory rail. He stepped forward with his left foot and propelled the leading edge of the butt-stock forward toward the terrorist's torso. He rotated his upper body and extended his right arm, locking his right elbow as he connected with Hoxha. His aim was high, or Hoxha ducked, and the weapon caught him across the face. The claw of the butt-stock connected with the man's temple. Hoxha crumbled to the ground, dead.

Mahegan saw the flesh and brain matter hanging off the end of his weapon and knew he had unleashed mortal fury onto the prisoner. He sprinted one hundred meters to Colgate's vehicle and found what he'd suspected: burning bodies. He reached in through the fire, his own shoulder burning from the shrapnel, and pulled at Colgate. All he got was charred skin coming off in his hands. He grabbed for Colgate's upper body and wrenched him out of the GMV, placing him on the ground. Patch and O'Malley were crawling over the burnt windshield to grab Coleseed. No one could find the gunner, Holmesly.

"Search away from the vehicle. He probably got thrown into the river. We'll have to search downstream," Mahegan said. Inside, he was a raging storm. Three more of his men were dead.

Eight left.

He stared momentarily at the trail vehicle in the distance, undamaged, with its crew of Copperhead, Inc. contractors standing stunned and motionless in the eerie darkness. Turning back to the burning vehicle, he only cared about piecing back together the bits of Colgate so that he could make him whole again. He was furious. He wondered how all the jammers, scanners, and thermal equipment had failed to defeat a homemade bomb in Nuristan Province, Afghanistan. In fact, there was only one way it could have happened and Mahegan refused to believe what he suspected.

As he stood over Colgate's remains, the charred flesh and the horrific grimace seared onto his face, he asked him, "Why, buddy?"

Pucino approached and said, "I don't know why, but I do know how, boss."

Mahegan, towering over the Italian soldier from Boston, looked down at the box in Pucino's hand.

"An empty MVX-90 box. From the bomb maker's hut. Made in the Research Triangle Park of North Carolina. Several more in there, unused," Pucino said.

Mahegan internalized this information. This was the only device that could have guided an electronic trigger signal past the jammers in Colgate's vehicle. And it had come from the U.S. of A.

The raging storm that had been building inside him for two months, ever since he had lost his first soldier in combat, finally unleashed. Mahegan howled with a primal ferocity that roared through the distant canyons, the valleys echoing with his anguish. Then he turned toward the Copperhead, Inc. private military contractors and stared at them, wondering why they were on the mission at all.

CHAPTER ONE

Mahegan knew he was being watched. After a year of drifting in eastern North Carolina, they had finally found him.

Which wasn't all bad.

The black Ford F-150 pickup truck had driven past his rented above-garage apartment on Roanoke Island one too many times. Mahegan had noticed the unusually clean exterior of the vehicle the first time. Here in the Outer Banks of North Carolina, a shiny, waxed truck was as obvious as a gelled playboy amongst seafaring watermen. The second and last drive-by, a day later, coupled with a slightest tap of the brakes, confirmed that either the Department of Homeland Security or the Department of Defense had located him.

He kept to his routine.

At five a.m. on a typically warm September morning, he ducked out of the Queen Anne's Revenge, a guesthouse owned by Outer Banks proprietor, Sam Midgett, and walked along Old Wharf Road of Roanoke Island. Mahegan slid around the fence that blocked the pavement a hundred meters from Croatan Sound, and found Midgett's twelve-foot duck-hunting boat. Pausing to listen to the bullfrogs and inhale the brackish odor, he shoved off through the low marshes, pushing through the reeds. A small white-tail deer darted past him, splashing through the knee-deep water. Stepping into the boat, he used the paddle to get some momentum and then he was in the deeper water of the sound, which was to the western side of the island. About one hundred meters out was an orange channel marker. He reached it, pulled a half hitch through a rusty cleat on the buoy, kicked off his mocs, and dove into the black water.

The sun was about an hour from cresting over the horizon of the Atlantic Ocean less than half a mile to his rear. He pulled with broad-shouldered strokes, the lightning bolt scar from the shrapnel of Colgate's vehicle explosion screaming with every rotation. The doctors had removed the embedded metal from just beneath his Ranger tab tattoo on his left deltoid and had told him to swim for rehab.

So he swam. Every day.

He preferred swimming this way, in the darkness. Alone, he was able to rehash the botched mission and its aftermath. And here he was also able to evade the vigilance of the Homeland Security noose that was tightening around him. He let his mind drift again, from being watched now to what had come before.

He latched on to the moment he had turned in his papers to resign his commission as a military officer. His teammates had written seven too-similar statements about how Mahegan had thwarted an escape attempt by the clever terrorist who used the bomb blast as a diversion. The Army Inspector General had balked at the carbon copy testimony of his teammates.

"What my team says is essentially true. But I let my emotions take over," he told his commander, Major General Bob Savage. "Colgate was dead. Hoxha may have given us something useful on Adham. Hoxha *did* try to escape, but he was still cuffed and gagged. I killed him. I failed. And we're no closer to Adham than before. It's that simple."

Mullah Adham was the nom de guerre of The American Taliban. Actually, Adham was an American citizen in his mid-twenties from Iowa named Adam Wilhoyt who had gone native with al-Qaeda.

General Savage nodded, trying to persuade him not to resign, but Mahegan never wavered.

"I could drive on like this never happened, but without my integrity, what do I have?" Mahegan said. Savage stared at the captain like a seasoned poker player.

"You know it was an MVX-90 that killed Colgate, Holmesly, and Coleseed. And I'm sure you have thought this, but once Hoxha was able to make that call to activate the trigger on the bomb, all you had to do was initiate a radio call to trigger the blast. Only the MVX-90, US manufactured and tested, could allow our radio signals, which operate on a very specific bandwidth, past all of the jammers that were operating."

Of course, it was all he could think about. He had technically killed his own men. In order to simultaneously jam enemy trigger signals and communicate to friendly forces, the American Army had developed the MVX-90. The device left discreet, protected gaps in the radio spectrum so that friendly communications could enter and exit while still searching for ill-intended incoming signals to block. The only way to find those gaps and know how to program a trigger device on the American frequency, Mahegan knew, was for the enemy to have an MVX-90 operating in the area. Effectively, it was like finding a programmer's backdoor into a software operating system.

A flash burst in his mind from the fateful radio call: *"Colgate—"*

Running his hand across his face, Mahegan said, "I know I killed them, sir."

After a moment, Savage responded. "Your radio did. Not you." Reacting to Mahegan's silent stare, he continued. "And whoever gave them the MVX-90."

Mahegan looked up at his commander and said, "I have an idea."

He explained as Savage listened, sometimes nodding and sometimes frowning.

"I have a different thought," Savage said.

Mahegan listened to his commanding officer, who pushed the papers toward him across the gray metal desk in Bagram Air Base. Mahegan looked down, shook his head, and pushed the papers back at his general.

"I've got to do this my way, sir," he said.

Savage nodded, saying, "You always do, Jake. But if you stay over here in the sandbox you can get your revenge for Colgate . . . and the rest of your team."

Mahegan grimaced. "You know what they say about revenge, sir."

"What?"

"It's all in the anticipation. The thing itself is a pain."

"Twain," Savage had replied. "Since we're discussing authors, then we might as well state the obvious: You can't go home again. You ought to take me up on my offer."

"I'll think about it, sir. Like I said, it's got to be done my way. And maybe there's another way to do it." Mahegan paused, and then said, "Thomas Wolfe, by the way."

"Roger. And that means you know what I'm talking about. You go back to America, especially with Homeland Security all over your ass, and nothing will look the same. You'll be blacklisted by that new moron they have running the nut farm at DHS and this list of vets she says are threats to society. You've gotten some press over this thing, too. And, Jake, General Bream, the Army Inspector General, is sniffing all around this faster than a Blue Tick Coonhound. He's an ass hamster of the highest magnitude and wants to be Army Chief of Staff. They are calling him the 'Chief of Integrity' or some such bullshit. If you go back, he will be gunning for you."

Mahegan shrugged. "Got a fair amount of that kind over here, too. I'll be okay."

"He's putting on his best indignant performance for the press. He's going for a dishonorable discharge, you know."

Actually, no. This was news to him. Bad news. He had fought with honor, risking his life for his fellow Americans and his teammates. Endless days and nights with no sleep, little food, and unspeakable danger.

"Didn't know that, sir." Mahegan looked away at the maps of Afghanistan on the plywood walls, reminders of firefights, combat parachute jumps, and helicopter raids everywhere.

"Don't sweat it for now, Jake. Cross that bridge when we get to it. Your team covered for you."

"They didn't cover for me, sir. They reported what happened."

Savage waved off Mahegan's statement and continued his sales pitch for Mahegan to stay in the Army.

"For the record, you belong here, with us, doing this," Savage said, pointing his finger at the maps. "This is your home. I took you in despite your psych evaluation, Jake. That counts for something."

Mahegan nodded, recalling how the Army psychiatrist had identified Mahegan's sometimes "impulsive, aggressive behavior," and recommended against inclusion in the elite force. Savage had stood firm and the "million-dollar man" was born. Oddly, Delta Force *had* been Mahegan's home, and he had left all that he loved.

"I just need time, sir," he told Savage. "Then, maybe I can do what you suggest."

Now, this morning, pulling hard through the black water, he wondered whether or not he should have accepted Savage's deal. The general had been right. Someone was looking for him and General Bream was gunning for a dishonorable discharge. He tried to push the black pickup truck and the Inspector General out of his mind.

His broad shoulders and powerful legs propelled him through the sound. After a shark incident while swimming off Wilmington's fabled Frying Pan Shoals, Mahegan was determined to appear dominant in the water. He swam with purpose, as if he were the apex predator, some kind of savage beast on the prowl.

His mind drifted from Colgate to The American Taliban, Mullah Adham, to his shoulder and to Martin Strel, who owned the world record for the longest continuous swim. Before beginning his swimming rehab, he had researched the sport. Strel swam 312 miles in the Danube River in 84 hours. Mahegan did the math. He was doing 5 miles max each way. Strel had cruised at a sustained rate of 3.7 miles an hour. Mahegan was doing something less than that, but not by much. Plus, Strel had a helping current while he was going cross-current. The tide was either coming in or going out, which was always perpendicular to his axis of advance. Mahegan knew he wasn't doing the miles all at once, of course.

He swam that way for an hour and a half until, on a downward stroke, his hand hit sand, touching the small beach of the mainland of North

Carolina. He pulled himself up, strode through the knee-deep water, and sat on the jutting spit of land that was the easternmost point of the Alligator River National Wildlife Refuge.

He sat about twenty meters back from the water, facing east, and watched the dawn appear over the Atlantic Ocean, Outer Banks barrier islands, and Roanoke Island. The sun cast an orange streak along the spreading vee of his swimming wake. The water rippled outward, inviting the coming day. The vee eventually disappeared, and he wondered about his life path. What was left in his wake so far? What more would there be? Would his trail simply blend back into the environment with no remaining signature?

As Mahegan stared at his diminishing path, he felt welcoming eyes surround him from behind.

He smiled. They had learned to come to him, or perhaps he to them.

The red wolves crept from their Alligator River refuge and joined Mahegan as he watched the sun and wondered about life. Mahegan had researched the terrain of Dare County Mainland, and among other valuable lessons, he learned that at one time there had been only sixteen red wolves left in the United States. The National Wildlife Refuge had tried an experimental repopulation program by placing a few of the sixteen in Alligator River National Park. Fierce hunters, the red wolves began to thrive on the abundant wildlife in the remote national park.

They traveled in family packs of adults and cubs. Mahegan turned and saw a youngster lying in some saw grass, staring at him. The pup looked more like a red fox than a wolf.

Mahegan felt a comfort here, removed from even the sparsely populated Roanoke Island. Drifting up the Outer Banks of North Carolina for a year, he had worked the odd job for a couple of weeks before moving on. He was a deckhand on a fishing boat out of Wilmington, a bouncer at a bar in Beaufort, and part of a landscaping crew in Hatteras. Remaining obscure was paramount.

But a year was enough. The one-year anniversary of his failed mission in Nuristan Province was tomorrow, and he was at the end of this particular trail.

Plus, they had found him. He needed solitude to finalize his plans. Today.

The first part of his plan, if he could call it that, was to borrow his new landlord's pickup truck, drive up to Arlington National Cemetery, and visit the gravesites of Colgate and the rest of his men who had been killed in action.

The second part was, well, complicated.

He stood and turned slowly, facing west. He counted the faces poking through the reeds and tall grass. Eight. Just like the remaining members of his team.

They seemed to be staring at his arm, where the scar that looked like a lightning bolt welt ran from his left shoulder to his elbow. Mahegan suspected that somewhere deep down in the psyches of these animals, they knew the threat to their species. Sixteen left. Just as families passed stories from generation to generation, these red wolves, Mahegan was certain, were passing the story of their near extinction to their offspring.

One of the wolves circled past him. He didn't know, but perhaps his kinship with these animals had something to do with being backed into a corner, the very essence of their being whittled to the core. Would they survive or evaporate into thin air? He closed his eyes, becoming certain of his connection with these predators. He relaxed and let his mind drift outward to them, and then opened his eyes. They had slipped silently into the bush, Mahegan catching the flipping tail of the pup.

He turned, waded into the sound, and began swimming.

As he glided into the water that was now showing some chop from a southerly wind, a distant, but enormous explosion shook the water around his body.

He stopped, stood in the chest-deep sound only twenty meters offshore and turned toward the mushroom cloud fueled by a large plume of smoke billowing upward like a miniature nuclear blast. He gauged the distance to be about ten miles away at a two-hundred-degree azimuth, southwest, in the center of Dare County Bombing Range.

Picturing the source of the burst cloud, Mahegan thought, *That's about right.* More than a year ago the Department of Defense had closed Dare

County Bombing Range, which oddly enough sat in the middle of the Alligator River Wildlife Refuge. In an attempt to appease a shunned contractor, the DoD had given the dirty job of clearing the bomb detritus to the private military contractor Copperhead, Inc.

As he began swimming back to Roanoke Island, Mahegan suddenly felt better about his decision regarding Savage's offer.

About the Author:

A.J. TATA is a career paratrooper and infantryman. Retiring as a Brigadier General, he commanded combat units in the 82nd and 101st Airborne Divisions and the 10th Mountain Division. A West Point graduate and Harvard University National Security Fellow, he is the award winning author of three critically acclaimed novels, *Sudden Threat*, *Rogue Threat*, and *Hidden Threat*. He was also a writer in Glenn Beck's New York Times Bestselling *Miracles and Massacres*. Tony has been a frequent foreign policy guest commentator on Fox News, CBS News, and The Daily Buzz. NBC's Today Show featured General Tata's career transition from the army to education leadership. He served as Chief Operations Officer for Washington, DC, Public Schools and then as the superintendent of Schools in Raleigh-Wake County, North Carolina, the sixteenth largest school district in the nation. An avid surfer, he is married to Jodi and has two children, Brooke and Zachary.

Connect with A.J. Tata Online:
Facebook /AJ-Tata-Author
Twitter @ajtata
Website www.ajtata.com

CPSIA information can be obtained
at www.ICGtesting.com
Printed in the USA
LVHW090226200421
684990LV00018B/80

9 781508 483786